WITNESS ELIMINATION

VIGILANTE JUSTICE

WITNESS ELIMINATION

VIGILANTE JUSTICE

NICK JUSTIN CHRONICLES

BOOK 2

by

SCOTT JOHNI

This novel is entirely a work of fiction. The names, characters, and incidents portrayed in it are the work of the author's imagination. Any resemblance to actual persons, living or dead, events, or localities is entirely coincidental.

Ebook: ISBN: 979-8-9988547-3-6

Paperback: ISBN: 979-8-9988547-4-3

Hardcover: ISBN: 979-8-9988547-5-0

Table of Contents

PART 2:
RISING TENSIONS AND BETRAYAL

PART 3:

HURRICANE MILTON AND THE FINAL SHOWDOWN

Major Charles Slovin, a decorated Air Force JAG, had uncovered something rotten running through Tampa Bay: a fentanyl and money pipeline linking private military contractors at MacDill Air Force Base to the Bruth'rs gang and to a faction of the St. Petersburg Police Department. When one of his informants vanished, Slovin grasped the circle was closing. He told his wife, Addison, if anything happened, the portable hard drive in their safe-deposit box contained everything—names, transfers, and proof of the network's reach.

Driving west on the Gandy Bridge, Slovin realized too late the trap had already been sprung. Headlights closed in. Tire spikes flashed across the asphalt. His SUV hit the strip, collided with the gang's black Mazda MX-5, and vaulted into the water below. Officer Gino Myers arrived moments later and swept the evidence before rescue crews reached the wreck.

Four days later, Nick Justin was celebrating the verdict of his career when Judge Armwell pulled him aside to deliver devastating news. His wife, Andrea, was in critical condition after a violent crash on the same bridge. That morning, she had helped Addison Slovin file death-benefit paperwork and had agreed to bring the hard drive to Nick. Somewhere between that promise and her trip home, the conspiracy struck again.

Andrea's Audi was forced off the bridge by a coordinated hit led by Myers and Sally Hinkins, a police officer with a Special Forces background. They planted fentanyl and bourbon to frame her for DUI. Andrea survived but slipped into a coma, leaving her husband with questions the cops refused to answer.

As Nick dug for the truth, the pattern sharpened. The RADD Squad, Myers's elite street-crime unit, was staging accidents, erasing witnesses, and laundering violence under the banner of law enforcement. Evidence disappeared, suspects died in custody, and every path pointed back to MacDill contractors and the Bruth'rs.

When community activist Shandra Greene stepped forward, her mask cracked. Her teenage son was murdered after encountering Myers. She revealed RADD had worked in concert with the contractors and the gang's distribution routes, which Major Slovin had been tracking. The same black Mazda and Dodge Challenger seen at Andrea's crash had been spotted near other staged accidents.

The deeper Nick probed, the more personal the betrayal became. His sister-in-law, Sarah Brown, was no bystander. Beneath her polished exterior, Sarah was Enigma, the unseen hand coordinating the contractors, the Bruth'rs, and RADD. Her lover and enforcer, Sally Hinkins, carried out the cleanup operations. Andrea's wreck had been a calculated sacrifice to protect their empire.

The revelation shattered Nick's world. Family dinners, shared grief, and every act of support Sarah had offered since the accident had all been camouflage.

When Sarah kidnapped seven-year-old Jessica Justin, the war turned overt. She demanded the hard drive in exchange for the child's life. The meeting place was in the shadow of the Gandy Bridge, where the first blood had been spilled. Nick went in armed with nothing but resolve.

Under the bridge's steel arches, the conspiracy collapsed. Nick rescued Jessica, and the police took Sarah into custody. A few hours earlier, they arrested Myers, stripped his badge, and exposed his RADD unit as a criminal front. But the fight was not finished. That night, Sally Hinkins broke into Nick's home, determined to erase the last loose end.

WITNESS ELIMINATION

Nick met her in the kitchen, bloodied and exhausted, and fought for his life. He swung a baseball bat once. The solid crack echoed, and Hinkins dropped unconscious. Nick called the police, and officers arrived minutes later to find the enforcer sprawled on the floor. By dawn, Myers, Sarah, and Sally were all in custody.

In the aftermath, Andrea woke from her coma and learned the truth about her sister's betrayal, Slovin's sacrifice, and the web of corruption that had nearly destroyed their family. Authorities dismantled the RADD Squad, seized Tagger Group International, and established a new multi-agency task force to pursue what remained of the network. Nick joined the effort alongside Sergeant Adams and Shandra Greene, determined to root out the rot.

Five weeks later, at Major Slovin's funeral, the honor guard folded the flag with crisp, deliberate motions. Nick and Jessica watched as the soldier laid the final triangle in the widow's palms. The price had been unbearable, but the resolve was stronger than ever.

Still, in Tampa Bay, corruption never stayed buried for long. The storm had passed, but the next one was already gathering on the horizon.

PART 1:
STORM ON THE HORIZON

PROLOGUE

THE COST OF FAILURE

Senator Eleanor Caldwell pressed her palm to the glass on the sixty-first floor as rain pelted the Miami skyline, neon bleeding down the city. Her breath fogged the pane. Her teeth clicked once as she shifted her weight, her fingers never quite settling.

Cream-colored leather chairs, a chrome console, and a steel sculpture made her office gleam. Bottles of single malt lined the wet bar, labels visible. Two bodyguards in tailored black suits stood at opposite corners, boots polished, hands near the edge of their jackets. Even here, sixty-one stories up, exposure prickled along her skin.

She slipped her phone from her pocket and thumbed a message to her aide in D.C. "Get out." She wiped the glass with her sleeve. The panic button under her desk clicked once, then twice. No response. The silence tightened, sharp at the edges. A chill crept up her spine. A faint tang of ozone leaked through the vents, storm-charged air sharpening the room into something deliberate.

The red clock above the credenza struck 22:00. Her phone buzzed.

Be ready.—V

No header. No code. She almost deleted it, but left it on-screen, a defiance meant for whoever was watching. She nodded at the closer bodyguard. He tapped his earpiece. The second shifted, steel creasing his jacket.

The comms panel blinked blue. She touched it. The lobby feed flickered to life: rifles set, eyes on the elevator. Her nearer guard clicked his mic, but his face went blank.

None of them should have been accessible. The fail-safes had failed. They were already inside.

She heard a voice, smooth, calm, Portuguese vowels softening the edges. "Observation is control, Senator. Always."

Her stomach clenched. Verdugo. She pictured the jagged scar through his lip, the way it must tug when he spoke. He was close. Watching. She could almost hear the phantom scrape of tissue with every drag of the scar, a faint grit of sound that set her nerves on edge.

Her chin lifted. "You've made your point. Say what you want."

Verdugo's tone pressed on, marked by an old injury, calm as the rain outside. "Your external detail is gone. You failed to protect Enigma and RADD. You neglected to cover your assets … two hundred million dollars. That is the cost of your failure."

On the lobby feed, the elevator opened. A janitor in a poncho pushed a mop bucket. The guards glanced once and turned away. Too late. He drew a suppressed pistol. Two bodies dropped before they realized they were dead.

Caldwell's throat seized, but her hands stayed steady as she ducked behind the desk and texted again, this time to her daughter.

Go. Now.

Her voice cracked hard and sharp. "That was the local police. Not mine to call. Nobody could have—"

"Nobody did," Verdugo cut in.

WITNESS ELIMINATION

The elevator in her foyer dinged. Her lead guard opened fire, shattering glass, dropping silhouettes as the doors fully slid open. For half a breath, Caldwell believed she might survive.

A flashbang clattered across marble. The suite erupted in white light, then darkness. Her protector smashed into a table. The second defender caught one and died with a hole drilled through his forehead.

Gloved hands seized her arms, her legs. Black figures moved with surgical precision, no insignia, no wasted motion. A scream caught in her throat. Only a rasp escaped.

"It was that attorney, Nick Justin. I did everything I could!"

Verdugo's voice filled the space—steady, unrelenting, every word edged with steel. His scarred lip curled as he delivered the verdict. "You understood the terms. There are no excuses. Only consequences. Tonight, you are only a lesson."

One man stripped her phone and jewelry, dropping them into a mesh bag. Another wiped her face with a rag, morgue-prep efficient. Her gaze caught a crayon drawing behind a glass award—blue sky, red house. Her daughter's gift from the first campaign. *If I'd left sooner ... burned it all down*

She twisted, one last surge of defiance. A black sack dropped over her head. The child's picture blurred in her peripheral vision.

The executioner's words rang in her ears—flat, indifferent. "Table cleared."

The balcony doors slid open. Rain slashed her cheeks. Verdugo's voice was almost kind. "Failure has consequences. Even the highest fall."

They hurled her into the darkness, and the storm swallowed her scream.

~

A thousand miles south, thunder rattled corrugated roofing. Servers glowed in the dark, their hum stitched with cigarette smoke. Carl "The Wrench" Walters lounged in a bomber chair, nicotine-stained fingers drumming on the armrest. A faded tattoo curled from under his cuff. His coal-black eyes tracked the feed: lobby breach, suite cleared, Caldwell's body vanishing into the storm. He exhaled through his nose, not with satisfaction but confirmation, like watching a machine finish its cycle.

He watched the fall. "Efficient." He flicked ash from an imaginary cigarette. Survivor habits carved deep.

La Reina stood behind him, the faint scent of jasmine threading the server's cold air, blood-red nails catching light. She tilted a silver ring on her finger, its stone worn smooth with use. Her gaze never left the screen. Her presence was a stillness, ancient, patience wrapped around danger.

But Carl's mind drifted to a memory from his last days with the Bruth'rs: the hard drive he'd spent sleepless nights cracking before the raid on his garage. *Carl saw the file structure: bank accounts, names of crooked politicians, dirty drug routes, all cross-referenced and airtight. He knew the hard drive wasn't a ledger; it was a map to the empire.*

"Once, I believed in justice, but justice waits too long. Now I believe in retribution, swift and absolute."

Carl nodded. "Protocol teams are working on it already. By morning, her detail takes the blame—blackmail, greed, whatever sells. Incriminating emails planted. Transfers queued. By the time the feds arrive, the book's closed." He slid a drive into the encrypted laptop. "For all their money, they never lock the right doors."

Her eyes cut to him. "You found shelter under me. Don't forget who owns your past."

His jaw set, but he didn't answer.

"No secondaries," she said. "Verdugo's completed his errand. Now we begin."

Carl muttered, "No loose ends. By sunrise, her legacy's tainted."

La Reina brushed lint from her sleeve, her voice sugar-sweet. "The senator failed me, and it cost me two hundred million dollars and the hard drive. Now, find the drive. The Americans must not touch what's on the Slovin package."

Carl exhaled through his nose—not to protest, but because he knew how they always played this game.

"Justin gave it to local cops," he said. "That's a problem."

WITNESS ELIMINATION

A thin smile crossed her face. "Only if we permit him." She turned to the window, lightning glare smearing the city below. "Let them whisper about the storm. What comes after is ours. Tempests pass. Empires don't."

The server hum merged with distant thunder. Carl queued the next phase: Slovin's drive, Justin, the Enigma. Outside the steel and glass, the city slept, oblivious to the lurking threat.

1

THE LINGERING STORM

September 24, 2024

Florida autumn was in full swing, the sky harsh and bright. The Ice Creamery hunkered at the end of a tired strip mall, its parking lot shimmering with heat.

Inside, Nick Justin watched his daughter devour a double-scoop ice cream. Jessica's nose, flecked with chocolate, wrinkled as she hunted the last bit of mint chip. He let his guard slip enough to smile for real. She looked up and offered him the tip of her cone.

He took it, knowing moments like this could vanish. "What was the favorite dog at the rescue today?"

"I liked them all." Her face scrunched. "Daddy," she asked, licking green from her wrist. "Did you ever have a dog?"

He nodded. "Oscar, a bloodhound. He ate the couch when I was ten."

She giggled. His laugh trailed off. The TV above the register crawled with news. "Hurricane Helene" swirled on the Gulf radar. Background noise for now.

Two teenagers stood outside, arms tangled. She wondered. "Are those two in love or being silly?"

"Could be both." Nick shrugged. "At times, you can't tell."

A pause. "Did you and Mom do that?"

"Yeah. Sometimes we still do, but it's different now."

The door banged open. A family spilled in, commotion echoing off the tile. Nick's gaze snapped to the glass.

Zara, Jessica's plush lioness, sat equally watchful, bead eyes narrowed at the shop entrance. Jessica shifted it again, angling the face toward the back of the store as if worried the danger could come from anywhere.

At the far edge of the lot, a black sedan idled. He recognized it before: 1st Street, then Publix. Too close to confront, too distant to forget.

Jessica caught his unease and adjusted Zara to face the window, marshaling defenses.

The lawyer in him wanted to log the plate and file a report. The father wanted to grab his daughter, to teach her that the world was never safe. He kept his face even and reached for her hand.

She squeezed hard. "Is something wrong?"

He lied. "Everything's fine."

Outside, the man from the sedan stepped out, bulky in a suit, gaze fixed on them. He tossed something into the trash and got back into the car. He could have been a bored PI, a threat, or nothing at all. The devil sometimes wore a smile and sometimes a blank face.

His pulse kicked, but he let the moment ride, choosing stillness. Jessica whispered, "He looks like the man in your court drawings."

He forced a shrug. "Maybe he lost his dog."

She smiled, but her grip stayed fierce.

The car eased away, a camera lens glinting, vanishing into traffic. Its presence lingered, leaving a bad taste in Nick's mouth.

~

Back home, Jessica sat at the breakfast bar, coloring pages of dogs, each in mid-run, ears flying. Her hands shaded carefully, moving fast, but her eyes kept flicking to the window. One drawing strayed from the rest: a lone puppy in the corner, watchful and small.

Andrea gritted through physical therapy, sweat bright on her brow, jaw set. The therapist coaxed her leg forward, but she refused to give in.

"Three, two, one, relax." She exhaled, half laughter, half surrender.

WITNESS ELIMINATION

"Nineteen more and I'll be ready for the Iditarod."

Nick paused, then smiled. "Jessica can coach you. She outran an entire pack at the rescue." Their daughter giggled, flashing green marker on her teeth. The sound was a gift, a brief respite from their unease.

Andrea's mouth tensed. "Do you wish we'd left Florida?"

He shook his head. "It wouldn't matter. They'd follow."

She flexed her twitching leg, face turned away. "Some are still out there."

"I know."

"Any names?"

"Carl's the real threat. Most of the others are gone. The rest …."

She tried to stand, her muscles giving a violent, involuntary tremor that forced her back down. She shut her hazel eyes, a sigh of frustration escaping her lips. "I hate how powerless I am."

Jessica dropped a marker and crawled under the stool—gaze sharp, scanning both parents— to snag it. She always watched. She always listened, even when they pretended she didn't.

"I'll get the mail." Nick rose, restless. He needed motion. Something to check, to fix.

Andrea's eyes flashed open. "Be careful."

Outside, the heat closed in. At the end of the block, a sedan idled. Different make, same intent. The window slid down a few inches, enough for a shadow to slip through. His heart thudded, but he stood his ground. Then he backed inside, locking the door.

Andrea turned to him, one thin eyebrow lifted. "Mail?"

He passed the envelopes. Jessica tucked her drawing into his hand, the lone puppy, wary and small. He taped it to the fridge.

~

Later, Nick thumbed through Major Charles Slovin's battered notebook. Addison had pressed it into his hands after the funeral, her grip cold and urgent. Cryptic notes, jagged sketches, frantic red circles. The top of one page read, "Don't trust anyone. See it through."

He searched for a pattern. Names scratched out, addresses, symbols he couldn't decode. One symbol caught his eye: a red crown drawn in sharp strokes, half-hidden in a margin. Beside it, Slovin had written a single word in block letters: "REINA."

Nick's pulse jumped. He remembered the name from whispered conversations in courthouse hallways, a rumor tied to backroom deals and cartel connections. La Reina. No face, no file, shadows pulling strings from a distance.

His mind drifted to the hard drive, "100% decrypted," he'd handed off to the undercover officer, Hank Kitchens, and the DEA when Jessica was missing—how weeks ago? Now it was buried behind "ongoing review." Every inquiry hit a wall.

He recalled Hank's face, tight with grim resolve, as they'd shaken hands in that sterile police station. "I'll keep a close eye on it, Nick. Don't you worry." Now, the department offered only silence. If Slovin had marked La Reina, then whatever the drive held dwarfed simple corruption. They were building something.

Nick snapped a quick photo of the page with his phone, thumb hesitating before sending it. He typed out a message to his investigator, José:

Red crown. 'La Reina.' Check everything you can.

He closed the notebook, tension coiling in his gut. Hank might have known something. He had tried the old number but got nothing, a sterile wall between him and his only real contact inside the narcotics division in the department. His hand hovered over the screen.

~

During homework hour, Nick and Jessica worked at the table, her worksheets spread out. Andrea called dinner from the kitchen, moving steadier than last week. The TV murmured about Senator Caldwell's violent death. The governor was expected to appoint a replacement soon.

Thunder rumbled outside. The phone rang, an unknown caller.

Andrea frowned. "Let it go to voicemail."

WITNESS ELIMINATION

Nick grabbed the phone. "Nick Justin."

A pause, static. "Nick, it's Tony from the old courthouse. Listen, there's been movement around the county jail. Guys from the old task force and some you wouldn't know. Visitors from Tallahassee. You didn't hear it from me."

Nick's palm hit the table. "What kind of activity?"

"Unusual. Late-night visitors. That's all I got. Don't call me back." The line cut out.

Jessica paused, pencil midair. Andrea didn't move. He pocketed the phone. Silence was heavy in the house.

~

That night, Nick pulled the round bottle from the cabinet, the one with the horse and jockey perched on the stopper. Blanton's. He poured two fingers and sat by the window, the pane streaked with rain. Thunder cracked. On TV, the mayor announced a new task force, Nick's name among the members.

Vanilla and oak drifted up, edged with a faint citrus-and-smoke bite.

Nick stared through the tumbler, the bourbon's glow bending the room's shadows, and thought about how truth had a way of biting the same way, warm at first, then sharp enough to sting.

He caught his reflection, tense and flickering. He never knew if he was the watcher or just a ghost in someone else's feed.

He turned off the lights one by one. Jessica slept on the sofa, her lioness plush still facing the window. Nick paused, counting four breaths—hers, then his—before the wind rattled the house. The silence afterward felt thick and foreboding

2

THE TRANSFER ORDER

September 26, 2024

Hurricane Helene closed in. Wind tugged at the gutters, pushing rain in heavy sheets that turned the yard into a blurred wash of gray.

Nick sat at the kitchen table with a legal pad and a pen. Crossed-out sentences filled the page, along with a small constellation of ink dots where he'd jabbed the tip when his thoughts ran out. His mug left a ring on the wood. He hadn't tasted the coffee since it went cold.

Seven weeks without more than four consecutive hours of sleep. His fingers shook when he tried to sign a check, and tension in his shoulders kept him rubbing his neck long past midnight. Vigilance had become a habit, constricting, familiar, hard to let go of. If he watched closely enough—locks, schedules, routes, faces at the perimeter—he could keep his family safe. But some mornings, when the house fell quiet, he wondered if he'd built a fortress or a cage.

Andrea came down the hall carrying Barrister the cat, slippers whispering, the belt of her robe knotted into a bow. She still favored her left side. She moved with a cautious, studied balance, as if anything sudden might topple her. Her short blonde hair framed her face, and she wore his old Stetson Law sweatshirt. She remained beautiful in a way that pulled a sharp ache through Nick's ribs and set his stomach twisting.

He hated cataloging the details: the small, involuntary tremor in her hand when she reached for her coffee, the slight bruise fading to yellow along her sternum where the CPR compressions marked her. It made him a watcher inside his own home.

Jessica padded in after her, lioness tucked under one arm, hair a wild blonde halo from sleep. Zara had become part of her body, especially since her aunt held her at gunpoint. She never strayed far from the stuffed toy. The lioness's bead eyes sought the door, the window, the hallway— the places where fear might come from. Today, they fixed on the kitchen door.

The TV flickered without sound. A red ticker cut along the bottom of a local morning show and then switched to the national feed. Andrea reached for the remote and raised the volume two notches. The anchor's posture changed, shoulders bracing, face tightening into the mask of breaking news.

"This just in. Federal authorities have confirmed the transfer of Sarah Brown and former officer Sally Hinkins to the ADX Florence in Colorado. The two women, central to last month's RADD Squad corruption scandal and multiple allegations of evidence tampering, will be moved under heavy security. For operational safety, the exact timeline are not being released."

Andrea halted halfway to her mug. Jessica stopped in the doorway at the sound of the television. He kept his gaze on the screen, but their eyes were a weight pressing down.

"Fast." Nick shook his head. "Too fast." Moves like that were never about security.

The broadcast cut to file footage showing Sarah crisp in a suit, posture straight, eyes a mask. Hinkins was in uniform, jaw set, blue eyes like chips of ice. The images were archival.

The real version was hollow-eyed in court, anger glossy as oil. Sarah's last statement unsettled him. "You will never be safe."

The old urge to triple-check the locks surfaced, but he reached for the mug and found it cold. "They want them gone before anyone asks the right questions."

Andrea's mouth pressed thin. "Or it's security."

"Maybe." Nick didn't say the part he believed. The system worked hardest to protect itself.

Andrea poured coffee into the cup he'd set out for her, the ceramic clinking softly against the counter. When she turned back, her phone flashed on the island. A message banner slid along the locked screen. In the beat it took him to glance back at the TV, she swiped and thunked the screen, making it go dark again under her palm. A small motion. A huge sound in his head.

He said nothing. He had no right to insist she live without corners to retreat to. Privacy wasn't disloyalty.

Jessica climbed into a chair, hugging Zara tight. "Is Auntie Sarah going to jail forever?" Her eyes widened a notch. She ran her thumb along the lioness's ear, a habit whenever worry crept close.

Nick and Andrea exchanged a glance, years of shared parenting settling the answer between them. He kept his voice even. "She made dangerous choices, and now there are consequences."

"Like a timeout?" Jessica asked.

"A long one." Andrea took his hand. Her wedding band was cool against his skin. Relief came sharply, like air returning after a held note.

The anchor moved on to weather, the radar a red-orange coil rolling up the Gulf, Helene's outer bands already poking the coast with wet fingers. Nick muted the sound again. The house reclaimed its hush, punctured by the storm.

"I should call Quincy."

Andrea nodded. "Tell him I said hi, and ask if the feds have it now, the drive."

He scrolled to Quincy's number and hit dial. One ring. Two. Three. He stepped out onto the back porch to keep his voice from waking the house. The sky had that bruised look it took on before severe weather. Under his feet, the boards creaked.

Four rings. Five. Six.

Voicemail. Quincy's gruff Boston baritone told him to leave a message after the tone.

He went back inside to the table. Jessica was nibbling at the corner of a slice of toast. Andrea watched them both, trying to be in two places at once and coming up short. The lioness sat upright in Jessica's lap, facing the door.

"Voicemail," Nick said.

Andrea winced in sympathy. "He's probably in a briefing."

"Or grabbing coffee." He pretended he agreed. He tried again. On the third attempt, he let it ring out and forced himself to speak. "Quincy, it's Justin. Saw the news. Reach out when you can." Nick almost mentioned "drive" instead of "news." He wanted to ask, "Is it secure?" He settled for, "Appreciate it."

He placed the phone on the table, screen up.

Five minutes later, it buzzed. He grabbed it at once.

"Counselah." Quincy's voice came clipped and cautious, that faint Boston edge curling the vowel, static hissing behind him.

"You knew?"

"Not officially. It was rushed. Paperwork's messy. Signatures don't line up."

"Why now?"

"Helene gives cover. Roads are a mess, and patrol squads are pulled for storm duty. Easier to move a convoy when everybody else is stacking sandbags. You didn't hear it from me."

Nick's hand tightened around the phone. "Route?"

A pause, more static. "East. Toward Lakeland staging. Strictly ground units. No air, the skies are already closed."

Nick's pulse kicked. "And the hard drive?"

Quincy's voice shifted, more guarded. Nick pictured him chewing on a toothpick, the way he always did when buying time.

"Quincy—"

"Nick." The warning was clear. "Keep your family close."

In the background, someone shouted, "Sarge, they want you in the briefing!"

"Gotta go."

"Understood."

"Give Andrea and Jessica my best."

The line went dead. He lowered the phone as the storm hammered their house harder than before.

Nick stood there until Andrea touched his arm, and he remembered to move. He set it down carefully, as if the hard plastic could break.

"What did he say?"

"That the system's working." He tried to smile. It felt like pulling a bandage off a wound.

Jessica hopped down from the chair and came around the table. She tugged his sleeve. "Can I draw while you talk lawyer stuff?" She made the request as if it required formal approval.

"Of course." Nick pulled a pad and a handful of markers from the drawer. She settled down, her attention focused. First, she drew a rectangle for a bus. Then windows. Then the rain slashed the paper from corner to corner. Zara watched, perched like a small queen on the edge.

Air rushed out. He hadn't realized he was holding his breath.

~

Inside, the command center burned blue-white, banks of monitors casting a glow across faces and gear. Carl liked the hum. It smoothed the edges in his head.

He sat with his back straight in a battered office chair. Fifty years had carved him into stone: square face, a thin scar that ran from his left ear to his jaw, visible only when the light caught it right. Scars marked his hands from old work and current hobbies, steady as he spun an unlit cigarette between his fingers. Carl didn't smoke during the planning. The cigarette served as a fuse, the signal that the mission went live.

"Blackbird weather system active." The filtered voice crackled on his secure line. The audio fuzzed for a heartbeat when lightning clawed close overhead. Carl didn't flinch.

Carl checked the corner thermal screen where Helene's bands swirled in hypnotic loops. "Acknowledged. Timeline."

"Target convoy eastbound on I-4. Branch Forbes' exit is in forty-five. Intercept corridor. State patrol reassigned to evacuation route by order."

"Perfect." Carl's tone was flat. He clicked a key and brought up traffic cams. Headlights appeared fuzzy as rain glazed the interstate. Another monitor cycled through team beacons. Alpha holding the cutover, Bravo ready at fallback, Charlie at the ramp, Delta sweeping law enforcement chatter with a sniffer he had borrowed from an old friend and never returned.

He toggled to the manifest. "Digital Storage Device, serial SLV-1984." He said it out loud to make it real. "You're the point of all this trouble." Carl believed in preparation. But the world still acted like a casino, and a wild card was always possible.

A young mercenary in rain gear moved closer. His voice was a hushed murmur. "Boss, outer bands are hitting Corridor Seven already. Drainage is garbage. Could bog the lead SUV before we make contact."

Carl turned his head slowly. The man swallowed. "Adjust your angles. You're not hunting deer. You're closing lanes. Box, not chase. We don't miss. Not today."

The operator nodded and vanished.

Another voice sounded in his earpiece. The Delta tech spoke up. "Federal encryption's still on. EPS jamming in place. Broadband backup has minimal bleed."

"Minimal is where mistakes happen. Clean it."

Carl ran the convoy schematic through his head. Armored SUV, transport bus, two support vehicles: one a decoy if they were smart, two if they were worth their salaries. Helicopter? Not in this weather unless the pilot had a death wish and an order he couldn't refuse. The hurricane wasn't cover—it anchored the plan. Storms slowed the world and turned authority into a suggestion. Communications degraded. Boundaries blurred. And law enforcement got busy with other people's emergencies.

An older team member, Gabe, scarred where his wedding ring used to be, stepped to the table. "What about Adams?" His voice was rough. "Last I heard, he was a problem."

"Adams has been reassigned to sandbag central. Disasters create priorities. We're not top of mind."

Gabe grunted. That was assent. The men drifted back to their stations, current-strong and coordinated.

Carl brought up an image of Corridor Seven. It was lower ground, two lanes each way with an overpass, and a narrow median was already forming standing water. A flashing banner at the bottom of the weather feed warned of flooding. He'd picked it for precisely that reason. No route changes without meeting a lake.

He stared at the clock. Time twisted inside him, both a blur and a crawl, like a film running at the wrong frame rate.

His pulse slowed the way it always did when the map got simple. Decisions were easier when the path narrowed.

"Alpha?" Carl keyed his mic.

"Here."

"Remember your tree line. The first shot's a doorbell, not a knockdown. We want the bus to think the ditch is its friend."

"Copy." The voice was crisp. Alpha always ran it straight.

"Bravo?"

"Here."

"You don't appear till you have to."

"Love being invisible." Bravo had a way of making ghost work sound like an inside joke.

"Charlie?"

"Standing by."

"You're the hand that closes the book. Don't read ahead."

Charlie didn't respond. He never did more than required. The closer didn't chatter.

Carl let the cigarette rest between his lips, the filter familiar at the corner of his mouth. He didn't light it. He never lit it until he had finished giving orders. Superstition, sure, but he and superstition had survived a lot of the same days.

He keyed the last command that pushed a staggered order through the teams: movement times, radio silence windows, fail-safes. The monitors flickered as confirmations came in, green across the board.

"Operation Windfall is active." He spoke to himself as much as to the listening ghosts.

Carl struck the lighter. Flame flared and then settled to a small, steady blue. He lit the cigarette and exhaled, smoke ribboning in the glow of the screens. "Storms clean the streets." He watched the convoy schedule crawl.

Thunder pounded the roof.

~

Nick found the kitchen again. Andrea set a steaming mug in front of him without comment, the handle turned the way he liked. She didn't meet his eyes. He recognized the careful courtesy. She was holding something she couldn't risk showing him. He was doing the same.

Jessica slid off her chair and padded to the window. She pressed Zara's muzzle against the pane and breathed until the fog around the spot widened into a cloud. "Look."

Nick didn't know if she meant the rain or the circle or something else entirely.

He moved beside her and rested a hand on her head. They stood like that for a minute, counting the seconds between lightning strikes. The wind rattled the screen. In the reflected room in the glass was a man he recognized only from old photographs where the eyes had too much fight in them to quit.

The news should have brought calm. It didn't. Relief required trust: in timelines, in signatures, in men who said "protocols" and followed them. It meant trusting the system to make the right decision when nobody was watching. He wanted to believe. He didn't.

Nick looked past their reflections into the storm. The road would be slippery and slow. If you needed to move a bus in that, you'd pick your moment and create your own weather. He didn't want his mind to go there. It went anyway.

Andrea's hand found the small of his back. "We'll get through this." Her voice had the careful weight of a closing argument, nothing wasted, every word deliberate.

"Yeah."

Outside, Helene's rain band swept through, turning everything behind the glass into streaks. Inside, Jessica kept the lioness pressed to the window.

Then the power dipped, the lights flickered, and the refrigerator clicked back on with a sputter. The moment snapped. He finished the coffee and set the mug down, empty, handle turned away from him like a verdict.

WITNESS ELIMINATION

The transfer order was supposed to be closure. Instead, it felt like the opening move in something darker.

3

HELENE'S ARRIVAL

September 26, 2024

Helene arrived as water.

Snell Isle's streets turned to brown channels, coursing fast around mailboxes and swallowing driveways whole. The bay pressed back against the seawalls in sodden breaths. Mangroves bent like drowned umbrellas. The impact glass in the living room held, but each gust caused a tremor.

Nick's eyes flicked toward the old Louisville Slugger propped near the back door, the wooden reminder of Little League seasons now a symbol of defense. He recalled how Louie had saved his life last summer, the strike to Hinkins's temple knocking her out before she could complete her intent to kill.

A few minutes later, he pulled open the drawer and drew his handgun, checking the weight, then sliding it back again. The bat felt honest. The gun was necessary. He waited. The storm did not. He watched the neighborhood drown. The television glowed, the power still on. The crawl never stopped. "I-275 exits flooded. Howard Frankland closed. Gandy underwater. Bay area shelters nearing capacity."

Floorboards creaked as the water rose. A trace of wet plaster mingled with Andrea's wine as she sat at the table, laptop shut, stem glass in hand. Meursault, smooth, buttery, floral. She rolled it once before sipping. The scar at her hairline pulled tight. When she shifted, a sharp, involuntary jolt ran through her arms. A brief touch at her throat, an unconscious tell betraying calculation behind her appearance.

Setting her drink down, she began packing a small bag for Jessica. Her daughter clutched Zara, then placed the lioness on the sill and left the room. Nick said nothing. Stopping his wife would've meant challenging her, and this wasn't the moment.

Nick's jaw clenched. He remembered the fentanyl, the wreck staged to look like carelessness, Sarah's smile in court while Andrea was broken. He didn't speak. He picked up the pen and wrote one word in the margin of Slovin's notebook, "Why?"

"Worst flooding in a hundred years," he muttered.

Jessica's door glowed a strip of blue. Headphones on, she was watching cartoons. Seven years old and already she knew when to vanish.

The feed cut to images of downtown Tampa. Ashley Drive vanished under the river. A trooper carried a dog through chest-deep water. The crawl read, "Federal transfer continues despite conditions."

"The orders were less like coordination, more like sandbags stacked too late," Nick said.

Andrea lifted her wine, eyes hard. "That again? Who signed off on that?"

Nick's phone buzzed against granite. Quincy.

Quincy's name flashed on the screen, and he pictured his friend's tall, solid frame and Boston accent.

DON'T BE ANYWHERE NEAR GANDY OR I-4.

A second line appeared.

Transfer moved. Lakeland site. Skies closed.

The vowels, the Bostonian edge, bled through the words.
He typed.

Whose order?

Three dots then nothing.

"Nick." Andrea's voice was even. "Are you listening to me?"

"Yeah." He pocketed the device. "It's nothing."

Andrea studied him, hand steady though her leg betrayed her. "Nothing makes you look like that."

Pinching the bridge of his nose, he let the silence stretch. "I'm watching."

"Nick, you don't simply watch. You tally. You build cases. Then you argue until someone breaks." She tilted her head. "That's fine. I like to know whether to put pillows on the stairs."

Pillows on the stairs, family code. A storm ritual born of Jessica's fear of bad weather. A survival drill disguised as a joke.

On-screen, a state official promised coordination. But the video feed displayed I-4 near Plant City: lanes backed up and drivers panicked. A cruiser angled sideways, lights spinning through floodwater.

Nick's stomach knotted. That wasn't damage. It was a choke point. Lower ground, no exits, escorts bunched.

Buzz. Unknown number.

STAY INSIDE. TRUST NOTHING.

Andrea lowered her glass. "Is it Quincy?"

"Not this one."

"Then who?"

"I don't know."

"You always know."

"Not tonight." He showed her the phone.

Her eyes didn't move. She had been an expert witness once, the kind jurors trusted more than surgeons. Even now, she parsed him like testimony.

"What would you tell a jury if they asked why moving anyone during a hurricane was the right call?"

"That it wasn't." He swallowed. "That a bigger risk outweighed the storm."

"National security." Her tone was dry.

"That's what they'll say."

"And you?"

"I don't have standing."

"You manage to find it when it suits you."

The phone buzzed.

ROUTES CHANGED. NOT PUBLIC.

He typed.

Where?

Nothing back.

Andrea frowned. "You think it's her."

Sarah's name didn't need to be said. Sarah, who had smiled in court while whispering, "You will never be safe." Even now, Nick could picture her unnaturally steady gaze.

Andrea touched her scar, a twitch running through her thigh. "Then lock the doors. Stop staring at windows you can't control." She stood looking around the house. "Nick, preparation for the storm is the best plan."

At Jessica's bedroom door, Nick knocked once. "Jess, sweetie, we have to stay close and get ready for this weather."

Jessica's voice came muffled. "Do I bring Barrister?" The cat's collar jingled.

"Bring him. He's part of the plan."

He gathered pillows and flashlights, then rechecked the locks.

～

An hour later, he cracked the front door and stared outside. The water had climbed another step, a darker stripe marking its rise.

His phone buzzed again. Unknown.

Stay inside. Trust nothing. Your daughter's guardian is a lie.

"If they knock, don't open it." His fist clenched.

Andrea pointed to the landing. "Pillows on the stairs."

The glass in the window frame shivered. A siren faltered and died. Helene pressed close, but something else was moving through Tampa tonight.

WITNESS ELIMINATION

His hand hovered above the deadbolt, rhythm ticking. His breath hitched, tight and shallow, matching the rising flood. Outside, a truck's headlights swept the drowned street.

For a beat, the world shrank to pulse and rain. His heartbeat thudded against the roar, waiting for what came next.

Weather whipped the windows so hard the frame shivered. Thunder rolled on their block. On every block.

～

The bus shuddered in the gusts, its metal skin strained as Helene's immense pressure tightened around it. Sally didn't flinch. "They think cuffs make a difference. They don't." Shackles clinked in rhythm with the downpour, a nervous percussion.

Sally—lean, buzz cut plastered to her skull, tattoos peeking from her sleeves—sat steady. Her blue eyes didn't blink.

The transport groaned through standing water, each turn a gamble between grip and glide. Rain hammered so hard the wipers carved gray slats that vanished. Inside, the air was thick, metallic, damp.

Sarah was in the second row, wrists cuffed, ankles chained. She ignored the bruises. Her gaze swept the cabin. Weaknesses everywhere. Daniel, in charge, pacing tightly, the driver chewing, another corrections officer slumped in his seat, three rear guards soft on posture. Timing would decide the rest.

Sally, beside her, poised as if she were back on stage, planted her feet and loosened her shoulders as she scanned the room with sniper calm. She glanced at Sarah.

The bus fishtailed through a flooded stretch. Chains clattered. A guard cursed. One inmate whispered a prayer. Then Sally angled forward. Her tone was level. "Breathe. It's the water, not the steering wheel. Get a grip or you'll slide off the road."

Daniel twisted around. His scowl was sharp. "Shut it."

Sally didn't look at him. Her focus held on Sarah. "Spacing's broken. Rear guards are soft. They'll bottle us soon." She lowered her voice. "Say the word, and I'll run point."

Sarah gave the faintest smile. "Patience. Timing matters."

The driver tapped the radio. His speaker hissed back muffled.

The change of route hadn't been a mistake. Sarah had been aware of the delay since the lawyer's last visit.

Daniel snarled into the mic. Static.

He turned. "If this thing rolls, you drown cuffed."

Sally tilted in. "She won't."

"You volunteering to save her?"

"Said she won't drown cuffed."

It was a warning. Daniel looked away first.

Sarah caught Sally's eye, and a flicker—sharp and acknowledging—passed between them, a shared, chilling amusement at the guard's limited imagination.

The driver muttered, "Orders said push through."

Sarah's smile barely registered. National security was the mask. Behind it were contracts, politicians, cartel money, the same decay that tried to kill Andrea.

"DOT would've flagged this. If it's still open, someone wants it open."

She nodded. "Exactly."

They crested a rise. Branch Forbes Road was ahead. Lanes torn apart, floodwater slicing across. The escorts funneled in. Trap set.

On the shoulder, a utility truck idled. A man in a county jacket waved a flashlight. Next to him, another figure moved with squared hips and balanced steps. Not workers but operatives.

Sally shifted. She turned her body to shield her conspirator. "Not a trooper stance, it's too calm."

Daniel gestured. "Open the door."

Her attention stayed on Sarah; she would kill or die at the signal. Sarah nodded once. At that nod, a cold, thrilling knot of certainty tightened in Sally's chest.

Sally eased her foot back, tested her range, and measured the lunge distance.

The driver cracked the door. The sound of the world outside—all rain and roaring wind—pushed into the bus. A plume of spray and air pressure rushed in, carrying the scent of diesel. The county man stepped closer, badge flashing authentic enough at a glance.

Daniel fidgeted, fingers brushing the seat seam.

Sarah's hazel eyes caught his. She leaned forward, her voice calm but cutting. "Relax." She cocked her head. "It's time." A smirk played at her lips.

Sally's nod was reverent. The guards hadn't realized yet. Death was already in the cabin.

≈

Lightning flashed, catching the jagged scar that split Carl's lip. He traced it without thinking. Smoke spiraled above the monitors.

He hunched in the gutted shell of a utility van parked along a Plant City frontage road. Fake company logos peeled from the doors, orange cones scattered across the shoulder.

The perfect cover. Roads underwater meant repair crews everywhere. No one looked twice.

Inside, equipment hummed. The laptop showed a grid of colored dots—convoy signals. They crawled eastbound, bunched at the washout. Rear escort lagging. Lead vehicle edging forward, hesitant.

He paused. The faintest smile touched his lips. Everything was in motion. The pieces were sliding into place.

A steady voice came over the comms. "Visual confirm. Bus boxed at Forbes. Driver rattled. Door cracked."

"Observation is control," La Reina had always said. Today, with every camera feed and comm signal, Carl made it true.

He keyed his mic. "Copy. Hold posture. No action until phase two. Let them sweat the rising water."

"Understood."

He checked the clock. Perfect. The one-day delay had bought this. By morning, flood rescues would drown out the headlines. A prisoner transport vanishing would initially register as storm collateral. Behind him, the crew waited without a sound. They wanted the weather to carry the blame. No footprint.

The laptop beeped. Convoy locked. He toggled a hacked street-cam. Grainy images but good enough. The vehicles sat boxed in, hazard lights reflecting. Guards hovered by the open door.

"Phase one complete."

"No cheers."

Noise was amateur. Professionals didn't hoot.

Next was redirection. Not Colorado. A black hangar at Lakeland Linder. A jet was waiting as a decoy. By dawn, the prisoners would be past jurisdiction, the paperwork buried in relief files.

Carl sneered, "Efficient."

The crew stirred. The praise was adequate.

He keyed the mic. "Hold. No action until the reroute clears. The storm takes the blame."

"Copy. They'll break soon."

Carl closed the laptop, dimming the glow. He waited. Phase two would begin the moment they believed they still had choices.

Outside, Helene howled, drowning everything in silence and rain.

4

THE BOTTLENECK

Rain slashed sideways across Branch Forbes, washing the blacktop into the ditches. The prison convoy crawled forward, headlights turned to blunted orbs in the downpour.

The lead driver braked hard. Engines groaned. The column bunched, the bus and SUVs packed together like caged animals.

"Jesus Christ," the sergeant muttered from the first SUV. He pushed open the door, boots immediately sinking ankle-deep in mud. Warm water soaked his trousers. Wind stung his face. He tilted his chin against the gale and stared at the ruin. "Road's half gone. Put any weight on it and we're swimming."

A younger guard leaned from the window, eyes darting, the brim of his hat dripping into his collar. "Orders say no stops. Straight through."

"Orders mean nothing if you drown in ten feet of water!" The sergeant's voice was granite. He scanned the stretch ahead. Floodlights snapped on. Engines idled. Amber strobes cut through the downpour.

A county truck blocked the detour, flanked by men in reflective vests and hard hats blurred by rain. They beckoned the convoy forward with steady, rehearsed sweeps—too precise for men battling weather.

The rookie brightened. He brushed wet hair from his freckled brow. "County crew. They've got us."

The men in vests stood unmoving. "Then why aren't they moving?" the sergeant grumbled.

He lifted his radio. Static roared, devouring his call for verification.

Behind him, drivers shouted over the engine rumble, some yelling to reverse, others to push through before the water took out the road. The ditch to the right churned like a river. On the left, cypress trees sagged under the weight of waterlogged branches.

"Nobody moves until I say."

His breath hitched once. "We're boxed in."

~

Sarah touched her throat. Hazel eyes steady, already calculating how long till the trap snapped shut.

Sally leaned. Chains clinked. Her blue eyes scanned the floodlit highway: the convoy was bunched too tightly, and the impostors signaled. Not work crews. Predators. They stood with squared stances, set their bodies, and watched the bus. Discipline like that came from combat, not the county payroll. She smirked.

Sarah studied the men, rain light playing across their stern features. Then she turned, that controlled smile tightening Sally's chest, anticipation tangled with loyalty.

"One way in." She smoothed a damp strand behind her ear, authority radiating from her calm.

Sally's pulse spiked. "It's staged."

The woman in cuffs leaned back, metal clicking. Sally tapped her wrist against her thigh, setting a rhythm she could own. "Of course."

The guard posted at the bus door. "Sit back!" His own hands trembled on his weapon strap, his tone edged, but his eyes wild.

Another pressed his face to the windshield, trying to read the detour through the foggy glass. "If we stall here, the flood washes us away." His voice carried across the vehicle.

Sarah tipped her head, listening to the storm. "Nature makes an excellent accomplice."

Sally's wrists flexed against steel. "They won't see it until it's too late."

"They never do." Sarah's eyes glittered with satisfaction.

WITNESS ELIMINATION

~

Water climbed another step on the stoop, wind rattling panes in staccato bursts, each gust pressing damp air into the house. The power failed, and the generator hummed, casting a thin yellow light across the living room and staircase, where pillows had been stacked into a fortress.

Andrea moved with purpose, her hair pulled back in a tight ponytail, inspected flashlights, and counted batteries aloud for Jessica to hear. "Three flashlights, two lanterns, twelve batteries. Again." She kept her voice steady, a deliberate tactic to keep Jess busy.

Jessica hugged Barrister, the cat's bell tinkling as he squirmed. His fur was damp and musky with warmth, making her clutch him tighter. "Do I have to keep him in the drill?"

"He's part of the family." Andrea checked the lantern. "We practice with everyone we protect."

"He freezes every time." Jessica set Barrister down on the lowest step. "He doesn't like storms."

"No one does," Andrea said.

Jessica sprinted upstairs, feet slapping wood, then raced back down. Her breath loud in the hush, she slid to a stop at Andrea's side, eyes shining with effort.

"Done!" She was breathless, triumphant.

Andrea managed a smile. "Perfect time, sweetheart. You passed."

The television's glow continued to convey the bad news. The storm and high tide overflowed entire neighborhoods. A sewage plant shut down. Warnings crawled across the screen. "Boil water. Don't flush toilets."

Nick leaned closer, his bald head reflecting the screen's cold light.

Andrea turned. "You're staring holes in the TV. What is it?"

"Flood damage. Nothing else."

Her gaze held him. She didn't believe it.

The girl's laughter was thin, nervous at the edges. She pressed her ear against Andrea's chest, listening for steadiness. She must have heard her mother's heart racing, because she hugged the cat tighter, sensing what neither parent said aloud. Barrister went rigid in her arms, not purring, not struggling, absorbing the fear that bled from their skin.

Nick's phone buzzed. Unknown number.

NOT COLORADO.

Colorado was the endgame—the supermax, the lockbox where Sarah and Sally would vanish forever. If the convoy wasn't headed west, the entire premise was a lie.

His lawyer brain dissected it, motive and opportunity—a diversion disguised as duty.

Andrea stepped closer, composure cracking a fraction. "Who is it?"

"Nothing." He adjusted the phone.

"Try again."

Her fingers tapped once against her thigh, a contained thunderclap. Her silence sliced. She didn't believe him.

Buzz.

STAY INSIDE. TRUST NOTHING.

He read it twice. The storm's rattling windows sounded like gavels. His teeth grazed his lower lip, an unconscious tell she filed away.

Andrea turned. "Pillows in place." She turned to Jessica, her voice steady as a metronome. "Lights-out drill next."

The girl looked between them. "Do we sleep on the stairs?"

"Only if we have to." Andrea smoothed the girl's hair. "Go again."

Nick didn't move. The texts replayed in his head. Not Colorado. Stay inside. Trust nothing.

He typed.

WHO ARE YOU?

No answer.

IF NOT COLORADO, WHERE?

Nothing.

WHY SHOULD I TRUST YOU?

Three dots pulsed.

YOU SHOULDN'T.

A photo followed. Branch Forbes. A swollen ditch eating into the shoulder. The lead SUV, the prison bus, and two trailing support vehicles sat idle, trapped.

How did they get this picture? They were involved, but why warn me?

She appeared at his elbow. "If there's something I need to know, tell me now."

"Quincy's not answering."

"Then tell me what we're preparing for."

He looked at her, at the scar beneath her hairline. What Sarah and Hinkins had cost them.

He turned away. He braced a hand on the wall, grounding against the rising panic. "We prepare for the worst, but we stay inside."

Andrea's mouth flattened. "Keeping me in the dark is not helping."

He exhaled. "This situation doesn't feel right."

∽

On the bus, everything tightened at once. Air. Cuffs. Voices.

Sally took a deep breath. The guard nearest her stopped pretending he wasn't scared. He kept cutting his eyes toward the floodlights, then back to Sarah. Her expression was thin and unchanging.

A rivulet found a seam above the window and dripped onto Sally's knee, shock-cold, real.

"Tell me." Sarah's voice was soft but carried absolute command. "What do you see that the others don't?"

Sally swallowed. "They want us to choose the road. Not because it's safe but because it's theirs."

Her smile was small and satisfied. "Good."

The transport lurched forward as the driver took the gap. Water climbed the wheel wells with a chewing sound. On the steps, the guard braced his shoulder against the door, as if he could keep the storm out by will alone.

~

At the first SUV, the sergeant lowered his hands to calm his men and turned to the rookie. "You, come with me. The rest stay. I need to warn the bus."

"Reverse!" He signaled back.

"We'll drown if we stall!"

"The shoulders are gone!"

He stood at the SUV's door, rain streaming off his cap. "Look at their feet." He nudged the rookie. The kid gripped his rifle so tight his knuckles blanched, freckles stark against his skin. "Spacing's wrong. They're not workers. They're a line."

Lightning strobed white.

The rookie swallowed. "If we sit here, water will make us hydroplane. If we turn, the prison transport jackknifes or lands in a ditch. If we go, we risk—"

"If we go, we're in someone else's plan."

The bus driver leaned on his horn. "Pick something. The water's rising." Thunder rolled across the sky.

Radio static answered every call. The men in vests didn't close the gap. They only gestured—unbothered, unblinking—leaving a slit of road no wider than a bus.

The convoy was already inside the trap, and the storm sealed the lid.

5

THE DIVERSION

The sergeant trudged from the lead SUV and stood in the prison bus doorway, his frame silhouetted by swaying, rain-streaked light. Water poured down his neck, soaking his collar, plastering his shirt to his skin.

He pressed the radio tight to his ear. Static. A hiss with no voice, no anchor—emptiness. He slapped the handset, motioned to the rookie to stay near, and scanned for any way out.

Engines strained against the current. Diesel fumes drifted back, mixing with the stink of wet canvas and the faint ammonia of prisoner sweat. Chains rattled. The sound set his teeth on edge. Thunder carried orders farther than radios ever could, cloaking intent behind a veil of rain.

The rookie crept closer, breath fogging. "County crew." His voice was thin. "They're waving us through." His hand trembled on the rifle, his thumb brushed the safety.

The sergeant narrowed his eyes. The figures weren't gesturing anymore. Their arms hung still, rainwater sluicing off their sleeves. Their boots hadn't moved—no shuffle, no bracing. In weather like this, men hunched against the gale. These didn't. They looked carved from the dark. Their tools caught the light.

"County crew, my ass." He shifted his stance, his footing against the current.

He leaned into the prison bus, slamming his hand on the console. "Back it up." He flicked two fingers to warn the driver.

The driver's Adam's apple bobbed. "Orders are clear. Straight line, no stops." He checked the mirror. Indecision clouded his gaze.

"Shut up and—" A muscle jumped beneath the sergeant's eye—the first crack in his control. He opened his mouth to shout again and never got the chance.

A pressure wave hit. The blast punched the oxygen out of his lungs. He flew backward out of the prison transport, sprawling onto the flooded roadway.

The lead escort SUV erupted in a geyser of flame.

It rose into the air, wheels spinning, headlights casting useless beams into the sky. Fire blew through its belly, the roof peeled back, metal shrieking. Windows burst across the bus, shards slicing faces and arms. The air reeked of acrid gasoline, burning rubber, and the copper tang of blood misting into the rain.

The rookie near his shoulder pitched left, half his jaw gone. Then the mud swallowed him.

Prisoners screamed, shackles clanging like mad bells. One slammed his forehead against the shattered window, trying to climb through it.

Sally's throat tightened. She pressed back on the seat, muscles taut, eyes searching for a sliver of opportunity. Her pulse synced with the rattle of chains—a rhythm she refused to let become fear.

The sergeant tried dragging the rookie with him as shrapnel streaked overhead. A fragment the size of a fist punched into the bus, hitting inches from his skull. The stench of burned hair turned his stomach. The rookie was dead. *Fuck. Thought I was saving you, kid.* His fingers tightened once on the kid's sleeve before he released his grip.

When the concussion rolled back, the SUV lay in the ditch, its front buried in mud, fire spitting beneath the hood. Black smoke billowed, thick and oily, laced with scorched metal.

"Contact!" His throat was raw. He fired, hands steady while panic surged around him.

Gunfire answered. Disciplined bursts, three at a time. Muzzle flashes flickered like fireflies—controlled, deliberate. Figures in dark gear slid through the tree line, masks glistening. They moved like shadows, rifles braced, aim unwavering.

Guards fired back—frantic, blind. Tracers hissed into the trees, vanishing. One officer spun as a round struck his chest, blood jetting hot into the rain. Another clutched his cheek, bone split, teeth spilling into his palm.

The sergeant's breath came fast. He squeezed shots into the rain, the recoil hammering against his wrist. The sharp bite of cordite fought the storm's rot in his nose.

A blast roared behind him.

Heat seared his neck. The rear escort SUV folded in on itself, tires shearing off, chunks of steel whistling overhead. A guard on the platform screamed as a shard tore through his thigh.

For an instant, fire lit both ends of the road.

The convoy stood boxed in by its own destruction.

"Trapped." A muscle along his temple jumped, eyes burning. "God help us."

Smoke crawled into his throat, each cough a reminder he was still alive. He wiped rain from his lashes, but the world stayed blurred.

The bus became a furnace of heat and iron.

A cutting charge ripped through its right flank, peeling metal back like foil.

The scene collapsed into shrieks and fumes. Seats tore loose from the frame, bolts snapped. Shards of glass swept over the prisoners, slicing skin, embedding in arms and cheeks.

The blast hurled Sally sideways. Her shoulder smashed into the seat bars. Pain burst down her arm. Her lip ripped open against the steel cuffs, copper flooding her mouth. She coughed, choking on soot. Her focus snapped tight as she shifted her body, trying to brace.

Guards staggered in the aisle. Ears leaked. Weapons slipped in their grips. One fell on a body. Another clawed at his eyes as blood ran between his fingers.

A guard lurched too close.

His rifle jerked in his shaking hands. The barrel knocked against seat backs as the floor tilted under him. His soles skidded on the mix of rainwater and blood spreading beneath him. His eyes were wild, unmoored.

Sally lunged. Her shoulders coiled, wrists snapping hard in the cuffs. The chain cinched into his throat. He gagged, eyes bulging as his nails scraped at the links. His breath came in wet spurts on her cheek. She planted her feet and pulled, muscles burning, tendons straining to the edge.

His heels hammered the metal decking. Each impact shuddered the frame. He slammed her into the wall—once, twice. Pain flared white behind her eyes, but she held tight. Her vision pulsed black around the edges. The stink twisted her stomach. She swallowed hard and refused to loosen her grip.

"Stop fighting." Cartilage crunched under her pull. His body jerked three times, then went slack. She let him slump to the floor.

Her hands tore at his belt, slick with blood. Keys jingled as she ripped them free, knuckles smashing the buckle. Her fingers trembled. The edge slipped, scraping the lock and cutting her palm. She tried again.

Click.

The shackle released.

Her wrists were raw, skin torn open by the steel, but she was loose. She dragged air into her lungs and fought the taste of smoke.

Around her, the other inmates—Bruth'rs gang enforcers—reacted with urgency.

"Sarah." Her voice was a rasp.

Sarah straightened. She brushed glass from her sleeve. She held out her wrists, calm and expectant, eyes bright with intent.

Sally shoved the key into the second lock. Metal clattered to the deck.

Sarah flexed her hands once, then knelt and pulled the dead guard's rifle free. She racked it, the motion smooth, practiced. A round slid home with a metallic click.

Wind forced its way through the ripped-open side of the bus. It whipped her hair across her face. Vengeance flickered in her eyes.

"Now it begins." Her voice was assured.

Sally felt something settle inside—steady, cold, necessary.

WITNESS ELIMINATION

Gunfire shredded the transport. Rounds punched through panels. Ricochets screamed off torn seat frames. Prisoners cried out, pinned, chained, bleeding.

Hot air churned with metal dust and blood-thick heat, stifling as steam. A prisoner crawled, dragging shackled legs through the aisle, until a burst caught him mid-scream and folded him forward. Sally flung the keys to another inmate. "Free the Bruth'rs!"

Guards yelled over one another, their voices fraying as orders dissolved into thunder and rifle-stutter. One fired blindly, lighting the haze, but his rounds chewed harmlessly into the seats. The return fire from the shadows was instant and silencing.

Sarah marked every movement. She had been bound like prey.

Not anymore.

Outside, boots splashed closer. Rifles cracked through the storm.

The trap had sprung. The bus was no cage now—it was a killing ground. And Sally and Sarah were the only predators left alive.

∼

Escort Vehicle Three was armored, providing tail security and carrying what mattered most.

Inside the SUV, agents Marcus, Keane, and Ortiz remained silent, their calm brittle and thinning. Radios hissed static, a greasy crackle filling the cabin. Rain streaked the windshield. Wipers dragged in fast, useless arcs. Diesel fumes seeped through the vents. Sweat and oil hung in the air.

On the seat between them sat the reinforced case—black, steel-edged, waterproof. The Slovin archive.

Agent Marcus kept one hand near it, fingers drumming the latch as if counting down. Older than the others, with a knife-thin scar on his jaw from a job that had gone sideways, he stared at the road. "Lead's destroyed." His eyes locked on the sudden bloom of fire where the escort had been. The world flashed white-orange—metal, rain, and screams blending into one electric blast. "Reverse. Move it! We're the target now."

The convoy ahead looked less like protection and more like a barricade carved open by violence.

"Then we hold." Keane braced himself in the passenger seat. He checked his rifle again, tension in every line of his posture. "That drive's a ledger of corruption—enough to topple governments or prop them up. Orders were clear. It doesn't leave this truck."

Ortiz sat behind them, sweat streaking down his jaw despite the cold seeping through the seams. His grip tightened on his Glock. "Orders don't mean shit if we're dead." He scanned the rear window in a search for escape that wasn't there.

The SUV jolted. A second blast illuminated the storm. Heat scorched the glass. Fire licked through the dark steel fragments raining across the road.

Marcus's gut clenched. "Rear's gone. It's us."

Static swallowed Keane's next callout. Then came a different sound—shrill, slicing through metal.

The RPG struck broadside.

The explosion engulfed them. The armored SUV flipped, rolling once, twice. Belts tore into shoulders. Glass shattered inward, carving skin. Airbags burst. The final crash plunged them into a ditch half-filled with water. Bones rattled from the impact.

Warm, muddy floodwater poured in through the torn frame. Gasoline and scorched plastic burned the air.

Ortiz coughed blood, streaking the seat. He clutched the case against his chest. "Rear contact!" His voice cracked.

Keane shoved his rifle through the blown-out window and fired. The flashes lit the trees. Shadows darted. Boots splashed closer—measured, practiced, no wasted steps.

"They're here!" He tore out his pistol and shot through the fractured windshield. Glass bit into his forearm as he leaned forward for a clearer line. Sparks skittered off the hood. A figure advanced through the haze, face hidden behind a rain-slick mask, rifle anchored tight.

Return fire shredded the SUV. Bullets punched through the opening. Keane gasped as three rounds pierced his vest and chest. "Get the drive out—"

He sagged sideways, breath rattling once before it stopped. Blood and hot fabric smoke twisted into the air.

"Push them back!" Marcus's voice frayed at the edges.

He fired in controlled bursts, each recoil drilling into already-bruised muscle. One attacker fell. Another dropped into the ditch, water erupting red. For half a moment, they could stall the assault. Then his slide locked dry. He slammed in a new mag and kept firing.

Ortiz clawed his way over the seat, dragging the satchel. Upholstery shredded. Stuffing floated around like ash. A round punched into his thigh; another ripped through his shoulder. He screamed but didn't release the case—fingers welded onto the handle by desperation and memory.

"Cover me!"

Marcus moved with him, crawling through twisted metal. Mud slicked his hands. Each breath seared smoke into his lungs.

Masked figures closed in, rifles raised. Their steps were sure, converging in an encirclement.

Marcus fired again. One shot clipped a leg. Another punched a shoulder. But they advanced anyway, methodical, inevitable.

He collapsed next to Ortiz. Lungs burned. Skin blistered where embers had kissed him.

Ortiz dragged the case closer. "I've got it!" He lifted his Glock with a trembling hand. His eyes flicked to the charred wreck of the convoy. Then he pressed the barrel against Marcus's temple. "I collect now."

A shape loomed in the overhead—masked, rifle ready.

"You were slow today, Ortiz."

Ortiz let out a shaking breath. "Damn. That was too close. Wasn't expecting the RPG." He raised a hand toward the operative. "Help me up."

The mercenary didn't move.

"La Reina requires a clean transition." The voice was cold as clipped wire. "Your payment was for efficiency, not survival."

"But I got you the delay— and the—hard drive—"

The shot cut him off.

Ortiz fell into the water, the satchel slipping from his grasp. Blood washed into the runoff. An operative scooped up the case. He wiped the handle once and sealed it into a larger waterproof satchel.

"Drive secure." Authority carried even through the mask. "Observation is control"—La Reina's creed—"and every angle is accounted for."

The SUV smoked in the ditch, half-submerged, its roof peeled back. Rain funneled through the wreckage, diluting the blood into pale spirals. The stench of gasoline, ozone, and burnt wiring hung in the air.

"Retrieve our fallen. Then move to the bus."

They disappeared into the hurricane, leaving three dead agents by the wreck.

The Slovin case rode in the satchel—dark leverage packed with names, accounts, and the rot behind the storm. Where it went next would decide everything.

~

The bus had become a slaughterhouse.

Sally tightened her grip on the pistol she'd ripped from the guard's holster, the handle slick with sweat and blood. A muscle jumped in her cheek. Her wrists still throbbed, but the steel didn't own her anymore. Smoke clawed at their throats; each cough was a reminder she was still breathing.

Daniel, the talkative guard, fired blind toward the shattered flank. His hands shook. His rounds tore into prisoners still bound to benches, their cries ending in wet rattles.

Sarah lifted the rifle—calm, deliberate—and shot once.

The round punched through his eye. His skull burst in a red spray against the window.

Sally waded through the chaos. Her boots slipped on the slick floor. A prisoner grabbed her ankle, his gaze desperate. Blood bubbled from his lungs.

"Not now." She kicked him free.

WITNESS ELIMINATION

He slid into broken glass and bodies. The chain clinked before stillness took over. The air reeked of bile and cordite.

Sarah lowered the weapon and met her lover's eyes. "It's done."

Sally's breath locked hard in her chest. Together, they climbed through the torn siding.

Rain lashed their skin, cold against the fire devouring the bus. Flames roared behind them, orange and hungry, clawing at the storm that spat down to smother them. The escorts were in ruins. Wreckage glowed like bones in a pyre. Bodies littered the asphalt—arms tangled, rifles dropped, faces slack in the downpour.

Around her, the other inmates—Bruth'rs enforcers caught in the sweep—lay scattered. Sally paused just long enough to lift two fingers in a small, silent salute. No time for more.

From the tree line, masked operatives melted back into the dark. The Slovin hard drive was already gone.

Sally wiped her mouth with the back of her hand. She smeared blood across her cheek.

"They hit everything." Her voice was rough.

"That was the point." Sarah stepped over a corpse without looking down. She tilted her head. She assessed the carnage the way some people reviewed case files.

Gunfire still cracked in the distance, but none aimed at them.

Sally shifted her grip on the pistol. "Where to?"

Sarah checked the rifle's chamber, eyes sharp beneath wind-whipped hair. "Forward."

Sally nodded once.

Side by side, they walked free—silhouettes carved in fire and storm, hardened in blood, alive when they shouldn't be.

6

GHOSTS IN THE STORM

Rain battered the Justin house, rattling the panes and pooling in the sills. The generator's thrum faded into the background, steady as a heartbeat. A faint vibration moved through the floorboards with each gust, as if the whole house were bracing its weight against the wind. Even the flicker of the television felt submerged, with the sound gone flat and distant, as if the house had sunk beneath the waves.

Nick stood in front of the TV, arms folded so tight his shoulders ached. His reflection hovered on the screen, ghostlike, eyes rimmed with sleepless hollows. He barely recognized himself—like a man waiting on a verdict he expects to lose. The crawl at the bottom scrolled in endless loops—floods, outages, shelters—but offered nothing he needed: no sign of federal transport, no hint of them.

He pictured Sarah adjusting her cuffs with that courtroom grace, each movement a statement of control. Sally, scanning exits—even in locked rooms. Their absence was a warning, a void too deliberate to ignore. The convoy had already been forgotten.

Andrea curled on the couch, legs tucked beneath her, while Jessica leaned in, small and tense. On the coffee table, her sketchpad spun with every rumble from the generator, the pencil tracing loose arcs. Barrister kneaded her thigh and flicked his tail in agitated bursts.

Lamps cast double shadows, corners thick with things unseen. The darkness stretched and breathed with them, hoarding its secrets.

Jessica hugged her knees. "Why don't they talk about the bus?"

Andrea opened her mouth, then closed it again. She smoothed a hand through Jessica's tangled hair, pausing at her temple to feel the flutter of nerves beneath. "The weather is big, honey. Bigger than anything else now." Her voice stayed soft, but her eyes flicked to Nick, asking questions she couldn't say aloud.

Nick's gaze never left the screen as he shifted his weight, tightening his stance. "Bigger than a federal transport ambushed in the middle of it?"

She shot him a sharp look, but he pushed on. "They'd never bury something like that. Not unless someone wanted it buried."

Jessica curled into her mother, quiet as Barrister, who was now asleep. Andrea kissed the top of her head. "Go check your flashlight, sweetheart. And maybe his treats too."

Jessica slid from the couch, careful not to wake the cat. She gathered her sketchpad to her chest like a shield and moved toward the stairs. At the base, she paused and glanced back, eyes moving from her mother to Nick as if trying to read the current in the room. Then she vanished upstairs. The storm drowned out her footsteps.

When her door clicked shut, Andrea turned, voice stripped of patience. Softness left her eyes.

"Stop. She doesn't need to hear it. Not tonight."

Nick ran a hand across his scalp, pressing hard enough to leave marks. "She asked."

"Jess is scared. She asked because she feels us coming apart."

Andrea moved to the kitchen, hands trembling as she braced against the counter. Her fingers splayed on the cold surface, the chill biting into her palms and keeping her from slamming a cupboard.

"What she needs is calm, not your conspiracies in a blackout. We don't know anything. For all we know, the transport made it."

Nick paced, bare feet on cool tile. "They know more than they're saying." He peered through rain-slick glass, as if answers waited in the space. A spike of pain throbbed behind his eyes. "It's not a conspiracy if it happened. I know what silence sounds like, and it's worse than a lie."

Andrea stared at the dark pane, where water etched shifting shadows. Her knuckles whitened on the counter. "You think you're the only one who sees what's happening? I see it too, but I don't get to chase ghosts. I have to keep her alive."

She still felt the phantom slip of Jessica's hand on that bridge, the moment her world had dropped out from under her.

Lightning strobed through the window, hitting close. The generator's steady hum stuttered and coughed, a tremor running through the floor as it fought to hold. It finally choked, plunging the television into brief darkness. The anchor's image snapped back on, flickering, before the generator regained its rhythm. Still nothing.

Nick's phone jolted in his palm with a text from an unknown number:

Not Colorado. Lakeland confirmed.

His hand tightened around it. His pulse kicked once, hard. He locked the screen, the device suddenly heavy.

Andrea dried her hands, shoulders tight as she turned. "What is it?"

"Nothing." He shoved it into his pocket, throat constricted. "You think I don't know the risk? This isn't about the storm. It never was. They're not phantoms, Andrea. Sarah, your sister, swore in court we'd never be safe again. Hinkins told me I was next."

Andrea braced on the counter, forearms twitching. "You're right. It's not the weather. It's choices. And now, you're choosing shadows over your family."

She leaned forward. Her voice dropped to a fierce whisper. "You don't know what it felt like when my heart stopped on that bridge. I have to keep her alive. She needs you here."

Upstairs, Jessica's door creaked, making a slight, scared sound. Nick's phone buzzed again. He flinched, pulling it out with a sudden, desperate motion.

By dawn, they will be ghosts.

Not memories. Warnings. Debts long past due.

He slipped it into his pocket, hands unsteady.

~

Thirty miles east, Carl's van sliced through water pooled on the highway. Night pressed on the glass, broken only by the blue console glow and the pulse of rain in the headlights. Tires hissed, and the van shuddered in the crosswind. Inside, one of the seat belts vibrated faintly against its buckle, rattling with each uneven gust.

Sarah sat in the rear, posture perfect, gaze serene, eyes half-lidded, as if meditating instead of plotting her next move. The cuffs were gone. She rubbed dark, angry grooves around her wrists. She had worn restraints before. These hadn't been the worst—just the latest.

Sally knelt on the floor, fingers sore and blood-slicked. A grin curled as she tucked the knife into her waistband. The van dipped slightly, forcing her to shift her balance to stay steady. Pain sparked with every flex. She ran her thumb along the blade until it bit, savoring the sting. Pain kept her sharp. It reminded her she was moving again.

Carl studied the monitors—grainy live traffic, drone feeds, and weather maps streaked with red. His scar caught the light as he sipped cold coffee. His mouth twisted at the taste. The hum of electronics breathed through the interior: fan whir, quiet processor clicks, the faint smell of warmed plastic clinging to the air.

From the front seat, one man spoke up. "Local stations are clear. No mention of the convoy."

"They wouldn't risk it. Silence is obedience."

Sarah's lips curved at the edges. "You're right. A lie invites scrutiny. Silence teaches people to accept." She adjusted her sleeves with precise, controlled movements. Chaos didn't sway her—it clarified things. "People prefer not to know."

Sally leaned back, cradling the blade's heft. "We're free. Imagine that."

Sarah met her eyes, calm and certain. "We were always free. The rest didn't know it yet."

Sally's grin tightened. She positioned the knife hilt at her waist, settling it where she liked it.

Carl watched the radar as rain bands crawled over the map. He tapped one of the dials out of habit, calibrating a display that didn't need it.

"Lakeland air traffic control is closed, but the restricted hangar there is prepared. By 0300, authorities will believe they have to lock the airfield before sunrise."

"And if they find out?" Sally's voice was tight, edged. "They always find something."

"They won't." Sarah tested her fingers again, satisfied. "The world only looks where it's told."

Carl's laugh slid through the interior. One of the men in the front shifted in his seat and glanced back, unsure whether to be impressed or afraid.

"Tonight, the storm does all the telling."

~

When the house fell quiet, Nick sat alone in the blue glow of the muted television. The faint tick of cooling pipes marked the silence, each ping drifting through the living room as the generator's distant thrum eased beneath it. It was the kind of hour that stretched too far, the kind that made the walls feel closer than they were.

Wind drove rain hard against the windows, a steady, relentless pressure. On the second floor, Andrea had carried Jessica to bed and tucked her under the blankets, Zara propped beside her like a sentry. A soft shift sounded above him—Jessica settling—a murmur through the ceiling. The weather wasn't just a backdrop; it cloaked sins, erasing evidence as fast as blood could spill.

Nick's phone buzzed. For a moment, he didn't move. His hand hovered over the device, thumb poised but hesitant, as if touching it would make the message real.

Lakeland airfield. The jet will be gone once this breaks. Miss the chance and they'll be out by dawn.

He stared at the words until his vision blurred. He'd known this was coming. A floorboard gave a soft protest from the second floor. Then Andrea's voice cut through the stillness from the stairwell: "No one touches her. Not ever."

Nick's breath caught. He closed his eyes briefly before turning toward the window. Outside, rain streaked across the glass, the TV's faint flicker reflected in warped lines. He stayed there a beat longer than he meant to.

Quincy wouldn't ask questions. He never did.

Nick shifted forward on the couch, leaning into the moment he'd been avoiding. He unlocked the screen and fired off a text to Quincy Adams.

7

TASK FORCE IN THE STORM'S

SHADOW

Nick leaned against the splintered porch rail, sweat soaking the old Tampa Bay Devil Rays T-shirt. The midnight air pressed in—thick, humid, Helene's signature. At least two feet of water, rot, and brine in every breath.

A faint tremor ran through beneath his palms. He nudged a toe along a warped board. He listened for the soft, warning groan of wood swollen past its strength. No buzz from the neighborhood line—dead line. He made a mental note to check the circuit breaker before dawn, another moving piece in a night already full of them.

He lifted his phone to his ear, thumb hovering near mute, his mind charting the next three contingencies. "You still vertical?"

José's voice came back raw but steady. "Barely. The generator kicked on. First floor's got a foot of water, but we're lucky. Our place sits a hair higher than the neighbors'. Cindi's running the Shop-Vac, cussing like a sailor."

The sloshing and the Shop-Vac's strained whine bled through the call—Cindi's curse-stream stitching over it. The sounds almost tugged a smile out of him.

He stepped inside long enough to test the deadbolt, fingers brushing the metal, then eased back onto the porch. "Tell her to keep the engine clear. Silt'll kill it faster than the water."

"Yeah, yeah. Silt's the devil." José's chuckle was nervous and exhausted. "We get another inch, FEMA'll need FEMA. City's gonna be scraping mud for weeks."

Cindi—red hair wild—was likely dragging that Shop-Vac through a flooded room, refusing to yield to disaster. He thumbed his phone, noting to look at the neighborhood Facebook page for help requests. "Anyone come by?"

"Sheriff's boys cruising in high-clearance rigs, but it's quiet. You?"

Nick's gaze swept the street—now a reflex. His old Ford sat on an incline in the drive, buried in wind-thrown debris. Nothing moved.

Except the white van.

It idled at the corner, logo worn to peeling streaks. Nick leaned slightly forward, tension rising at the base of his skull. He searched for movement behind the glass.

"The usual, power crews and city trucks. A vehicle's been sitting close by for thirty minutes. No markings. Could be nothing, but I'll send a pic."

He slid the phone into his palm, took a quick photo of the van's profile in the ambient gloom, and sent it to José.

Scan for this panel van—parked by the house.

A second passed—long enough for doubt to nibble at him. Overreacting? Or too slow?

José replied, "I'll scrape cameras for the plate at first light."

Inside, a lamp snapped on, slicing through the dark. Andrea stepped into the doorway with a towel draped across her shoulders, shifting her weight carefully to favor the leg she still guarded. She dabbed her neck and caught Nick's eye.

"You tell him about the roof?" Her voice was calm.

Nick set the phone to speaker. "She's here."

Andrea cupped her hands. "Next time you borrow my saw, don't leave it on the deck during a hurricane!"

José's tone crackled with static and stubborn humor. "Duct tape held. Ham antenna's gone. Might be my best engineering yet."

Andrea smirked. She gave Nick a quick, wry glance. "As long as we keep what matters dry."

Nick brushed her fingers as she passed. A faint tremor lingered under her skin. He lowered his murmur. "I texted Quincy about the Lakeland airfield a few hours ago. No response. Doesn't mean they didn't move, but if they did, they didn't loop me in."

José's tone shifted, clipped and professional. "Don't expect a reply, Nick. If they diverted resources, the task force won't admit it to you."

"I'll check on you in the morning," Nick said.

"Roger that."

Andrea dropped onto the porch swing, pushing off with her foot to start a slow sway. The towel slipped against her shoulder. She settled. Fingers adjusted it in a practiced motion. "I can't believe this swing survived. Silly forgetting to take it down."

Her hair clung to her cheekbones. Her eyes tracked Nick before sliding to the deep shadow stretching across the yard. She drew her legs in and rubbed her knee—a restless little ache she never quite lost after the accident.

"You think it's over?"

He wiped sweat from his scalp. The porch light caught a faint glint of skin. "Helene's headed north. Should break for Tallahassee by dawn."

"That's not what I meant." She let the swing ease to a stop. "You think this is done?"

Nick's jaw flexed. His eyes drifted over the drowned block. He took a breath before he answered. "Storm's the first act. The cleanup comes after."

Andrea reached across the narrow space and squeezed his hand. Her grip was firm—steadying, but laced with its own worry. "If you get the call, go. I'll keep the house standing."

His gaze flicked to the van, then down the hollow stretch of street. "Task force is spinning hard. Senator Maxwell's everywhere—shaking hands, promising action." Nick shrugged, the motion weary. "Looks like another opportunity for him, not a solution."

"They want this to pass as a one-off." Andrea straightened as the swing rocked. "Sweep everything up before anyone asks questions. So what's our move?"

"We bunker down. See who surfaces when the water drops and the cameras fade."

He wiped his forehead with the towel Andrea had used, pausing where her scent lingered—shampoo and salt. He settled beside her. The night closed in, heavy with storm residue, every sound dampened as if the city were holding its breath.

She nudged his knee.

Relief trucks thumped down the avenue. Somewhere east, a siren faded. Even in a disaster, St. Pete was restless. Beneath the hush, a pressure built—something circling in the static, waiting its turn.

Andrea rested her head on his shoulder. "Let's go inside and try to get some sleep."

He rose with her. His fingers stayed curled around the phone, thumb hovering—already bracing for the next emergency.

～

The call came at 3:11 a.m., slicing through Nick's sleep. He flailed for the vibrating phone, pinning it under his palm before it could wake his wife. The number was unfamiliar, but the digit pattern spelled government or hospital. No one in this city called with good news after midnight. Even in the pre-dawn, St. Pete was alert. The place kept an eye on its own secrets.

He answered, heart pinched tight. "Nick Justin."

The voice was clipped. "You're needed at the substation, Justin. Twenty minutes."

No explanation. The call ended as he opened his mouth to respond.

Nick stared at the device, letting the dark screen settle into him. Something cold clicked behind his ribs. He pulled on yesterday's jeans, a clean shirt, wool socks, and work boots. He tested the deadbolt then eased outside, careful not to wake Andrea.

WITNESS ELIMINATION

His boots squelched on the porch, boards slick with rain. The stench of fertilizer and crushed leaves stung his nose. He scanned the block. The panel van was gone. He wanted to believe that meant relief, but the street held its breath.

He backed the old Ford down the driveway, headlights striping the flooded asphalt. The engine coughed, caught, and the dashboard lights flickered before they settled. Water lapped at the curb, palmetto fronds tangled under abandoned cars, gutters gurgled up what the storm had tried to hide. The place appeared cleaner than it was if you didn't look too close.

He eased the truck south, past the shuttered Dunkin', its drive-thru sign pointed at the dirt, billboards half-ripped, awnings peeled back. At every intersection, traffic lights blinked like wounded eyes. He crawled and checked for the sudden gleam of oncoming headlights. He counted three squad units in the first mile, each with a single cop slumped behind the wheel, scanning the wreckage for survivors or threats.

Downtown was mostly dark. Only the blue glow of the hospital and a scatter of county buildings broke the gloom. Mirror Lake had become a slow, oily pool, swallowing sidewalk and curb, reflecting broken neon from the heart of the city.

He parked under a live oak, its branches sagging from the wind. He killed the engine. A distant siren wailed. The faint drip of runoff sliding off awnings, no other sounds. He jogged to the city annex through ankle-deep water.

Inside, the air was thick with the stale stink of old carpet and the relentless, grinding buzz of the backup generator. Its vibration ran through the floor and up into Nick's teeth. Furniture had been jammed above the waterline, pushed back as if to clear a path for something bigger than people. Down the corridor, an emergency light flickered over a knot of waiting faces.

A uniformed officer with stubble checked a clipboard. He jerked his chin. "Captain said to go straight in."

Nick gave a short nod and elbowed the door open. A wave of coffee and sweat hit him. Manila folders, maps, and damp police reports littered the table. At the head, Judge Armwell—pencil mustache crisp over a task force polo—spoke in a quiet voice to two stone-faced Feds. He turned as Nick entered, eyes unsparing. He pointed.

"Mr. Justin, take a seat. You are late."

Nick glanced at the wall clock. 3:59. He dropped into the chair, feeling every stare. The room seemed to hold its breath along with him.

Others waited—a mid-level state attorney, a wiry guy with windblown hair. At the far end, Sergeant Quincy Adams sat hunched, massive arms folded. His skin was deep brown, his frame linebacker-solid from his Boston College days. Built to absorb a riot without flinching, he kept his gaze fixed on the tabletop, hands clasped tight. His knuckles blanched.

Judge Armwell flipped the folder open and slid it across.

"New developments."

Nick sifted through the pages. At the top: Senator Eleanor Caldwell. A photo of a body under a tarp at the foot of a Miami skyscraper. A banking sheet for Tagger Group, one hundred and fifty grand, July 2024. A familiar heat crawled up his spine. That much money didn't move without a purpose. Someone had bought something—loyalty, silence, or worse.

Nick's stomach knotted. Everything with Sarah was beginning to unravel.

He turned another page, each one heavier. "It appears Sarah Brown, ex-CEO of Tagger Group, had some business with the late senator."

Nick met Judge Armwell's stare. "Excuse the impatience, but you didn't drag everyone out before dawn to discuss a U.S. senator's death from a couple days ago, even if there are ties to my beloved sister-in-law." He let out a brief, humorless exhale. It never reached a smile.

The harsh overhead lights buzzed, the generator hummed, and outside the water kept rising.

Nick sat in the metal chair, the chill cutting through his jeans. He shifted the seat a fraction, bracing himself as he scanned the faces at the table: bureaucrats, exhausted cops, two Feds with matching frowns. Papers fanned across the surface, manifests and maps curling at the edges from the rain. It all read official, but the chaos was baked in.

Judge Armwell spoke up. "I will also address a resource allocation issue from early this morning. Mr. Justin, your unsolicited, anonymous

WITNESS ELIMINATION

tip regarding a pre-dawn flight at Lakeland Linder Airport resulted in the diversion of state and federal resources away from the primary containment zone. The airfield was found secure, the plane was stationary, and the report proved false. That is the kind of reckless action we cannot tolerate during disaster response."

At the far end, Quincy Adams took up more space than the chair allowed, arms folded, jaw locked as he scanned the whiteboard. A slight flex tightened along his forearm every time the hallway voices spiked. He had the stance of a man who'd tackle a hurricane if it came through the window.

Shandra Greene stood to the side, notebook pressed against her chest. She wore a thrifted windbreaker, jeans, and the look of a person let in only because she wouldn't go away. Skepticism and stubbornness marked her stance. Nick caught her eye. She nodded, and her foot tapped once, a pulse of agitation.

A pair of county lawyers argued over flood maps. Under the flicker of a single bulb, a battered satellite phone sat in a salad bowl at the center of the table. Every so often, someone picked it up, listened to the static, then set it back down.

An image flickered onto the wall. Nick squinted. "Are you telling me they destroyed a prison bus and three support vehicles?" He glanced at the sergeant, who only grunted.

Nick snorted. "Yet, Judge Armwell, you dare to scold me on resource usage, when I was correct that the convoy was in danger. Do your job, so the citizens don't have to." For a moment there was silence.

"Restraint." Quincy's voice was even, a hint of Boston buried under the fatigue.

Shandra shook her head. Disbelief tightened her features. "You don't lose a prison transport, a trio of trucks, and an entire crew by accident, not in this region." She gestured at the windows, where stormwater trickled over the glass, and flood maps bled color at the edges. "You all know it doesn't add up."

Tension pulled across his back. A decision formed, tenuous but real. "Everyone's fighting the storm, but nobody's asking how a federal convoy gets hijacked in Hillsborough County. No cams, no bystanders, nothing."

Quincy traced a finger over the timeline on the whiteboard. His shoulders rolled under his damp shirt. "Convoy left Pinellas County jail. Breached fourteen miles short of Lakeland Federal. Air cover grounded. Everything else goes wicked quiet." He tapped the board, eyes narrowed. "It isn't only the weather."

A thin fed with a windblown tie pushed his glasses up. "Logistics was a mess. Communications down, crews displaced, assets out of position."

Nick raised an eyebrow. "Chaos is an excellent disguise for bad intentions or terrible luck."

Shandra leaned in. "How many times do you see the same faces at these tables, Nick? Same faces, same answers. Nothing changes." Her eyes flicked toward Armwell.

He gave her a wry smile. "In this city, the more things change, the more the stink stays the same."

Adams looked up. "Someone flagged you. Not random. Is your texter friendly or a foe toying with you?" His vowels rolled longer, words dropping off at the end like he was back in Southie. He sweated through his uniform in this battered room.

Nick cracked his neck to the side, the sound small. His mind went to the missing prisoners. "Sarah Brown and Sally Hinkins." He hissed the names. "Could be anyone pulling strings. Whoever it is, they want this controlled."

Shandra's brows drew together. "People like that don't disappear; they get disappeared."

Quincy's voice lowered, steady as a drumbeat. "Heard Maxwell wants this wrapped quickly. Wants it sealed tight. And believe me, when a politician from up north says 'contained,' nothin's gettin' out."

Water streaked down the window. Storms only ever revealed what was already broken.

Nick studied the projected map. "Let's figure this out and lock it down before the flood takes it for good."

In the hush that followed, the old building shuddered under another gust. Somewhere, a siren wailed and then faded.

8

MYERS INSIDE

Nick slumped against the cracked leather of his truck seat, the annex shrinking in his rearview mirror. The meeting's implications crystallized. Sarah Brown and Sally Hinkins were gone, flawlessly extracted in the heart of a hurricane.

He punched the wipers on high, cutting streaks through the muck on the glass. He drove by a lot that had become a shallow lake. Two blocks away, a traffic light swung from a single cable, its dead eyes a perfect metaphor for the city's blind spots.

He pulled his phone from his pocket, thumb hovering over José's contact. He hit dial.

"Tell me you're not still in that meeting." José's voice was thick with exhaustion.

"Just finished. They called me in about the prison transport between Pinellas and Lakeland Federal. They ambushed the convoy. The chaos wiped out a bus and three support vehicles."

"Fuck. Casualty count?"

"Unknown. That's the official line." A sheriff's cruiser splashed through the lot, lights off, moving with the cautious detachment of someone surveying damage, not hunting criminals.

"Two prisoners vanished from the wreck—Sarah and Hinkins."

"Hell of a time to run a field trip," José countered. "Storm gave cover to all kinds of sins."

Nick stared through the windshield, rain sliding in heavy sheets. "Yeah, makes you wonder which ones will ever wash up."

He pressed his thumb to his brow, trying to quiet the throb building behind his eyes. "You should've seen their faces. Judge, feds, local brass—all staring at maps like they barely recognized the county anymore. As if this was an act of God instead of a coordinated hit."

"What was the route?"

"North on 275, then east on I-4. Standard run to Lakeland Federal—right up until it wasn't."

The line went silent, leaving only José's breathing and papers shuffling. "That's four jurisdictions, minimum—Feds, state troopers, Hillsborough Sheriff, DOC transport. Somebody with clearance had to flash badges or flip switches to let a convoy get struck that clean."

"My thoughts exactly." Nick pulled over. Silence magnified every sound.

He slumped back, neck rolling against the headrest, eyes shut. Each crack of lightning sent a pulse through his skull. Fatigue weighed him down, his body heavy and his nerves jangling, until a surge of adrenaline snapped him upright. How much more could he take before something broke? His mind was crowded with thoughts of his daughter, asleep at last, and his wife, probably gazing with determination at the ceiling, waiting for him to come back home.

"I need eyes and ears, José. Maxwell's already talking containment, which means the investigation's compromised before it starts."

"You want me to track in a flood zone?" José's laugh was brittle. "I'm good, but I have limitations. I can't walk on water yet."

"You know the players. You've got contacts I don't." Droplets raced down the side window, merging and splitting like the city's alliances. "Sarah wouldn't go quiet. She'd leave breadcrumbs to prove she could."

"For whom? You? The feds?" José sighed. "What about your family? You thinking about their safety in all this?"

The question hit harder than expected. Nick stared at the dashboard glow. For a few seconds, his own heartbeat was the only sound, quick and uneven. Images of Andrea—eyes glinting—and Jessica—hair wild as she curled in bed with Barrister—pressed in.

He let out a hard breath. "Every second."

"Then maybe—"

"If Sarah's out, we're already on her list." Nick's voice was sharp. "She's got nothing to lose now. Containment won't protect us."

"Fair enough." José's voice dropped. "I'll tap my old network, check with my port contact. If they needed to move bodies, living or dead, a shipping container's cleaner than a hospital."

"And check—"

"The private airstrips, I know. But anything that got off the ground during Helene had clearance from someone with significant pull."

His shoulders eased a fraction. José always thought three moves ahead and never required the obvious spelled out.

"At least that cockroach Myers didn't escape," José said. "Small mercies."

Nick's thoughts snagged on the name Myers. The one man tied to the entire system—Bruth'rs, RADD, and Sarah's crash—who hadn't vanished. The lockup wasn't confinement for him; it was a secure staging area. He was the one who'd manipulated evidence in Andrea's accident, linked to the street crew and the department's corrupt operations.

Nick thumbed a note into his phone:

County visitor logs—Myers?

He was sitting at a twisted stop sign, windshield fogging. Outside, the world blurred, smeared into shifting shapes. He pressed a palm to his chest. The beat was frantic. He waited for it to slow.

"Myers is still in lockup?"

"Last I checked. Why? You think he's connected to this?"

"Sarah never made a move without purpose. She chose her time and her allies. If she's out, it's because someone inside pulled it off."

"He's still locked up." José's tone shifted. "Could be useful, having eyes on him, though jail isn't exactly fertile ground for intel."

"Unless he's waiting for something." Nick turned the ignition. "I'm heading home to check on Andrea and Jessica. Call me the second you hear anything, no matter how small."

"Roger that. Watch your back. With natural disasters like this, people disappear in plain sight."

The line went dead. He checked the rearview—once, twice. Every passing set of headlights was a threat.

His beams caught the water spilling across the street, carrying debris: plastic bottles, broken branches, a child's shoe tumbling end over end in the current. The evidence of lives disrupted, swept away by forces larger than themselves.

He turned toward home, to his family. The wipers beat a rhythm that matched his pulse. Someone had orchestrated the prison break with military precision, using the hurricane as cover, the same person who might already be watching them.

Sarah was free, and that changed everything. The question wasn't whether she would come for them, but when. And in the prison's belly, under the hum of dying lights, Myers was still waiting.

~

D-block corridor flickered between darkness and sickly amber light, each stutter revealing a different tableau of prison life. Myers leaned against the wall, shoulders squared, eyes tracking the room. Power had cycled on and off for six hours, the generators straining to keep the lights on. With half the guards pulled for flood duty, the ratio of blue shirts to jumpsuits tipped dangerously. The air reeked of sweat, disinfectant, and men testing boundaries.

Myers cataloged the room: twenty-three inmates. Four guards. Too many bodies, too few badges. Trouble in here always started with simple math.

Down the corridor, boots scraped on wet concrete, a puddle reflecting the ceiling in broken patterns. Conversations dropped to whispers whenever Myers repositioned.

They knew who he was. What he was. Ex-cop in general population— a death sentence anywhere else. But not for Myers. Weeks here only sharpened what the military and the streets had taught him.

The overheads died again. Blackness swallowed the room. Nervous laughter rose to cover real fear. After eight seconds, the generator caught, and the fluorescents sputtered back to life.

WITNESS ELIMINATION

In the brief darkness, something had changed. Ruiz, a Bruth'rs enforcer with slabs of muscle, edged closer. Too close. His eyes held the flat calculation of a man measuring coffins.

"Water's rising outside, cop," Ruiz sneered. "Heard that convoy got taken out. Shame about your friends."

Myers kept his face blank, but the words landed clean. The block already knew about the hit. Information spread faster than water in a flood. La Reina had pulled the strings as promised. Now all he had to do was wait for her to tug the next one.

"Back up."

"Or what? Half the screws are out playing lifeguard." Ruiz rolled his shoulders, tattoos stretching across his neck. "You're not as protected as you think."

Three other inmates drifted in, forming a semicircle. Not close enough to draw the guards, but sufficient to block sight lines. A classic inmate move: create a blind spot, exploit it fast.

Disasters didn't erase evidence; they gave cover to anyone willing to use them.

The ex-cop stayed neutral, posture loose, one hand near his hip and the other hanging free. He'd survived Afghanistan by reading bodies before they moved. Prison was no different.

"Last warning."

The lights flickered, dimmed, then held. In the brownout, Ruiz made his move, a shoulder check. Not a real punch but enough to send a message to the block that the cop could be touched.

The shove clipped him high—rookie mistake.

The movement was automatic. He pivoted using Ruiz's momentum to slam him face-first into the concrete wall. He drove a knee into the back of Ruiz's thigh. The bigger man collapsed. As he buckled, Myers hooked two fingers under his chin and wrenched, neck torqued.

"Is that the best you've got?" He tightened his grip until Ruiz's breath broke into strangled gasps.

He jerked once, but Myers pinned him against the wall, locking the larger man in place. The other inmates backed off, eyes dropping to the floor tiles.

He could end it here. Should end it here. But lessons needed witnesses, and witnesses needed memories that wouldn't fade.

Myers let go of Ruiz's jaw and hammered three precise strikes to his kidney. Textbook pain compliance, taught at the academy, perfected on St. Petersburg streets. Ruiz folded, dropping hard.

"Stand up."

Ruiz gasped, struggling to rise. Myers waited until he was halfway up, then stomped the side of his knee. The crack echoed through the block. Ruiz collapsed, screaming, clutching his leg.

Myers straightened, breath hot and fast in his throat. He flexed his hand, knuckles aching, stung by a glancing cut where Ruiz's teeth had caught him.

The ex-cop knelt beside him, patting Ruiz's pockets with the easy rhythm of a man checking his own coat. His hands moved with practiced detachment, though his knuckles still flared with pain. He found a sharpened toothbrush handle, palmed it, then leaned close to his ear.

"Next time, don't telegraph. And don't come alone."

Two COs approached at last, moving with the weary slowness of men who'd watched this play out before.

"What's the situation, inmate?" Diaz's tone made it clear the question was a formality.

Myers stood, slipping the shiv into his waistband. "This inmate slipped. Wet floor." Myers gestured toward the leaking window.

Diaz nodded. His eyes flicked to the others, who now found the ceiling tiles fascinating. "Medical's stretched thin. He'll have to wait."

"I'll help him to his cell." Myers offered, all cooperative patience.

The guards retreated, leaving Myers to haul Ruiz up by his collar. Ruiz stifled groans as Myers dragged him to the cells, jostling the ruined knee with each step.

"You think you know how this place works, but you're still thinking like street muscle. In here, patience beats strength. Information trumps force."

Myers dumped Ruiz onto his bunk. The narrow cell gave momentary privacy from the block's curious eyes. From his pocket, he produced a small white pill, contraband painkillers worth more than cigarettes these days.

"This buys twenty minutes of straight answers." Myers held the pill out of reach. "Starting with who told you about those transports."

Ruiz's eyes flicked between the tablet and Myers's face. Pain beat pride. "A guy on cleaning duty heard the guards talking. Four vehicles were hit during the storm. Everybody's saying it was the weather, but nobody buys it."

Myers dropped the pill into Ruiz's trembling palm. For a flash, the memory surfaced—the first time he'd traded for a secret, years ago in a squad car, when he learned information could buy more than a badge ever could.

"Who else knows?"

"Whole joint's buzzing. Word is somebody important got taken out or set free. Depends on who you ask."

Myers nodded once. Ruiz swallowed. "You picked the wrong day to make a name for yourself, Ruiz."

"Wasn't personal," Ruiz grunted through clenched teeth. "Block's watching. Had to make a move."

"I know." Myers straightened his shirt. "That's why you're still breathing."

The lights flickered again, holding this time. When they steadied, Myers was already at the door.

"Consider this a professional courtesy." He kept a hand on the frame. "Next time the power drops, stay in your cell. Mother Nature washes clean, including evidence."

He left the Bruth'rs enforcer cradling his shattered knee and returned to the common area, where inmates parted before him like water around stone. Inside, the hierarchy was restored. Myers took his post at the wall, watching, waiting, his message delivered in the universal language of pain.

~

Water swirled pink, then washed clear, carrying Ruiz's blood in thin spirals. Myers worked the soap into his knuckles, methodical, unhurried. The staff bathroom's lone bulb threw harsh shadows across his face, sharpening the hollows beneath his cheekbones, the flat calculation in his eyes. No cameras watched here by design—a blind spot in the prison's surveillance.

He rinsed his skin again, letting the sting steady him. Disinfectant mixed with mildew, dragged up a flash of Kandahar: sweat, grit, the iron tang of violence before he shoved it down. Boots scraped on wet concrete somewhere down the corridor, wind whistling through the seams of the old stone. Perfect cover for conversations. He waited a beat longer. The steps didn't turn back.

The right joint had split, more from Ruiz's teeth than the wall. A clean tear, unlikely to draw attention. He flexed his fingers. The ache was manageable. Required.

Violence was currency inside these walls. Spend it with care. Spend it when you must. And when you do, leave a mark. Kandahar had taught him that much. The rules never changed—only the backdrop.

A heavier gust rattled the doorframe. One more power spike and the cells would lock down, a fail-safe designed to trap everyone in the place the system believed they belonged.

The door creaked open. Myers didn't turn. In the spotted mirror, Toomey slipped inside. His expression didn't shift; the reflection gave him all he needed. Young guard, ten months in, shoulders already sagging under the compromises he'd made. His Adam's apple bobbed as he thumbed the flimsy lock.

"Area's clear." Toomey's voice was thin. "Shift supervisor's tied up with the flooding in C-block. We've got five minutes."

Myers shut off the tap and dried his hands. The motion was slow, deliberate. He leaned against the sink, posture casual, his gaze locked on the guard.

"You look nervous, Toomey. That's not good for either of us."

"I'm not. I—" Toomey fumbled in his pocket. He produced a cheap burner phone. "Came through Wilson in receiving. Said it was 'the package' you were expecting."

He didn't reach for it. "They mention me by name?"

"No. He said it was for our friend in D-block." Toomey swallowed. His hand shook just enough to betray him. "After Ruiz and the transport, I figured —"

WITNESS ELIMINATION

"You figured you'd cover your bases." Myers extended his hand. "Smart man."

The phone was light in his palm. He rubbed the seams with his thumb, checking every imperfection. He turned it over to scan for tampering. It was insubstantial. This wasn't his first contraband delivery, but caution had kept him alive on both sides of the law.

"Any word on the prison convoy?"

Toomey glanced at the door. "Official line says 'severe weather event.' But the chatter's different. One bus, three support vehicles hit at once. Comms jammed."

"Casualties?" Myers asked.

"No survivors."

Myers nodded. This was not luck, not nature—it was coordination. Sarah should already be halfway to the safe house, Hinkins in tow. But extraction was only half the equation. Now it would take strings, political strings, pulled hard and high, to finish the job.

He powered on the phone. The contacts contained one number. The entry listed no name, only a Venezuelan country code. Carl's people were right on schedule.

He turned and braced himself against the sink. He centered his breath.

"I need a few moments. Watch the door."

Toomey hesitated. In the spotted mirror, the guard shifted. The silence stretched, filled only by the distant whistle of wind through the vents.

"I should get back before—"

"Two minutes, Toomey. Then you can go back to pretending you're another underpaid CO." Myers's voice hardened. "Unless you'd prefer I mention to Ruiz who's been bringing in those pills you've been selling?"

Toomey moved to the door. He pressed his ear against it, playing lookout with the desperate focus of a man who'd glimpsed his own precarious future.

Myers dialed the single contact. The line connected after one ring, silent except for the faint sound of road noise. He didn't wait for a greeting. Too much time had already bled away.

"Confirm package status." His tone was clipped.

A man replied, his voice thick with an accent. "Package secured. Delivery proceeding as scheduled despite conditions out there."

"I need you to relay a message." Myers kept his tone neutral. His eyes stayed on Toomey's back. "Tell La Reina that schedule changes are in effect. Nick Justin connected with the task force at 0300. The feds are involved, but containment protocols are active."

"Understood. Additional instructions?"

This was the delicate part, balancing need-to-know with deniability. "Tell Sarah that the Gandy approach is compromised. Clearwater route only. And remind her our friend at the port moved it up two days, not one."

The voice repeated the message verbatim. Carl's people never missed.

"One more thing," Myers added. "Justin's investigator, Dominguez, is tied to the Port Authority through a contact. A nurse there. Flag him as a priority."

"Elimination?"

Rainwater leaked through the ceiling, a dark drop crawling down the plaster. "Not yet. Monitor. He's leverage."

"Understood."

Toomey shifted by the door. His foot tapped with nerves. "Sixty seconds," he mouthed.

Into the phone, Myers gave the last instruction. "The flood begins inside before it reaches the streets. No deviations."

The voice repeated the phrase verbatim.

Myers added, "She'll know. And she'll move the politicians when it's time." That was the real play. Extraction was muscle. Freedom would take politics. Myers killed the call, pulled the battery, and held both pieces.

Toomey turned. "We need to go. Shift change in two minutes."

Myers handed him the fragments. "Trash them. Different cans, different wings."

"Jesus, Myers, I'm not your—"

He flinched back a half-step, nowhere to go.

Myers stepped in close, not touching but erasing the gap. "You became mine the day you took cash to sneak contraband through the wire. We're past negotiation."

Toomey's shoulders slumped. "Is it true what they're saying about Brown, that she's tied to Senator Maxwell?"

WITNESS ELIMINATION

Myers studied him. He calculated how much truth was useful. "She's tied to everyone. That's what makes her valuable. And dangerous."

The lights flickered again, longer this time. Myers moved to the door, hand on the knob.

"When this ends, you'll have a choice. The smart ones always know which way the current's running before the flood."

He left Toomey under the buzzing bulb. Back in the common area, inmates parted around him. The Ruiz lesson still held. Myers resumed his station at the wall, neutral, patient.

The hierarchy reformed in the wake of violence. The pieces were moving. Sarah was free. La Reina had her signal.

The move was coming, and only the prepared would survive it.

9

THE WRENCH'S SIGNATURE

September 28, 2024

Nick hunched over his laptop at Neighborhood Joe, broad shoulders crowding the small café table, the light glinting off his bald head. The rim of his coffee cup was forgotten against his lip. Three tabs displayed wreckage photos. A fourth showed surveillance stills from the convoy breach. The clean fractures of steel and glass filled the screen. Outside, St. Pete whirred back to life after Helene. Inside, the steady click of his cursor and the café's background hum created a bubble of focus. Something wasn't right.

A hard blink reset his vision. The shop buzzed with post-hurricane energy—laptops open, phones charging at every available outlet, conversations laden with storm stories. Neighborhood Joe had escaped flooding, its power grid miraculously intact, transforming it into an impromptu community center. The familiar scent of espresso and warmed pastries provided a thin veneer of normalcy that Nick clung to, though he knew it wouldn't last.

"Refill, counselor?" The owner appeared at his elbow with the pot in hand.

Nick nodded. He slid his cup forward without looking up. "Thanks, Thomas."

His fingers tapped a steady rhythm on the scarred tabletop as he enlarged the image of the wrecked bus. A gash split its reinforced side, the metal edges too clean, too precise for flying debris.

He flicked through the images, his legal instincts sharpening into forensic focus. Two strikes, each to cripple. One to kill the engine block. One to breach an extraction point. Power out, comms down, first responders stretched thin. This was surgical work.

Nick's jaw tightened as he pulled up the convoy files, the transport carrying the hard drive, the core to Slovin's investigation. The report blamed "catastrophic structural failure from extreme weather." But the photos proved otherwise: too neat, too deliberate to be nature's work.

A precision blast took out the convoy's lead SUV, halting the caravan near an overpass, shelter from both the weather and satellite eyes. A second charge hit the rear, boxing in the prison bus and the evidence vehicle between walls of fire and steel.

He cross-checked the two breaches side by side. Same approach. Same tools. Same mind.

The air conditioner kicked on, blending with the surrounding chatter. Nick's focus didn't waver. A professional had used the hurricane as a perfect cover for two strikes.

He pulled up an older case file from his archives, a wrongful death suit involving structural failure at a construction site. The defense had claimed storm damage, but Nick's expert witnesses had proven deliberate sabotage. The cutting patterns, the structural knowledge, the precision, they all mirrored the destruction on his screen.

"Forensic engineering." He tracked every detail. Both incidents required an intimate understanding of vehicle design, specialized tools hard to obtain, and split-second coordination in hurricane conditions.

His pulse quickened.

He closed the reports and opened a fresh search window. He weighed the options. His fingers hovered over the keys before he typed, "Professional breaching experts criminal Florida." The results scattered across the screen: security consultants, military contractors, nothing useful. He refined the query, sharper this time. "Vehicle extraction, evidence tampering."

The results narrowed, but nothing substantial emerged. Nick leaned back. The chair creaked under the shift. This type of expertise wouldn't show up in public records. He needed deeper sources.

Nick turned to his phone and scrolled through his contacts. He paused on a name he rarely touched, a former client with ties to Tampa's underbelly, a man who knew which doors opened without a key. The message was brief.

> **Looking for info on high-level breaching experts active in Florida. Professional work. Discretion appreciated.**

The response came faster than expected.

> **Sounds like The Wrench. Nobody else in the state works that cleanly. Ghosts in, ghosts out.**

Nick froze. A pulse ticked in his throat. His fingers hovered. He typed back:

> **Carl Walters? Thought he disappeared after the Bruth'rs bust last summer.**

The pause stretched this time, long enough to sharpen the edge of unease.

> **Never left. He moved upstream to bigger fish. Word is he works directly with the Venezuelans.**

Nick set the phone down. The pieces slid into place. Carl "The Wrench" Walters—mechanical genius, former gang leader, tied to international players. The perfect executor of a dual-strike operation demanding precision and flawless timing.

The images were different now, sharper, more damning. If Walters was involved, both incidents reached far beyond local corruption. This wasn't about freeing a dirty cop or stealing evidence; it was a display of power.

He closed his laptop.

Two separate attacks, one signature hand. A network with reach he'd scarcely believed existed.

And now they held the hard drive, the one thing that could have dismantled them.

~

A sweep of motion filled the doorway as José stepped inside and scanned the crowded interior. Compact and broad-shouldered despite his modest height, he moved with the wary grace of a fighter who'd never stopped training, the scar above his brow caught in the café's light.

Nick tracked him through the shifting bodies. Tightness bunched in his friend's shoulders. When José spotted him, the subtle nod they exchanged held the weight of shared understanding. This wasn't a casual coffee meet-up.

Nick had already cleared his table of extraneous materials, the laptop screen positioned for José's eyes only, its images of precision-cut metal again frozen on the display.

José slid into the chair opposite Nick and exhaled. "You look like hell." His voice carried the gravel of exhaustion, roughened by old fights and late nights. He flexed his hand on the tabletop. The absent pinky caught the eye as much as the scar over his brow. "The storm or the case?"

"Both. Coffee?"

José shook his head to dismiss the offer. "Let's get to it. Your message sounded urgent."

Nick rotated the laptop toward him. He angled the screen into view. "Quincy sent photos over." He tapped the image. "Bus breach, convoy hit—identical method, identical tools. These weren't opportunistic crimes during a hurricane. They were strikes by a person with knowledge."

José leaned in. He studied the images. His eyes narrowed. "You have a name in mind."

"Carl Walters. The Wrench."

The effect was immediate. José's posture snapped rigid. He drew a sharp breath, his gaze sweeping the café before settling back on Nick. His voice dropped to a whisper. "The Wrench? Bastard cut my pinky off.

We almost had him when the arrests went down at his garage, but he vanished in the chaos."

"Tell me what you know." Nick's tone was steady despite the churn in his gut.

José glanced over his shoulder, then leaned closer. "Walters was a mechanical prodigy. He could tear down and rebuild anything by the time most kids learned to drive. So he set up a chop shop for the Bruth'rs, and within a few years he was running them, until Sarah stepped in with Hinkins and that ex-cop, Myers. His workshop was a fortress of tools and tech, years ahead of ground-level work."

Nick tipped his chin. "That kind of expertise would explain the heft in both operations."

"More than that. Walters didn't breach security—he rewrote it. When he ran the gang with Sarah, he hijacked every CCTV camera on the Gandy Bridge for their street races and fentanyl runs." José's eyes, fixed on the laptop screen, traced the scars in the metal. "His specialty was creating blind spots and making things vanish from digital records." His expression hardened. "Sarah and Sally Hinkins had the cartel pipeline: drugs, laundered cash through shells."

Nick grazed his lower lip. "And now he's with La Reina?"

"That's the word. My contacts say he went international after the Bruth'rs collapsed. La Reina pays a premium for his kind of expertise." José's tone dropped. "As for how they connected, anything from recruitment to …."

"So, he moved in-house. The higher the stakes, the better the resources." Nick's voice tightened. "Could he run two separate ops during a hurricane?"

José gave a humorless laugh. "That's his specialty. The Wrench reads systems—weather, traffic, emergency response, like blueprints. The hurricane wasn't an obstacle; it was a tool."

The noise from the café dimmed. "The method makes sense. He exploits vulnerabilities, uses cutting-edge tech, and leaves nothing traceable."

"Exactly. He doesn't force his way in; he finds the weak spot. Not a prison break or evidence theft at all—a message. They were showing how deep their reach went."

"And the hard drive was the ultimate prize." Nick shut his eyes. The weight of it pressed in. "Everything Slovin built, every connection he died for is now in their hands."

A shadow crossed José's features. "My contacts say The Wrench was in Tampa a week before Helene. Specialized equipment came in, too: cutting tools, signal jammers, custom electronics. Nothing suspicious alone, but together ...."

"That's the toolkit for a perfect-storm op." Nick met his gaze. "Planned well in advance. They knew the transfer schedule, knew the route."

His hand curled into a fist. "Must be someone inside the department, the courts, or both." José's fists clenched. "Positioned to access sealed schedules. Secure enough to feed it out. The one who arranged that one-day delay."

Nick rubbed his face. If Walters was behind the strikes, the conspiracy ran far deeper than they'd uncovered, outside the RADD Squad, far past local corruption. Fatigue seeped through. "How do we find him?"

"We don't. The Wrench is a ghost. No address, no footprint. Works through intermediaries, encrypted comms." He tapped the laptop screen. "These cuts are his signature. By the time you see it, he's gone."

Around them, the café carried on. Conversations flowed. The espresso machine's hiss, the steady swing of the door. At their table, the air had thickened with realization.

"We're not fighting dirty cops." José's laugh was bitter. "We're up against a professional network with reach we can't track."

A grim nod answered him. "And now they've got everything Slovin uncovered before his death."

The question pressed between them, heavy and unspoken: what now?

~

The coffee shop door swung open, admitting a shaft of harsh Florida sunlight that momentarily silhouetted Andrea's and Jessica's figures. Nick's breath caught. His family in public still triggered an instinctive threat assessment.

WITNESS ELIMINATION

He tracked their path through the crowded café. Andrea's short hair brushed her cheeks. Beside her, Jessica clutched her mother's hand. Blonde hair spilled past her shoulders, the purple backpack bouncing against her slight frame.

José's look shifted. Both men straightened as they approached.

"Uncle José!" Jessica's hazel eyes lit up. Her voice rose above the café's hum. She broke from her mother's hand and wove through tables with fearless energy.

A warm smile broke across José's face. He bent to meet her. "There's my favorite artist. How's Professor Roar doing after the storm?" He gestured to the stuffed lion peeking from her backpack.

"Zara was brave, like you. And she is not a professor." Jessica scrambled onto the chair next to him and pulled out a worn sketchbook. "I drew what our street looked like after."

Nick met Andrea's eyes over their daughter's head, the unspoken message clear. *Not now.*

Andrea gave the slightest nod and settled into the chair beside Nick. She leaned close. Her hand slipped into his under the table—a quick squeeze, their private code for caution. "We were driving by and saw your car. Thought we'd surprise Daddy for lunch."

Nick forced a smile. "Best surprise of my day." He reached out and tugged one of Jessica's braids. "Hey, Jess, do you think you could get me another coffee while I talk to Mom for a minute?"

Jessica glanced up from her drawings. Her eyes narrowed with the suspicion of a child who recognized adult deflection. "Are you talking about the storm? Because I already saw it. The Mitchells' roof is gone, and Mrs. Delgado's car got crushed by a tree."

"It's boring legal stuff, honey. Could you get your dad that coffee? See if they have those chocolate croissants you like." Andrea brushed Jessica's hair back from her forehead, eyes steady despite the faint pallor of her recovery.

Jessica let out an exaggerated sigh but slid from her chair. "I know when I'm being gotten rid of." She held out her hand to Nick, who slipped her a twenty. "I'll take my time." She wove toward the counter.

The moment she was out of earshot, Nick leaned in. "We've identified who orchestrated the bus breach and the convoy hit. Carl Walters."

"Sarah's old ally?" Andrea stayed composed, though her eyes widened. Her fingers tightened around her purse strap. "Of course. My sister's comrade."

José cut in. "The Wrench is working with La Reina now. These attacks were arranged at the highest level. Your sister and Hinkins are players, but only pieces in a bigger game."

Andrea absorbed this, eyes narrowing as the implications set in. "If this Carl planned both operations during a hurricane …."

"Then we're up against an organization with resources we've hardly grasped." Nick's gaze flicked to Jessica at the counter before he went on. "Advance intel on secure transports, specialized gear, coordinated teams at multiple sites, all pulled off in the middle of a Category 4 storm."

"That's not street crime," Andrea said.

José shook his head. "Not even typical cartel work."

Nick nodded. "It's corporate and sanctioned at the government level." He rubbed his temple, the pressure mounting. "We've been thinking too small. The RADD Squad corruption, the evidence, that was only the surface. The hard drive mapped it all: money laundering, political protection, international channels."

"And now they have it," Andrea said.

The café's air conditioner droned, masking their hushed voices. Jessica's animated chatter with the barista drifted over—a fragile reminder of normalcy in a world tilting out of balance.

"The enemy isn't local corruption." Nick's words were measured. "It's a network with deep pockets and no boundaries. They pulled off two precision operations during a hurricane—took the targets, erased the traces, vanished in hours."

"And now they own the playbook." José's fingers drummed an anxious rhythm on the tabletop.

Andrea's mind was already racing. "The hard drive doesn't merely incriminate them; it maps our entire case: witnesses, evidence chains, strategies." Her voice stayed steady, but a tremor shook her hands. "It's a blueprint."

Nick voiced the question, though the answer was clear. "For what?"

"Containment," Andrea whispered.

WITNESS ELIMINATION

Silence broke as Jessica returned. Her tongue tucked at the corner of her mouth, she balanced a coffee cup and a plate with two chocolate croissants. "These are the last ones." She slid back into her seat. "The lady said there wouldn't be more until tomorrow because of the hurricane."

"Good timing." Andrea's smile did not quite reach her eyes.

Her daughter broke a croissant in half, chocolate smearing her fingers, her face alight with simple pleasure. The contrast between her innocence and the darkness pressing in tightened her chest.

Jessica wandered toward the wall display of pre-storm photographs. The moment she moved out of earshot, Nick leaned close, his voice dropping to a private register.

"They want us dead, and they've taken our best weapon." His eyes locked on Andrea. The hard drive was no longer evidence but a blueprint for their elimination.

Andrea's jaw trembled before she forced it still. She gave a small nod. Her eyes flicked once to Jessica, then returned to Nick. The question was unspoken, but sharp, *What now?*

Nick had no answer. Not yet.

10

COURT OF SHADOWS

September 27, 2024, afternoon

The villa loomed like a fortress of glass overlooking the Caribbean Sea. A faint trace of jasmine hung in the cooled air while manicured gardens and a fountain shimmered on the terrace. La Reina reclined on a pale-silk divan, Mateo, the small boy, on her lap. He turned a smooth gray stone over and over in his palm, its surface worn from years of handling. The stone clicked softly between his fingers, a steady rhythm he used whenever adults talked around him. She stroked his hair with a blood-red fingertip in the dim light.

A flatscreen on the wall played silent news: a helicopter's view of waterlogged streets, debris adrift under storm-dark skies. A calm voice narrated "unforeseen chaos," omitting every crucial truth.

Opposite her stood El Verdugo, motionless in a tailored suit, posture exact. A thin white scar ran from his jaw to his temple. His steely eyes swept the room, cataloging furniture for leverage. Once a soldier, he had become an instrument of a more elegant war.

"The breakout succeeded." His tone was smooth, curling around a distinct Portuguese accent. "Sarah and Hinkins are secure. The Slovin hard drive is en route."

La Reina's gaze stayed on the screen, where a gaunt senator's face flickered by. The boy's fingers clenched the stone, and she placed a hand on his back in quiet reassurance. He leaned into the touch, and she allowed it for a moment before shifting back to business. "Collateral damage?"

"Within expectations," the Brazilian merc replied. "Three federal agents, twelve DOC guards, six Bruth'rs inmates—lost under the storm's cover."

She tilted her head, eyes cutting to him like a blade through shadow. "The lawyer—Justin—he has a family? A son?"

"A daughter. Jessica."

A faint smile curved La Reina's lips, the muted triumph of someone who'd already won an unseen game. "A king's cub."

El Verdugo held steady, attuned to threat, immune to invitation. The child was never the point. The father was.

"Myers is our contact inside the jail. He warned us that Justin and Dominguez are active. The feds are entangled but contained. The storm gave us a blank canvas. The flood started beneath the surface before it hit the streets. No deviations."

"Excellent." She rose, lifting her hand from the boy's back. He stirred but stayed still, attuned to her rhythm.

Across the room, a panel of monitors waited. She expanded one feed: a peaceful suburban street punctuated by a boarded-up building. Painted on its facade was a lioness, blood-red splatters staining her chest like war paint.

"Send a message, something visceral that exploits his weakness."

El Verdugo replied, "The lioness will run red."

She turned, her silhouette filling the room, eyes shadowed and commanding. A thin, merciless smile teased her lips. She had risen to the top of the cartel with calculated grace, never mistaking silence for softness. One word perfectly timed could gut an empire.

"Opportunity wears many masks," she said. "This one has roared."

~

September 28th afternoon

WITNESS ELIMINATION

The whetstone whispered along the steel, a comforting sound in the townhouse's hush. El Verdugo held the recurved blade at a perfect twenty-degree angle, each stroke slow and exact. Afternoon light slanted through the blinds, catching on the metal and revealing flaws invisible to lesser eyes. He paused, tested the sharpness with his thumbnail, and frowned. Not yet.

Water beaded on the glass beside him, condensation tracking down to pool on the polished mahogany. The townhouse's furnishings spoke of money: tasteful, expensive, forgettable. Exactly what he required.

The following day, Verdugo arrived back in St. Petersburg, a ghost among the wealthy residents of this exclusive enclave.

The knife made another pass across the stone. Another. Another. The motion centered him, breathing practice for a man with bloodier intentions.

El Verdugo's hands bore the marks of his profession—not scars but precision. An economy of movement. Nothing wasted. He turned the blade to catch the slanting light: eight inches of high-carbon steel, its handle wrapped in cord for a secure grip under any condition. An extension of himself, like a sidearm, only closer. More honest.

The clock nudged forward: 4:17. His associate would arrive soon with confirmation. The job was almost complete. The cartel required tight preparation and execution.

He set the knife down, reached for a cloth, and wiped an invisible smudge from it. The recurved blade gleamed.

From his case, a smaller stone came next—a finisher. Its grit was nearly imperceptible, meant for final touches.

He worked, mind drifting to training days. A special forces instructor stood over him, not a hair out of place despite the jungle heat. *Excellence isn't a goal—it's a condition,* the man had said, clipped and cold. *A weapon is only as good as its edge. And you are a weapon.*

Four-twenty-two. Footsteps approached the front door, hesitant. A key turned in the lock. Alvarez had temporary access. The door opened then closed. A pause in the foyer.

Footfalls betrayed a man's mind. These spoke of uncertainty. Fear.

Alvarez appeared in the study doorway, a man in his mid-thirties, his expensive suit pulling at the shoulders. His cologne arrived first, aggressive and overconfident. A sheen of humidity clung to his hairline, as if he'd jogged to the door.

His eyes flicked to the knife, then away. A small tell.

He cleared his throat and rubbed his palms on his thighs.

"It's done." Alvarez forced the words flat. "The message was delivered."

The enforcer didn't look up. "Sit."

A command, not an invitation. Alvarez hesitated then took the chair opposite, perching on its end, hands clasped.

The whetstone whispered, a metronome counting down to something only El Verdugo understood.

"Tell me." His Portuguese accent gave the words a musical chill.

"The marina." Alvarez spoke too quickly. "Symbol on the boathouse wall. Red. Visible from the main dock." He swallowed. "It'll be discovered by morning."

El Verdugo's gaze flicked up. "Not paint."

Alvarez flinched. "Blood. As ordered."

The whetstone rasped. Three more strokes. He tested the edge against his thumb. Better. Not perfect. He resumed.

"And the other matter?" His voice was level, detached.

Alvarez shifted. His suit rustled, cheap lining beneath a showy exterior. A man playing at importance. He had seen hundreds like him. Ambition without discipline. Hunger without control.

"The senator's aide understood our position. He won't be a problem."

"Did you watch his face when he understood?"

Alvarez nodded. "Yes."

"Good."

Alvarez's right leg bounced. His collar darkened with sweat despite the cool air.

"There is …" Alvarez licked his lips. "There may be a complication."

The whetstone stilled. "Continue."

Alvarez's hands unclenched, then clenched again. "The boathouse. As I was finishing the lioness, I caught movement on the adjacent dock. A witness."

The clock ticked.

"Describe."

WITNESS ELIMINATION

"An old man. Fishing. He turned when he heard me. I don't think he saw clearly between the buildings, but he noticed something."

The stone was set down, aligned square on the table.

"And this man. What did you do?"

"I got out of there before he could see me. Didn't engage. I figured it was better to report in than take any action on my own."

El Verdugo's expression didn't change. "You left a witness."

"He was far. In the shadows. He couldn't have—"

He lifted the knife, inspecting its edge. "What was the distance?"

Alvarez blinked, calculating. "Maybe thirty yards? Across the water. And like I said, it was between buildings."

"Between buildings." El Verdugo nodded, as if confirming something. "Yet you recognized him as an old man. You saw enough to assess his age but assume he saw nothing?"

A sheen of sweat gathered on Alvarez's upper lip. "I can find him. Tonight. It won't be a problem."

"It is already a problem."

El Verdugo rose in a fluid motion, knife in hand, and crossed to the window. He stared out at the manicured lawn.

"The lioness was a signature. A message meant for the lawyer. It required discretion."

"I know, and I—"

"Not finished."

He turned. The sun behind him cast his face in shadow.

"Messages require clarity. When they become unclear, they lose value."

Alvarez nodded, too fast. "I understand. I'll fix this. I know the marina, so I'll find him tonight."

"Tonight is too late. Word travels. The witness may already have spoken."

El Verdugo moved from the window, circling behind Alvarez.

"Stand."

The subordinate rose, his knee clipping the chair on the way up. His tie hung loose, slightly askew. The disorder was obvious.

"You know what La Reina values above all else?" Verdugo's delivery softened, almost conversational.

Alvarez latched onto the change. "Loyalty?"

"Control."

The enforcer stepped forward, stopping precisely three feet from the man.

"Command requires information discipline. When details escape, control weakens."

"I can still salvage this." Alvarez's voice frayed. "The old man likely didn't even register it. And if he did, who would believe him? The police are already in Maxwell's pocket."

El Verdugo tilted his head slightly. "Perhaps, but now we have uncertainty where there should be none."

He examined the knife, turning it so the light traced its edge.

"Unacceptable."

Alvarez's eyes widened. His hand moved toward his jacket, where a holster might be. The motion caused no concern.

"Wait." Alvarez raised a hand. "I've been loyal. I can fix this."

"I know you believe that." Verdugo's tone was calm, almost gentle. "But belief without capability is merely another form of error."

Alvarez backed into the chair. "Please." His voice cracked.

"La Reina trusts me to maintain standards." Verdugo stepped forward. "Your role was to execute, not to create problems requiring solutions."

Alvarez's hand reached his jacket, fumbling.

In one smooth motion, he closed the distance. The blade found its mark—angled beneath the ribs, upward. Clean. Professional.

Surprise flickered in Alvarez's eyes, then understanding.

El Verdugo caught his weight, guiding him down to prevent blood from reaching the imported rug. He lowered the body with care, maintaining eye contact as life ebbed away. Respect for the process. For transitions.

"You see now"—the words were a low murmur—"why precision matters."

Alvarez's mouth moved soundlessly. His eyes fixed on the ceiling then emptied.

El Verdugo checked his watch. 4:31.

WITNESS ELIMINATION

He rose, knife in hand. He scanned the room. No spatter. Minimal pooling. Contained. Cleanable.

A moment later he returned to the chair, wiped the blade on a black cloth, and resumed sharpening.

The witness would need to be addressed. A loose end.

Calculate. Plan. Execute.

The whetstone whispered again, its rhythm unchanged.

Clarity settled. One task was complete, another identified. The mission continued.

Outside, the light softened toward evening, stretching shadows across the villa floor.

The recurve caught the filtered sun.

Perfect.

11

NIGHT VIGIL

September 28, 2024

Jessica lay in bed in the near-dark. It wasn't the wind anymore. This was something else. The electric thrum of the dehumidifier in the living room. The moan of settling timber. A sharp, mildewed tang in the air, decay deep in the bones of the home. No cleaner could reach it. Hurricane Helene was gone, but its ghost remained.

From downstairs, her father's voice rose. Her mother's was a soft counterpoint. Not shouting. Not yet. Worse than yelling. Each word aimed to wound. Their discontent seeped through the floorboards like salt-bleached water, corrosive and unrelenting.

Jessica pulled Zara tight against her chest. It was a witness to everything. The days of clinging had matted the fake fur. Her father had given it to her after she'd parted with her unicorn, left it in the arms of Mrs. Addison at her husband's funeral. The lioness wasn't merely a toy. It was her protector.

Below, her mom's voice cut through the vents, raw and unfiltered, laced with fury.

"We could've died."

That rage had been building since the floodwaters first crept toward their house, born not of fear but of helplessness.

Her father responded with a muted, defeated rumble, frustration buried in the sound. It hit Jessica square in the chest.

His jaw would be clenched—the look he wore when justice slipped through his fingers.

"This isn't about the house." Andrea's tone was tight. "It's about the risk. We shouldn't have to live like this. In this …."

In this what? The rest was lost.

Her mother would be gesturing toward her neighbors' homes, the storage pod units in yards, the appliances rusting at the curb. All of it, the wreckage that still choked their street, wasn't only a mess. It was stress made visible. A permanent, ugly reminder of what they'd lost.

Jessica turned Zara over in her hands, aiming its amber eyes at her bedroom door. The plush didn't flinch. Didn't cry. Jessica got out of bed and moved to the door.

Downstairs, the volume rose. The cadence shifted. No longer careful, now combative.

The conversation had become a cross-examination.

"Did you phone him?" her father snapped.

The question wasn't about a phone call. It was about trust and the deep seismic shift that had cracked open their relationship since the storm.

"Who? José?" Andrea's voice jumped. "He's family. You know that. We have to learn how to defend ourselves."

"It's an investigation," Nick said. "He's putting himself in the jury box."

Her father's law talk bled into "precedent, submitting evidence, due process." But there were no rules for the fear that hung in the air.

A stair creaked, one sharp groan, then silence. One footstep. Someone was listening. The stillness hit harder than noise ever could.

It was the quiet moments that truly terrified her.

Jessica padded back to bed, Zara clutched tight. Her small world was fracturing, and the only two people who could hold it together were fighting. They spoke in terms she didn't understand.

But the fear wasn't in the words. It sat in the distance between them, in the space those words opened up.

WITNESS ELIMINATION

Jessica pulled the thin sheet to her chin. She pressed her face into the lioness, its bead eyes fixed on the door. Her whisper barely stirred the air.

"You'll watch for me," Jessica whispered. "Tell me if they come."

A car door slammed outside. Then nothing. The kind of silence that made everything feel heavier. Jessica sat up, her gaze snapped to the door, unblinking. The sound had come from the right side of the house. No driveway there. Only debris. And the place where that shadow had been earlier.

She inched to the window and peeked out. Something moved in the darkness. They were being watched.

12

THE STREETS FLOODED

September 29, 2024, morning

Nick drove his old Ford F-150. Adams sat in the passenger seat, wearing a damp, wrinkled polo shirt and cargo shorts. Stubble shadowed his chin, and deep-purple bags pooled beneath his eyes.

They rolled through neighborhoods. Mattresses sagged on curbs, yellowing in the sun. Couches, bloated and salt-bleached, were like beached whales in the grass. A refrigerator was on its side, a rusted metallic casket. The soundscape was a chorus of machines: the thrum of generators, the whine of chainsaws. This wasn't recovery. It was a crime scene.

Adams stared forward, a professional mask in place. "The senator's office wants a quick cleanup." His voice was clipped. "They want the city to look functional. Optics are everything."

Nick kept both hands on the wheel. "Optics don't find a perp."

Adams pulled out a tablet and scrolled through a map peppered with red markers. Flood zones. He was a man of data.

They turned onto a street marked by a brown waterline staining the peeling paint on the houses. Ahead, the road was clogged. A small crowd had gathered around an emergency relief vehicle. A man, face etched with exhaustion and frustration, broke from the group when he spotted their truck. His eyes locked on Nick's.

A former client. A mechanic he'd helped with a messy traffic case two years ago.

The man approached, his steps slow but steady. "Officer." His voice was a rasp. "They say someone rerouted the FEMA aid. Why? We've got nothing here."

The words were theater. A coded cover for their meeting.

Adams leaned forward. He played his part. "Resources are being allocated as fast as possible."

It was an empty promise.

The man stepped in, his voice dropping to a conspiratorial whisper, barely audible over the thumping of the nearby generator.

"I saw them," the man said. "One looked like a contractor. Big guy, covered in grease. They were pushing something on a flatbed. Tryin' to be real quiet. Not a soul around. I heard it." He glanced at Adams, then back at Nick, eyes opening a fraction too much. "They haven't stopped bringing drugs in. The storm's their cover."

A chill hit Nick's blood. "How do you know it was them?"

The man's eyes darted to Adams, then back to Nick. "I was ... associated. With the Bruth'rs. Back before you took down the old crew." He swallowed. "The way they moved, the way they kept watch. You don't forget that kind of presence." His voice dipped, rough with paranoia. "Heard 'em talk about FEMA trucks. That's how they were movin' the cargo."

The informant's whisper landed like shrapnel. Direct, unvarnished truth in a world of lies.

"And yesterday"—he breathed the words—"I spotted a lioness mural on that boarded-up building over there." He pointed at a ruined storefront. "Swear it was bleeding. Marked with something red. I heard 'em say it was a message. 'The king's cub is now fair game.' Gotta go."

Nick's blood ran cold. The lioness. A warning that cut deeper than the law. He checked the rearview, but the man had already vanished into the crowd. "What do you think, Quincy?"

WITNESS ELIMINATION

Adams shook his head. "Local intel's unreliable. The informant is stressed. Hallucinating. We can't divert recovery teams based on rumors."

The warning lingered, unseen but heavy, like a phantom limb he couldn't shake.

Nick shifted gears. "Have you heard anything official about Hank? I know witness protection is tight, but he hasn't returned any of my messages."

Adams sighed. He rubbed the bags under his eyes. "He's restless, Nick. The system doesn't reward men who blow the whistle; it buries them. He's been complaining he can't run a new lead, something about a 'Red Crown' symbol and the ports. I told him to let it go. His job is to stay safe, not chase leads."

"La Reina?" The name was barely a whisper, the confirmation chilling.

Adams shook his head. "It's stress, Nick. You can't be chasing rumors now either."

He turned to Adams. "What about the marina?"

Adams's face remained a mask of exhaustion. He checked his digital map. "The area is marked as a flood zone, Nick. It's a logistical nightmare. These are legitimate resource shortages, not political maneuvers."

Nick searched his face. He found only the strained discipline of a cop trying to manage the unmanageable position.

It was a lie.

Adams was following orders from higher up. Those same directives had diverted FEMA trucks and matched the local man's warning a little too well.

As they drove, the lioness mural painted on a boarded-up storefront loomed into view. Its fierce eyes locked onto his. On its chest was a splash of red paint. Like blood.

It was a message. No doubt about it.

And it was for him.

13

TASK FORCE ISSUES

September 29, afternoon

Nick shouldered through the door, stepping over a sandbag barrier that had failed to hold back the flood. He steadied himself on the frame a moment—too many days of adrenaline and too little sleep making the world tilt by an inch. Three days after Hurricane Helene, the converted annex near Mirror Lake still bore her fury: brown stains climbing four feet up the walls, tacky linoleum squishing beneath his boots. Overhead lights cast a sickly glow over a collection of government personnel who were as waterlogged as their surroundings, their expressions drawn with the peculiar exhaustion that follows disaster.

A window-unit air conditioner rattled in its death throes, pushing around little more than heat. Nick scanned the room, cataloging each person with the precision of a man used to reading juries. Three FBI representatives clustered near the coffeepot, their blue windbreakers pristine against the squalor. State emergency officials huddled over laptops powered by orange extension cords, their lines snaked across the floor like synthetic vines. At the center, a battered conference table groaned under manila folders, topographic maps, and Styrofoam coffee cups.

Sergeant Quincy Adams stood apart, tapping a rhythm on his tablet. He'd found time to change into a uniform, which was rumpled but remained tucked in. He caught Nick's eye and gave a tight nod.

"They've been waiting." His voice was sharp. "Feds are anxious to get this over." His fingers drummed faster at the term, a tell Nick hadn't seen from him before.

Nick flexed his jaw, tension gathering. "I'm sure they are."

The lead FBI agent, a gray-haired man with the posture of someone who'd been military before the Bureau, lifted his head as Nick approached. "Mr. Justin, we were about to begin without you."

"As always, I'm right on time." Nick pulled out a folding chair, its scrape against the floor drawing all eyes. He sat deliberately, placing his leather portfolio on the table. The metal was cold through his jeans. Everything in this place was cold. "Where are we with the prisoner transfer manifests?"

The agent—Holcomb, according to the credentials around his neck—glanced at his colleagues. "We're still processing the documentation from the county. The storm has complicated matters."

"Complicated. Sarah Brown and Sally Hinkins were in custody before Helene made landfall. The authorities should've logged it the moment the cuffs went on."

Holcomb's face stayed impassive. "There are jurisdictional protocols. Information is distributed on a need-to-know basis."

"And I need to know." Nick leaned in, forearms on the damp table. "I'm the task force liaison appointed by the mayor. Or did that memo get lost in the flood, too?"

A woman in a Department of Justice blazer cleared her throat. "Mr. Justin, we understand your frustration, but these procedures exist for a reason. The investigation is ongoing, and with Senator Maxwell's office taking a personal interest—"

"Personal interest?" Shandra Greene's voice cut through the room like a blade. She'd been so still she was nearly invisible. Now she stood, her chair skittering behind her. "Is that what we're calling political interference now?"

WITNESS ELIMINATION

Shandra moved to the table, her steps measured but forceful. She wore her fury like armor, back straight, eyes sharp, unblinking. She slammed her palm on a file, the sound cracking like a gunshot.

"My son's killer, Gino Myers, is sitting smug in county jail, arraigned, but justice keeps dragging its feet. The RADD Squad's getting shuffled around, same faces, different titles. And now two key suspects vanish during a hurricane?" Her voice trembled with contained rage. "This isn't a jurisdictional issue. This is a cover-up."

The room fell silent. Even the dying air conditioner held its breath.

"Ms. Greene." Holcomb's square jaw twitched. His tone dipped into something patronizing. "We understand your personal stake in this matter, but—"

"Don't." Nick cut him off, standing beside Shandra. "Don't diminish her concerns. Where are the manifests? The prisoner tracking logs? The chain-of-custody documentation from Tagger Group International?"

Adams shifted. "The senator's office wants this contained. Recovery crews are back out, so they're chasing optics."

"Optics?" Nick let out a brittle laugh. "How does letting corrupt cops and cartel-connected suspects vanish during a natural disaster inspire anything except fear? Is there even a manhunt underway?"

~

The day unraveled fast. Equipment failures mounted. Servers were down, backup generators were sputtering, and connections were timing out. Every request faced a bureaucratic wall. People demanded signatures, authorizations stalled, and systems rebooted.

By late afternoon, the fluorescent lights pulsed in time with the throbbing in his temples. When Holcomb suggested an hour-long break, Nick was grateful. He stepped outside into the air. The sky hung gray, threatening more rain for a city already drowning.

When he returned with coffee, Adams sat alone at the table, his face grim.

"They've cleared out back to Tampa."

Nick stared at the empty spot where the file boxes had been. "Where are the manifests?"

Adams didn't look up. "Gone. Holcomb checked them out for 'secure transport' back to the regional office."

"The originals?"

"Everything." Adams lifted his head. "They said copies would be available tomorrow, after processing."

Nick crossed to the storage cabinet, where he'd locked his supplementary files earlier that day: his own records of the prisoner transfers and the evidence logs he'd painstakingly compiled. The lock was intact. But when he opened the door, only bare folders remained.

For a heartbeat, the absence was louder than any alarm.

"Someone had a key." Adams eyed the empty drawer. "The Feds take what they want."

The rot from the streets had seeped inside, unseen but unmistakable. It wasn't the city decaying after the flood; it was the very system meant to hold it together.

~

Shandra Greene materialized from the shadows of the hallway outside the briefing room. She positioned herself directly in Nick's path, shoulders squared beneath her blazer, her bold brown eyes locked on his with an intensity that made retreat impossible. The light flickered, casting her face in alternating amber glow and shadow, revealing the taut line of her jaw, the slight flare of her nostrils, subtle signs of fury held in check. Nick glanced over his shoulder. They were alone in this forgotten corridor, water stains marking the ceiling.

"They're burying it." Shandra's voice was razor-edged. "All of it."

Nick nodded.

"Those manifests didn't walk out." Her hands trembled. Anger or fear—he couldn't tell. "Someone wants Sarah and Hinkins to disappear into the system or out of it entirely."

"We'll request new copies." The offer sounded hollow.

Shandra's laugh was sharp, humorless. "You still think this is a functioning bureaucracy? The files are missing. The backups will be corrupted. Timestamps altered." Her fingers curled into fists. "Ten months fighting for justice for my son, Jaquez, and now, vanished evidence, recanted witnesses, stalled investigations. I know the pattern."

A maintenance worker shuffled by, mop dragging across the damp floor. Nick angled his body to block her from view, creating the illusion of privacy. When the man turned the corner, Shandra leaned closer.

"I have copies." Her voice dropped to a whisper. "Not everything, but enough. The ballistics report from Officer Myers's service weapon. The dashcam footage they claimed was corrupted. Documentation linking the RADD Squad to the contraband moving through MacDill."

Nick's pulse quickened. "Where?"

"Somewhere safe." Her eyes never left his face, measuring his reaction. "If they keep stonewalling us, I'm taking it to the press. All of it."

"They're too big, Shandra." He kept his voice steady. "Too connected. Senator Maxwell has half of the Tampa Bay media in his pocket. They would bury or discredit the story within hours."

"Then I go national and make it impossible to contain." The fierce determination in her tone allowed no room for doubt. "They're protecting someone. Someone bigger than Myers, bigger than Hinkins. A name worth letting murderers walk free during a natural disaster."

Nick ran a hand over his face, the stubble of four unshaven days rasping against his palm. The exhaustion of the past weeks settled on his shoulders.

"That makes you a target. The kind that doesn't get warnings. These people have ties to the Venezuelan cartel. You know that."

Shandra's eyes flashed. "I'm already in danger." Her voice caught. "They took my son. Shot him down and called it justified. What else can they take from me?"

She straightened, and her composure snapped back into place. "At least this way, if something happens, everyone will know why."

Behind Shandra, across the street, stood a building, one of many damaged by Helene's fury. The plywood over its broken windows had become an impromptu canvas. Another spray-painted lioness crouched there, fierce and protective, its outline stark against the weathered wood.

A red mark on its chest pulsed in the late-afternoon light. *The king's cub is now fair game.* The memory sent a chill through him, despite the hallway's oppressive heat.

Shandra followed his gaze. Her eyes found the mural. A grim smile touched her lips.

"Appropriate, isn't it? They think they're hunting us." She met his eyes. "They don't realize we're the ones with teeth."

Nick studied her face. Beneath the activist's armor lay the grieving mother. In the ten months since her son's death, Shandra Greene had turned pain into purpose, grief into action. She wouldn't back down, couldn't. And he couldn't let her face this alone.

"We need to be smarter than they are. If we use what you have, the timing has to be perfect."

"So, you're with me?" She appraised him.

"I'm for justice." Nick held her gaze. "But we do this my way. No leaks unless we both agree. And we meet where they can't monitor us— not here, not your office, not mine."

Shandra considered this, then gave a single, sharp nod. "The community garden on 22nd. South side by the shed. Seven tomorrow. The volunteers will provide cover."

"I'll be there."

They parted. Nick's cell buzzed in his pocket. He pulled it out, angling the screen away from her. No sender. The ten words that made his blood run cold.

She wasn't the target. Your daughter was. Check your home.

His fingers went numb around the device, but he forced himself to slide the phone away. What flickered in his eyes sent Shandra a step back.

"What is it?"

"Nothing." The lie came smoothly. "Confirmation we're making the right move."

WITNESS ELIMINATION

He walked off. His mind raced, measuring risks and calculating fallout. Behind him, the lioness on the wall watched with painted eyes.

The king's cub is now fair game.

The warning hadn't been about Shandra at all.

14

INK & VENOM

Ink & Venom sat between a pawnshop with a blacked-out window and a laundromat that never had more than two machines working. The storefront glowed purple from a strip of neon tubing. José stepped through first. Nick followed, letting the heavy door thump shut behind him.

A chemical sting clung to the room—ink, antiseptic, metal. Flash art covered the walls in tight clusters: skulls, blades, saints with broken faces. A single figure bent over a client's arm in the chair. Coins jingled from the chains looped across his vest—hence the nickname. Coin didn't look until the machine stopped.

He lifted the buzzing needle, wiped the man's shoulder in one practiced stroke, and snapped his gloves off. The tattoo was of a smoldering wolf's head, teeth gripping a cracked crown. Clean lines. Heavy black. Focused craftsmanship.

Coin turned. "Didn't expect both of you."

José nodded. "We need a word."

Coin jerked his chin at the client. "Tank—grab a beer in the back."

Tank rose, flexed his arms, and disappeared behind the curtain. The flap settled.

Coin faced them. "Say it."

José didn't ease in. "Sarah and Hinkins escaped. Six Bruth'rs died."

Coin's jaw pulled tight. "I inked those guys. I heard their plans, their fights, their victories. Those six? They were steady hands. Now they're on slabs while Sarah and that ex-cop walk free. A split's coming. You can feel it."

Nick frowned. "The manifest doesn't track. They moved the crew but left Myers behind. Why?"

Coin grunted. "Yeah. It raised eyebrows here, too."

"Does a split help?" Nick asked.

"Helps no one," Coin shrugged. "Some still pledge to them. Others want blood. The tension burns from the inside out."

Nick showed a photo on his screen. "I'm getting messages. Anonymous. Whoever it was had eyes near the bus hit. Sent images close to the blast. Then they shoved us toward a fake flight out of Linder. Nothing lines up."

Coin studied the image. "Someone's steering you. Maybe toward truth. Maybe toward a ditch."

José crossed his arms. "You hear anything about the transfer delay?"

Coin rubbed a thumb across a dent in the counter. "A badge pushed for a one-day shift. FBI. No name. Pressure from someone with reach. Storm rolls in, transfer still moves. Means national security got thrown on the table. The only reason anyone forces a run like that."

Nick felt the logic tighten. "And the replacement bus?"

"Only one in the yard without a camera," Coin said. "Rushed. Clean order. Somebody wanted it blind."

Nick asked, "Could the texter be Bruth'rs?"

Coin shook his head once. "Bruth'rs talk plenty, but their chain of command is tight. The rank-and-file spill stories. The ones running the show stay quiet. If someone's whispering, I can't tell you which tier they came from. Could be inside. Could be a badge. Could be someone who moves pieces without ever stepping on the board."

José pulled a folded stack of cash from his pocket and set it on the counter.

Coin looked at the money, then up at Nick.

"And the next legal jam is on me," Nick said. "Pro bono."

Coin took the cash and slid it under a towel. "Good. Because I've got one last thing."

He paused, voice dropping. "A cartel's cleaning its mess from the summer. Quiet moves. Quick hits. Anyone who failed them is getting erased, starting with that senator who went airborne off a balcony. Word is her 'security promise' didn't hold. That was strike one. More strikes are coming."

Nick felt the air thicken. "They're tying the transfer to her death?"

Coin nodded. "If a cartel thinks you're part of their problem, you don't get warnings. You get taken off the board. And six dead Bruth'rs? That wasn't the main event. That was warm-up."

Nick absorbed it. "Anything else?"

"Yeah," Coin said. "Stay alert. If your phantom texter reaches out again, assume they're holding more than a phone." He raised his voice toward the back. "Tank—get back out here."

Tank pushed through the curtain with the beer still in his hand. Coin pulled on new gloves and pointed at the chair.

"Sit. Let's finish this wolf."

The machine buzzed again, filling the shop with its steady hum.

José and Nick stepped outside, the violet glow brushing their faces before the door thumped shut behind them.

José stared at the street, scanning the parked cars. "If he's right, we're not just hunting a leak. We're standing in the middle of a war."

Nick checked the phone in his pocket. It was still dark. "Let's move before the next strike lands."

They headed toward the car, the night tightening around them.

15

JESSICA'S FEAR

September 29, 2024, night

Jessica's fingers traced the stain on her windowsill, following its outline like a map to nowhere. Although their house fared better than others, water still seeped into its foundation. A sour smell of damp rose up, something no bleach could fix. Night had fallen hours ago, but sleep stayed far away. The patched window rattled in its frame as the wind pushed at it, testing for a way in. A mosquito whined along the glass, its thin body silhouetted in the floodlight.

The harsh beam outside glared against the pane. A prickle crawled up the back of her neck. The light flickered, plunging her room into darkness, then sputtered back to life. The power grid in St. Petersburg was still patchy, lines failing and holding in uneven stretches. The generator thrummed outside, its deep, steady drone a constant reminder that life was different.

"Dad should be home by now." The words were just breath.

She climbed onto her bed and reached for her sentinel. Tonight, she needed it. Her hands shook. She gripped Zara tight.

She moved Zara to the window, its weight comforting in her hands. The white glow outside cast long shadows across the room, making the stains on the ceiling crawl like living things. Jessica adjusted its paws, turning its face toward the yard.

"You have to watch." She straightened the ears. "Tell me if they come."

The house groaned around her, the same sound from every night since the storm. The wind pushed harder, slipping through cracks in the patched-up walls. Each creak made her spine go cold. Mom always said it was the house settling. But she didn't believe it. Houses talked. And this one was warning her.

She pressed her forehead against the warm glass and stared into the dark. The lawn was full of broken stuff: tree branches, roof pieces, a plastic chair tipped on its side.

Her breath fogged the pane. She wiped it away with her palm, leaving a smudge shaped like a handprint.

"I saw the lion painting." She stroked the lioness. "The one with the red spot. Dad said I didn't see it … but I did."

Zara only stared back, unblinking and quiet.

Outside, limbs cast splintered shapes across the grass, turning familiar things strange. The house gave another creak, and her shoulders hunched. In the corner of her ceiling, the security system her uncle José had installed blinked its tiny warning light, fixed on her.

Aunt Sarah. She understood why they hadn't gone to see her in jail, no matter what Mom had once promised. That night under the bridge came back. Sarah's perfume mixed with bay air, and the gun pressed cold against her ribs. That was when she learned her aunt's smile could turn sharp and dangerous.

She hadn't been in the SUV, but the story had been whispered again and again: how it flipped on the Gandy Bridge, how Mom didn't wake up for days in the hospital. What stuck with her most were the machines, the steady beeping while Dad told her to be brave. When Mom finally came home, she was using a cane and trembled.

All of it—Sarah's gun, Mom's coma, the crash—was tied to the hard drive Sarah wanted from Dad. Why did it matter so much? It turned her aunt into someone she barely recognized. How could the same person who used to bring her sparkly hair clips and stuffed animals be the one who hurt Mom, rattled Dad, and held her at gunpoint?

And now Sarah wasn't even locked up anymore. She'd escaped with that ex-police officer who terrified her even more.

A flicker of movement broke the memory. At the far edge of the yard, where the security light's reach thinned into dark, something slid along the fence, like a shadow unhooking itself and moving on its own. Her muscles locked, waiting for it to appear again.

Jessica blinked, clutching Zara tighter. The shape was gone. Had it been there at all? A person? An animal? Or the light playing tricks as the floodlight sputtered?

"Did you see that?" Her voice was almost lost beneath the drone of crickets outside. A bird was trapped inside her chest, pounding against her ribs.

The yard was empty now, nothing moving but ripples spreading in the puddles. She pressed her face to the glass. She scanned the fence line, the hedge, the driveway. Nothing.

She took a step back from the window, then another. Her gaze locked on the spot where the shadow had slid. Her stomach clenched. Aunt Sarah's gun was cold against her ribs, perfume in her nose—like it was happening all over again.

The bedroom door was shut tight, and the crack beneath it was black. Downstairs, Mom would be half-asleep on the couch, her medicine making her drift. She almost called out. Instead, she crept back to the window, lifted Zara, and hugged it hard to her chest.

"Maybe it was nothing."

The floodlight sputtered again, harder this time, throwing her room into quick flashes of brightness and dark. In the stuttering flicker, the water stains on her wall twisted into faces, animals, monsters. She squeezed her eyes shut until the glare steadied.

When she dared to look again, the yard was the same, but the safety was gone. Zara stayed quiet in her arms, its glass eyes catching only the shaky glow.

She set it back on the sill, turning its face toward the spot where the shadow had been. Her hands shook as she adjusted its paws. "Tell me if they come." She smoothed the fur. "Dad said we're safe, but I don't know if that's true."

Outside, a faint breeze rattled loose shingles and scraps of plastic across the yard. Any footprints that had marked the soil were gone.

~

One second she was on her bed, staring at the floodlight flicker against her walls, and the next, her bare feet were on freezing concrete. It was a switch only dreams could make, sudden and strange. Iron bars climbed on both sides of her, going up so high she couldn't see the top, only darkness. The air stung her nose, sharp and sour. No need to wonder. A prison.

The one from the news clips. Dad thought she wasn't looking. The place where they kept Aunt Sarah before the bus.

The hallway stretched forever, tight and straight, like it wanted to trap her inside it. Lights buzzed above her head, some dead, some twitching on and off, painting the block in sick yellow. The empty cells gaped on either side, metal doors hanging wide like mouths waiting to bite. The floor froze her toes until each step hurt. She wished she could turn back, but in dreams you didn't get to choose.

A siren screamed, so loud it made her teeth ache. Red bulbs flashed on and off, turning the walls bloody for a second then dark again. Voices shouted somewhere distant, too jumbled to make sense. But they were scared. Heavy doors banged shut, and keys rattled like chains. Feet pounded closer.

Jessica's ribs pressed tight, too small for the pounding inside her. She wanted to run, but her legs felt stuck in syrup. Every step dragged slowly. The shouting grew sharper, closing in. At the far side of the hall, a guard appeared, his shirt stained with something black. He froze when he spotted her, his mouth opening as if he meant to say her name. Then he vanished through a side door, leaving her alone with the siren's scream.

She saw her.

Aunt Sarah stood at the end of the corridor, tall and straight, as if nothing could touch her. She wasn't in an orange prison suit. She wore one of her fancy outfits, the kind she used to show up in when she brought gifts. Not a wrinkle on it. Her blonde hair was pulled into a tight knot, clean and perfect, like the shouting and chaos hadn't happened at all.

WITNESS ELIMINATION

She looked exactly the way she had that night the police came. The same way she looked before Dad's face hardened whenever Jessica said her name.

"Jessica." Aunt Sarah's voice cut through the sirens, sweet and steady. "Come here, sweetheart."

Her smile was the same one she used when she handed over presents—sparkly clips, bright pens, the toys she'd given Jessica not so long ago. Only now that grin sat wrong, too strained, too practiced, like she'd put it on instead of feeling it.

Her aunt grew larger, her posture filling the flashing red light. Her shadow stretched over the floor, long enough to reach her feet.

She wanted to tell her to stay back, but nothing came out. Her mouth moved, yet the alarms swallowed the sound.

Sarah walked forward, calm, as if nothing around her mattered. A guard appeared, shouting, his club raised. She only tilted her head, and then he was down. The club spun across the ground like a toy top before it stopped with a clatter.

Another officer toppled. Then another. The cells that had been empty moments ago now held shapes, arms reaching out, grasping, grabbing at the air. The flashing red light turned it all into broken images, like a nightmare, like pictures passing too fast on TV.

And still Aunt Sarah came closer, grinning, her eyes locked on Jessica as if she was the only person left in the world.

"I've been waiting for you." Her voice was louder than the alarms yet soft as if she were whispering into Jessica's ear. "It's time to come with me. Your father has something that belongs to us."

Jessica tried to step back, but the hallway behind her had vanished. Only a blank wall pressed against her shoulders. Sarah was so close now that Jessica could see her own reflection in her aunt's eyes: a small, trembling girl, trapped, with nowhere to go.

Her aunt's hand stretched forward, fingers long and polished, reaching like the claws of something that pretended to be human. "We need you to send a message, sweetie. It won't hurt. Much."

Jessica's neck locked tight. Invisible hands squeezed the air from her. She opened her mouth to scream, to call for Dad, for Mom, for anyone, but nothing came out. Sarah's fingernails hovered inches away, the alarms shrieking, the red lights flashing faster and faster until the whole world felt like it was fracturing.

"*Dad!*" A scream ripped out of her throat, raw and desperate. She jolted upright, sheets knotted around her legs, sweat soaking through her nightshirt.

The prison corridor was gone. She was in her room. Only the steady blink of the security system's red light cut through the dark. She clutched the lioness so tightly its seams stretched, the stuffing bulging like it might burst.

The door flew open, slamming against the wall. Mom filled the frame, one hand braced for balance. Even in the dim glow, her mother's face shifted—first alarm, then relief; then she tried to look brave.

"Jess." Mom's voice was thick. "It's okay, baby. Just a dream." She moved toward the bed. Each step looked like it hurt.

Jessica's sobs came in hiccupped bursts. "She was coming for me." Jessica gasped. "Aunt Sarah, she said ... she said Dad has something."

"Shhh." Her mom eased herself onto the mattress. It dipped under her weight, pulling Jessica closer. "Aunt Sarah can't harm you. Not anymore."

She drew her daughter into her arms. Jessica pressed her face against her mother's shoulder, breathing in the mix of warm skin and the faint antiseptic smell that never left after the hospital. Andrea's embrace enveloped her.

"It felt real." Jessica whispered into her mother's neck. "The prison, the alarms, everything."

Andrea stroked her hair, fingers catching in the tangles. "Dreams can feel that way," she murmured. Her voice was steady, but a tremor ran through her hand. "But you're safe here. With me. With Dad."

Jessica pulled back. In the dim glow, her mother looked older than she remembered, with new lines etched around her mouth and eyes. "Where's Dad?"

Andrea's face flickered, like a shadow moving under her skin, before she smoothed it away. "Working late. He'll be home soon."

Her eyes slid past Jessica to the window. Outside, the light wavered, making shadows crawl across the walls. Andrea's arm tightened around her daughter.

"Let me stay with you tonight," she said, her gaze never leaving the glass. "We'll chase the bad dreams away together."

Jessica nodded and settled down. But even as sleep tugged at her, her mother was tense, eyes fixed on the dark outside, as if she was watching for something.

16

FIRING RANGE

September 30, 2024

The warehouse door groaned on rusted tracks as Nick dragged it open enough for Andrea to slip inside. The air struck them— mildew from the floods, metal dust, and beneath it all, the sharp tang of gunpowder. José stood waiting in the half-light from broken skylights. Three folding tables formed a makeshift counter, their surfaces crowded with pistols. Nick's throat tightened. The law had always been his weapon. Not these.

"Let's get working," José said. His face stayed impassive as his eyes tracked Andrea's cautious gait. There was a subtle tremor in her left side.

"How's the pain today?"

Andrea lifted her chin. "Manageable."

Nick remembered the sound of her muffled sobs behind the bathroom door that morning, the prescription bottle lying open on the vanity—two pills gone instead of one.

Hurricane Helene had left the warehouse district a patchwork of ruin. This building had survived better than most, the concrete frame still scarred but solid. José had reshaped the space into a functional firing range: sandbags stacked against the far wall, water-stained where the flood had reached, and wooden pallets raising gear above the damp floor.

"We have little time," José said, nodding toward the table. "Inspection crews are coming next week. Once they mark this place, it's gone."

Nick stepped closer, taking in the lineup with a lawyer's eye: three Steyr pistols, two Glocks fitted with tactical lights, and a pair of Berettas, their black finish drinking in the meager light from the skylights.

"These are all unregistered?" Nick asked, his voice flat, more statement than question.

José didn't blink. "You want a paper trail after what they did to Andrea?"

Nick's jaw tightened. Only a day had passed since the lioness mural with its blood-red chest, but it had stripped them of sleep, of peace. The threat against Jessica had reset every line he thought he wouldn't cross.

"Show me," Andrea said, stepping forward. Her eyes locked on the weapons. Nick found himself staring. Her resolve caught him off guard.

She lifted one of the Steyrs, its heft a shock in her palm. Cold. Dense. She turned it over, tracing the handle with her thumb, her finger hovering near the trigger guard as if anticipating the recoil. For a heartbeat, she closed her eyes, steadying herself. When she opened them, the hesitation was gone.

"Understanding it first is key," José said, moving closer. "Feel its mass, its balance, how it answers when you fire. This is your lifeline now."

Andrea nodded. Her fingers adjusted around the textured frame, gripping it until her knuckles turned white. Anchored and steady. A dark determination settled in her eyes. She gripped the weapon not with fear, but as if she were finally holding the answer to keeping Jessica safe.

"Now, let's talk about stance," he said, planting his feet shoulder-width apart, knees bent, arms loose but ready. She copied him, the Steyr in her hands.

"Firm but not white-knuckled," he corrected, nudging her grip. "This isn't about strength. It's about control."

She breathed once, twice, settling into the posture like she'd been born to it. For the first time since the crash and the threats, fragility didn't cling to her. She stood prepared.

WITNESS ELIMINATION

Nick watched Andrea mirror the position. She no longer looked like the hospital administrator who used to agonize over budgets. Pain had stripped that away, leaving something harder beneath.

"Now, you," he said, turning to him. "This isn't theoretical, Counselor."

The Glock sat heavy in Nick's hand—cold, charged, more burden than tool. His jaw clicked, a reflex he hadn't noticed in years. "I have one at the house." He knew its mechanics from training, but it still pressed against his conscience. He mimicked José's stance, yet his body balked, aching for the simple weight of a Louisville Slugger—something that belonged to him, not to violence.

"Trigger discipline," José said, his eyes sharp. "Keep your finger off it until you're ready to fire. Never point at anything you don't mean to put a round through. Line up your sights, fix the picture, steady your breath, then press the trigger."

Andrea absorbed the instructions with unnerving focus. When José set a paper target against the sandbags thirty feet away, she stepped to the firing position without hesitation.

"Protective gear first," José said, passing out ear protection and glasses.

The first shot cracked through the warehouse like a thunderclap, hitting a sandbag. Andrea flinched at the recoil but steadied, adjusted, and fired again. A third followed, then another, each one more controlled. By the time she dropped the magazine, holes peppered the target, seventeen with thirteen clustered tight in the center mass.

José's eyebrows rose, the closest thing to surprise Nick had ever seen on his face. "You've done this before."

Andrea ejected the clip and lowered the pistol, her hands trembling faintly from the kick. "My father," she said. "Back in college. He thought a woman should know how to protect herself." Her laugh came dry, without mirth. "He was thinking muggers in parking lots, not cops on payrolls and cartel hitmen."

When Nick's turn came, the Glock seemed to gain weight with every heartbeat. All the courtroom talk he'd spun about ballistics, trajectory, physics—none of it steadied his resolve. His first shot tore into the sandbag wall, a foot shy of the target. The recoil jolted up his arm, less a reminder than a reprimand.

"Tighten your grip," José said. "Anticipate the kick, but don't flinch before it happens."

Nick forced his breath steady and fired again. This one punched the target's outer ring, but at least it marked the paper. Brass casings clattered onto the cement, their metallic clatter like wind chimes from some nightmare carnival.

The gunfire continued, each shot cracking against the concrete. The air grew thick with the acrid tang of burned powder, stinging Nick's nose and throat. By the last magazine, his hands throbbed and his ears rang even through the muffled protection. Across the line, Andrea sagged with exertion, but her shots still clustered tight on the sheet. It was as if her body remembered something deeper than practice, absorbing the mechanics even through the drag of fatigue.

"Enough," José said, checking his watch. "A gun only helps at distance. Up close, it's dead weight." He set the pistols aside and dragged the exercise mats into place with a kick. "Now we focus on fighting stance, movement, and strikes."

"Is this smart?" Nick's eyes flicked to Andrea's left leg, where a sudden, slight tremor betrayed the struggle to hold her balance.

José's eyes went cold. "You think anybody's gonna go easy on her because of her knee? Nobody fights fair out there." He walked to the center of the mat and braced his feet. "Stand like this. Weight balanced. Real power starts in the legs and hips. Arms just finish the job."

Andrea stepped forward and settled into place. She mimicked him cleanly, adjusting her shoulders, bending her knees with a confidence that surprised Nick. Years of swimming and tennis were still there, written into her body's memory. Watching her find her stance, steady and sure, stirred something in Nick's chest—pride. Pain hadn't broken her. It had carved her into something harder, someone ready to stand and fight.

"Fists up," José demonstrated. "Protect your face. Chin down. Eyes on their center, not the hands."

José guided her through the basics—jabs, hooks, knees—each motion deliberate. Pain tightened her face when she pivoted, but she didn't falter, didn't complain. She blinked hard, forcing the pain behind a mask of calm. This wasn't sport; it was survival. Sweat traced a line down her temple, but what he saw wasn't weakness. It was resolve, iron forged. She was already stronger than the men who'd tried to break her.

When Nick's turn came, something in him stalled. His punches landed, but they lacked force. He'd sparred with José enough to know the rhythm, the patterns, the openings. But practice didn't matter here. His body pulled back from that reality even as he swung.

José saw it instantly. He stepped closer, eyes narrowing. "You're pulling back," he said. His voice carried no anger, only cold finality. "You know the moves, Counselor. But this isn't the ring. There's no middle ground here. Commit or walk away. Half measures won't fail you—they'll get your family killed."

Nick reset his stance, the old boxer's rhythm settling into his limbs. He forced himself to picture the faceless men who had run Andrea off the bridge, the ones now circling Jessica. Heat rose in his chest. He drove his fist into the bag, solid contact but without teeth.

"Now think dirty," José said, stepping in close. "Fight like your life depends on it. Go for the throat, the eyes. Don't just hit. End it."

This time, Nick's punch came loaded with fear and fury. Each strike was no longer practice but a promise, every blow a father's answer to the threat against his family.

José gave a single nod, grim and final. "That's where you start."

~

José unspooled the beige wrap, his scarred knuckles moving in tight, economical patterns around Andrea's smaller hands. The cotton whispered against her skin, winding beneath the palm, between each finger, locking her hands into weapons. Nick watched from the edge of the mat, catching the flicker in his wife's hazel eyes as the tab snapped into place. She was changing under José's guidance, sharpening, hardening. The sight stirred both pride and unease in him.

"These protect your fists, not your target," he said, and slipped the focus mitts over his calloused hands. He squared his hips. "Now show me that cross jab we practiced."

Andrea threw two punches. The gloves gave only a muted pop. Her strikes were light, tentative. She was unsteady. Her muscles caught between old limits and this new, unforgiving violence.

"Stop thinking about your balance," José said. "Your mind builds boundaries. Your body knows what to do if you let it."

Andrea's jaw tightened. She reset her stance, weight balanced, eyes fixed. The next jab snapped forward, knuckles popping against leather, the sound echoing through the hollow warehouse. A flicker of surprise crossed her face before she buried it beneath focus.

"Better," José barked. "Again."

Outside, the late-afternoon sun filtered through broken skylights, stretching shadows across the concrete floor. The building was cut off from the city, a pocket of silence where normal rules no longer applied. Andrea wasn't a hospital administrator with a titanium rod in her leg. Nick wasn't a lawyer clinging to statutes and precedents. In this place, they were stripped down to something rawer, two people learning how to survive.

"Think about the Challenger that hit you on the bridge." José moved the mitts in an irregular pattern, forcing her to track and strike. "Think about the fear when you knew they weren't stopping. Channel it."

Andrea's next punch snapped forward with sudden ferocity. Something dark flashed across her face. The follow-through cross nearly forced José back a step.

"There it is." A curl tugged at his lip. "Use it."

Sweat traced down Andrea's temples. Her breath came in steady, measured breaths. The hesitation was gone, replaced by something harder, sharper. She pivoted. Pain crossed her face but never stayed. The punch landed with a crack that echoed through the cavernous warehouse, the sound of someone refusing to be broken.

"Again."

For fifteen minutes, José pushed her through combinations: jab, hook, duck, weave, uppercut. Andrea's shirt clung with sweat, her breathing roughening into uneven exhales. Her leg muscles twitched at every pivot, the resistance obvious, but she never slowed.

"Last sequence." "Everything you've got. One, two, three, two."

Andrea drew from somewhere deep, a reservoir Nick hadn't seen since this ordeal began. Her punches snapped forward, each one fueled by months of rage, the crash, the coma, the danger aimed at Jessica. The final cross cracked against José's mitt with such force that even he faltered, his eyes widened in rare surprise.

This was someone forged from pain into steel, a partner who refused to bend. For the first time in weeks, Nick thought they might actually stand a chance.

Then it was over. Andrea's strength bled away in an instant, her body folding back into a support beam. Her chest rose and fell in jagged bursts. Sweat plastered her hair to her forehead. Her wrapped hands, so fierce a moment ago, now trembled.

José crossed to a cooler and returned with a bottle of water. "Drink."

Andrea fumbled with the cap, twisted it off, and drank deep. Water ran down her chin. Her body couldn't get enough. When she lowered the bottle, halfway empty, she swiped her wrist across her face, leaving a dark streak where sweat and wrap residue mixed.

"I didn't know I could do that." Her voice was raw with fatigue and wonder.

Nick, watching from the edge of the mat, felt pride surge past his worry. For weeks, he had seen her broken, fragile, uncertain. Now, even shaking and spent, she was unbreakable.

José studied her for a long moment. "Fear isn't your enemy. It's a tool. Most people let it control them, paralyze them. Discipline transforms it, turns it from weakness to weapon."

Andrea's eyes locked on his, something new burning behind them. The water bottle crackled in her grip as if it couldn't contain the shift happening inside her. Nick knew that look. This was determination.

"Your turn." José raised the mitts. "She's set a high bar."

Nick stepped forward, the mat soft beneath his shoes, aware of Andrea against the beam. She was still trembling, sweat streaking her temples, but she radiated strength. It caught him off guard.

"Don't fight pretty." José's voice was cold. "You know how to win points. That won't save you in a warehouse or alley. Forget defense. Go for the break—the throat, the eyes, the kneecap, the groin. There's no ref, no bell. You end it or you don't walk away."

Nick froze, the years of sparring and rules of the ring colliding with the raw edge in José's tone. Andrea's eyes held him—steady, expectant. Commitment fused inside him, tangled with the memory of Jessica's voice screaming for him in the dark.

José gave a quick nod, the barest invitation. Nick answered with a textbook jab—clean, sharp, but José caught it, twisting his wrist hard enough to send pain spiking up his arm.

"Dirty." José released him. "There's no honor in a real fight."

Nick took a breath. He drove a palm toward José's nose, pivoted, and went for the knee. They circled. Nothing pretty, nothing for the scorecards. The moves were ugly, efficient, meant to buy seconds, not rounds.

José nodded. "That's survival. That's what keeps your Jessica breathing."

Fifteen minutes later, Nick's arms burned with unfamiliar exertion, sweat stinging his eyes, his knuckles throbbing despite the wraps. The difference was raw, desperate improvisation, the willingness to do whatever it took. In his chest, something shifted. The knot of helplessness that had been tightening since the first threat against his family gave way.

José called time with a sharp clap of the mitts. "Enough for today. We'll go again tomorrow."

Andrea steadied herself without support, though fatigue carved deep lines around her eyes. She peeled the tape from her hands. The cotton was stained with sweat. "Will this be enough?"

José packed the gear with mechanical precision. "This isn't only physical. It's psychological. Most people never learn what they're capable of, what they'll do when cornered." His eyes lifted, pinning them both. "Now you will."

Nick crossed to Andrea and helped her gather her things. Their eyes met, the silence between them carrying more than words ever could. The woman he'd married nine years ago was gone. In her place stood someone reshaped by pain, sharpened by fear. And in her gaze was the same stern resolve tightening inside his own chest.

On the walk to the car, neither spoke. José's lesson pressed against them more heavily than the night air. This wasn't training anymore. It was preparation for the versions of themselves they were afraid to meet.

~

Nick killed the engine and listened to the tick of cooling metal. Beside him, Andrea's breathing had steadied, though the set of her jaw betrayed the pain she wouldn't voice. The dashboard clock glowed past eight. In the passenger seat, she flexed her fingers, working out the stiffness from seven hours of training—seven hours of learning how to hurt people. How to kill. He reached across the console and covered her hand, feeling the raw knuckles beneath his palm.

"Cindi came by." Andrea nodded toward the garage where Cindi's SUV sat under the porch light. "She said she'd stay until we got back."

Nick nodded, relief and guilt tightening together in his chest. There was comfort in knowing it was Cindi, someone who understood how high the stakes had become, who didn't need explanations. While he and Andrea trained for a world that no longer honored old rules, she guarded Jessica with the calm alertness of a friend who missed nothing.

They entered through the front door, Nick steadying Andrea as she navigated the two steps up. The house greeted them with its familiar scents: laundry detergent, the faint must of floodwater that never quite left, and the rich trace of Cindi's spaghetti sauce lingering in the air. Cindi stood in the kitchen, her green eyes sharp, but too discreet to ask questions.

"She's been asleep for about an hour." She slipped her purse off the counter. "Had trouble going down. Another nightmare, I think, but she wouldn't talk about it."

Nick pursed his lips.

After Cindi left, Nick moved through the first floor, testing each lock and window. The security panel by the stairs blinked its steady red assurance. Outside, the house generator's hum filled the silence, masking the neighborhood's flickering power.

"I'll check on Jess." Andrea's hand was already on the banister.

She climbed, every step measured, her body rigid from the day's work. The faint creak of the staircase followed her until the carpet swallowed the sound. Warmth rose in his face as she pushed forward, undercut by guilt for the pain carved into her stride.

When she returned minutes later, her face had softened. "She's out cold. Zara is back on the windowsill again."

He smiled despite the ache in his chest: Zara, the toy watching for dangers no child should even imagine.

The kitchen light flickered once then steadied. Outside, the floodlights echoed the surge, shadows sliding across the yard like restless phantoms. The power grid still limped along after Helene, and every falter carried the same unspoken reminder: their safety was fragile, temporary.

Andrea moved to the refrigerator, retrieved two bottles of water. She passed one to Nick, their fingers brushing, enough contact to remind him of what he was trying to protect. They drank in silence, the generator's hum filling the space. She leaned against the sink, and he sat at the island. The counter was more than furniture; it was a fault line that hadn't existed before the threats.

"I'm sorry for all of this." Nick's voice was low.

Andrea's head snapped up, eyes hardened. "Don't." She slammed the bottle onto the countertop hard enough to splash droplets across the granite. "Don't apologize for fighting back."

"I brought this into our lives," Nick pressed. "The RADD Squad. Myers. Every thread I pulled—"

"Stop." Andrea rounded the island, closing the space between them. She radiated a fierce energy that caught Nick's breath. "Sarah chose this, not you. Myers ran me off that bridge. They threatened our daughter." Her voice dropped to a whisper. "They're the ones who should carry the shame."

The security light outside wavered, throwing restless shadows across Andrea's face. Pain and determination had carved new lines there, sharpening her into someone different. The woman from the warehouse was back, the one who had driven her fists so hard that even José had shifted back.

"I'm terrified," he admitted. "Not for me. For you. For Jessica. I'm afraid I've marked you both in ways that can't be erased."

Andrea stepped closer, close enough for him to feel her warmth, catch the faint trace of sweat and gunpowder left from training. "And I'm scared this has made me weak." She gestured to her twitching leg. "That when it matters most, I won't be able to protect her. Or you."

The rawness of her admission cracked something open in him. He pulled her close, feeling the heat of her body, the way her fingers clutched his back like she was anchoring herself against a tide.

"I keep hearing what José said," she murmured into his shoulder. "That fear's a tool. I've been trying to shove it down, pretend I'm not terrified every time Jessica's out of my sight. But maybe that's wrong. Perhaps I need to carry it. Use it."

Nick buried his face in her hair, breathed in the mix of sweat and something essentially Andrea that no trauma could touch. "When I watched you on that firing line today, drilling the center again and again … I wasn't looking at my wife. I was seeing someone who could terrify me."

She drew back enough for their eyes to meet. Her smile didn't reach her eyes.

"Good. Fear's a weapon. Let them fear me. Let them fear us."

Andrea's hand slid into his, fingers locking tight. She led him upstairs. Each step was deliberate, measured so as to disguise pain behind resolve.

They passed Jessica's room, and the cracked door allowed them to glimpse her safe in her bed.

In their bedroom, she turned to him, her face half-lit by the glow of the light. She reached for him with a hunger that drove the same rawness he felt. The day's training had stripped them down to something elemental—life and death separated by margins too thin to measure. They came together with an urgency born less of desire than of survival, shedding clothes in careless piles on the floor.

Andrea pulled him onto the bed, her hands urgent, tracing him as if to memorize the body she might lose. Her touch carried an intensity sharpened by fear, a fierce affirmation of life in the shadow of violence.

When Nick hesitated, cautious of her injuries, she drew him closer, her eyes leaving no room for doubt.

Afterward, they relaxed in each other's arms, sweat cooling on their bodies, their breathing slowing into something steady but not calm. The house shifted around them with its storm wounds, timbers creaking, plaster settling. The floodlights stuttered beyond the window, and they threw jagged shadows across the yard, reminding them that peace here was borrowed, never earned.

Andrea's hand traced idle patterns on Nick's muscular chest, her head tucked beneath his chin. When she spoke, her voice was so soft the words were a vibration against his skin.

"If they want to break us," she whispered, "they'll have to kill us both."

He tightened his arm around her shoulders, drawing her closer, feeling the steady beat of her heart pressed to his side. Outside, the shadows continued their restless dance, but inside this room, something had solidified, a resolve hard as steel.

17

MAXWELL'S SHADOW

Senator Maxwell's manicured fingernails drummed once against the polished oak of the witness table. The Dirksen Senate Building's hearing room smelled of furniture polish, a familiar comfort as he surveyed the packed gallery. Cameras tracked his every movement. He adjusted his American flag pin, then leaned toward the microphone.

"Mr. Chairman, distinguished committee members, thank you for the opportunity to address the federal response to Hurricane Helene." His voice carried the cadence of a man long rehearsed in public duty. "The devastation across Florida's Gulf Coast, Georgia, and North Carolina demands our full attention and resources."

The gallery before him was all contrast: senators in crisp suits, fresh from air-conditioned offices, and local officials with shadowed eyes and rumpled shirts, their faces marked by exhaustion from crisis management. Reading the power dynamics instantly, Maxwell shaped his testimony for every audience at once.

"Within twenty-four hours of the hurricane's landfall, my office coordinated the deployment of three thousand government personnel," he continued. "We established emergency distribution routes that delivered over two million gallons of drinking water to affected communities."

He sipped his coffee, letting the performance sink in. The chairman nodded on cue. Maxwell suppressed a smile. The numbers were real, but the claim of his personal involvement was a lie. State crisis teams had built the supply chains, their work folding neatly beneath the banner of "federal response."

Shifting in his seat, Maxwell drew eyes to his immaculate navy suit, tailored to suggest authority without ostentation. Silver hair caught the light, framing features crafted to project trust on camera. The contrast was deliberate: behind him, the FEMA director slumped in a creased jacket, her exhaustion from nights in the office plainly visible.

"The allocation of national assets has prioritized critical infrastructure," he said, his gaze sweeping the committee with practiced warmth. "Power to hospitals, water systems, emergency services, and clearing operations has been restored at unprecedented speed." What the charts didn't show was the cost—whole precincts pulled into debris removal, FEMA offices short-staffed, patrol cars running storm duty instead of manhunts. The system was stretched past its breaking point, and everyone in the room knew it.

Tapping the folder before him, he offered a visual cue of the data backing his claims. Inside were graphs curated to showcase progress while concealing delays. Missing entirely was the truth: federal appropriations funneled toward political allies, even as neighborhoods like South St. Petersburg waited for basic aid.

The questioning began with softballs from supporters, allowing Maxwell to elaborate on foresight and preparedness. He settled into a rhythm, each measured answer reinforcing his narrative of competence and control.

"Senator, could you address concerns about the uneven distribution of FEMA support?" asked a junior member from Michigan, eyes fixed on a scripted card.

Maxwell nodded gravely. The question warranted reflection—or at least the appearance of it. "The appearance of inequity often stems from the necessity of triage in disaster response. Critical needs must be—"

"Senator Maxwell." The voice cut through, sharp as a blade. "Tampa Bay Times."

Maxwell's eyes found the source, a reporter rising from the media section, recorder extended. His press badge dangled from a frayed lanyard, and his sports coat was a season out of fashion. Not polished. Not Washington. A local.

The chairman tapped his gavel. "Sir, this is not a press conference. Questions will come from committee members only."

But the reporter's persistence carried. "The public deserves answers about Senator Caldwell's assassination and the prison transport ambush during Hurricane Helene. Will you comment on reports linking these events to corruption in your office?"

The question hit like a blow. Maxwell's measured breathing faltered for a split-second of shock before training locked back into place. His fingers tightened on the water glass until the skin over his knuckles went white.

The room froze, tension sharp and electric. The name "Caldwell" rankled him, dangerous, forbidden. Eleanor Caldwell: ally, rival, and now his victim. No one could prove it, not with the evidence sealed away.

Maxwell's smile came a fraction too late—imperceptible to most, glaring to anyone watching closely. "I have no comment on ongoing investigations," he said. His gaze slid to the back of the room, where his chief of staff, Richards, stood with arms crossed.

Richards gave a slight nod. Crisis containment was already in motion—phones buzzing in pockets, staff tracking the reporter, tracing his sources, preparing counters before the story could take root.

The chairman's gavel cracked again, louder this time. "Order! This hearing will maintain order!"

But the damage was done. Security moved the reporter toward the exit, his voice still carrying Sarah Brown's and Sally Hinkins's names— names that should never have entered this room. The press corps, once lulled by predictable talk of crisis management, snapped awake. Notebooks opened, screens lit, fingers tapped.

Maxwell drew a careful breath, recalibrating. "Mr. Chairman, if I may continue …."

The chairman nodded, grateful for the return to normal procedure. Maxwell's tone steadied, his expression settled—concern blended with resolve, the model public servant addressing natural disaster response. But beneath the table, his left hand clenched so tight, his manicured nails dug into his palm.

For years, he had maintained separate worlds: public service and private enterprise, policy and shadow operations. Now, the wall between them had its first hairline crack. Small. Almost invisible, but present. And cracks only multiplied.

While cameras kept rolling and Maxwell spoke smoothly about flood mitigation funding, his mind was already racing: calls to make. People to silence. Evidence to erase. The lioness mural had carried its warning to Nick Justin about his daughter. Perhaps it was time to send more than warnings.

The air conditioning hummed, white noise beneath procedural exchanges and scripted answers. Maxwell's testimony rolled on without further incident, composure restored. But in the press gallery, whispers rippled, questions formed, connections took shape.

Something had changed. His world of careful manipulation had become more dangerous, both for himself and for everyone tied to him.

≈

Sergeant Quincy Adams shifted his weight outside Conference Room B. The thin carpet over the marble offered no comfort. His uniform, pressed and perfect on the Tampa flight that morning, now felt constricting after three hours of questioning. He checked his watch. 4:17 p.m. Senator Maxwell's aide had told him to wait, that the senator wanted a private word. A commendation, perhaps, for his remarks on St. Petersburg's recovery needs. But the aide's tone hummed with warning, like a tuning fork on stone.

The door opened with a whisper of expensive hinges.

Senator Maxwell emerged, silver hair catching the light, hand already extended. Moments ago, he had been at the center of a political maelstrom. Now he was refreshed, focused entirely on Adams, the earlier disruption erased.

"Sergeant Adams." Maxwell captured his hand in both of his, a practiced show of intimacy. "Your statement was invaluable. The committee needed to hear from someone with boots on the ground."

WITNESS ELIMINATION

Adams nodded, conscious of the gulf between them, a local sergeant facing a U.S. senator. Yet Maxwell's manner suggested equality, colleagues in service. The handshake lingered a beat longer than necessary, firm and calibrated for trust.

"Please come in." Maxwell indicated the conference room. "We will not be disturbed."

The room was small by Senate standards but luxurious compared to the briefing rooms he knew in St. Petersburg. Dark-wood paneling absorbed sound, creating a cocoon of privacy. A crystal pitcher waited on the table, with two glasses already poured. Planned down to the minute.

"I was impressed by your command of the situation back home," Maxwell said, settling into his chair and gesturing for the sergeant to join him. "Most officers of your rank wouldn't have the comprehensive grasp you showed."

The sergeant settled into the leather, cool against his back. "I've been coordinating with emergency services since before Helene made landfall, Senator."

Maxwell nodded as if the sergeant had offered wisdom, not a routine procedure. "That dedication will be remembered, Sergeant." He sipped his water, studying him over the rim. "Have you considered your long-term trajectory?"

The question caught him off guard. He had expected a debrief on recovery necessities, not professional advice from a senator. "I'm focused on the job at hand, sir."

"Admirable." Maxwell set down his glass. "But vision separates leadership from service. St. Petersburg requires men like you in positions of genuine authority."

The implication hung between them. Chief of police. Unspoken, but loud. His pulse quickened despite himself.

"The department has a chain of command," Adams said, his Boston accent thickening under stress.

Maxwell smiled, smoothly and unhurried. "Chains can be climbed faster with the right support." He leaned forward, lowering his voice—a private confidence. "The recovery after Helene presents unique opportunities. People will remember those who distinguish themselves now when they fill posts."

Adams took a sip of water, buying a moment to compose himself. His frustration at being passed over for promotion was no secret. But hearing it echoed by a man with Maxwell's influence sparked a dangerous feeling.

"St. Petersburg faces critical challenges. Beyond the physical reconstruction, there's law and order." His tone warmed with practiced concern. "Certain elements are exploiting the chaos. Vigilante justice is rising in the vacuum."

The sergeant stiffened. "If you're referring to specific incidents, Senator ...."

"Nick Justin," Maxwell said. "A lawyer behaving as if he's above the institution he once served."

Adams's face stayed impassive, but his mind raced. Justin had been operating in gray areas since his wife's accident—investigating without authority, pressuring witnesses, and collecting evidence by questionable means. Yet he had exposed corruption, and the system ignored it.

"Justin's had a difficult time since his wife's accident. He believes there was foul play."

Maxwell nodded once. "Tragedy can distort perspective, push good men across lines they'd never cross." He paused. "But we can't allow chaos, Sergeant, not when the city is this vulnerable. The rule of law must prevail—especially now."

"What exactly are you suggesting, Senator?" An edge crept into his voice.

Maxwell reached into his jacket and produced a slim black phone, featureless and cold. "Encrypted end to end, directly to my office." He placed it on the table, within reach but not offering. "St. Petersburg needs eyes and ears on the street. Someone who understands the difference between justice and revenge."

Adams stared at the device. Its presence turned theory into transaction. "You want me to spy on Nick Justin."

"I want you to protect the city from well-intentioned men doing irreparable harm." Maxwell's voice hardened, the paternal warmth gone. "Justin's obsession with the RADD Squad, with Myers, with imagined conspiracies—it threatens your department's stability during a critical recovery period."

Gutted streets back home filled his mind, flooded stations, half his officers still diverted to storm duty. No wonder the prison ambush hadn't triggered the manhunt it should have. There weren't enough boots left to chase shadows, not with debris still choking half the city.

His fingers twitched, neither reaching for the phone nor pushing it away. The career path Maxwell dangled required a first step, and this was it. Chief of police, authority to implement the reforms he had long pushed for, to clean the department from within. But at what cost?

"I report to Captain Phillips," Adams said, testing the boundary.

"Of course," Maxwell replied. "This arrangement ensures critical intelligence reaches federal hands quickly. A parallel channel, not a replacement." His eyes hardened. "Especially given certain … irregularities in how information moves through official channels in St. Petersburg."

People couldn't trust the department itself. Not entirely wrong. The corruption Nick Justin had exposed ran deep.

"Consider it." Maxwell tracked his hesitation. "Sergeant, the city needs leaders who understand nuance. Black-and-white thinking is a luxury we can't afford during reconstruction."

Adams reached for the phone, fingers closing around its smooth case. "I'll keep my eyes open."

"That's all I ask." Maxwell rose. The meeting was over. "St. Petersburg is fortunate to have you, Sergeant Adams. I look forward to watching your career develop."

The sergeant pocketed the phone, weightless yet feeling heavier than his service weapon. As he followed Maxwell to the door, his mind ran angles, risks, plays, and countermoves. Protect Justin. Report to Maxwell. Play both sides. Refuse.

Maxwell extended his hand again, the politician's grip warm and confident. "Safe travels back to Florida, Sergeant. I'm sure we'll speak again soon."

He nodded, the phone a silent weight against his ribs. The path forward wasn't clear, but he knew one truth. He had entered a game where every move had consequences he couldn't control.

PART 2:
RISING TENSIONS AND BETRAYAL

18

DIVIDED

The safe house command center wasn't much to look at: two battered folding tables, a dozen mismatched chairs, six monitors rigged into a lopsided grid, extension cords snaking from a generator next door. Sarah Brown paced the perimeter, checking each angle.

Her jeans had smudges on the thighs, and a faded T-shirt was streaked with dirt and sweat. She paused under the largest window. Garbage bags sealed over jagged glass. The black plastic caught the screen light, rippling with each breath of wind. She scarcely registered the grime on her sleeves or the scuffs on her sneakers. Vanity was a luxury long abandoned.

Sally Hinkins watched from the corner of a metal table, limbs folded so tight her forearms knotted like rope. A coiled viper tattoo, visible under the hem of her collar, traced its head down her neck. Old burns striped both biceps, silver ridges stark against sun-darkened skin. Her buzz-cut made her blue eyes blaze in the cold display glow. She shifted her weight, boots scraping across linoleum scarred by fire.

The space stank of ozone and fuel. On the screen, a local reporter faked a smile through the catastrophe: downed lines, impassable roads, sections of the city dark, and rumors of a new system spinning over the Yucatán.

Sarah muted the broadcast with a click and tapped the back of the laptop, waking it. "We're still missing full manifests from the police." Her voice was flat. "Without them, we can't confirm the disposal crews ever finished the sweep of the evidence room."

Sally's jaw flexed. "Maybe you should ring in another favor." A dare, acid-edged with something close to admiration. "Senator's people still pick up on Sundays?"

Sarah blinked. "Maxwell's staff is only useful if we keep giving them outcomes. No outcomes, no protection. And you know what happens then."

"Yeah." Sally uncrossed her limbs, rolling her shoulders until something popped. "I get the order and do my little sanitation dance. Or I end up dead."

Sarah's gaze dropped to the scarred skin, reading its history like braille. "You signed up for this. Don't play the martyr now."

Sally snorted and hopped off the table. Her boots scraped the scorched linoleum, scuffing the remnants of old Bruth'rs graffiti. "I signed up for extraction, not babysitting a box of files. Why am I stuck here when I could be out making sure rivals don't torch another site?"

Sarah flipped open a folder and slid out a single sheet. Her fingernail tapped a staccato rhythm before she held it up between two fingers. "You see this? The complete handoff log for the Port of Tampa. You know how much work it took to clean this up after my sister's husband screwed it?"

Sally's lips curled into a partial snarl, but before she could speak, Sarah's glance turned to ice.

"All problems are ours now." She let the paper drift back to the table. "If Justin had stayed in his lane, we wouldn't be on the run covering up all these stray threads." She sliced her hand through the air, cutting off the thought. "And each so-called stray thread draws more heat. We can't afford mistakes, not with the Bureau sniffing around and part of the city screaming for resources after Helene."

Sally's hands closed around a battered coffee mug, fingers drumming its rim. "What's the next move?"

They locked eyes for a long moment. On the displays, surveillance feeds cycled through: loading docks, the police station, and the battered courthouse facade. One feed carried a muted weather report—a swirl of clouds over the Caribbean, forecasters calling it "a disturbance worth watching." No name, no tracks yet, only uncertainty.

"I want a full sweep of the MacDill chain tonight," Sarah said. "Use only people we can trust. No ties to SPPD." She set a second file on top of the first, aligning the corners with care. "You coordinate. If there's even a hint of outside interference, we're out. Understand?"

"Fine." Sally's grip tightened on the mug. "But tell me why you're suddenly spooked about the Air Force assets when you've had me watching the Justin house for two days straight."

Sarah's voice chilled. "Because there's a child involved. The moment we make a move on the family, everything gets louder. That's not how this operation succeeds."

Sally's eyes glittered. "But you want to, don't you? Rip off the Band-Aid. Take the little girl because it works."

Sarah's smile strained. "I want to win. That's not the same as being reckless."

Hinkins set the mug down with a sharp click. "You say that, but the only time you look alive is when you're pulling strings. Any time someone pushes back, you flatten them."

Sarah regarded her with cool detachment, as if weighing a chess piece for sacrifice. "Is that what you want, Sally? To be challenged?"

The silence stretched, heavy and sharp.

"No." The defiance left Sally's voice. "I want to be useful."

"You are." Sarah gathered the files, squared their corners, and slid them into a fireproof envelope. "When the time comes, you'll do what's necessary. Until then, follow the plan. Don't go off script." She turned back to the screens, the conversation dismissed.

But Sally stayed rooted, her fingers brushing the ridged scars on her forearm. "What happens to Jessica Justin?"

"You'll handle it. You always do." Sarah sneered. "I'm planning a special family reunion."

Sally nodded, small and tight, then turned away, crossing the floor in angry strides. She slipped into the dark beyond the display light, her silhouette shrinking, but not fading.

Sarah stood alone in the center of the building, the generator's drone vibrating through the concrete. She checked her reflection in the black glass, smoothed a line in her jacket, and adjusted a lock of hair.

She straightened her lapels and whispered to the empty room, "Blood doesn't matter."

A distant rumble traced along the horizon, but the real storm was already here, coiled in the city's bones, invisible and electric.

~

Sally Hinkins claimed a corner of the warehouse, the farthest spot from Sarah's orbit. Shadows pooled there, the lone bare bulb overhead casting more gloom than light. The plywood wall behind her was unfinished. Someone had hammered raw sheets over old cinderblock, and the surface was splintery and pale.

She rolled a knife in her palm, letting its weight steady her thoughts. Combat steel, balanced and honed to a wraith-thin edge. She liked the discipline of sharpening—each pass of the whetstone a ritual, each rasp a reminder that even the hardest metal could be ground down if you pressed long enough.

The room was thick with oil and humidity, layered over the mildew that never left. A dry wind rattled the boarded window, sending needles of dust through the light. Perspiration beaded on her brow, slid down her jaw, and turned bitter on her tongue.

She'd watched the other woman for a year. They were lovers. No one else had ever known what to do with her, not even the hit squads down south. *You aim me, and I attack.* But Sarah didn't aim—she placed. Each order was part of some larger geometry, each task a move on a board only she could see.

Hinkins respected it. Feared it even. But lately, something had slipped—cracks in the calculus. Sarah's eyes darted to something unseen before snapping back. The way she obsessed over the Justin girl, pretending not to care, yet monitoring her with cold fascination.

Sally pressed the knife to the stone, then set it down with a deliberate click. From her jacket pocket, she pulled a tiny, grainy, black-and-white photo, a snapshot taken from a drone camera or a long lens. Jessica Justin, small beside her mother's leg, clutching a lioness plush. Eyes wide as quarters, face streaked with mud and snot.

Her fingers flexed on the picture, creasing it. How did it feel to be clutched so tightly, to be protected that much? The last time anyone had touched her with tenderness, she'd been too young to recall. Everything after had been drills, inspections, punishment.

She folded the photo, slipped it back into her pocket, and picked up the knife. Her thumb traced the edge, found a spot still rough. As she worked the whetstone, her eyes drifted to the plywood wall. Her first job for the CEO surfaced—killing the philandering husband, dead weight in their threesome. A dark snicker escaped her. She pictured the mural—a lioness crouched in blood-red paint, its chest tagged for the kill. In their world, any animal got tagged prior to the slaughter, and now that target was a child.

She licked moisture from her upper lip, tasted salt. "One day it'll be me."

The burn scars on her left arm never healed right—ridged and shiny, a map of each careless mistake. Her fingertip traced the worst of them, the texture shifting from raised and hard to soft and nerveless where the flesh had melted away. The doctors deemed it a miracle she'd kept the hand. Dumb luck.

Knife in hand, she turned to the wall. She wanted to leave something behind, something Sarah couldn't polish or erase. She pressed the steel to the plywood and dragged it down in a ragged arc, the sound heavy and satisfying. Then another, crossing the first. Two lines, gouged and ugly, a scratch that meant nothing to anyone but her.

She wiped the edge on her thigh and studied the scar. It could have been a warning. Could have been a signature.

Outside, the dry wind rattled the siding. The rhythm was steady and sure. It sounded like something alive, stalking in the dark, waiting for the right moment to pounce.

~

Carl worked from recall. The Slovin drive was long gone, handed back to La Reina after the prison-bus hijack, but he didn't need the hardware anymore. The files had imprinted themselves on his mind.

Three monitors glowed before him, lines of code crawling across black screens. The apartment was small and close, heavy with the smell of old coffee and the heat of the processors. Outside, traffic murmured somewhere below, a city half-asleep and indifferent.

He wasn't rebuilding the archive for anyone else. He was recreating the structure for himself—the logic of it. The way Slovin's encryption folded back on itself, how metadata nested in recursive loops that hid routing numbers inside contract references. The pattern remained visible. The rhythm of his keystrokes from the night when he broke it open echoed.

Back then, he had assumed it was another smuggling ledger, maybe a decoy. When he was called in again to verify the data before it disappeared into La Reina's custody, the truth hit him. It was genuine. Not a trap. A map, shell companies, defense contracts, offshore trusts, and campaign donations—an entire ecosystem of corruption coded into silence.

Now he typed from memory, rebuilding the lattice one variable at a time. Each command unearthed another buried image: a timestamp, a balance sheet, a name. He paused only to jot notes on a legal pad.

He was crafting what he called a protection file, a compact packet that would activate if anything happened to him. It was insurance holding fragments of retained data and a key sequence pointing to storage nodes he controlled. Any effort to erase him would trigger its release.

WITNESS ELIMINATION

When the framework stabilized, he leaned back and let the screens blur into a wash of light. His recollection sharpened further. One folder had contained correspondence between La Reina's logistics network and a private account registered through a Caribbean trust. He typed the numbers he retained, reconstructing them character by character until the pattern matched the one in his head.

The result appeared: an offshore bank code belonging to Senator Maxwell. Fifty-seven million dollars. He stared at the number for a long time, its pulse audible in the silence. Money moved like blood, invisible and constant. This was the artery that fed power.

He opened another window and sketched the wider network from memory—defense contractors tied to Maxwell's committees, county officials and donors fronting shell firms, agents and police officers listed as "consultants." Each name tightened the circle.

He didn't celebrate the discovery. This was a map, and maps did not judge. They told him only where to move next.

When the pattern was complete, he encrypted the protection packet under three layers of keys and stored it on isolated drives. The file held no stolen data, only the ghost of it—enough for him to rebuild the truth again if needed.

For a moment, he considered going further. With what he knew of Maxwell's routing codes, he could reach that account, maybe even divert the funds into escrow sooner than anyone noticed. Fifty-seven million was leverage on an empire. But power used too soon was a flare. He wasn't ready to burn.

He wrote one last note at the bottom of his pad, "When necessary, divert. Not sooner."

Then he shut everything down. The room cooled as the processors wound down to silence. He rubbed the tension from his neck, and the monitors faded to black.

The data might belong to La Reina now, but the knowledge lived with him. That made him the most dangerous variable in the game.

19

NICK'S RELUCTANCE

October 2, 2024

Nick fumbled the magazine, his fingers betraying the certainty that once ruled courtrooms. The smooth metal slipped, snagged on the pistol grip, then clattered to the patio concrete. Sweat stung his eyes as he bent to pick it up. José's disapproval weighed on him. Three seconds gone. Moments in which, as the investigator never tired of reminding him, a man could die.

José clicked the stopwatch with his thumb. "Again." His eyes betrayed a flicker of frustration. "And this time, don't look down. Feel the mag seat."

Nick exhaled hard through his teeth and ejected the empty clip from the Glock. The backyard range was exposed. The fence offered no real cover. Several doors down, a neighbor's generator hummed, its drone marking the rhythm of post-disaster life. Six days after Helene, half the neighborhood still lacked power.

Mountains of debris lined the curb, its backdrop a waterlogged mess of drywall, salt-stained furniture, and family photos warped beyond recognition. Ordinary lives wrecked, made extraordinary by water and wind. The lawyer had dragged a sheet of plywood across two sawhorses for a shooting bench, targets propped against the oak that had almost crushed his garage.

"Focus," José snapped. "This isn't a deposition. You don't get a recess when rounds are coming at you."

He slammed the fresh clip home with more force than necessary. The metal-on-metal crack rang out, sharp and final. He racked the slide, raised the pistol, and fired five shots into the paper target's center mass. They came quickly. Two went wide.

"Reload."

Nick thumbed the release. Another fumble. Another beat gone. José's sigh weighed more than a shouted reprimand.

"You've been at this three days," the investigator said, scratching his jaw stubble. He'd traded pressed slacks and button-downs for tactical pants and a faded T-shirt, muscle stretching the fabric. "You should be fluid by now."

"I'm a lawyer, not a soldier." Nick wiped his palm on his jeans before grabbing another magazine. Dummy rounds rattled inside. "This isn't—"

"Natural? Yeah, I got that part." José reset the stopwatch. "You think the Bruth'rs care? You think the cartel's worried about your comfort zone?"

The air between them thickened. Nick loaded again, ejected again, loaded once more, his movements sharpening with each repetition but lacking the flow his friend demanded. A lawyer's precision versus a soldier's instinct. His mind grasped the mechanics, but his body resisted the weapon's lethal simplicity.

"The Venezuelan cartel doesn't send diplomats," José said, the edge still there. "And Sarah Brown's not filing motions anymore. She's moving pieces around a board, and you're a—"

"Pawn. Yeah, I get the metaphor."

He set the pistol down and flexed his fingers. The calluses were wrong, foreign to the hand that had built a career on handshakes and persuasion.

He crossed to the weathered bench where his Louisville Slugger leaned. The handle still carried the impression of his grip. He picked it up, the weight familiar, stance and swing returning without thought.

"This saved my life before." Nick traced the nicks and scratches that marked those fights. "I know where it'll land, how it'll feel. With the gun, I'm still counting steps in my head."

José shook his head. "The bat works against street thugs. The men coming now won't fight you on your terms."

"These terms, you mean." Nick gestured with the wood toward the pistol. "Your terms."

"Reality's terms." José's voice hardened. "You've seen what they're capable of. What they did to Andrea wasn't an accident. It was a test run. A gun isn't optional anymore."

Nick's jaw tightened. The bat was light in his hands, inadequate against the threat described. The old rules had ended the night Andrea's car rolled over on the Gandy Bridge. Every compromise since—the security system, the panic room, the firearms—was another step away from the life they'd built.

"I've taken everything from men like that in the courtroom," he said, setting the bat down. "Built cases that left the untouchable broken and scrambling."

"In a system that worked." José tapped the stopwatch face. "Those cases took months. You've got days, maybe hours, before they make another move."

A portable radio on the bench crackled with a weather bulletin. The automated voice cut through their argument, flat and clinical: "The National Hurricane Center is monitoring a broad tropical disturbance over the Bay of Campeche. The system will probably strengthen as it enters the Gulf of Mexico later this week. Residents along Florida's west coast should remain alert for updates."

The two men exchanged glances. Another storm threat so soon after Helene. The air was dry but carried the sick-sweet stench of mildew from water-damaged homes. A reminder that they were still reeling from one disaster while another loomed.

"Perfect timing," Nick muttered. "Nothing like a hurricane to flush out the rats."

"Or give them cover." José picked up the Glock, checked the chamber, and handed it back. "Which is why we don't have time for philosophy. Reload again."

Nick took the pistol, its weight still foreign. His fingers found the release, and this time the movement came cleaner, faster. The stopwatch clicked. He focused on the rhythm—eject, reach, insert, rack. Dummy rounds clacked into place, a hollow echo of what would happen if the drill turned real.

He finished the reload in under two seconds.

"Better," José said. "Now do it fifty more times until you can do it without thinking."

The lawyer nodded, swallowing the argument that rose in his throat. The bat might have served him once, but the past was gone. Washed away with the storm surge, dissolved in the salt water that had claimed so much of their city. He began again, learning the precision of survival.

~

Andrea laid the Steyr's components in perfect alignment on the white towel, each piece gleaming under the overhead light. The ritual calmed her: barrel, slide, spring, magazine—a puzzle she could solve by touch alone. She methodically cleaned every part with a discipline that belied the fatigue that made her shoulders tremble.

The kitchen radio murmured about a tropical disturbance over the Gulf, warnings delivered in the same flat cadence as every forecast. She tuned it out, focusing instead on the metallic click of parts fitting together. The sound was more reassuring than any voice on the airwaves.

She shifted in her chair. Her left leg spasmed—a reminder of her sister. The doctors used words like "fortunate" and "remarkable recovery," but Andrea measured progress by steps taken before pain flared, by how long she could push herself before needing to sit.

Her hands never faltered. The barrel gleamed beneath the cloth as she cleaned it. The slide moved smoothly under her touch, spring tension giving with satisfying resistance. Three months ago, she would have recoiled at the thought of her hand on a weapon. Now its weight was another compromise—like the security alarms.

The radio announcer broke through the background murmur. "A disturbance over the Gulf could strengthen over the coming days.

WITNESS ELIMINATION

Emergency management officials urge residents to review disaster preparedness plans, particularly in areas still recovering from Hurricane Helene."

Her fingers paused on the slide assembly. Another storm, when the city hadn't finished bleeding from the first. She pushed the thought aside and returned to her task, slotting the recoil spring into place with a soft click.

A floorboard creaked in the doorway. Andrea looked up, her hands sliding the gun parts closer together on the towel. Jessica stood there, the lioness plush pinned to her chest, her eyes wide and steady. Her pajama pants were already too short, another growth spurt her mother had nearly missed while she was in the hospital. The girl's gaze locked on the disassembled firearm, curious more than anything else.

Neither spoke. The radio filled the silence with talk of a tropical system and the need for caution.

The rehearsal played in Andrea's mind: whisking the pistol out of sight, distracting her with comfort. But looking at the child's face—her careful study, her lack of fear—the speech died in her throat.

Jessica already knew. Maybe not in the details, but she understood their world had changed. The nightmares, the security checks, the hushed conversations that stopped when she entered a room—she had been assembling her own puzzle components.

"Come here." Andrea patted the chair beside her. "If you're curious, I'd rather you understand than wonder."

The girl climbed onto the seat, the lioness plush tucked in the crook of her arm. She studied the parts on the towel with the same concentration she gave her science homework.

"That's a gun."

"Yes. A Steyr M9-A1." Her tone remained matter-of-fact. "I'm cleaning it and putting it back together."

Jessica's finger hovered over the barrel. "Dad has one too. I saw him practicing in the backyard with Uncle José."

Andrea nodded. "Your father and I both need to know how to use these safely."

"Because of the bad people?" The girl's voice kept steady, but her grip on the lioness plush tightened. "Like Aunt Sarah and her friend Officer Hinkins."

An ache spread through Andrea's chest, sharper than any pain from the accident. She'd hoped to shield Jessica, but children noticed everything, piecing together truths adults tried to hide.

"Yes," she admitted. "There are people like Aunt Sarah and ex-Officer Hinkins, who want to hurt our family."

"Is that why we need guns now?" Jessica's gaze met her mother's, unflinching. "We didn't have them before."

She weighed the answer. The easy thing would be to soothe her, say they were simply being careful, but that kind of comfort was as false as the safety they once believed in.

"We need them because the rules have shifted." She picked up the slide, showing how it moved along the frame. "Remember when you learned to ride your bike without training wheels? It was scary because the guidelines were different. You had to balance, pay attention in a fresh way."

Jessica nodded, leaning closer.

"This is like that. The world shifted, and we need unfamiliar skills to keep our balance." She slid the pistol back together. "But we don't let fear control us. We prepare."

"Like the hurricane supplies?"

"Exactly." Andrea allowed herself a small smile. "We don't panic about the storm. We get water, batteries, and make sure the generator works."

Jessica considered this, her brow furrowed. Zara dipped from her chest as she relaxed slightly. "Dad yells when he practices. I heard him growing mad at the gun yesterday."

Andrea suppressed a laugh. "Your father's always relied on his mind. This is strange to him." She finished assembling the pistol, the last piece locking in with a satisfying click. "It was strange for me, too, but I had time to practice while I was growing better."

"You don't yell at your gun."

"No, strong isn't loud." She paused, surprised by the words, which seemed to come from a deep maternal place. "Prepared is strength."

Jessica repeated, "Prepared is strength."

Andrea picked up the clip, pistol angled at the wall. "This is important, Jess. See this magazine? This is how you verify if it's loaded." She pressed the release, checked the chamber. "Empty. Always verify, even if you're certain."

Jessica watched with the same intensity she gave multiplication tables. Not with fear, but with the solemn sense that this mattered.

"Can I ..." she hesitated. "Can I touch it?"

Andrea shook her head. "Not yet. First, you need to learn the safety rules. When you understand those, then we'll talk about supervised handling." She secured the weapon and set it aside. "But you can always ask questions."

Jessica nodded. Her small hand reached out, not for the gun but for her mother's fingers. Andrea clasped it, feeling both the fragility and the strength she was trying to protect.

The radio murmured about shifting pressure systems and preparedness plans. Outside, the light deepened to copper as sunset neared. From the backyard came Nick's voice, then José's deeper reply. Two men were preparing in their own way for the storms ahead.

"Mom?" Jessica's voice pulled Andrea back from her thoughts.

"Yes, baby?"

"I'm glad you're teaching me." Jessica's fingers tightened around Andrea's. "It's better than being scared and not knowing."

Tightness constricted her throat, but she forced a swallow. She brushed her daughter's hair back from her forehead. "That's my brave girl. Now, how about we make dinner while the boys finish their practice?"

Jessica slid from the chair, the lioness plush tucked to her chest again. Her posture had shifted. Shoulders straighter, chin lifted. Not carefree, but not cowering. Prepared.

It wasn't the motherhood Andrea had imagined. Teaching her eight-year-old about firearms instead of cookies or braids. But as she watched Jessica move in the direction of the refrigerator with newfound purpose, she realized she was passing down a different strength, to face reality without flinching, to prepare rather than pretend.

The Steyr, reassembled and locked, rested on the table. Andrea rose carefully, testing her weight on the injured leg before stepping after her daughter and whatever came next.

~

The cemetery was almost empty. Late sunlight slid between the oaks, turning the rows of headstones into pale islands in shadow. Shandra walked the narrow path in her worn sneakers, a paper cup of gas-station coffee cooling in her hand.

She stopped at the marker that bore her son's name.

JAQUEZ GREENE

Born October 3, 2004—Died January 17, 2024

He ran his race with heart.

She brushed away the leaves that had gathered at the base and set the drink beside the flowers. Her fingers lingered on the carved letters.

"Hey, baby," she breathed. "I used to say you'd run faster than me one day. Guess you proved me right. Tomorrow would've been your birthday." The words caught in her throat.

The air was still, heavy with the sweetness of cut grass and the faint salt drifting in from the bay. A sad smile touched her lips. "You remember the hurdles? You always said they looked easy until you were the one jumping. That's how life turned out, huh? An entire line of obstacles nobody warned us about."

Her smile faded as the warmth of memory gave way to the weight of everything that followed.

"You were so damn bright, Jaquez. St. Petersburg College. First in the family. I still keep your acceptance letter on the fridge. I bragged to everyone I met how proud I was. Still am."

She sat on the stone border and ran a hand through her hair, her skin glistening under the last trace of sun. "You'd hate what's happened here. The uniforms, the judges, the politicians. They protect their own. But we got some of them, didn't we? Myers is sitting in a cell waiting for trial, and the other one, Hinkins, is on the run. Don't you worry. She won't stay hidden."

A breath trembled out of her, caught between laughter and grief. "You always said, 'Mama, you can't fight the whole system.' Maybe not. But I can battle the rot that took you. And I'm close. A senator's tangled in it now. Maxwell. His name's all over the files."

Overhead, the sky was blue-orange—the color of dusk.

"I know what you'd say. 'Be careful.' I hear you."

For a moment she traced the edge of the stone with her thumb. She reached to the top corner of the headstone, pressing against a small ornamental carving shaped like a lily. A hidden latch clicked.

The panel slid open enough for her to reach inside. She drew out a legal-size envelope sealed in plastic.

"Still running hurdles," she whispered. "Still chasing the finish line."

She slipped the envelope into her messenger bag, closed the compartment, and brushed the dust from her jeans.

"Love you, baby. I'll be back soon."

The wind stirred the grass.

Shandra turned toward the gate, the last light falling across her as the graveyard settled into silence.

20

PRESSURE POINT

October 4, 2024

The conference room was a temple to bureaucratic rot. The air reeked of a losing battle between mildew and industrial bleach. Above, ceiling tiles sagged—a map of decay, water stains spreading like brown, cancerous continents.

Nick tracked one aggressive stain while Agent Holcomb droned about "procedural delays" and "jurisdictional challenges."

Eight days since Hurricane Helene, and the government still moved with the toxic inertia of silt.

Three empty chairs stood as silent witnesses—resources reassigned to "higher priorities," per conveniently timed memos.

He shifted. The chair scraped across tacky linoleum still damp from the deluge, the sound sharp in the tense silence. Maps plastered the walls, red zones marking the city's drowned arteries. The task force room was an island of pretense in a sea of real crisis.

Under the table, Shandra slid a slim manila packet toward him. "Meant to give you these at the garden. Got pulled into something and forgot to call."

Nick kept his eyes on Holcomb.

Holcomb straightened his documents—a white monument to nothing. "The prisoner-transport manifests are pending reconciliation through the proper channels. We anticipate certification within the week."

"A week?" Nick's tone dropped to a growl. "Sarah Brown and Sally Hinkins have been missing for eight days. Every hour that passes—"

"We're working diligently to resolve this administrative issue," Holcomb cut in, jaw tight beneath his gray-flecked beard.

Nick's fingers brushed the envelope, a reminder of the risk she was taking.

The two junior agents scribbled in their notebooks, eyes down. The DOJ rep, Levine, checked her watch for the third time.

"Administrative issue? It's always something with you folks, isn't it?" Shandra remained in her seat. She let her head tip back against the wall and stared at the ceiling tiles. A humorless smile touched her lips. "My son's killer sits in county. His accomplices disappear because of paperwork."

Holcomb aligned the edges of his file folder with the corner of the table. He didn't look up. "We operate under emergency protocols, Ms. Greene. We lack the luxury of perfect clerical work."

"Bullshit." Nick kicked the empty chair next to him. It skidded across the linoleum and hit the wall with a hollow thud. "Don't give us that run-around. You lost two high-value targets, Holcomb. That's a fucking disaster."

He paced the length of the small room, hands balled into fists at his sides. "I want the chain of custody. I want the surveillance logs. You tell me you don't have them, and I'm going to tear this room apart."

Levine flinched as Nick passed her. She fixed her gaze on the scuffed floor. "The storm damaged the physical proof. The facility experienced significant high water."

Nick stopped pacing. He leaned over the table, crowding Levine's space. "How convenient," Nick growled. "We've both seen what happens when records go missing. This isn't weather—it's obstruction."

Adams shifted in his seat at the end of the table, his uniform impossibly crisp despite the humidity. "The senator's office has clarified that public trust is the priority throughout recovery. They want this handled quietly."

"Public trust?" Nick's laugh held no humor. "Two suspects tied to a Venezuelan cartel vanish inside a Category Four hurricane, and you're worried about optics?"

A young staffer appeared in the doorway—nervous, clutching a stack of binders like a life vest.

"The, uh, archival retrieval you requested, sir." He set the stack on the table, eyes flicking toward the overturned chair against the wall. "Everything we could recover from the backup servers." His volume dropped. "Senator Maxwell's people already collected the originals. Said something about a high-level cooperating source requiring immediate review?"

The temperature in the room fell. The silence was absolute.

Holcomb's eyes flashed a warning at the staffer, who paled.

"That will be all," Holcomb said.

Nick caught the change in Adams's posture—a stiffening, the faint tightening of the jaw. The look of a man hearing confirmation of something he'd rather deny.

"Maxwell's office," Nick said. "What source is Maxwell working with?"

Holcomb gathered the materials with mechanical precision. "That information is classified. The session is adjourned until we can compile the necessary documentation."

Nick stepped forward. "We need access to those files now. Every minute those women are free, more evidence disappears, more witnesses recant."

"I'm sorry, Mr. Justin," Holcomb said, "but protocol must be followed." He signaled to his agents, who began packing tablets and notebooks with the efficiency of a tactical retreat. "We'll reconvene when we have actionable intelligence."

The group dissolved in a shuffle of papers and scraping chairs. The federal team filed out, relieved to escape. Only Adams remained, fingers tapping a nervous rhythm on his binder.

"This is bullshit." Shandra walked to the door, latching it.

"They're burying it," she said, turning back to join him at the window. "All of it."

Nick nodded, jaw tight. "I waited for you in the garden. Left messages. I figured something pressing pulled you off."

Her eyes flicked toward him, a brief acknowledgment. "It did, but you have them now."

Nick pocketed the envelope, the material crackling like a fuse. He turned to her and Adams, his decision solidifying.

"The task force is dead," he said. "Our work continues off the record."

≈

The records room had once been a janitor's closet. Now it smelled of paper, bleach, and sweat.

José hunched over a folding table. The overhead bulb threw hard light across towers of printed Texter logs. His glasses drooped low on his nose.

Shandra leaned against the wall—close enough that her shoulder brushed his when she shifted. In that cramped space, any movement was personal.

"Start here," José said, tapping the page. "This is two weeks prior to Helene making landfall. All correspondence in or out of the five numbers linked to Bruth'rs leadership is logged here."

Shandra nodded, eyes tracing columns of timestamps and digital tags. The content was gone—wiped clean—but the metadata remained, digital footprints in bureaucratic sand.

"What am I looking for?" she asked.

"Patterns," José said. "Bursts of activity or periods of silence. Anything that didn't fit."

He spread the pages in order, his movements fluid and practiced. A boxer's discipline turned forensic.

"Here." He circled a cluster of identifiers. "September 25th. Twelve texts from this source to three others in seven minutes."

Shandra leaned closer, her braids brushing the paper. "What happened at 2:13?"

The investigator slid a prison-transport schedule forward. His finger landed on a highlighted line.

"2:15. Sarah Brown was reassigned to a secondary bus after a 'mechanical issue.' That replacement vehicle didn't have cameras." He paused. "You see it?"

Shandra's jaw tightened. She flipped open her handwritten timeline. "Next day, September 26th, 10:07 am. Same contact. Another burst."

José nodded. "At 1:50 p.m., prisoner transfer was diverted by flooding."

Shandra frowned. "High water didn't start till after two."

A chill fell over the room. José circled more clusters, the ballpoint biting through the paper. Shandra matched him move for move until she stabbed through the sheet.

"This contact was in each round of activity," she said. "Our source."

José studied the digits, committing them to memory. "We'd run it, but it wouldn't be under a real name. Burners, shells, cutouts. They know the game."

"Not perfectly," Shandra said. She flipped back a few pages, her finger stopping at a later burst. "September 28th, 9:22 p.m. Nick's house alarm. This spike hit fifteen minutes earlier."

José's throat tightened. He remembered the call that night—Nick's voice breaking through static, Jessica clutching the lioness plush as the floodlights died.

The doorknob twitched. Testing.

A faint mechanical whine slipped through the crack and vanished.

José's hand shot to his hip. No gun.

Shandra didn't move. Her eyes stayed fixed on the sliver of light until the shadow slid away.

Footsteps. Silence.

She whispered, "We're burned."

José exhaled slowly. "Nick's house?"

"No, too obvious. They're watching him."

She swept the papers into a folder. José grabbed his phone, photographed the logs, and uploaded them to his private server. Insurance.

He tapped the circled number. "This couldn't be random chatter. They knew when to pull the trigger. An insider was feeding them."

"Inside the system," Shandra said. "Closer than we wanted to admit."

The air thickened with betrayal. For the first time, it ceased being about bureaucracy.

It was about a traitor choosing the other side.

José straightened the table, wiped the surface, and stacked the boxes back into anonymous neglect. Then he unscrewed the lone bulb overhead, plunging the room into black.

Before stepping out, he sent a single encrypted note:

We're burned. Watch your six.

That would be enough to raise the hair on Nick's neck.

~

Adams stood by his cruiser, phone in hand, the streetlight flickering.

"Quincy," Nick called. "Hold up."

Adams looked up, face blank. The light blinked out, casting the lot into darkness. When it sputtered back, a shadow crossed his features before he buried it.

He pocketed his device. "Nick, heading out?"

Nick moved between him and the car door, jaw tightening.

"You're feeding them intel." No preamble. He had the certainty of a man who'd seen enough evidence to know.

Adams stiffened, posture morphing from casual to defensive. His hand twitched toward his belt then stalled midair before dropping back to his side. "That's a serious allegation from an outsider without jurisdiction."

"Jurisdiction? That's your defense?" Nick closed the distance, collapsing the buffer Adams was trying to keep. "We trusted you. After everything last summer ...."

"You don't understand the pressure—"

Nick cut him off. "I understand betrayal. While we've been hunting Sarah Brown, an insider's been warning her every step of the way. Transport schedules and secure protocols aren't public knowledge. A source is feeding her."

WITNESS ELIMINATION

Adams's eyes flicked left, scanning the lot for witnesses or exits. Finding none, he squared his shoulders. His fingers weren't steady as they tugged his collar.

"You think it's that easy?" His tone dropped, hardened—a cop closing ranks. "Good guys and bad guys. This isn't your courtroom, Counselor. You can't object and expect reality to comply."

Nick's reflection warped in a puddle between them, his features stretching into something feral. "Clear enough. Myers tried to kill my wife. Sarah Brown staged a prison break during a hurricane. Now evidence vanishes every time we close in. Someone's making it possible."

Adams's jaw tightened, teeth grinding. The light stained his face a sickly amber, the lines around his eyes carved into crevices.

"I follow orders," Adams said. "So do you, when the money's right. Let's not pretend your hands are clean."

Nick's eyes narrowed. "What's that supposed to mean?"

"You've turned a blind eye when clients cut corners. Argued damages you knew were padded. Pushed claims for people gaming the system. We all bend rules, Justin. The only distinction is which side of the table we're sitting on." He leaned in, voice dropping to a harsh whisper. "We're all compromised. The only difference is who signs our checks."

Nick's hand shot out and gripped his lapel. Wool bunched in his fist. "Don't equate negligence cases with this. My wife nearly died. My daughter—" His voice cracked, fury bleeding into something raw.

Adams didn't resist. That passivity only fueled Nick's anger. He shoved him back, the sergeant's back thumping lightly against the patrol car.

"Who are you working for?" Nick demanded. "Maxwell? The cartel? How deep does this go?"

The question hung in the humid air, the streetlight catching droplets like suspended glass. Adams dragged a hand over his face, shoulders sagging with sudden exhaustion. He blinked twice.

"Orders don't come from me," Adams said. "They come from Maxwell. The feds are cutting a deal with Gino Myers. Maxwell's pushing to get him released under federal supervision, leaning on the governor and the Bureau."

The admission jarred Nick. Rage and disbelief left him lightheaded, his chest hollow.

"You knew?" His tone was raw, scraped. "Myers tried to kill Andrea."

Adams wouldn't meet his eyes, staring into the middle distance. "I didn't have a choice. Politics runs above my pay grade."

"That word," Nick spat. "That what we're calling attempted murder now?"

Adams leaned back against his car, suddenly older in the sodium light. "Maxwell thinks Myers has leverage to take down the Venezuelan cartel's operations."

"So they let a dirty cop walk." Nick's volume dropped. "The man who ran my wife off the Gandy Bridge gets a deal."

"The senator has friends in Washington," Adams said, resignation thick in his tone. "The type who make U.S. attorneys change priorities. The sort who end careers with a phone call."

Gone was the crisp sergeant with Boston slang and sports metaphors. In his place stood a man boxed in. The realization didn't ease Nick's anger, but it shifted the target.

"When?" Nick asked. "When does Myers walk?"

"Tomorrow. 10 a.m. transfer to federal custody. After that, he's protected."

Adams straightened his uniform where Nick had grabbed it. "I wasn't supposed to tell you. They know what you'll do."

"And what's that?"

"Try to stop it. File motions, call in favors, raise hell in the press." Adams met his eyes. "They're counting on it. They want you distracted while they move the real pieces."

Thunder rolled over the lot, vibrating through Nick's shoes. The storm was still far off but closing.

"Why tell me now?" Nick pressed, suspicion cutting through the fury.

Adams glanced around. "I know what Myers, Sally Hinkins, and your sister-in-law did to your family."

Nick stepped back, disgusted. Lightning split the sky, flaring through the clouds massing overhead.

"This isn't over," he said. A promise. A threat.

Adams gave one curt nod. "It never is."

WITNESS ELIMINATION

Nick turned toward the blackness. Thunder followed, closer now. The storm was coming, and they all knew it would be worse than the last.

~

The records room was buried in the county building's basement, a concrete tomb for bureaucratic remains.

Shandra scanned the badge she'd borrowed from a friend. The lock clicked open, soft as breath. None of the three guards looked up.

The door groaned on swollen hinges. She slipped inside and latched it quietly. The air smelled of mildew and ozone. A single fluorescent tube buzzed overhead, casting more shadow than light.

Rows of shelves vanished into the gloom. Floodwater had left a tideline chest-high, the paper below it warped and gray. The room still breathed the storm that had drowned it.

Shandra moved quickly, silent on the thin carpet. She'd memorized the filing system on a previous visit, shadowing a clerk: Three aisles in. Second unit from the barrier. Top shelf above the flood line.

Her fingers found the black folder. "Port Security Protocols 2023–2024."

The clock read 11:42 p.m. Twenty minutes, maybe less.

She carried the file to the desk in the corner, the stapler and tape dispenser next to each other. She noted the order and would leave everything exactly the way it was.

The chair squeaked when she sat. She froze, counting heartbeats until the silence settled again.

The binder's cover was stamped "Restricted." A dim smile touched her lips as she cracked it open. The spine popped—a dry, reluctant crack in the quiet.

"Personnel. Infrastructure. Patrol Schedules."

"Resource Allocation."

Sheets flipped beneath her fingers. Budgets. Rosters. Inventory logs. Nothing. Nothing. Nothing.

Then, her hand stopped.

"William H. Maxwell, United States Senate." The letterhead glowed faintly under the light. His signature sprawled across the document. March 17, 2024. Addressed to the Coast Guard Commander and the Port Authority Director.

The language was camouflage: "strategic reallocation of monitoring assets," "temporary surveillance modifications."

But beneath the jargon, the reality was stark: he'd moved Coast Guard patrols. Pulled them off specific sectors. The coordinates aligned with the Bruth'rs' shell docks exactly.

Her pulse spiked. That date—days before the fentanyl surge hitting St. Petersburg.

The windows aligned. The shipments slid right in as the Coast Guard was elsewhere.

Maxwell hadn't turned a blind eye. He'd built the doorway.

Every document confirmed it—fresh memos, fresh "modifications," all bearing his signature, carving another hole in the net.

The cartel hadn't infiltrated Tampa's ports. It had inherited them.

The task force had been chasing ghosts at MacDill while the real invasion unloaded in plain sight.

The overhead light flickered, casting the room into darkness before buzzing back alive. Shandra's pulse hammered. She couldn't risk taking the originals; their absence would raise alarms.

She raised her phone. The shutter click cracked through the silence.

Sheet by sheet, she documented Maxwell's betrayal—the senator who preached against corruption had become its architect.

When she finished, she replaced the papers perfectly, the binder flush with its neighbors. Not a trace left.

A small television in the corner glowed silently, captions scrolling across a muted weather report. "Tropical Storm Milton strengthening into a hurricane." Spaghetti models looped the Gulf. St. Pete was dead center.

One storm ending, another beginning. The rhythm of Florida life.

Shandra checked her watch—11:58 p.m. The guard's next round would start any minute. She scanned the carpet for stray fibers, shifted the chair back into its groove, and smoothed the pile where her shoes had turned it.

WITNESS ELIMINATION

Before leaving, she opened her encrypted app, uploaded the photos to José's secure server, and typed:

Confirm receipt. Urgent.

If she didn't make it out, the truth would.

The hallway outside was empty, lit by emergency bulbs that painted pools of sickly yellow along the ground. She slipped through the checkpoints as easily as she'd entered. The guards barely looked up, distracted by storm briefings and phones.

By the time she reached her car three blocks away, the wind had begun to tug at the trees. She unlocked the door, slid inside, and let out the breath she'd been holding.

She pulled up the clearest photo, the one with Maxwell's signature, and texted Nick:

"Maxwell shielding marina operation. Confirmed expansion into port. Pretty sure Carl's involved.

Her thumb hovered above the screen. The weight of it sat heavy on her chest—corruption, betrayal, the certainty that knowledge like this carried a price.

She sent the message anyway. It whooshed into the digital ether—irreversible.

The phone dropped on the seat beside her, evidence burning hot in its circuits. She started the engine.

A flicker in the rearview. Movement—small, deliberate.

Not her imagination.

A shift of breath from the backseat.

A wire looped around her throat and pulled tight.

Her hands flew to the garrote, nails scraping metal that only bit deeper. Her reflection stared back—eyes wide, mouth open in soundless panic. Behind her, the man's expression was calm, cold.

"May you find peace with your son," he whispered, his accent clear.

She kicked against the dash. Fingers carved bloody crescents into her neck. The world narrowed to black.

And then she was gone.

21

THE ALLIANCE

The villa's terrace opened onto a strip of dark water framed by royal palms. A single lamp cast a circle of amber light across the table. Senator Maxwell stood inside it, jacket folded over one arm, bourbon in hand. Beyond the reach of the glow, La Reina sat in shadow, her posture composed, her face unreadable.

"Thank you for the discretion," Maxwell said. "Bimini suits the purpose."

La Reina lifted a small glass of rum. "Bimini suits discreet people and silent business." Her voice carried easily. "You asked for off the record. Consider it granted."

The empty pool deck offered stillness. "Then let's be direct," Maxwell said.

"Please," La Reina replied.

"Is the Greene matter resolved?"

"The activist will not trouble your committees."

He hesitated a beat, unsettled. "Can it be traced?"

"Only by those who already know."

He nodded slowly. "Unfortunate."

"Necessary," La Reina said. "She mistook conscience for armor. It never lasts."

Maxwell took a deliberate sip and set his tumbler down. "Then we're aligned again."

"We were never out of alignment," she said. "Only waiting for the noise to stop."

The breeze moved across the terrace, salt-heavy and warm, brushing the tablecloth. Below, the surf rose and fell like measured breathing.

"We have to address the rest," Maxwell said. "Loose ends. Testimony. Optics."

"Say the names."

"Gino Myers," he said. "He can still be useful. The Bureau is prepared to transition him—federal supervision, sealed identity, new placement. He'll be packaged as a cooperative asset who protects ongoing investigations."

"Witness protection," La Reina said, "for an executioner."

"For a source." Maxwell's correction was smooth, practiced. "He understands the chain of command inside RADD. He can redirect heat onto the right target. If he stays quiet, he lives well. If he talks, it'll be what I tell him to say."

"And Adams?" La Reina asked.

"Contained," Maxwell replied. "He's getting a recommendation for a promotion in Gainesville. Small market, low-profile jurisdiction. Far enough from the cameras to forget he ever wore a task-force badge."

La Reina's glass turned once between her fingers. "Tucked out of the way," she said. "I prefer that to graves."

"So do I," Maxwell said. "Burials attract eulogies. Transfers do not."

"You and I share that preference," she said. "Clean work over mess."

"Agreed," Maxwell answered, "which is why we're here."

La Reina continued, "The ports will remain accessible and close when I require it. If your Coast Guard friends need language, I'll provide it—preparedness, readiness, repositioning. You'll ensure Tallahassee stays grateful and Washington looks elsewhere."

"Tallahassee and Washington are handled," Maxwell said. "Between my office and your logistics, very little can't be justified."

"Handled," La Reina repeated. "A generous word."

He leaned forward, catching the glint of crystal but not her face. "Our arrangement endures because we understand the distinction between favor and dependence. I don't beg. I negotiate."

"And I don't flatter," she said. "I deliver."

Maxwell withdrew a slim leather folio from his coat and pushed it to the edge of the light. "Committee authorizations, draft language for emergency procurement, and next quarter's deployment schedules. The signatures you require will appear after the fact."

From the dark, a small cigar container glided forward with a fingertip. "Port manifests. Contribution flows. Identities of those asking questions and those paid not to."

Maxwell palmed the box and slipped it inside his pocket. "You make it sound sordid."

"Only when spoken out loud," she said. "On paper, it's civic life."

He refilled his drink with the ease of a man who had negotiated in a hundred private rooms. "One more thing. I'm being encouraged to form a presidential exploratory committee."

"National interest demands access to the keys," La Reina said. "The presidency is a larger stage. The lights are brighter. The microphones multiply. You'll require steadier nerves."

He smiled. "I have steady hands."

"You have consistent appetites," she said. "Steady hands are rare."

He looked toward the water, catching his reflection in the glass. "If this moves forward, appearances will need cleaning. Old alliances minimized. New counsel installed. Donors curated."

"Image is marketing," La Reina said. "I prefer engineering, but I'm charitable. Tell me what you require cleaned, and I'll name the price."

"I demand distance from disorder," Maxwell said. "Shandra Greene was chaos. She's now absent. That's acceptable. Myers becomes order. That's the story we tell."

A soft knock sounded from inside the villa. A bodyguard opened the sliding door two inches, set a phone on the credenza, and disappeared again. Maxwell didn't turn.

"I won't be the one saying your name on a stage," La Reina said. "I don't clap from the cheap seats. But I expect the doors I unlock to stay accessible when I need them."

"And when one of yours needs a new identity," Maxwell said, "you'll have it. You have my word."

"I prefer proof."

"You have both," he said. "The governor won't obstruct me. The Bureau's aligned. Washington desires results it doesn't have to explain. Tallahassee wants ribbon cuttings and headlines. They all want clean hands. I provide the sink."

La Reina's gaze was that of a collector assessing a fragile acquisition. "You're a useful man, Senator."

"I aim to be indispensable."

"Careful," she said. "Vital men end up in portraits. Portraits don't move."

He finished his drink and set it aside. "You like the reminders."

"I value accuracy," she said. "You sell stories to people who need them. I trade stability to people who understand its price. We work in adjacent markets."

Silence followed—neither awkward nor empty, only final, like a ledger closing.

Maxwell tapped the folio. "We'll say the ports are crucial to economic security. Federal redeployments are, let's say, part of readiness. We'll say nothing about the names that benefit. If the media asks, they'll get numbers and enthusiasm."

"And if the media receives more than figures," La Reina said, "they'll get silence from those who matter."

He nodded once, a small motion with the weight of ritual. "You're content with our course."

"Yes," she said. "As long as you remember who writes the route."

He almost laughed. "You think I'd forget?"

"I think men who love podiums mistake applause for permission," she said. "Applause is free. Permission is not."

His device lit. A Washington number scrolled across the screen. He silenced it with his thumb and laid the phone back on the credenza without breaking eye contact. "You see," he said. "Controlled."

"Tallahassee and Washington," she said. "Controlled, as you promised. Keep it that way."

He gathered his coat and slid one arm into it, then the other. "Our partnership continues."

"It does."

WITNESS ELIMINATION

He waited, perhaps for a blessing, maybe for another condition. The dark offered neither. Nodding toward the shadow where her eyes waited, he turned for the door.

"Senator," she said, "when the exploratory committee becomes a campaign, recall who arranged the silence that paved your way."

"I remember everything that matters."

"Good," she said, "because I do too."

Maxwell stepped inside. The door closed on its track with the soft precision of a file drawer. On the terrace, the lamp hummed. The faint breeze moved across the table and faded. In the glass, the sea's reflection swallowed his image, leaving only the empty chair in shadow.

22

JESSICA'S COURAGE

Sunday, October 6, 2024

Andrea's knuckles whitened on the steering wheel as she threaded through the gauntlet Hurricane Helene had left behind. Ten days after landfall, St. Petersburg was still a jigsaw puzzle of wreckage. Tree limbs speared through sodden mattresses, overturned mailboxes leaned out of murky puddles, roof shingles were scattered like playing cards. In the rear passenger seat, Jessica sat, her fingers clenched around Zara, eyes tracking every car on the road with a burden of vigilance no eight-year-old should carry.

"Remember to look for the Wallgreens sign," Andrea said, shifting her weight as a sharp ache stabbed through her ribs from the compressions that had restarted her heart. A spasm rippled down her right arm, quick and mean, rattling the leather before it passed. She masked the twitch with a controlled breath and guided the Audi through a pothole filled with oily rainwater that shimmered with a toxic rainbow sheen under the weak light.

The radio crackled through static before the announcer's voice cut in. "Tropical Storm Milton has strengthened to Category 1. Forecasts show rapid intensification, possibly Category 4 or 5 prior to landfall on Wednesday. Emergency officials urge residents to finalize evacuation plans now."

Jessica's fingers tightened around the lioness, her eyes sweeping the streets. The stuffed animal's fur bunched between her knuckles, golden threads pulling free from seams.

"Two hurricanes in less than a month," Andrea muttered, flicking the turn signal. "And Milton of all names. Who calls a hurricane Milton?"

She risked a glance at her daughter, hoping for even the ghost of a smile. But Jessica stayed fixed in her watch, shoulders taut, gaze unbroken. Another casualty of their new reality was the absence of her daughter's easy laughter.

They passed a FEMA distribution center, the lines of residents curling around the block. Faces followed their car—some sharp with envy, others flat with resignation. National Guard troops in sweat-streaked fatigues waved traffic past a fallen power cable, their gestures brisk but fraying at the edges. Andrea kept her eyes forward, unwilling to meet the hunger staring back at her.

The radio host's voice cut through the static, frustration on full display, "Callers report stalled debris removal throughout St. Petersburg. Mayor Wilson insists Hurricane Milton preparations won't hinder Helene cleanup."

Andrea snorted at the lie. "There aren't any cleanup efforts to hinder," she muttered.

In the back, Jessica's small body went rigid. The silence was so sharp it pressed against Andrea's chest like a heavy hand.

They stopped at a red light on 4th Street, the Walgreens sign glowing two blocks ahead. Andrea drummed her fingers against the leather, calculating how long it would take. Her ribs still ached, every shudder a reminder she remained broken. Her pain prescription was ready.

"Mom." Jessica whispered, "Turn now. Someone's following us."

Andrea checked the rearview. A dark sedan was several cars back. She hadn't registered it earlier, but now the pattern was clear. It had been shadowing them since they'd departed the neighborhood.

Her grip tightened on the wheel, a tremor sparking through her arm as adrenaline surged against her bruised chest. "How long?" she asked, her analytical mind cataloging details even as her pulse hammered.

"Four turns," Jessica said, her voice steady but thin. "Dad told me more than three isn't a coincidence."

WITNESS ELIMINATION

The light flipped green. Andrea yanked the wheel hard left, cutting over oncoming lanes during the narrow gap before cross-traffic surged. A horn blared in protest.

"Hold on." She gunned the Audi down the side street.

The road was a gauntlet of ruined furniture, storm-soaked couches, and splintered dressers stacked like barricades. A shopping cart was toppled in their lane. Andrea jerked the wheel, swerving past it. Pain, sharp enough to steal her breath, flared over her ribs with the movement, and a spasm rippled down her arm before she forced it still.

In the rearview, the sedan made the turn, too, closing the gap as it barreled forward.

"Still on us," Jessica reported, eerily calm. She had twisted in her seat, peering through the back window, the lioness clutched tight against her chest.

Andrea snapped the wheel left onto 22nd Avenue, barely easing off the gas. The neighborhood here was a maze of detours and debris, but she fixed on the Snell Isle Bridge. It was the quickest path home if she could make it through.

Up ahead, a utility truck blocked half the road, and crews swarmed around a downed power line. Andrea's pulse spiked as she eased off the accelerator, calculating angles, lungs constricting with every shallow breath. In the mirror, the sedan bore down, its dark bulk eating distance.

"Hold tight," Andrea said, flooring the gas toward the narrow gap between the truck and a parked car.

Metal shrieked as the Audi's side mirror clipped the utility vehicle. The car jolted hard, shuddering violently, threatening to tear the wheel from her grip. Shouts erupted from the workers, drowned by the roar of the engine as she forced the car through and lurched free.

Two more sharp turns, chosen at random, carried them deeper into the neighborhood. Andrea's breath came shallow and measured, every jolt of the pedals sending a flare of pain. A tremor ticked through her fingers, dulled by adrenaline as she kept her focus on the mirrors, scanning for shadows.

The sedan never reappeared, but her pulse refused to slow.

At last, five relentless minutes later, she swung into their driveway.

"Do you see them?" she asked Jessica, who was still twisted in her harness, eyes on the road behind.

"No," Jessica said after a long moment, "I think we lost them at the truck. But we need to get inside."

Andrea didn't wait. She was already out of her seat, door swinging open as she half-fell onto the pavement. She yanked the back door wide, fingers fumbling at the buckle, breath coming fast. The harness released with a sharp click.

"Come on, baby."

She scooped Jessica out, one arm around her back, the other shielding her as she pivoted toward the house. Keys. Door. Light. She didn't stop moving.

Inside, with the door slammed and locked, Andrea finally crouched, hands shaking as she brushed damp hair off Jessica's face. Her fingers lingered on her daughter's cheek, as if confirming she was real, here, safe—for now.

"How did you know, Jess?" she asked, though she already suspected. Nick's lessons, whispered in the dark.

"The lioness told me," she said. Not the comfort-seeking answer of a child but code.

Nick's voice echoed in her memory. "Watch the animals. They see danger first."

She nodded, accepting the truth and the fiction intertwined. Walgreens could wait. The prescription wasn't worth the risk.

"Well," she said, forcing a lightness, "please thank the lioness for me."

Jessica's grip tightened on Zara.

~

Jessica pressed her face to the living room window, the cool pane easing the heat in her cheeks. Zara stood guard in her arms, its bead eyes fixed on the street where shadows stretched long in the late light.

Andrea moved through the ground floor, each gesture dressed as routine but serving a tactical purpose. She checked the front deadbolt, then tested the sliding patio door while watering the houseplants, and checked the driveway through the kitchen blinds as she filled a tumbler of water. Her grip trembled once, an involuntary shake that sent a ripple through the liquid, before steadying it.

"Anything out there, Jess?" she called, her tone shaped to sound curious rather than anxious.

Jessica didn't turn from her vigil. "No cars. Mr. Wilson's fixing his fence again."

Andrea nodded, unseen. The neighbor's persistence meant extra eyes on the street, witnesses if the sedan returned. She crossed into the living room, chest tightening with each careful breath. She eased onto the couch, forcing her body into stillness. On the table was a cold mug and Jessica's math workbook, pages dog-eared from repeated struggles. She picked up the remote and lowered the volume as the television came alive.

The Weather Channel glowed from the corner, its map a swirling bruise of reds and oranges. A meteorologist gestured at a spiraling mass in the Gulf. Hurricane Milton was upgraded to Category 2 and could reach Category 4 prior to landfall. Evacuation graphics crawled along the bottom of the screen. The danger registered in a glance, and she clicked the sound lower still.

She checked her phone. No new messages. Nick's last text, hours old, was characteristically terse:

Meeting with Adams. Check in later. Stay alert.

She typed a quick update about the sedan, then stopped. He already had plenty to carry. She'd tell him face-to-face.

At the window, Jessica's lips moved in a silent litany to the lioness. The habit had begun after the nightmares. Ritualistic, unsettling. Andrea had once thought children were supposed to outgrow talking to toys, not begin at seven.

"What's she telling you?" Andrea asked.

Jessica didn't turn. Her small face reflected in the pane. "She says Milton is bringing the bad people with it."

The matter-of-fact tone chilled Andrea. It was the same tone Nick used. The cadence of an analyst cataloging threats, not sharing fears.

"Jess." Andrea patted the couch. "Come sit with me for a minute."

Jessica lingered at the window, eyes combing the street one last time before turning away. She crossed the room with the careful steps of someone carrying a burden too large for her age, the lioness clutched tight against her chest. The couch dipped as she climbed up, her small body settling into the space beside Andrea.

"Are they coming back?" Jessica asked, barely audible above the television's drone.

Andrea weighed her answer. The administrator in her craved precision; the mother longed to promise safety. She split the difference.

"Not tonight," she said, wrapping an arm around Jessica's shoulders. "And if they did, they'd have to get through alarms, locks … and Mr. Wilson, who sleeps with a shotgun resting on his lap."

The humor landed dark. Jessica's gaze, sharper than any child's ought to be, searched her face for cracks.

"Dad says we must always be prepared," Jessica murmured, fingers combing the lioness's matted fur. "That's why he taught me about being followed."

Irritation flared, but she tamped it down with reluctant gratitude. They'd fought over the extent of what Nick told their daughter, where protection ended and burden began. Today, his paranoia had likely saved them both. The thought scraped her raw. Her eight-year-old was already absorbing the world like a trainee, not a child.

"Your dad is smart about keeping us safe," she conceded. "That's why we practice. So we're prepared, not scared. Like fire drills at school."

Jessica nodded, seeming to accept the framing. She curled against Andrea's side, her small body loosening by degrees. On the television, the meteorologist had moved on to evacuation zones, his finger tracing the coastal neighborhoods most at risk.

"Will we have to leave because of Milton?" Jessica asked, her eyes fixed on the storm's spiraling image.

"Maybe," Andrea said. "We'll decide tomorrow when Dad gets home."

While Jessica watched the screen, Andrea's gaze shifted to the mantel where the locked Steyr case blended with framed photos. To an outsider, it looked decorative, but the combination was burned into her mind, the weight of steel waiting inside a heavy promise. José's recent drills echoed in her mind. She was prepared now, or as capable as a person could be.

Andrea's jaw set. Her chest ached with each shallow breath. A nerve in her hand still twitched, but that wouldn't stop her. Not if they came for her family. Not again.

Jessica's breathing softened into the rhythm of sleep, her head heavy on her mother's shoulder. But Andrea stayed vigilant, one arm protective around her daughter, eyes shifting to the windows, ears tuned for any creak of the house. In the Gulf, Milton gathered force. In St. Petersburg, Andrea prepared to meet a different storm.

23

SALLY MOVES IN SHADOWS

Sally's back slammed into the canvas wall, the metal frame groaning beneath her weight. Sarah pressed close, her bob brushing Sally's cheek, sharp strands framing high cheekbones and slicing the air between them. The pocket of space thickened with musk, mildew, and tension suspended like a held secret.

The contrast twisted in Sally's gut, Sarah's elegance against the surrounding rot, power wrapped in ruin.

Sally's forearms tensed, the ink along her flesh catching shadows in the dim light. Her inhale hitched as Sarah's fingers traced up her neck, nails carving heat into her skin.

"Look at me," Sarah said, soft but unyielding.

Sally obeyed. Sarah's face hovered inches away, hazel eyes sharp with calculation. Nearly two weeks had passed since their escape, and Sarah still looked like she could walk into a boardroom—hair cropped close, bob-line perfect, composure intact. Only a flicker of wildness betrayed how far they'd fallen.

"You belong to me," Sarah whispered, fingers digging into Sally's buzzed stubble, pinching hard enough to send sparks of agony down her spine. "Say it."

Sally's breath caught. "I belong to you."

Sarah smiled—tight, joyless. Then she kissed her.

It lacked softness. It lacked sweetness. It was hungry, teeth and breath, and the press of power. Greedy. Sally gasped, the edge of sting mixing with heat as Sarah claimed her mouth. When she pulled back, Sally was trembling.

"Again," Sarah breathed.

"I belong to you," Sally said, pulse hammering beneath Sarah's thumb at her throat.

The safe house walls pressed in around them, canvas curtains strung from a rusted frame, forming a private alcove within the gutted warehouse they'd claimed after the storm. Outside, water still pooled in the sunken corners, and the roof leaked with every thunderclap. But inside this enclosure, Sarah had arranged her world in her command center. Controlled.

A weather-worn duffel sat nearby, half-zipped. Inside were cash, IDs, go bags. One of many fallback kits scattered across the state.

Sarah's hand slid to Sally's collarbone, nails tracing the ridge, a touch balanced between caress and threat. "You did well with Nick's former client, that informant today."

Pride bloomed in Sally's chest before she could stop it. The man had cracked fast, spilling all he knew about Nick Justin's investigation.

"He won't be a problem anymore."

Sarah's eyes didn't blink. "And the body?"

"Where no one will look." Sally swallowed. "At least not until after the next storm."

Sarah's lips curved. "Proving your devotion every day." Her grip tightened on Sally's jaw, tilting her head back, throat exposed. "That's why I need you. Why I chose you."

The praise cut through Sally like wire, pleasure sharp enough to hurt. They'd begun as partners, mirrors of hunger and ambition, until Sarah's control seeped in like a slow toxin. She had unmade her, peeled away everything that didn't serve.

Sarah leaned in, her body flush against Sally's. The cheap vodka on her breath clashed with her otherwise perfect composure.

"No one else understands what we're building," she murmured. "They think it's about money. About drugs."

Her lips brushed Sally's ear. "They can't see the bigger picture."

Sally's knees weakened. Sarah knew exactly how to play her, every act a calculated dose of intimacy and command.

"When do we strike Justin?"

"Soon." Sarah's fingers slid lower, slipping beneath Sally's shirt to find bare skin. "But first, we need leverage. The hard drive isn't sufficient anymore."

"What kind of leverage?" Sally's voice came thin, distant. Her focus fractured under Sarah's touch.

"His daughter," Sarah said. "Jessica."

Something cold uncoiled in Sally's gut. They'd used the girl before, Sarah's first move to pressure Nick, and it had backfired. Badly.

"She's a kid."

Sarah's nails dug into Sally's side, above the viper tattoo curling up her thigh, hard enough to bruise. "She's a tool. Nothing more." Her hazel eyes turned to steel. "Prove your allegiance. Tell me you grasp this."

An image surged, Jessica clutching that silly lioness, eyes wide with fear. Something violent twisted in Sally's chest. She imagined ripping the plush open, stuffing spilling like innocence torn apart, the texture of it against her skin, the seams unraveling. The fantasy frightened her, yet thrilled her.

"I understand." Her voice was steadier than she felt.

Sarah studied her, reading her for hesitation. Finding none, she kissed her again—slow, claiming, a taste of control wrapped in promise.

"No one else matters," she murmured against Sally's mouth. "Not the girl. Not her mother. Only what we're building."

Heat pooled in the space separating Sally's legs, desire and ambition tangling into something she couldn't separate. This was what Sarah did, blurred the lines between want and need, loyalty and survival.

"What's the play?" Sally asked when Sarah finally pulled back.

"We watch. We wait." Sarah straightened, smoothing her blouse. "The storm is coming, Hurricane Milton. Evacuation orders are already going out. When the city empties … the lioness and her cub will be alone."

The canvas drapes rustled in the stale breeze from a fan, drawing Sally's eye. Beyond their alcove stretched the remains of their force: cartel soldiers, crooked cops who'd followed her out of loyalty or fear, and mercenaries Sarah had hired through offshore accounts.

All were waiting for her command.

Sally nodded, but something twisted in her chest, not quite resistance, not quite doubt, but a fracture forming in the foundation of her devotion. Sarah had promised power, equality, a place at her side. But moments like this—Sarah's hand on her jaw, positioning her like a chess piece— would she ever be anything more than a weapon?

"I'll set up surveillance on the house," she said, stepping back from the wall. The space between them chilled her, but it also cleared her head. "We'll know their routines before we move."

Sarah caught her wrist before she could leave the alcove. "Remember who saved you, Sally." Her thumb pressed against her pulse. "Remember who you are without me."

Sally met her gaze and saw it, the warning beneath the warmth. Without Sarah, she was nothing, a disgraced cop with blood on her hands. With her, she was something else. Something dangerous.

"I remember," Sally said, both truth and a lie.

As she slipped through the canvas curtain, leaving Sarah to her planning, Sally's hand drifted to the knife at her hip. The metal was cool against her palm, grounding her. Sarah might control her future, might own her loyalty—but there were parts of herself she'd kept hidden.

Ambitions Sarah hadn't discovered yet.

The drapes rustled closed behind her, sealing Sarah back inside her command center. Sally exhaled slowly, forearms tensing beneath inked skin as she released the air she'd been holding too long.

She belonged to Sarah.

For now.

～

The safe house felt claustrophobic, the atmosphere thick with moist wood, perspiration, and the stale echo of old violence. It was a ramshackle building, decades overdue for condemnation, but the cartel had hardened it into a maze of guarded rooms and dead-end stairwells. Power flickered from a patched generator rigged to a stolen transformer, its steady hum barely masking the tension underneath.

WITNESS ELIMINATION

Sally Hinkins stood near the door, arms folded, biceps taut beneath the soaked tank top. She swept the room, her gaze sharp and unblinking. The coiled viper tattoo on her left leg peeked out where her cargo pants rode low on her hip, less a decoration than a warning.

"Sarah's not here," one of the men sneered, leaning back in his chair. "We don't take orders from you. We listen only to La Reina and Sarah."

Sally didn't flinch. The cartel soldiers had been growing bolder, testing lines, probing for cracks. With Sarah focused elsewhere, they'd started circling off the leash.

"Sarah's the real boss anyway," another spat in a thick Spanish accent. "Hinkins, you're her slutty plaything."

Sally's fists clenched at her sides. Rage bloomed hot and clean. She stepped off the wall, the space tightening as she closed the distance.

"Funny you should say that," she said, her voice razor-edged, "because you're about to find out how much I enjoy playing."

She struck before they could blink.

Her boot slammed into the first soldier's knee, the joint folding with a wet pop as he collapsed, howling. Chairs scraped. Shouts erupted. Two others surged, but she was already moving, controlled fury in motion.

She drove a fist into the second merc's ribs. Something cracked. He folded, gasping as he hit the floor.

She pivoted, catching the third man with an uppercut that snapped his head back, blood spraying as he crashed into the table.

The last man backed away, eyes wide.

This was her moment. A calculated display of force. Sally fought to remind them who she was and what happened to anyone who forgot.

The last man turned to bolt.

Too slow.

She grabbed his collar and slammed him into the wall, rattling the frame. He froze.

"You think you can disrespect me in my own space?" Her face was inches from his. "You don't get to choose who's in charge here."

With a swift punch to the jaw, she dropped him. The crack echoed off the cinderblock. He crumpled.

Sally stood over him, boots planted. Then she spat, forceful and deliberate.

"Recall that next time you talk about my boss or me."

The room remained silent.

She straightened, muscles buzzing with adrenaline. Around the table, none of the men moved. The message had landed.

Sally rolled her shoulders. "That was a warm-up."

Her gaze swept the room, cold and unblinking.

"If Milton hits as violently as they say, we can't afford weakness. Not from any of you. And especially not in front of La Reina."

~

The overturned trash cans reeked of spoiled milk and sodden cardboard, their contents spilling across the cracked asphalt like entrails. Sally crouched behind them, the grit-laced wind off Tampa Bay stinging her eyes and gluing her clothes to her skin.

Two houses down from the Justin residence, she had clean sight angles on both the front door and the flank windows, their yellow light burning against the dusk. Hurricane Helene had left the road wild, as if nature had clawed it back, with fallen branches and broken furniture barricading the curbs, sagging power wires strung between leaning poles, the asphalt buckled where floodwater had eaten its foundation.

Perfect conditions for surveillance.

Her blue eyes tracked every movement across the property, unblinking. Her legs flexed with every shift of her weight, the muscles in her thighs tight from the crouch. Most neighbors had abandoned their ruined homes; those who remained were too consumed with recovery to notice a shadow out of place.

Sally adjusted the binoculars, the rubber eyepieces warm against her skin. The moon hung bloated and yellow above the bay, its glow diffused through haze that bruised the sky. Streetlights flickered on and off, ghosts of a broken grid. With every stutter of illumination, the surrounding shadows shifted, resettling like living things.

She'd been in position for nearly four hours, logging movements. Nick Justin was still gone, likely out with his investigator, José Dominguez. But Andrea and Jessica were home. Their silhouettes passed through the house in a rhythm that felt alien against the backdrop of storm wreckage.

Andrea walked slowly, her posture guarded, every step calculated. Jessica stuck close, a small shadow at her mother's hip, never more than an arm's reach away.

Movement at the front of the house drew Sally's focus. The porch bulb flared to life, casting sharp angles across the warped concrete. Andrea stepped out first, her gait uneven as she eased down the walkway. Jessica followed, clutching a reusable grocery bag in one hand and the lioness plush in the other. The toy dangled limply, its short fur catching the fractured beam.

Sally's pulse quickened.

Sarah had been clear: monitor Nick's movements, identify weak points, locate any evidence he might be holding. But she'd said nothing about the lioness. Nothing about that symbol the girl wouldn't let go of.

Sally recalled that Jessica used to whine about wanting her unicorn.

Now she carried a lioness.

Sally's jaw clenched. The unicorn was childhood. The lioness meant guardian.

Andrea unlocked the trunk of their second car, an Audi sedan that had survived Helene untouched in the garage. She loaded the grocery bags carefully, one hand bracing her ribs. Jessica lingered on the walkway, the plush now hugged tight to her chest, her face turned toward the darkened road.

For a moment, the child looked directly at her.

Jessica's gaze swept the pavement, slow and searching, like she knew where the shadows should end, and where they didn't.

Sally flattened against the brick wall of the neighboring house, the rough surface catching at her shirt. She stilled her breathing, slowing it to a whisper. The daughter couldn't have seen her. Not from that distance. Not in this gloom.

Still, the hairs on her arms lifted. That primal thrum buzzed beneath her skin.

Mother and daughter disappeared inside as the door closed. Sally exhaled slowly, the tension in her shoulders easing by degrees. She shifted position, circling toward the edge of the Justin property where a large oak tree cast long, concealing shadows. Wind stirred the debris-strewn asphalt—candy wrappers, palm fronds.

The neighborhood hummed with broken routines: an air pump two houses down, the staccato rhythm of late-night roof repairs, voices rising in argument over insurance claims.

Through a window, Sally caught sight of Jessica entering her bedroom, the plush still clutched in her hand. The girl crossed to the glass—the same opening that haunted Sally's sleep after Sarah's plan had failed. She paused there, her small face solemn in the lamplight, and placed the lioness on the sill with slow precision.

Facing outward and watching the night.

Something twisted in Sally's chest—a knot she couldn't immediately name. The plush sat upright, its glass eyes catching the room's glow in twin pinpricks of vigilance.

It wasn't sleek or perfect. It wasn't powerful. But it endured. And that, somehow, made it dangerous.

Sally edged closer, moonlight beaming around her as she hugged the deeper shadows. From this angle, the sentinel seemed to stare straight at her, eyes fixed, accusing. Her hand drifted to the combat knife at her hip, the grip familiar, grounding. Her pulse kicked faster now as she imagined closing the distance. Pressing the blade to the pane. Reaching through. Taking the plush. Shredding it.

She could see fabric tearing, stuffing drifting like ash across the hardwood. Innocence undone. The fantasy felt real, almost tactile, with the seams unraveling in her mind.

Her breath thickened, clouding in the muggy night air.

This wasn't part of Sarah's plan, but the guardian meant something. And whatever it was, it needed to be destroyed.

Perhaps it was the girl's safety.

Or maybe it was something else, something in Sally that still recognized the lioness as the last piece of what she used to be.

Inside, Jessica stepped back from the glass, her face still visible through the window. She said something to it. Sally couldn't hear but didn't need to. A child's ritual. A whispered plea for protection against the dark.

"The lioness will be mine." Sally's voice was cold.

WITNESS ELIMINATION

Jessica turned at her mother's call, disappearing into the house. The toy stayed behind, its bead eyes catching the room's light and throwing it back at the night. Empty now. Watching still.

Sally's grip tightened on her knife ... then relaxed.

Not tonight.

She still had a job to do. Sarah wanted intel: routines, weaknesses, leverage. That came first.

But she'd be back, and when she returned, the plush would be the first to fall.

Sally slipped into deeper shadow as a gust of wind stirred trash and sea rot from the bay. Overhead, power lines swayed like nerves exposed. The forecast called for Hurricane Milton to make landfall soon, a second storm in less than a month. The perfect cover for Sarah's plan.

But Sally had plans too.

They started with a child's lioness staring out at a night that had already let the monsters in.

24

MOVING PARTS

Monday, October 7, 2024

The marina district stretched a mile south of downtown St. Pete, where floodwaters had finally drained from the lower streets. Buckled pavement forced Nick off balance, and thick electrical cables sprawled across the ground like sunning snakes.

Power crews had already restored electricity here, proof that money made all the difference. Intact vessels bobbed in their slips, fiberglass hulls gleaming under the merciless sun. Some jutted up at grotesque angles, masts resembling broken fingers clawing at the sky.

José waited beside a maintenance shed, his slender frame half-swallowed by shadow, eyes fixed on the security monitors with the patience of a man who'd built a life on noticing what most overlooked.

"Over here." José didn't turn, his voice pitched low.

Nick slipped into the darkness beside him, back pressed to the wall. "Holcomb dragged the committee meeting past sanity. They had no intel on Sarah or Hinkins. Not enough boots to run a post-storm search."

José nodded, his expression tightening. At thirty-eight, he looked older. The scar above his brow stood out sharper on sun-darkened skin.

"Look at the cameras." José tilted his chin at the nearest pole. "Notice anything?"

Nick studied the setup—standard waterproof housing, indicator lights solid, unnaturally steady. "They're working. After a hurricane that size, that's something."

"Too fast, too perfect." José pushed off the wall, motioning for Nick to follow down a narrow service path. "Every camera in the district went dark for at least forty-eight hours after Helene. But here? Back online in twelve, except for the blind spots."

They stopped at the corner. José pointed in the direction of a loading area where several trucks were parked. "That zone has no coverage." He tapped a pole with two fingers. "Southeast pole's angled too far west. Northeast pole's tilted down for faces at the gate but skips the bay completely."

Nick's jaw tightened. "Someone designed it that way."

"A person with access." José's voice dropped. "Friday night, Shandra sent me an email. Time-stamped 11:58 p.m. Documentation tying Senator Maxwell to shell companies with controlling interest in Port Authority contracts. The same entities are behind the Bayboro security install and the Coast Guard asset shuffle. What I've cracked is surface-level, fragments, redactions. There's a deeper layer locked down tight, something she buried."

The pieces snapped into place. "Maxwell controls who sees what at the marina."

José nodded, eyes flicking constantly over their surroundings. "The money trail runs from Maxwell's shells to Tagger Group International, then through three more cutouts before it lands in accounts tied to La Reina's cartel."

"What else did Shandra say in the email?"

"Use this if I don't check in by Monday." José's mouth thinned. "It's Monday. She hasn't answered calls or texts. I went by her house this morning. There was no sign of her."

A cold weight settled in Nick's gut, an echo of the day when Andrea's SUV flipped on the Gandy Bridge. "I visited her house yesterday. Locked up tight. Mail is still in the box. No lights. Her car is gone. But I got one text from her with an image of Maxwell."

José's jaw flexed, a flash of anger tightening his scar. "That's as direct as it gets."

"Friday night. Right before she went dark." Nick slid a hand down his face, the stubble rasping against his palm. "As if she knew what was coming."

"When did you last hear from her?"

"She skipped today's task force session," Nick said. He closed his eyes, replaying her voice when they spoke—flat with nerves but edged with conviction. "But at an earlier meeting, she handed me an envelope and said it was everything the feds didn't want us to see."

José's head tilted. "What was in it?"

"Copies of records that were supposed to be sealed or already seized. Stuff Maxwell's people took possession of. Shandra must've slipped into the office before the files were moved. Copied them. Risked it all." Nick's jaw tightened. "Prison intel on Sarah and Sally. Transport schedules. Phone numbers. Witness lists. Evidence that should've been on the table but got buried."

José swore under his breath, sharper this time. "And you're just telling me this now?"

"I wanted to cross-check before I dropped it on you," Nick said. "But if Maxwell knows she got her hands on it ...." He didn't need to say more.

"Trouble," José grimaced.

"She was chasing a new lead." Nick pushed off the wall, frustration mounting. "We must check her office at the community center."

José answered, "Already did. The place was tossed. Not obvious, but someone professional. Drawers slightly ajar, computer still there but the hard drive swapped. They wanted what she had without broadcasting a break-in."

Nick's eyes tracked a Port Authority worker walking the main path, radio hissing at his belt. The man glanced their way a beat too long before continuing on.

"The Bruth'rs are transporting product through here," José said once the man was gone. "They're using hurricane reconstruction to shift more than lumber and drywall."

"And the cartel's cash funnels back to Maxwell through those contracts." Nick's fists clenched. "We need to move on this now, José. If they've got Shandra—"

"We need to be smart," José cut him off. "This isn't street level. It's Maxwell. Federal muscle. Cartel enforcers. Go in blind, we end up like Shandra or worse."

Nick's cell buzzed. He angled the screen away from view. Unknown number. One line of text.

Tonight. Tide hides footsteps. Dock C.

He showed it to José.

"Could be Shandra," Nick said, his mind jumping ahead. Dock C, Bayboro. High tide after midnight.

José's eyes narrowed. "Could be a trap."

"Either way, I'll be there." Nick pocketed the phone. "I need to check on Andrea and Jessica before the Milton evacuation kicks in."

"I'll tap my port contacts and see who's working Dock C tonight." José clasped Nick's shoulder. "And, Nick, wear the vest I gave you. The real one."

Nick nodded. The current might hide footsteps, but it wouldn't stop bullets.

~

Nick's key scraped in the lock, the familiar sound carrying extra weight. Inside, the house had morphed from home to command post—maps spread across the dining table, bottled water stacked in neat rows, flashlights stationed at every corner. Andrea knelt by a duffel in the living room, sliding a first-aid kit into place. The cane was abandoned on the couch, forgotten now. Outside, the sky hung gray, air pressure dropping as Hurricane Milton gathered strength over the Gulf, ready to deliver a second blow to a city still staggering from the first.

"You're ditching the cane," Nick said as he shut the door. The deadbolt clicked with a finality that matched the darkening clouds.

Andrea looked up, with a ghost of a smile flickering across her face. "Dr. Patel said I could try without it. Timing's not ideal, but …." She straightened, testing her weight. The grimace Nick had grown used to was gone. "Feels strange. Weak but free."

"Like everything else these days." Nick crossed over to her and kissed her forehead. His gaze shifted to the bay window, where Jessica sat cross-legged, arranging Zara on the sill. Its glass eyes stared outward.

"Jess has been keeping watch," Andrea whispered. "She says the lioness tells her when people are outside."

A gust pressed on the windows, and the house groaned. The weather stripping they'd installed after Helene whistled thinly, a high counterpoint to the deeper creaks of the frame.

"Roads are already jamming," Nick said, helping Andrea zip the go bag. "Evacuation's mandatory by morning, but we should leave if …." He stopped. The phone was heavy in his pocket.

Andrea's eyes narrowed. "If what?"

Nick pulled the cell free and showed her the screen. The message glowed in the dim room.

Tonight. Tide hides footsteps. Dock C.

Her gaze flicked to his face, lips pressed tight, her hazel eyes hardening. "Who sent this?"

"Unknown number. But it came right after José and I were talking about Shandra's disappearance. She's been missing since Friday. House locked, office ransacked."

"And you think this is her?" Andrea took the device, studying the text as if the letters might rearrange themselves into something safer. "This isn't Shandra's style, Nick. It's bait."

"Perhaps. Or maybe she's in trouble and couldn't risk spelling it out."

Andrea handed the phone back and snapped the duffel's buckles closed with sharp clicks. "We're leaving for Tampa tonight. All three of us. They already canceled Jessica's school. My mother's expecting us."

"If Shandra reached out—"

"Then she can reach out again when we're safe." Andrea's voice held steady, but her fingers betrayed her, trembling as she adjusted the bag's strap. "I won't let you walk into another trap, Nick, not after everything we've been through."

"And if it's not a trap? If she's holding evidence that could bring down Maxwell and the cartel?" Nick dragged a hand over his face, rasping stubble under his palm. "I can't ignore that, Andrea."

"You mean you won't." Her tone carried no accusation, only the weary certainty of someone who knew him too well. "Even after Sarah and Hinkins used Jessica to reach you. Even after what Myers did to me on that bridge."

The house shuddered as another gust pressed into it. Outside, a neighbor's trash can clattered across the street, a hollow drumbeat in the wind.

"I'll take precautions," Nick said, stepping closer. "José will back me up. We'll handle it together."

"There's no precaution for people like this," Andrea cut in, eyes flashing like before the crash. "Cartel connections. Federal backing. You think a vest and your investigator friend are enough for that?"

Jessica's head turned slightly toward them, though she stayed at her post by the window. The lioness stared out while Jess watched her parents. Her breath fogged the pane.

"We've never backed down," Nick said, softening. "Not when Myers framed you. Not when Sarah took Jessica."

"And look at what it has cost us," Andrea said, gesturing to her leg and the scars beneath her clothes. "Look at what it's still costing. Jessica wakes up from nightmares about Sarah every night. I wake up gasping, back in that car rolling on the bridge."

Nick started to answer, but his phone buzzed in his hand. Another message.

They found Hank. He needs you. Don't be a coward.

Nick went cold. Officer Hank Kitchens was key to taking down the Bruth'rs last summer, hidden in witness protection ever since. Only a handful knew his true identity.

"Whoever sent this knows about Hank," Nick said, showing Andrea. Her face drained of color. "That doesn't mean Hank's in danger. It means someone's working hard to manipulate you."

"Or warning me." Nick's jaw clenched. "Either way, I need to know."

"Dad?" Jessica's voice came small but clear from the window. She hadn't moved, her back still to them, the lioness still facing the street. "There's a person out there."

Nick crouched beside her. The area looked empty except for storm debris—branches, newspapers, a lawn chair overturned on the grass. The sky pressed lower, heavy with Milton's fury.

"Where, Jess?"

"Gone now." She adjusted the plush slightly, angling it toward a different stretch of road. "But Zara saw them."

Andrea joined them, her hand on Jessica's shoulder. Outside, the palms bent under the rising wind.

Nick's thumb hovered over his phone. He typed.

Who are you?

The message was sent with a soft whoosh. They waited. Minutes stretched. No reply.

"We need to leave," Andrea said at last, her voice steady for Jessica's sake. "Whether you meet this person, Jessica and I are going to Tampa tonight."

Nick kept his eyes on the empty street. "I'll get our things together."

The house creaked around them, timber and nails straining against the gusts, as if something else were testing their defenses, probing for weakness, waiting for night to finish what the storm had begun.

25

THE GANDY BRIDGE

Monday, October 7, 2024, 11:30 p.m.

Nick's knuckles whitened on the Audi's steering wheel as he threaded through St. Petersburg's fractured streets. Gusts rattled the chassis. Debris skittered along the glass, a frantic scratching sound. His gaze shifted between the road and the rearview reflection, a reflex sharpened by months of watching for tails and threats. Beside him, Andrea sat rigid, her hand massaging her leg. In the back, Jessica clutched Zara as they drove toward the Gandy Bridge and the relative safety of Tampa.

"You'll call José when we reach my mother's?" Andrea's tone carried more demand than doubt.

Nick nodded, downshifting around a fallen palm frond sprawled across the asphalt. "As soon as you're settled."

Andrea pulled her phone out. "I'm texting him now. Telling him you're running late so he doesn't panic."

The Louisville Slugger rested in the passenger footwell, leaning against the center console, its worn grip within easy grasp. It had become his security blanket, harmless to explain, brutal up close. The Glock stayed tucked beneath the driver's seat, insurance if things went sideways. To anyone else, it looked like a father's sporting gear, nothing more.

"Daddy?" Jessica's voice drifted from the back. "Is Hurricane Milton bigger than Helene?"

Nick met her gaze in the rearview, offering a smile that never reached his eyes. "The weatherman says it's strong, sweetheart. Bad timing, coming so soon after."

The Audi's tires splashed through a puddle, brackish water cascading over the hood. Helene had left St. Petersburg a maze of ruined homes and sewage-choked streets. The new storm promised to worsen the misery, already compared to the Tampa Bay Hurricane of 1921.

"There's a car," Jessica said, peering out the rear window. "It keeps making the same turns we do."

Nick's throat tightened as headlights flared in his mirror, twin orbs floating in the dark. They'd been there for three blocks, holding steady, not close enough to threaten, not far enough to be chance. His jaw clenched as he took a deliberate right turn at the next intersection, adding minutes to their route.

The sedan followed.

Andrea's posture shifted. She'd seen it too. José's paranoia had once seemed excessive; now it felt necessary.

"Jess, honey." Andrea met her eyes in the reflection. "Why don't you count the traffic lights until we reach the bridge? See if you can remember how many there were last time."

Jessica nodded, distracted by the game. Andrea's hand slid to the glove compartment, the casual movement hiding its intent.

"Four cars back." Nick pushed through a yellow light. "Black sedan. Tinted windows."

The pursuing vehicle surged forward, closing the gap with alarming speed.

Nick stabbed the brakes, dropping behind a box truck, then floored it again, spoiling their angle.

His hand dropped to the Louisville Slugger beside Andrea's leg, fingers brushing its familiar grain. "Andrea—"

"I see it." Her voice hardened. The glove compartment clicked open. "Jess, lie down on the seat now. Cover your head with your jacket."

WITNESS ELIMINATION

The vehicle swung into the right lane and accelerated alongside them. The passenger window rolled down, revealing only darkness inside. Nick pressed the accelerator, the Audi's engine climbing higher.

The first shot cracked through the night, followed by the shattering of the rear windshield. Shards peppered Nick's neck as he yanked the wheel, trying to ram the attacking car. The Audi skidded across debris-strewn asphalt.

"Down!" Andrea shouted, reaching into the glove box.

The second tore through the space Nick's head had filled a heartbeat earlier. Wind screamed through the broken pane, Milton's distant fury riding the gusts into the Audi. Jessica's cry rose from the back seat, frayed with terror.

Andrea raised the Steyr, the gun settling into her grip. She racked the slide once, checked the chamber, then brought the sights up. Her breath hissed—a rhythmic, sharp intake.

The pistol barked, the muzzle flash lighting the cabin in strobes as Andrea fired out her window, shots steady despite the Audi's lurching. One. Two. Three. The third round hammered the sedan's windshield, spiderwebbing the glass. Startled, the driver jerked the wheel. The car slammed into the concrete guardrail, tires screaming.

A muzzle sparked from the wreck as it crashed, a wild shot punching through the Audi's rear window.

Nick yanked the wheel hard, widening the gap as the sedan smashed into the barrier with a crunch of metal and cement. It rolled across two lanes before coming to rest on its roof, wheels spinning uselessly in the gust-lashed dark.

Jessica screamed as shards rained around her. The lioness plush slipped from her grasp, tumbling to the floor as the car leveled out.

"Jessica!" Andrea twisted, the Steyr still clutched in one hand. "Jess, are you—"

"Mommy!" It broke from her in a sob, thick with terror and pain.

Nick's eyes snapped to the rearview. A red stain spread across Jessica's sleeve, stark even in the dim light. Blood. His daughter's blood. His vision narrowed, the windshield dissolving until only one thought burned clear.

They'd been hunting his family all along.

~

Red streaked the leather, stark against the tan. In the reflection, Nick saw it, his stomach knotting cold. The bullet had grazed the outside of her upper arm, leaving a shallow but bloody furrow, tiny glass fragments stippling her cheek and shoulder. She was rigid in shock, her slight frame locked in place, tears cutting clean tracks through the blood on her cheeks. Andrea's harness clicked free. She twisted toward the back, her movements sharp and economical despite the strain on her healing leg.

"Keep steady," Andrea said, her voice unnervingly calm as she leaned between the seats. "I need to see how bad it is."

Nick pressed the accelerator, the speedometer edging over a hundred. Gusts buffeted the car, pushing it sideways as he swerved around a pickup crawling in the left lane, horn blaring as he blew past.

"It hurts." Jessica whimpered. "Mommy, it hurts."

"I know, baby. I know." Andrea wedged into the back, her hands working. She tore a strip from the bottom of her shirt, folding it into a makeshift compress. "This will press hard, but it'll help."

Nick fumbled for his phone, thumb smearing crimson across the screen as he dialed 911. Each ring dragged. When the dispatcher finally answered, she sounded distant and maddeningly calm.

"911, what's your emergency?"

"My daughter's been shot." He clenched his teeth. "We're eastbound on Gandy Boulevard toward Tampa General. She's eight years old, bleeding steadily but conscious. I need an ambulance to intercept us."

Silence stretched, crushing. "Sir, with Hurricane Milton approaching, EMS resources are limited. What's your exact location?"

"Did you hear me? My daughter's been shot!" Nick's voice cracked, raw. "We're in a silver Audi past the east end of the bridge. She needs help now."

"I understand, sir. All available units are deployed under evacuation orders—"

Nick slammed his palm into the wheel. "Then alert the hospital. Silver Audi, gunshot victim, pediatric. We're coming in hot."

WITNESS ELIMINATION

He ended the call, the phone slipping from his bloody fingers to clatter onto the console. In the back seat, Andrea held pressure on the wound, murmuring reassurances into Jessica's ear. Her face was chalk-pale, freckles stark against the skin.

"Daddy," she whispered, voice trembling, "my lioness fell."

Nick glanced at the floor where the toy was, its tan fur already darkened with blood. Andrea freed one hand from the compress to lift it and set it gently on Jessica's chest. Her fingers closed around it at once, clutching with desperate strength.

"How bad?" Nick pitched his voice low for Andrea alone.

"Graze on the right upper arm. Painful but not life-threatening if we keep it clean." Andrea's clinical tone barely hid the fury underneath. "Glass cuts on her face and neck, nothing too deep. She's in shock but stable."

He gritted his teeth as the realization hit. The texts, the timing, the attack—each piece fitting together into one design aimed at Jessica. Worse, the texter hadn't been warning him; he'd been steering him.

The informant's words echoed in his mind with sickening clarity. *The king's cub is now fair game.*

"This was planned," he seethed. "They wanted us on that road at that time. The message about Hank, the marina meeting. All of it was bait."

Andrea's eyes met his in the rearview glass, her features hardening. "Sarah."

The name hung between them, heavy with history and betrayal. Sarah Brown—Andrea's sister, Jessica's aunt, the architect of their suffering. Escaped now with Hinkins at her side.

"Has to be," Nick agreed. "Who else would know about Hank?"

Jessica whimpered as the car jolted over a pothole, her small body jerking with the impact. The plush soaked her tears, its fur darkening with blood until it looked almost alive.

"It's okay, sweetheart," Andrea murmured, her bloodied fingers smoothing Jessica's hair back. "Hold on to Professor Lioness. She's watching over you."

"Her name's Zara," Jessica corrected. Even in shock, some boundaries held.

Nick met Andrea's eyes in the mirror. Despite everything, a flicker of pride passed between them. Their daughter, stubborn even now.

Tampa General's emergency entrance glowed ahead, stark in the gust-driven dark. Nick swerved into the ambulance bay, brakes squealing as he stopped short of the automatic doors. A security guard waved him forward, flashlight cutting the gloom to clear a path for the battered Audi.

"Stay with her." He shoved his door wide into the wind.

He sprinted around the car, grit and salt stinging his face, his shirt snapping around his body. A medical team was already surging through the parted glass doors, gurney rolling fast to meet them.

He yanked the rear handle. Jessica looked impossibly small amidst the blood-smeared upholstery, her skin drained of color. Andrea had fashioned a crude sling for the wounded arm. The bandage held most of the bleeding, but fresh crimson still spotted her sleeve and streaked the lioness's fur.

With infinite care, Nick lifted his daughter into his arms. She was lighter than he remembered, breakable as thin glass. The lioness stayed pressed to her chest, its stained body an extension of her own. As he lowered her onto the waiting stretcher, gusts shrieked around the building's corners, whipping the trees and rattling the ambulance bay doors on their tracks.

The storm had found them after all.

26

NICK'S SPIRAL, ANDREA'S FIRE

Tuesday, October 8, 2024, 12:15 a.m.

Medical staff swarmed Jessica's gurney, their voices clipped and urgent as they steered it down the fluorescent corridor. Nick stood frozen at the threshold, his daughter's blood tacky on his fingers. The antiseptic air hit him hard, separating him from Jessica as surely as the panels that swallowed her form.

"BP dropping. She's in shock." A doctor strode alongside. "Start fluids wide open. Get OR 3 prepped, now."

His daughter was impossibly frail amidst the white sheets, her pale face half-hidden by an oxygen mask too large for her features. The bloodstained lioness plush rode on a stainless steel tray, its glass eyes catching the lights as it jolted with every bump in the tiles. Nick's chest tightened as the gurney vanished behind swinging doors marked "AUTHORIZED PERSONNEL ONLY."

A nurse placed her hand on his shoulder, halting his instinctive step forward. "Sir, you need to stay here. The surgical team will take good care of her."

The squeak of rubber soles echoed down the corridor, sharp in the silence he carried inside. His gaze drifted to a mounted television where a meteorologist gestured at Hurricane Milton's swirling mass, now officially a Category 5. Its eye stared back from the screen, a predator circling its prey.

"Projected landfall within twenty-four hours," the meteorologist intoned, her voice lost beneath the rattle of wind battering the windows. "Unprecedented gale speeds exceeding 160 miles per hour."

He stared at the map. "Of course."

His knees buckled, and he dropped into a molded plastic chair bolted to the wall. His hands shook, fingers still curled as though cradling Jessica's weight. He stared at his palms. The crimson had dried into the creases of his skin, a map of the violence he'd invited home. He scraped a thumbnail across the stain, trying to erase it, but the color held fast.

The tremors built until his whole body vibrated with contained rage and fear. He had failed her, failed to protect his own child. Every decision, every pursuit of justice, had led here to his daughter's blood on hospital sheets while another storm gathered outside.

A security guard passed, radio crackling with updates. "Non-essential personnel out by sixteen hundred. Critical patients stay with skeleton staff."

Nick's gaze locked on the entrance, willing it to open, to show Jessica whole and safe. But it stayed shut, sealing away whatever was happening beyond.

The elevator at the end of the corridor slid wide. Andrea emerged, her clothes stiff with dried blood, her arms scrubbed pink to the elbows. Her face held rigid control, but behind her eyes burned wild fury that mirrored his own.

She walked to him, her steps measured. Damp hair clung to her temples, and wind-driven grit speckled her shoulders from outside. Beyond the glass, gusts rattled the panes, each blast timed to her heartbeat.

"Surgery?" she asked, leaving so much unspoken.

Nick nodded, a knot in his throat. Andrea lowered herself into the chair beside him, her movements careful, controlled. She braced a hand on her thigh, muscles twitching from the adrenaline crash. A wince tightened the corner of her eye as she took the weight off her bad knee, but she forced her breath steady.

The scent of hospital soap mingled with the metallic tang of blood.

"It was Sarah," Andrea said after a long silence. Not a question, but a fact—cold and certain. "She's always been possessive of Jessica. Now she's using her to get to us."

Nick's fists curled on his knees. "I led us straight into it. The texts, the timing, they played me."

"They gamed us both," Andrea corrected, her jaw tight. "I should have seen it. My own sister."

A nurse emerged from the OR, her face carefully neutral. "Mr. and Mrs. Justin? Jessica's in surgery. Dr. Lynn is one of our best pediatric trauma surgeons. The bullet only grazed her upper arm—soft tissue damage, no bone or major vessels hit. She's stable, but the team needs time to clean the wound and close it properly."

Andrea nodded—stiff, automatic. "What about evacuation plans? The hurricane—"

"Critical cases and essential staff will stay. Everyone else evacuates by morning." The nurse's eyes flicked to the window, where gusts rattled the frames. "We've got protocols: generators, supplies, flood barriers. They held during Helene."

As the nurse retreated, Andrea's hand found Nick's, her fingers intertwining with his. Her skin was cold despite the building's oppressive warmth. When she spoke again, her voice had dropped to a pitch that raised the hair on the back of Nick's neck.

"This doesn't end until they're dead," she growled. "Sarah, Hinkins, all of them."

~

Hours had passed. The wind pressed into the windows, the sound cutting through the corridor. A new hardness set her jaw, and fire lit her eyes. This wasn't the Andrea who argued for caution, for legal solutions, for playing by rules their enemies had abandoned. This was a mother whose child had been hunted.

A technician wheeled a cart past, Jessica's bloodstained lioness perched on top. Its amber eyes caught the light, flashing like twin points of fire. Andrea snatched it, clutching it to her chest.

She positioned Zara on a small table facing the OR doors. Nick recognized the gesture—Jessica's ritual, her way of creating guardians against the darkness. Now Andrea adopted it, the blood-crusted plush standing vigil while their daughter fought for her life past those panels.

The squeak of nurses' shoes punctuated the silence. An astringent smell burned Nick's nostrils, mingling with the metallic tang still clinging to his skin despite repeated scrubbing. Beyond the glass, gusts pressed at the windows, the frames groaning in protest.

"We finish this," Nick said, his voice steady. "Whatever it takes."

Andrea's fingers tightened around his, her nails digging into his palm. They sat side by side, shadows stretching behind them as the corridor lights flickered—two figures remade by violence into something harder, more dangerous.

Outside, Milton gathered its strength.

Inside, vengeance did too.

~

The Louisville Slugger settled across Nick's knees, its polished grain catching the corridor's dim light. The worn handle carried the memory of countless grips: Sunday batting practice with his daughter, the odd pickup game with colleagues, and now a weapon for darker nights. Nick's thumb traced the manufacturer's stamp, the indentation as familiar as his own heartbeat. He squeezed the handle, testing the resistance, needing to feel something solid in a world that had turned liquid and chaotic. Beyond the reinforced walls, Milton's distant bands clawed at the Gulf Coast, but here in sterile purgatory, time stretched like wire drawn too tight, ready to snap.

A wall clock read 2:03 a.m. An hour earlier, Jessica had come through wound care—sedated, bandaged, and wheeled into a pediatric room where Andrea kept vigil. Nick had stepped out, claiming he needed coffee but really to escape the monitors' steady beeps.

Wind knifed through the building's seams, slipping through microscopic gaps in the hospital's defenses. The fluorescent lights flickered then steadied. In that flicker of dark, the ambush replayed:

WITNESS ELIMINATION

headlights blooming in the mirror, the black sedan easing alongside, the passenger window lowering into shadow. The crack of the first shot. Glass bursting. Jessica's scream ripping through it all.

His fingers tightened around the bat's handle. The Louisville Slugger had been his companion since Andrea's "accident" on the Gandy Bridge—a compromise when the Glock seemed foreign in his hand. It had put Hinkins on the floor with a single swing. But now, with traces of his daughter's blood still beneath his nails, the bat seemed useless—wood against bullets.

"That's the lawyer from the commercials." The whispered fragment floated down the corridor as two night-shift nurses passed, their rubber soles squeaking in rhythm. "His family has been in the news non-stop." They glanced at Nick, cutting off the moment they saw him.

He glared at the older nurse. She flinched but didn't look away. "Vitals are stable," she said, sliding into professional calm. "Dr. Lynn says she's responding well."

He only nodded. The nurses moved on, whispers resuming once they thought him out of earshot. He didn't need the rest. They all knew his family had been targeted. These wounds weren't random. They were messages.

Another gust rattled the windows, the frames groaning against the pressure outside. Tampa General was built to withstand hurricanes, its reinforced structure a monument to Florida's endless war with storms.

On a wall-mounted television, the overnight meteorologist projected Milton's path. His voice was calm, detached, as if describing a detour instead of an approaching cataclysm. "Hurricane Milton is maintaining Category 5 strength with sustained winds of 165 miles per hour. Current models show landfall Wednesday evening, October 9th, twenty-four hours from now."

The meteorologist's finger traced the projected path across Tampa Bay. "Mandatory evacuations remain in effect for all coastal zones. This could be the most dangerous storm to strike the region in a century. Unlike Helene, this will be a wind event."

Nick's eyes slid from the television to the dark windows. Beyond the glass, gust-driven haze already blurred Tampa's skyline, the city lights smudged to faint glows. The evacuation order meant nothing. Jessica couldn't be moved, so neither would they. They would face the hurricane as they had every other—together, backs to the wall, daring it to break them.

His phone vibrated in his pocket, jolting him like a live wire. Since the ambush, every sound set his nerves on edge. He pulled the phone free with deliberate calm, half-expecting another message from the faceless sender who had baited them into the trap.

The screen glowed blue in the dim corridor. Unknown number.

Finish what Hank started.

Nick's breath hitched. The air in the corridor seemed to thin, sucking the oxygen from his lungs. Officer Hank Kitchens had gone into witness protection after testifying against the Bruth'rs. His undercover work had gutted their network, but one snake slipped away—Carl.

The connection hit him hard. The Bruth'rs had rebuilt under cartel guidance. Tonight's attack wasn't random. It was payback for Hank's work—and for Nick's. But why go after Jessica? Why not him? Why not Andrea?

Unless the goal wasn't revenge but retribution.

He gripped the bat until his knuckles blanched. The wood thrummed with his rage, an extension of him waiting for release. The message could be another trap, but almost no one knew Hank's work, and fewer knew what "finishing" it meant.

A nurse stepped out of Jessica's room, her face drawn with fatigue. "Mr. Justin? Your wife is asking for you."

Nick rose, the bat in his grip like a natural part of him. The nurse's eyes flicked to it, then back to his face, a question forming but left unsaid. The staff had already made exceptions for his family—the bat, the law enforcement posted outside Jessica's door. They understood, even if they couldn't admit it.

"Tell her I'll be right there."

As the nurse retreated, Nick turned to the rattling windows. Wind swept across Tampa Bay, a reminder of nature's indifference to human suffering. But unlike the storm, the threat to his family wasn't random. It was human, deliberate, and stoppable.

WITNESS ELIMINATION

His phone weighed heavy in his pocket, the message seared into his mind. *Finish what Hank started.* It was a way forward.

He would find them—Sarah, Hinkins, the shooters, the ones pulling their strings.

No one would stop him. He pushed off the wall, his shadow stretching long and jagged across the linoleum, a dark promise cast before him.

27

SARAH TIGHTENS THE NET

October 8, 2024, 6:00 a.m.

The stocky cartel man sat slumped in a battered metal chair, scarred hands trembling, a dark stain spreading across his shirt. He was one of two who'd crawled out of the wreck. The third died when the sedan rolled. Survival hadn't spared the others from Sarah's disappointment. His eyes flicked up as she circled him. Her boots made no sound. She adjusted her cuff, aligning the fabric perfectly. Order amidst chaos.

She studied him for a long, level moment. He wouldn't meet her gaze, fixating on the table's surface where her fingers drummed an arrhythmic pattern.

"Explain." Her tone was calm, almost patient. "The plan was simple. You had one job. Watch. Wait. Remove the obstacle. Instead, he's alive and protected at a hospital with his family."

He swallowed, eyes flicking up, then away. "They spotted us."

Sarah glared. "The lawyer and the housewife made you?" She leaned closer to show the cold edge in her hazel eyes. Her nose wrinkled. The smell of him—old sweat and fresh fear—clotted the air. It disgusted her. "We don't tolerate failure. You had one task. Hit the target. Make it clean. Disappear."

His lips moved, scrambling for an excuse. "It spun out of control. I tried—"

"You tried." The echo dripped with poison. She straightened, letting silence cinch tight around him. "Was it fear? Or do you lack the stomach for it?"

He shook his head, jaw clenched, blood drying at his collar. "I did what I could. If Hinkins had—"

Hinkins should have handled this. Sally wouldn't have missed, wouldn't have left witnesses, and wouldn't have failed. Sarah's fist clenched at her side, nails biting into her palm until the sharp sting grounded her.

She let him squirm. "You know what happens when mistakes are made." She dragged a chair across the floor, sat opposite him, elbows resting on her knees. "Tell me, if you had another chance, would you get it right?"

He nodded fast.

Sarah smiled, cold as glass. "You won't get another opportunity."

She rose, crossed to the battered cabinet, and drew a slim blade from its drawer. She tested the weight, the balance familiar and comforting. She knelt beside him, the metal glinting under the light.

"I want you to deliver a message," she whispered. "Failure is not an option. Not for you. Not for anyone. Next time, I expect results."

She pressed the edge enough to score his jaw, a sharp line of blood welling instantly. His entire body went rigid.

"Leave." She rose. "And if you speak of this, if you breathe my name with mercy, I'll finish what you started on that bridge."

He staggered to his feet, clutching his side, eyes wide with terror. Sarah watched him go, the weight of her disappointment settling over the room.

When she was alone, she let her fury simmer for a moment, a silent, burning wish that Sally Hinkins had been the one in that car. Next time, she would make sure.

~

WITNESS ELIMINATION

Sally perched on the windowsill of her safe house bedroom, combat knife balanced across her thighs. Outside, a waterlogged mattress slumped beside a telephone pole, its surface stained the color of weak tea. The whetstone sat cold in her palm as she drew it along the blade. The rasp of metal on stone was a steady, rhythmic hiss.

Scrape. Pause. Turn. Scrape.

The routine anchored her as the world threatened to spiral beyond control. Her muscles remained coiled tight, tension locked inside like a spring wound to breaking. She squeezed her eyes shut, but the image burned: the body crumpled in the corner where Sarah had dumped it, the silence that followed the violence, Sarah's flat voice delivering the verdict on loyalty.

Sarah hadn't known Sally was watching and had not seen the stiffening in her shoulders when the blade bit. But the message had landed clear. Loyalty required demonstration. Sarah had shown exactly what happened to those who failed her test.

The knife's edge caught the dim light filtering through the rain-streaked window, flashing in a thin, perfect line. Sally tested it against her thumb, the steel biting calloused skin. Not sharp enough yet. Nothing in her life had seemed sharp enough lately. Not her instincts, not her resolve, not her place in Sarah's operation.

"Loyalty requires demonstration," she whispered, mimicking Sarah's cultured tone.

Two weeks since their escape during Hurricane Helene. Two weeks of watching Sarah rebuild. The balance had shifted. What had once been a partnership was twisted, manipulative, but still shared. Now she had become just another asset, another soldier in Sarah's private army.

Water dripped from a corner of the ceiling, the steady patter a counterpoint to her whetstone's rhythm. The safe house, formerly a cartel stash, had weathered Helene poorly. Milton would likely finish what the first storm had started.

Sally's burned forearms flexed as she adjusted her grip on the knife, scars stretching taut across her skin. The humidity made the old wounds itch, a phantom heat rising from the tissue. Each mark was survival etched in flesh. She hadn't lasted this long by ignoring shifting loyalties.

"One day, Sarah," she whispered. "One day."

Wind rattled the window frame, Milton's early bands clawing at the city. Forecasts called it catastrophic. This was the perfect cover for whatever Sarah planned next.

She squeezed her eyes shut, picturing Jessica Justin's lioness plush soaked in blood as paramedics rushed the girl into Tampa General. She'd seen it clutched tight, the glass eyes catching the emergency lights, flashing like beacons straight at her as she watched from the stolen ambulance in the parking lot. The girl was a pawn, Sarah's pawn, as were Sally, the lieutenant, and the man bleeding out somewhere in the dark.

A pulse throbbed at her wrist—a rhythmic reminder of borrowed time. How long until Sarah's gaze, that calculating assessment that missed nothing, turned on her? How long until some perceived disloyalty marked Sally for demonstration purposes?

The same instincts that had kept her alive through South American operations, through the corruption of the RADD Squad, through Sarah's manipulations, now hummed with warning. The scales had tipped. Sarah was no longer the calculated risk Sally had chosen to follow out of prison. She had become something else, untethered from consequence and treating people as expendable pieces in a game only she understood.

Outside, a gust sent a palm tree swaying, its fronds whipping in the wind. The glass panes rattled in their frames as Milton's early bands pushed ashore. What had been distant lines on a meteorologist's map, colored swirls on radar, was turning tangible. Inevitable.

Sally left the knife standing in the sill, a monument to unspoken rebellion. She crossed to the small table where her Glock was disassembled, its parts arranged in precise order on a cleaning cloth. The weapon embodied what she had become: authority corrupted, protection twisted into threat.

Her hands worked from memory, reassembling the pistol with practiced efficiency. Each piece clicked into place, the action requiring no conscious thought. Unlike her relationship with Sarah, where each word, each touch, each moment now demanded calculation.

Sheets of water hammered the window. Through the warped glass, the street below broke into shifting shapes and shadows, as if the city itself were coming apart under Milton's reach.

WITNESS ELIMINATION

Sally checked the Glock's action, the slide smooth under her hand. The weight was right. Balanced. Reliable in a way people never were.

The floor creaked outside her door. Sally's muscles tensed, her body still as boots approached. Heavy, deliberate. Not Sarah's precise clicks. A cartel soldier then.

"Hinkins." The voice was male, accented. "Meeting in ten. Command center."

"Copy that," she answered, tone flat, revealing nothing of her thoughts.

The boots retreated. Sally holstered the Glock on her hip and crossed back to the window. She pulled the knife free in a single smooth motion. The wood held the scar of its blade, a mark that would outlast her.

Like the one she meant to leave on Sarah when the time came.

28

THE GHOST IN THE MACHINE

Tuesday, October 8, 2024, 11:30 a.m.

The steady beep of the heart monitor kept time like a metronome, each pulse a reminder that Jessica was alive. Nick watched the jagged green line and her pale face on the starched pillow. Thick gauze wrapped the spot where the bullet had grazed, the bandage climbing over shallow cuts from flying glass. Twelve hours had passed, and the spray of crimson still haunted him. She clutched her lioness plush even in drugged sleep, fingers locked around it with the desperate strength of a child holding an anchor.

The October light slanted through half-closed blinds, casting bars across the sterile tiles. Beyond the glass, Tampa was under a deceptively gentle blue sky—the hush before disaster. In the corner, a television played silently, a meteorologist in suspenders pointing at swirling red and yellow graphics of Milton's projected path. The second major system in less than a month pressed toward a region still bleeding from Helene.

"I updated Judge Armwell and Agent Holcomb about the shooting," Nick said, turning from the window. "They're dispatching a detail, but the storm has resources stretched thin. It might be a while until they get a guard on the door."

His eyes met Andrea's. "Let me handle this. Florida's a stand-your-ground state. We did nothing wrong."

Andrea nodded once.

"They'll want the gun for ballistics."

"I told Holcomb it's secured and ready for them when they arrive," Nick added.

"Fine," she said. "José gave me spares. They can have this one."

Nick swallowed, the casualness of the reply hitting him harder than the ambush. Multiple guns. He had to protect their friend. His voice dropped to a fierce whisper. "Let's keep José out of it."

"Understood."

Andrea sat rigid in the vinyl chair, her purse at her side, one hand hidden inside its opening. The pistol never left her grip. She pressed her hand to her thigh to steady a twitch. It came less often now. Each flare was a weakness she fought to master, masking the slip with focus, eyes locked on the bag, mind rehearsing the motions of field-stripping the weapon. Not yet reflex but close, built through repetition and stubborn will.

Nick studied her, the new lines at the corners of her eyes, the set of her jaw. In the twelve days since Helene, she had hardened. The woman who once hesitated over taking ibuprofen during pregnancy now treated a nine-millimeter as standard equipment.

Jessica stirred, a small whimper slipping out. Both parents froze, watching her face tighten, then smooth back into restless dreams.

"Doctor said the sedatives should wear off by tonight," Andrea murmured, tightening her hold on the concealed weapon. "She'll have questions."

"What do we tell her?" Nick rubbed his palms against his jeans, rough with the residue of three sleepless days. "How do we explain this?"

Andrea's knuckles stilled on the leather. "We tell her the truth. Bad people tried to hurt us, and we're going to stop them." When she lifted her gaze, a hard glint carried the words. "No more lies, Nick. No more pretending we can shield her."

The monitor's rhythm jumped, then steadied. Nick leaned forward, brushing a strand of hair from Jessica's forehead. A few inches one way and they would be planning a funeral.

His phone buzzed, shattering the stillness. José's name lit the screen. Nick moved to the window and answered.

"Tell me you have something," he whispered.

"The encryption's cracking," José said. "Shandra's file, fragments are coming through. Redacted memos, partial audio, and location tags. But I need you here. One wrong choice and we lose it. Power's still unstable."

"I don't have a car, I parked the SUV in the garage, it's evidence."

"I'm way ahead of you. Cindi should be there soon. Take her truck, and she'll sit with Andrea," José said.

Nick looked at Jessica, then Andrea.

"Go," Andrea said, reading his face. Her free hand found his. "This doesn't end here. Not until they're finished."

He crouched beside her, voice quiet. "I shouldn't leave you."

"We need leverage. Whatever Shandra uncovered could be it." Her eyes shifted to Jessica. "Go find it. Then we make them pay. Don't worry about the police or FBI. I won't say anything without counsel."

He rose, pulling his jacket from the chair. "Call me if she wakes. I'll be back as soon as I can." Andrea nodded, her focus already returned to their daughter, one hand resting on the pistol hidden in her lap.

At the door, Nick paused. Three months ago, they had been planning kitchen renovations and the new school year. Now they were soldiers in a war they had never chosen.

His phone buzzed again, no sender ID.

Found her yet? The wind will cover her tracks. Don't trust what you hear.

Nick's grip tightened. The texter was always too accurate, always a step ahead. He wanted to believe it was Carl, to give the ghost a name. But the truth gnawed at him. Until the source slipped, they were chasing shadows.

He slid the cell back into his pocket without replying and stepped into the hall, leaving Andrea and Jessica behind the door.

～

The metal roof of the garage rattled with each gust, a reminder that the storm was drawing closer. Nick killed the truck's engine and sat for a moment. Dust and leaves skittered over the windshield, the world outside rippling in the shifting light. José had chosen an abandoned repair shop five miles northwest of downtown St. Petersburg, isolated from neighboring buildings, its hurricane-damaged sign hanging by a single bolt, squealing in the wind. The perfect place to hide from the law and from those operating beyond it.

He shoved the door open, the gale snapping it back before he forced it shut. The side entrance yielded to his key. José changed locks at every temporary base. Inside, the air reeked of motor oil and mildew.

"José?" The name echoed against concrete walls scrawled with faded graffiti.

"Back here."

Nick followed the sound through a maze of tool cabinets and rusted car parts to what had once been an office. Now it served as José's command center: a tangle of blinking monitors casting harsh light across the room. The former boxer turned fraud specialist hunched over a keyboard, his silhouette etched by scrolling code. Three laptops formed a tight semicircle, each displaying fragments of data. Cables sprawled over the floor to a pair of generators in the corner, their exhaust vented through a rough cut in the wall.

José didn't look up. The screens' blue-white glow shone onto his tired face. Four days of stubble shadowed his jaw. An abandoned protein bar and a scatter of empty energy drink cans marked his vigil.

"You look like hell," Nick said.

José's fingers never paused on the keys. "Pot, kettle."

Nick pulled out his phone and tried Shandra's number again. Straight to voicemail, as it had for the past seventy-two hours. Her recorded greeting instructed him to leave a message. He ended the call without speaking.

"Still nothing?" José asked.

"Nothing." Nick pocketed the device. "What have you got?"

José tapped the center screen where progress bars crawled across the display. "Encrypted email hit my burner at 11:59 p.m., triple encrypted, military-grade. It carries a private header only a few hands would know, and Shandra didn't invent that segment."

Nick leaned closer. "Someone helped her."

"This is the level I flagged back at the marina," José added. "The fragment Shandra buried deeper than the rest."

"Or she found it and copied it." José dragged a hand down his face. "Either way, it was a dead man's switch. If she missed a twelve-hour check-in, the files sent automatically. I broke a section of it yesterday. That's what we went through before. But there's a core layer here. What's cracking now is the heart of it."

The implications settled in Nick's gut like lead. "She knew she was in danger."

"After what happened to her son and your daughter? We're all in danger." José's tone carried no accusation, only fact. "I've been running decryption since it hit. First layer broke yesterday. Second cracked an hour ago. The last one's running now."

Nick edged closer to the screen. "How much longer?"

"Minutes, maybe. Power surges keep forcing restarts." José nodded at the generators. "We've got six hours of fuel left. After that, we're on borrowed time."

Nick paced the narrow space, each second grinding against him. Andrea and Jessica were exposed at the hospital. Shandra was gone, almost certainly dead. And Milton edged closer with every hour, the whole city bracing for impact.

"There." José's voice cut through Nick's thoughts. "We're in."

The progress bar blinked *complete*. Files spilled across the screen—dozens, organized by date. José clicked the most recent, stamped two days before Shandra vanished.

"Damn," he muttered.

The document bore Coast Guard letterhead, CLASSIFIED across the header. It detailed the redeployment of assets from St. Petersburg to the Florida Keys, effective September 28 through November 30. Not weather evacuations; these were strategic repositioning. At the bottom, Senator Maxwell's signature authorized the move through Homeland Security.

"This is classified material," Nick said, his voice low. "Possession is a federal crime, José. Step away from the console. If they kick down the door, I'll take the weight."

The investigator didn't flinch. He just offered a sharp, humorless grin. "A bit late for that. My fingerprints are digital, and they're all over this. Besides, I'm not letting you go down alone."

Nick exhaled, accepting the loyalty he couldn't afford to reject. "Then we need to lock this down. Cold storage. Somewhere Maxwell's reach can't wipe it until we find a badge we can actually trust."

"Way ahead of you," José said. "Mirroring to three offshore servers as we speak. But look at the geography."

"The Coast Guard base is less than a mile from Bayboro Marina," Nick said, the pieces slotting together. "They emptied it two days before Helene hit."

"Prior to landfall, they were gone," José added. "The order runs through November. They couldn't have known Milton was coming, but it made their job easier. No patrols, no eyes on the water, and a wide-open port a mile away."

José pulled up an aerial map, docks marked in red. "These are the slips they cleared. Look familiar?"

Nick leaned in. "Private berths. High-security access only."

"Perfect for unloading cargo unseen." José flipped through more files: shipping manifests, shell companies, bank transfers routing through Panama and Venezuela. "Shandra wasn't bluffing. She found the pipeline and the money."

He paused, scrolling to the bottom of the folder. A single audio file sat apart, time-stamped 11:59 p.m. the night she disappeared. José double-clicked.

The speakers hissed, then Shandra's voice filled the room, steady despite the edge of fear beneath it.

"Nick, if you're hearing this, it means I didn't make it out. The conspiracy runs higher than we thought. Maxwell isn't simply shielding the marina. He's coordinating with the cartel. The shipments during Helene were only a test. The real payload arrives within the week, military-grade weapons diverted from federal stockpiles and funneled through Bayboro's private slips. Follow the money. Don't trust official channels. They're compromised."

The audio ended with a click, as if she'd cut it herself. No struggle. No death rattle. It was her final act of defiance, preserved in the machine.

Nick gripped the edge of the desk, knuckles white. Her words still echoed in the room—calm, deliberate, terrified beneath the control. She had known she might not walk out of that file room. She had left him this breadcrumb and then gone dark.

"Play it again." Nick's voice was hard.

José complied, isolating the final seconds. No struggle. No gunfire. She cut off by her own choice, as if she'd decided to leave the rest unsaid.

"They caught her afterward," José said. "She knew the walls were closing in even as she recorded it."

Nick's cell vibrated in his pocket. He pulled it out, already knowing what he would find. Another anonymous text.

She should have trusted the wind's cover, not her own secrets. Find her body.

These weren't warnings—they were taunts. Whoever sent them had been there when Shandra died, close enough to hear her last breath.

Before he could stash the phone, another message appeared from a different number.

Sergeant Quincy Adams wrote:

Have you heard from Hank?

Nick typed back:

No. Why?

The reply came, blunt.

He slipped his detail. Gone dark.

Nick stared at the screen, unease threaded into the storm already rising. If Hank Kitchens was out there chasing leads, he was a walking target.

"José." Nick held out the cell. "The texts started right before the prison transfer."

José read the messages, his expression hardening. "They're playing with us." He paused. "Hank's not the type to sit still."

"No." Nick took the device back, staring at it. "They're hunting us. Using the coming storm as cover, like they used Helene."

Wind gusted through the rafters, rattling the corrugated siding. One generator sputtered before catching again.

"We need to recover her body," Nick said, the words tasting of ash. "Not for evidence. For justice."

"With Milton tracking closer? The evacuation orders are already going out." José gestured at the radar on one of the monitors. "We've got maybe eighteen hours before this place is gone."

"Then we must move fast."

Nick's phone vibrated. Andrea's voice came through, low but steady.

"Tampa detective stopped by. She wanted a statement."

"What did you tell her?"

"That I'll wait until counsel arrives. I won't say anything without you."

"Good," Nick said. "José will meet me there. I'm heading back now."

PART 3:
HURRICANE MILTON AND THE FINAL

SHOWDOWN

29

JESSICA'S AWAKENING

Jessica surfaced through layers of fog, each breath pulling her closer to wakefulness. The medicinal sting of the room hit her before she opened her eyes. It tasted metallic, like a penny held under her tongue. The heart monitor counted her existence in steady beeps. A blanket pressed on her chest, and an IV tugged at her arm. In her left hand was the lioness, still with her.

Her eyelids fluttered open to stark white walls and the silhouettes of her parents: her mother rigid by the bed, her father a dark outline in front of the storm-pressed pane.

Pain came next, a hot throb in her right shoulder, beating with her heart. Jessica blinked her vision clear. Outside, gray clouds bruised the sky, heavy on the glass. But it was her mother who commanded her attention.

Andrea sat straight in the hospital chair, the vinyl squeaking beneath her posture. Her purse rested on the small table next to her, the zipper drawn closed but not secure. She focused her eyes on Jessica, mind already rehearsing the questions she knew would come. She smoothed the sheet over her daughter's legs, pleating the fabric between her fingers to keep them from trembling.

Nick stood at the window, shoulders hunched under an unseen weight. The Louisville Slugger leaned beside the wall within reach. At the sound of Jessica's blankets rustling, he turned, his brown eyes meeting hers.

"Hey, sweetheart." His voice was roughened by worry but gentle all the same. "How are you feeling?"

The question felt enormous, beyond anything Jessica could answer. She looked down at the thick white bandages wrapping her arm from shoulder to elbow, like a strange cocoon. The memory jolted back, the shattering glass, the sting, the sudden pain.

"Are the bad people gone?" she asked, frightened, yet direct in the way only children manage.

Andrea's hands stilled, the towel twisting once in her fingers. Her gaze moved from Jessica to Nick, a silent current the girl felt more than understood.

"Not yet." Andrea drew a slow breath, reminding herself that the detectives would return soon and every word would matter. "But they will be."

Jessica nodded, accepting the answer with a solemn wisdom beyond her years. She looked down at the lioness in her hand. Its golden fur had been washed, Andrea's careful work, though faint red stains still shadowed the right arm, a reminder of the wound she carried herself.

"She got hurt too," she whispered, holding her stuffed animal up for inspection. Her fingers traced the stiffened spot where the crimson didn't wash out.

Her mother leaned toward Jessica, every bit of attention anchored on her daughter. She touched the stained fur lightly. "Yes, she did. She was protecting you."

"Zara was keeping watch," Jessica said, propping the lioness upright by her side. "She's still on guard."

Andrea's face shifted, hardening around the eyes, resolve setting in. She nodded once. These were not the hands that tucked notes into lunch boxes or braided hair. They smelled faintly of sanitizer now, not cookie dough. Her jaw had set in a way Jessica had not seen before last year.

"I will make them pay," Andrea promised.

Nick left the window and stood behind her, resting a hand on her shoulder. His face had hardened too, unflinching. The parents Jessica had known prior to the bridge were still there, but their naïveté had been scorched away.

Jessica nodded. She shifted the lioness so its eyes stayed fixed on the door.

"Like the storm," Jessica said, nodding to the glass where raindrops spattered the surface. Milton's edge had reached the coast. "It changes everything when it passes through."

Andrea's hazel eyes widened at her daughter's quiet wisdom. She smoothed Jessica's hair from her forehead.

"Yes." Andrea met her gaze with steady intensity. "Like the storm."

Nick moved to Jessica's other side, easing around her bed. The heart monitor beeped, oxygen hissed, thunder rolled closer, an uneasy symphony of danger and safety. Jessica pressed Zara to her cheek, the washed fabric faintly stiff where the stains had never fully lifted regardless of her mother's scrubbing.

"Will we be protected here?" she asked, her voice small against the rumble outside.

Nick squeezed Jessica's uninjured hand, forcing a smile meant to steady her regardless of the ache in his chest. "Aunt Cindi's right here, and an FBI agent's in the hall. José will be here soon. You're secure, sweetheart."

He brushed a stray lock from her forehead, his thumb gentle. "Family sticks together. I'll be close. You're never alone, not for a second."

Jessica clutched the lioness tighter, her fingers wrapping around its worn foot. She nodded, a silent pact of trust passing between them.

She kept the lioness upright once more, its glass eyes fixed outward, a silent sentry where hers had drifted. "She'll keep watch," Jessica whispered, eyelids already growing heavy.

Her mother observed the window. The lioness observed the door.

For a moment, the room was still. Jessica's breathing settled into the steady rhythm of the monitor, her slender fingers curled around the lioness's paw.

Then came a knock.

Nick turned first. Through the glass panel, he caught a glimpse of dark suits, badges clipped to belts, and the muted reflection of blue hospital scrubs moving past behind them.

Andrea straightened in her chair, her hand brushing the purse at her side before falling still.

The door opened a fraction.

"Mrs. Justin? Detective Leone, Tampa PD." The woman's voice was gruff. A second figure stepped into view. "Special Agent Burkett, FBI. We heard Mr. Justin was back."

Nick moved closer to the door, keeping himself between the agents and his family, his shoulders squared to block their view of the bed.

Burkett nodded toward the clipboard in his hand. "We'd like to get a brief statement about the shooting, if you're up to it."

Andrea's gaze flicked to Nick. He gave a small nod. The approaching storm rumbled in the distance.

~

Nick followed Detective Leone and Special Agent Burkett into the private waiting area outside the recovery wing. Andrea walked beside him, composed, alert. A few empty chairs lined the wall, their plastic backs dull with wear.

Burkett opened his notepad. "Thank you both for coming out. We need a brief statement for the record."

Nick kept his tone even. "We'll cooperate through counsel. Let's keep it short."

Leone nodded. "That's fine. Tell us what happened."

Nick spoke carefully. "We were ambushed while approaching the eastbound span of the Gandy Bridge during the storm evacuation. One sedan pulled across our lane without warning. There were at least three hostiles inside: a driver, a front passenger, and another in the rear driver's-side seat. They opened fire. Andrea engaged to protect herself and our daughter. Her round shattered their windshield, and the vehicle impacted the guardrail. Someone in the back shot again, and that round caught Jessica. We do not know the status of anyone in that wreck. I called 911 and rushed us to Tampa General Hospital."

Burkett looked up from his notes. "Your wife discharged the handgun, correct?"

"Yes."

"We'll need to take that weapon for ballistics."

Andrea set her purse on the table and opened it. The pistol was wrapped in a folded towel. She placed it between them. The towel muffled the steel, the weight settling on the laminate. "Unloaded."

Leone gestured to the uniformed officer behind her. The officer verified the chamber was empty then sealed the firearm in an evidence bag and logged the chain of custody.

Nick reached into his pocket. The plastic felt greasy with sweat. He slid the Audi's key fob across the table, settling it beside the bagged weapon.

"You'll need to process our vehicle as well. I moved it to the parking garage. Third floor, spot 357. The rear window is blown out, and there are likely shell casings in the cabin."

Leone nodded to the officer, who bagged the keys.

Burkett reviewed the paperwork. "Is this firearm registered under either of your names?"

Nick met his eyes. "Florida law doesn't require registration. It was lawful self-defense. Stand Your Ground applies here."

Burkett paused his writing. "Do you have any idea who might have targeted you?"

Nick's voice stayed steady. "Ask Judge Armwell and Agent Holcomb. They're familiar with the task force tied to all this. My family has been a target since before we helped bring down the largest fentanyl ring in Florida. Look at the prison-bus escape involving Sarah Brown, my wife's sister. If you want suspects, start there. Or check the Venezuelan cartel. Or the RADD Squad if you're ready to confront corruption in your own ranks."

Leone's expression tightened, a vein pulsing at her temple. "Those are serious accusations."

Nick didn't flinch. "They're not accusations. They're facts. It's been on every news channel for two months."

Burkett closed his notebook. "Are you declining to provide further detail?"

"I'm refusing to speculate. I provided you with potential leads. Any other questions will need to go through counsel. Unless you're charging us, we're finished here."

Burkett regarded him for a moment then nodded once. "We'll be in touch."

Leone gathered her papers, slid a card across the table, and rose. "For when you're ready to talk again."

Nick picked it up, testing the sharp corner against his thumb. "We'll be represented."

The two officials collected their materials and left.

Andrea released a slow breath. "They'll be back."

Nick folded the card and slipped it into his jacket. "Let them. Next time, they can bring a warrant." He watched the detectives turn the corner, the evidence bag in hand. The pistol was gone, but the larger fight had only begun.

Nick waited until the hallway was clear before opening the door. José and Cindi were in Jessica's room, their faces drawn from the same sleepless strain that gripped him.

Cindi rose first, a gentle hand touching his arm. Her fingers were warm, a stark contrast to the chill seeping from the walls.

"Everything all right?" José asked.

"The agents took a statement," Nick answered. "And the gun."

José's jaw flexed. "There's a lounge down the hall. Let's talk there."

Nick nodded and turned back toward the recovery wing. Andrea joined him, steady but pale. Together they walked the short stretch in silence, each step carrying them farther from interrogation and closer to what came next.

WITNESS ELIMINATION

~

The lounge was like a temporary shelter, a neutral zone between battles. Overhead lights hummed, casting the room in a sickly pallor that made the living look half-dead. Cindi guided Jessica's wheelchair through the doorway, the IV pole rattling beside them like an unreliable companion. In the corner, the television commanded attention, its volume low but the weatherman's expression making words unnecessary.

"Hurricane Milton has reached Category 5 strength with sustained winds of 165 miles per hour." The meteorologist's suspenders strained as he gestured toward the swirling radar. His voice carried the forced calm of a man delivering a death sentence. "Some weakening may occur before impact, but residents of Tampa Bay should prepare for a catastrophic event within twenty-four hours."

José shifted, his boxer's frame cramped in the molded plastic chair. His eyes flicked between the screen and Nick, searching for what only he noticed. Cindi steadied him with a hand on his knee, her wedding ring a brief spark of gold in a room of beige and gray.

"The exact path remains uncertain." The weatherman's finger traced lines along the coastline. "But each model shows Tampa Bay taking a direct or near-direct hit."

The window rattled as a gust pressed into the glass, proof that Milton was approaching. All heads turned except Jessica's. She stayed fixed on the swirling graphics, her fingers working the lioness's patched fur. Its faintly stained arm rested on her bandaged one, wounds reflected in fabric and flesh.

Nick met Andrea's gaze across the room. Milton advanced. Emergency crews would be overwhelmed, power grids would go down, and roads would be cut off. For most of Tampa Bay, disaster. For them, cover. The same darkness their enemies would use to hunt them could be turned to their advantage—nature's fury creating a lawless window where rules no longer applied.

Andrea's mouth tightened. Message received.

José cleared his throat. "I've secured a safe house in Ybor City. Generator's ready. Supplies in place. We move once Jessica's stable."

On-screen, the view shifted to street level, where evacuations continued. Cars crawled along highways, police waving them through clogged intersections. "Mandatory orders are in effect for Zones A and B in Pinellas and Hillsborough. Zones C and D are voluntary for now, but that could change within hours. Unlike Helene, which flooded us, this one's a wind event. Stay away from windows and hunker down."

Jessica's eyes never left the screen. "The eye," she blurted, small but clear. "That's where it's calm."

The room quieted, watching a child who grasped both the meteorological truth and its deeper weight. The hurricane's center— destruction circling a pocket of stillness. Nick set a hand on her uninjured shoulder.

"That's right, sweetheart. But we have to get through the eyewall first."

Cindi leaned forward, checking Jessica's pallor and IV line. "The facility transferred non-critical patients. What's the doctor saying about Jessica?"

"They want to keep her through the storm." Andrea's tone left no doubt she found this unacceptable. "Monitoring for infection, shock, and blood work."

The unspoken understanding hung between them. This meant riding out Milton in a concrete fortress right on the bay, trusting protocols and generators untested by a hurricane this size.

"You hide from flooding and hunker from wind." Cindi scratched the stuffed animal gently. "This one's all wind. This building will hold. Jess, Zara, and I will be fine." She took Jessica's hand.

José's phone vibrated on the table. He checked it, expression darkening. "My port authority contact confirmed that all Coast Guard assets have been 'repositioned for preparedness.' Sound familiar?"

Nick's jaw tightened. The same language they'd heard before Helene when Maxwell cleared the way for cartel shipments.

"They're using the weather." Nick's voice was clear. "Again."

WITNESS ELIMINATION

He looked to Andrea. "We're going back to the house. It keeps us within striking distance. If we don't cross the bridge now, the evacuation cordon will lock us out."

Jessica shifted in her wheelchair, wincing as the bandage tugged at her skin. She set the lioness on her lap, its gaze steady.

The windows rattled under a stray gust, a reminder that Milton's reach was already brushing the coast. Landfall was still many hours away, but the outer bands advanced.

Andrea stepped beside Nick, their shoulders touching. Her hand found his, fingers locking with quiet resolve. Her gaze lingered on Jessica then moved to Cindi. The handoff was agreed to. Their daughter would be safe here.

Beyond the window, a scatter of raindrops peppered the glass, not the storm itself but the whisper of its approach. Each impact counted down what remained.

José met Nick's eyes. A quiet question. A quiet nod. Andrea added her own, her voice steady. "Then let's finish this."

"It's time to go hunting."

They would find their enemies in the storm's eye.

30

PRESSURE MOUNTS

October 9, 2024, 10:00 a.m.

Senator Maxwell gripped the podium with the manicured hands of a man who had never known labor, his pressed jeans and rolled-up sleeves a carefully staged costume of emergency leadership. Cameras caught his expression of concern from every angle, broadcasting to Floridians huddled in darkened living rooms, listening for hope in the storm.

Nick watched from his own home, the screen's flicker leaving shadows across the walls as Milton's outer bands tested the structure in probing gusts. Andrea sat at the far end of the couch, one leg tucked beneath her, eyes sharp as glass. Her jaw worked in rhythm with Nick's, anger simmering under her reserve.

"Government resources have been pre-positioned throughout Tampa Bay." Maxwell leaned into the microphone. "FEMA teams and utility crews are staged at Tropicana Field, Tampa International Airport, and Raymond James Stadium, ready to deploy as soon as conditions allow."

The camera panned over the press corps, their rain-damp suits and skeptical faces exposing the gap between Maxwell's polish and the weather outside. Nick recognized several reporters he'd dealt with before—good journalists who knew theater when they saw it.

"This unprecedented federal response," Maxwell continued, "represents the culmination of my office's efforts to ensure Florida's safety."

Nick's neck tensed. Andrea's hand found his, anchoring him. The window frames ticked as another gust pressed the glass. José sat beside them.

"Under my watch," Maxwell's chest swelled, "we've allocated resources that will enable first responders to reach communities faster than ever before."

Andrea's lips twisted. "All he's ever led is a parade … in his own honor."

"Leadership?" Nick turned from the screen. "He chaired nothing but witch hunts."

"Watch," José murmured. "He's building up to something."

As if on cue, Maxwell's face shifted into the "solemn duty" mask Nick remembered from dismantling the task force.

"I'm announcing today that my office has secured a key cooperating witness with vital intelligence on recent criminal activity. Former Officer Gino Myers has agreed to provide federal authorities with testimony on the prison bus attack and the assassination of Senator Caldwell."

Nick's blood turned to ice water. Myers—the man who flipped Andrea's SUV on the Gandy, planted evidence, fabricated charges—was now being paraded as credible.

Andrea's voice dropped to a growl. "Of course. There's always room for a cop with dirty hands if he tells their story."

"Because of the sensitive nature of Officer Myers's statement and ongoing threats to his safety, he has been placed in federal witness protection," Maxwell continued.

Nick's fist slammed the coffee table. A glass jumped, spilling across Jessica's school photo. "Son of a bitch."

Andrea snatched a towel, blotting quickly, eyes locked on the screen. "Let it go, Nick. Don't give him the satisfaction."

"They're cleaning house. Covering their tracks."

A reporter shouted over the wind, "Senator Maxwell, are you saying the Justice Department has granted immunity to an officer charged with multiple felonies, including attempted murder?"

Maxwell's smile never wavered. "Officer Myers has provided information so critical that certain accommodations were necessary. Today, we've taken a significant step forward."

Nick shot to his feet, pacing like a caged animal. "Myers walks while Jessica lies in a hospital bed, while Andrea carries scars he gave her, and Shandra's body is missing."

Andrea scowled. "All it took was the right enemy, the right crisis. That's justice now."

"This was always their endgame," José said. "Discredit witnesses, eliminate evidence, control the narrative."

Nick's phone buzzed. Sergeant Quincy Adams.

He stepped into the kitchen and answered in a whisper, "Adams."

"You heard from Hank?" Static rode the sergeant's tone but not uncertainty.

"No. Why?"

"He slipped out of protection three days ago. Said he had a lead. I've got a ping near Tropicana Field. You wouldn't know anything about that, would you, Counselor?"

Nick forced his voice steady. "No, but if Hank went after a lead, you know why."

"Yeah," Adams snapped. "Because people like you kept whispering in his ear. He trusted you more than the badge. And now he's missing." The line went dead.

Nick returned, jaw set. "Hank's missing. Ditched protection. Adams has a lead near the Trop."

On TV, the meteorologist's tone sharpened. "Update on Hurricane Milton: sustained winds have decreased to 145 miles per hour. Milton has been downgraded to Category 4 but remains catastrophic. Landfall in thirteen hours."

Andrea's mouth tightened. "Cat 4 or not, it's cover for them."

Nick's phone buzzed again. An anonymous text.

Hank would be proud. Find the dock with the red crown.

He read it aloud.

"Dock' doesn't have to mean the waterfront," José said. "In logistics, it's any loading bay. Tropicana Field's full of them."

"And the red crown?" Andrea asked.

Nick thought it over. "Days prior to Helene, Slovin's notebook had a red crown scrawled beside La Reina's name. I thought Hank would've recognized it." His voice hardened. "Carl's twisting that memory into bait."

Another gust slapped the siding. Rain hissed.

Nick grabbed his jacket. "Let's move now, before Maxwell's people sweep it."

Andrea blocked his path. "I'm going with you."

José snapped his laptop shut. "The baseball stadium loading docks. If it's a trap, we'll see it coming. Hang on for a few minutes, I have a way we can get access to the Stadium parking lot."

~

The wipers fought a losing battle against Milton's outer bands, each pass clearing the windshield for only a second or so prior to fresh sheets of rain blurring it again. Nick gripped the wheel, steering the F-150 through flooded streets. Beside him, Andrea sat rigid, posture taut, while José worked from the back seat, his tablet glowing with satellite imagery of Tropicana Field. Through the downpour, the stadium's dome rose like a ghostly apparition, an island in a city bracing for the worst.

"Checkpoint ahead." José leaned forward between the seats. "National Guard. Standard hurricane protocol. They'll be watching for strays."

Nick eased off the accelerator, eyeing the cluster of military vehicles near the main entrance. Soldiers in ponchos waved cars through with clipped efficiency. Three transport trucks idled in the lot, diesel engines rumbling under the wind.

"Think your credentials will get us through?"

"Better than nothing." José pulled a PI license, a laminated emergency personnel badge, and a folded high-vis vest with "Red Crown Logistics" stitched across the chest. He rubbed his thumb over the embroidery, tugging at a loose thread before adding a waterproof work order stamped with a QR manifest. "If they scan it, the system will spit out a contractor listing. Looks legit enough."

Andrea's hand shifted inside her jacket. "And if it doesn't?"

"Then we improvise." Nick steered toward a side gate with a lighter guard presence.

Water sheeted over the hood as the truck pushed through standing runoff. Two Humvees loomed as Nick stopped at a chain-link barrier. A weary guardsman approached, rain dripping from his helmet.

José leaned out the window, credentials ready. "Dominguez, here for an insurance assessment. Pre-storm documentation. Red Crown Logistics subcontractor. Heard inside is bunk city for the crews?"

The man frowned, keyed his radio, and waited. Static and clipped voices answered. After a beat, his shoulders eased. He waved them through. "East yard's full. Make it quick. Mandatory evac in three hours."

Nick nodded, guiding the truck inside. The service road curved around the dome, opening onto a staging ground lit by flood lamps. Since Helene, Tropicana had become FEMA's default hub—utilities, Guard units, even food trucks crammed the lot—an entire city's lifeline stacked under one roof. Workers hauled crates and lashed down tarps. Beneath the concourse, cots and tents sprawled along the floor, a storm shelter for the crews trying to hold the city together.

"The texter said a dock with a red crown." Andrea scanned the perimeter. "We're nowhere near the water."

They climbed out, rain slapping their hoods, gusts tugging them sideways. Andrea's eyes swept the stacks as they pressed deeper into the yard. Water ran in sheets over the concrete, each step splashing shallow runoff. Floodlights cut through the downpour, casting jagged shadows spanning stacked pallets and tarps.

Andrea halted, chin lifting toward a service bay door. "Nick."

Fresh red paint on the corrugated metal, a crude crown mismatched for FEMA, unmistakable in intent. The pigment wept in the humidity, trailing crimson streaks down the steel like an open wound.

Nick's pulse spiked. "There."

José's voice went flat. "Not an agency mark. That's La Reina's."

Nick's phone buzzed. He pulled it free, raindrops stippling the glass. The message glowed.

You're looking in the wrong place for your friend. The game is over. —Carl.

Nick's grip tightened. The plastic creaked under the pressure. "Carl. He used the red crown because Hank would've chased it, and he knew I'd follow. Pure bait."

Andrea's jaw clenched. "Then he wanted us here. Not for evidence. For the trap."

José's gaze swept the yard, every muscle tense. "Shandra. Hank. Now us. He's erasing the list."

Somewhere nearby, a Guard officer barked orders. A tarp tore loose, snapping like a banner in the storm.

Nick shoved the phone into his pocket. "Cindi's with Jessica. She's safe, which means Carl's game is us."

They sprinted back to the truck, splashing through runoff. Behind them, the red crown bled in the rain, not a clue but a signature—Carl's mark, daring them deeper into his storm.

31

ADAMS: FINAL STAND

The service tunnel door gave way beneath Nick's shoulder with a rusted groan, hinges protesting from wind and age. Outside, Milton battered Tropicana Field, turning the dome into a giant drum, each gust booming through the concrete corridors. Moisture seeped through hairline cracks, rivulets tracing the walls like veins. Nick swept his flashlight across the dark, Andrea and José close behind, three shadows advancing through a building that felt alive with the storm.

"Maintenance level should be down this way." Nick's beam caught a corroded sign, arrows pointing toward a stairwell. The air was thick with mildew and wet steel, a taste of rot.

Andrea followed, weapon steady in her hand. Her light swept corners and doorways in clean arcs. "How sure are you about this?"

"Adams said Hank had a lead near here." José's phone painted his face an eerie blue.

The steps descended into deeper darkness, slick with condensation. Nick's boots sent hollow reverberations chasing down the shaft. The air grew denser with every level, pressing colder on their skin. A deep rumble—thunder or the foundation itself—vibrated through the concrete, a bone-deep reminder of Milton's growing fury.

Nick paused once, tilting his head to listen for another set of steps in the dark. No sign of Adams. Only their own sounds, fading.

Three levels down, they emerged into a maintenance tunnel that stretched through the stadium's belly. Emergency lights flickered at irregular intervals, power struggling against the storm, casting the passageway in strobing amber that turned ordinary shadows into lurking threats. Water cascaded from a ruptured pipe, a shimmering curtain that fractured their beams into prismatic warnings.

"This way," Nick said, checking the turns against memory. Every step felt heavier. If Hank had come here, this was where the trail ended.

The hallway split then split again, a concrete maze under the stadium's weight. Their footsteps echoed down barren halls, phantom followers dogging their pace. Every few minutes, the steel frame shuddered beneath a violent gust, swaying like a ship at sea.

José pointed toward a heavy door stenciled "Storage Section C."

"Should be through here."

Nick tried the handle. Locked. Andrea was already pulling a slim case from her jacket, tools catching the light as she bent to the task. Her fingers moved fast despite the cold. Thirty seconds later, the lock surrendered with a dull click.

"Since when do you pick locks?"

Andrea met his eyes, something harder in her gaze than he remembered. "Since Myers rolled me and my SUV on the Gandy." She pushed past him into the storage area, weapon steady in her hands.

The room opened before them—a cavernous space cluttered with equipment, spare seats, and shrink-wrapped pallets of concessions. Their beams crisscrossed the dark, momentary constellations searching for any sign of Hank.

Nick froze. Somewhere beyond their light, a footstep echoed—one beat too many to be theirs. Then silence.

The air hung heavy with cardboard and lubricant, undercut by something sharper, metallic, unmistakable.

Blood.

"There." José's beam fixed on a figure slumped against a far wall, half-hidden behind a stack of folding tables.

Nick broke into a run, caution gone. His light fixed on a figure lashed to an exposed pipe. It was Hank Kitchens, head sagging against his chest.

Blood had dried in narrow streaks from a gash above his eye, stiffening his shirt in a collar of rust.

"Hank!" Nick's shout rang in the cavern as he dropped to his knees. His fingers pressed into the man's neck, searching for a pulse beneath cold skin. Nothing. He shifted, tried again, desperation clawing higher.

Andrea knelt beside him, her beam catching what his had missed: the swollen wreck of the officer's hands, wrists chewed raw by zip ties. His face was a map of punishment: one eye swollen shut, lip split, cheekbone cracked beneath purple flesh.

José stayed back, his phone clicking through the scene. Each flash froze the brutality into sterile evidence, stripping the horror down to record and code.

"He's gone," Nick said, anguished. "No pulse. Cold." He forced himself to look closer. Hank's knuckles told the story: nails torn, bone shattered. His ankles bore the same raw cuts as his wrists. He'd been held, beaten, and broken before the end. Nick's chest tightened. Every planted clue had led them here. Not to save Hank but to witness what was left of him.

"It's a message. Shandra. Hank. They're erasing everyone who brought down the cartel last summer."

The storage room door slammed open, denting the wall and sending the sound cracking through the concrete. Sergeant Quincy Adams filled the doorway, jacket soaked dark, water streaming from his broad shoulders to pool at his boots. His massive frame blotted out the corridor's emergency glow, a silhouette cut from shadow. In one hand, his shotgun hung low, muzzle slick.

Nick knew him even before the light caught his face: the rigid stance, the steady breathing of a cop who'd sprinted in, ready for a fight.

Quincy's flashlight swept the room, pinning José first then Andrea with her weapon half-raised, before stopping on his friend's broken body.

"No." Quincy's whisper came out thin, swallowed by the stadium's groan. His light wavered in his grip, the first crack in the iron steadiness that had always marked him. "No, no, no."

Three strides carried him to the victim. He dropped to one knee, a broad hand hovering over the shoulder, unwilling to confirm what his eyes already knew. Nick stepped back, giving him space, watching as the sergeant's fingers touched cold skin.

"Damn it, Hank." Quincy's voice cracked, the cop's armor giving way to something raw and human. For a long moment, only Milton's distant roar and the drip of water through rusted pipes filled the room.

Quincy rose, and in the space of a breath, the grief of a friend was gone. Rage had taken its place, his features set like stone. His knuckles strained against the shotgun's stock.

"What the hell are you doing here?" he demanded, Boston vowels sharpened by anger.

Andrea slid between them. Her weapon hung at the ready, muzzle down but prepared. "Same thing you are. Following leads."

"Leads?" Quincy spat. "This is a crime scene, not a scavenger hunt for your brand of vigilante justice." His radio hissed at his hip, storm noise bleeding through, but he ignored it, eyes locked on Nick. "You've got no badge, no authority. You're civilians trampling a murder scene."

Nick stepped up beside Andrea, unwilling to stand behind her shield. "He followed a lead. That's why we're here."

"Bullshit." Quincy shifted his grip on the shotgun, barrel angled down but tense in his hands. "Hank wasn't dumb enough to reach out to a civilian instead of his own department. Last time we talked, I asked if you knew where he was. You lied."

"Unless he didn't trust his own department."

Quincy's face darkened, a vein throbbing at his temple. "You think I wouldn't protect him? That I'd let someone in my unit become a target?"

"The system's compromised," Nick said, motioning toward the body. "How else does a cop in protection end up like this? Who knew he was here? Who had access?"

Quincy drove forward, stopping inches from Nick's face. His coffee breath hit in sharp bursts. The shotgun dipped as he leaned in, its muzzle hovering shy of Nick's chest, accusation turned into a physical threat. "You fueled him. Fed his paranoia. Kept pushing when he should've backed off."

"Hank was onto something real—"

"He's onto something dead!" Quincy roared. He jabbed a finger into Nick's chest. "You're a vigilante playing cop, Justin. An ambulance chaser who should've been disbarred. You've got a hero complex that makes you think the rules don't apply to you."

Nick's fists clenched, control slipping. "And you're a coward in uniform, letting men die behind your badge. Hank knew the risk. He chose it—because he understood what was in play. Maybe he even saw you as Maxwell's man."

"His life was the wager!" Quincy's face twisted, grief breaking through the anger. "His family. His future. All gone because you made him believe you knew better than an entire department."

José stepped between them, his phone glowing in the dim light. "Sergeant, we've got records. Messages. Leads Hank followed." He tried to show Quincy the screen, but the sergeant batted it away.

"Evidence?" Quincy's laugh was harsh, stripped of humor. "Like the evidence that got your finger cut off? Or the evidence that nearly got Justin's daughter killed?"

Andrea glared. At the mention of Jessica, her tone dropped cold. "Careful." That halted Quincy in his tracks.

The stadium shuddered as a violent gust slammed the dome. Dust sifted from the fixtures, settling over Hank like a shroud.

"You know this runs higher than street level," Nick said. "Maxwell. The cartel. The weapons. Hank was tracking all of it."

"And now he's dead!" Quincy's voice broke, raw grief punching through the cop's veneer. He jabbed a finger toward the body. "You think this is chance? Hank follows a lead, and you find him like this? They wanted you here, Justin. You're dancing on their strings."

The accusation hit home, scraping against Nick's own doubts. He started to answer, but Quincy had already turned away, jamming his radio with a force that looked better suited to a fistfight.

The shotgun twitched as his grip tightened, anger barely held in check. "Officer down at Tropicana Field service level. Send units now." His voice was flat again, professional, though fury still bled through. "CSU and medical examiner. Priority response."

A burst of static led to a garbled confirmation. Quincy faced them once more, jaw set so tight it looked carved from granite. The shotgun never wavered. "You have about twenty minutes. After that, I arrest you for obstruction."

"We're on the same side," José said.

"No." Quincy's eyes locked with Nick's, two immovable objects with no give between them. "We're not. Not anymore."

The partnership that had been forming, the tentative trust built over shared information and common enemies—all of it was shattered on the concrete floor, as broken as Hank's body.

Nick held Quincy's gaze, refusing to look away first. "When your people arrive, they'll secure the scene, document everything by the book, and then the evidence will disappear, like it always does." He stepped closer, lowering his voice. "And you'll be left wondering if you could have prevented the next death by listening to me now."

Quincy's jaw worked beneath his skin, muscles bunching and releasing. "Get out. And stay away from my investigation."

Andrea touched Nick's arm, a gentle pressure signaling retreat. Outside, Milton battered the dome, wind tearing through the upper levels like a beast seeking entry. Inside, the pressure was worse—a storm no concrete could contain.

Nick backed away, holding Quincy's stare until the door was narrowed to a sliver. His last glimpse was of the sergeant on one knee beside the body, broad frame bowed under a private grief no badge could shield.

The door shut with heavy finality, sealing off more than the room. Whatever thin thread of trust that had tied them to official channels was gone.

Milton's roar shook the walls, but Nick barely heard it. The texter had pulled them in and now meant to turn the storm back on their heads.

32

GINO MYERS

Gino Myers sat in the safe house living room, body loose in the armchair, eyes never still. The khakis and button-down issued by witness protection chafed at his neck, a daily reminder that he now belonged to the government. Beige plaster. Beige flooring. Silence. Three days in this coffin of anonymity and the room already pressed in tighter.

The house was built for erasure: walls the color of old bone, carpet the shade of cigarette ash. The couch and seat carried the same faded blue stripes, furniture chosen to vanish from memory. In the kitchenette, a lone coffee mug sat in the drying rack, stamped with a discount-store logo no one would recall.

He walked the perimeter twice a day, cataloging every exit and every potential tool. The block in the kitchen offered four blades—two chipped, one dull, and one solid chef's knife sharp enough to open a throat like his old Ka-Bar. A fire extinguisher by the back door had the right heft for a skull strike. Even the ceramic lamp by the couch could cause a concussion if swung hard.

His fingers drummed the armrest, muscle memory searching for the service weapon that wasn't there. They'd taken it, of course. Ex-cops in witness protection didn't get to keep their guns, a bitter joke that gnawed at him daily.

At 7:34 p.m., a knock split the quiet. Three sharp raps. Wrong timing. Wrong tone. The handlers weren't due until tomorrow, and they always called first. Myers rose in one smooth motion, slid to the side of the door, spine flat on the wall.

"Federal agent," called a voice. "Security check."

"Identification," Myers said, tone flat, adrenaline flaring.

A badge appeared in the peephole's narrow view, gold shield catching the porch light. Proper formatting, proper font. At a glance, legitimate. Myers unlatched the locks and cracked the door enough to study the man outside.

The visitor stepped in wearing a suit pulled straight from a mannequin. Pressed lines. Hair regulation-neat, smile assembled. Real Bureau men carried wrinkles by noon and smelled of coffee.

"Agent Daniels," the man said, extending a hand Myers left hanging. "Routine check before your testimony." His teeth were uniform as piano keys. "Senator Maxwell wants to be sure you're … comfortable."

"Maxwell sent you?" His tone stayed casual as he gestured toward the table, guiding the man with his back to the window. "Didn't know senators handled witness security personally."

The smile didn't move. "The senator takes a personal interest in high-value witnesses, especially those with information critical to national interests."

Myers sat. The man took the other chair.

The tells stacked quickly. Shoes were expensive leather but scuffed along the sides, never polished. Tie clip was an inch too high. Sloppy mistakes, invisible to most but not to the veteran officer. And the eyes—one blue, one hazel—never still. Not a fed's eyes.

"How's the coffee?" the man asked, tapping a finger against the table in a syncopated rhythm that itched at Myers's nerves.

"It's coffee." Myers eyed the rough hands. Callused, trigger-worn, a professional. "It does the job."

The jacket shifted as the man leaned in, flashing the holster beneath. "Quite a career, Officer. Afghanistan. Patrol. RADD Squad. Now a star witness." His voice dropped, confidential. "The senator values loyalty, especially under pressure."

"Loyalty," Myers echoed. "Is that what we're calling it now?"

The smile thinned. The rhythm stopped. "Consistency is all we ask. Match the testimony you've already given. Nothing more."

WITNESS ELIMINATION

"And if it doesn't?"

The man's hand drifted toward the coat. "Then other arrangements will be made."

Myers struck first. He clamped the wrist before it reached the holster, twisting. With his other hand, he snatched the steak knife he'd taped under the table and drove it up toward the throat.

The impostor jerked sideways. The blade caught the edge of the jaw, skidding up across cheekbone, tearing a jagged furrow through skin and muscle. Crimson spattered hot over Myers's forearm, into the man's mismatched eyes.

The wound was savage but not mortal. The man roared, fury boiling over pain, and clawed for the throat. They collided, momentum toppling the table in a splintering crash.

They hit the floor hard. Myers kept the knife, but his grip on the wrist was the anchor. The impostor's knee slammed into his gut, blasting the air from his lungs. He rolled with it, refusing to let go. Blood poured from the torn cheek, streaking the beige fiber in jagged arcs.

Snarling, Myers smashed the man's head against the floor once, twice. The body bucked with surprising strength, fingernails raking across his face, burning fresh welts into his skin.

Blood slicked the handle. The impostor wrenched hard, tearing the knife from his grip.

The holster brushed his palm. Myers ripped the pistol free.

The impostor lunged for it. Both men locked on the weapon, the muzzle jerking between their faces, steel and sweat inches from deciding the fight.

Myers slammed his forehead into the man's nose. Cartilage crunched. Blood burst anew. The grip faltered. Myers forced the firearm sideways, shoving cold metal into the temple slick with sweat.

He leaned close, breath hot and ragged. "Tell Maxwell next time to check the stitching."

His finger closed. The shot cracked like thunder in the suffocating beige. The man convulsed once then stilled. Myers rolled off, chest heaving, pistol searing in his grip. The air stank of copper and burnt powder, acrid in the stale room.

Thirty seconds. That was how long it took to prove witness protection couldn't protect anyone.

～

Myers checked his watch. 7:41. If the impostor had a check-in protocol, he had thirty minutes at best before alarms went up. Enough time, if he moved with purpose.

He dropped to a knee and stripped the body. He shoved the ruined Italian wool jacket and blood-stiffened shirt aside, moving to what mattered: the shoulder holster, its leather worn perfectly to fit; a well-tuned sidearm with three spare mags; a backup piece strapped to the ankle; an encrypted phone and credential wallet. Quality gear, all of it. Whoever sent this cleaner had invested in tools, not brains. He kept the essentials, leaving the spoiled clothes in a heap for the cleanup crew to erase.

He pulled a slim billfold from the inside lining and flipped it open. The laminate read, "Thomas Daniels, Federal Bureau of Investigation." Badge number, credentials, holograms—all looked right at first glance. Even the photo could pass in bad illumination. Others wouldn't see it: a lamination seam and the faint ripple of aftermarket sealing.

"Amateur hour," he muttered, sliding the leather into his pocket.

Myers retrieved the Glock from the coffee table. Standard issue, well cared for, its custom night sights glowing dull green in the gloom. He ejected the magazine—one round shy of full. Chamber check: live. He racked the slide, savoring the smooth precision of a weapon maintained by someone who took pride in his craft. The pistol slid into the shoulder holster, the weight settling against his ribs like an old companion.

The badge came next. He polished it once with his thumb, the silver face catching the lamplight, the eagle and justice seal shining through its worn scuffs. Power in miniature—he knew that authority well. People didn't see the man, only the shield. He clipped it to his belt with deliberate care, a small ritual that made him stand straighter.

He knelt by the body again, applied the still-warm fingers to the phone's scanner. The screen unlocked with a pulse of blue, intel spilling out in encrypted fragments. Myers scrolled, eyes narrowing, then sharpening with satisfaction.

Coordinates. Names. Timetables. Maxwell's contingency plan for Hurricane Milton laid bare: assets pulled from St. Petersburg, sensitive material shifted out of holding, and—buried but clear—the exact location of the senator's refuge, a fortified estate outside Jacksonville with its own power grid and guards.

Myers's lips curved into something close to a smile. The cleaner's device wasn't merely a kill order—it was the whole playbook.

He moved to the desk, the dead man's cell glowing in his palm. His thumb hovered then tapped out a text to a number he'd carried in memory for months.

The game is not over. It has just begun.

He studied the words before sending them, savoring the thought of Nick reading them. The lawyer had torn his life apart, yet Myers still breathed, while the other man's family bore the scars.

Myers hit send. Satisfaction settled as the text vanished into the ether. Let Justin feel it—that cold finger of dread, the reminder that his enemy was alive, watching, waiting.

In the hallway mirror, the reflection was a stranger. Stubble. Close-cropped hair. Jeans and a black T-shirt made him another face in the crowd. Not the protected witness. Not the cop. Something leaner, coiled tighter. A man with nothing left to lose and everything to reclaim.

He shut the door softly behind him, final. The street outside was quiet, nothing but the hiss of water in the gutters. Drops darkened his cotton, but he moved as though he didn't notice—spine straight, stride unhurried. Ordinary weather meant nothing to a man who carried greater storms inside.

He slid into the shadows of the road, one life ending in his wake as another began. The hunt was on. And this time, Myers wasn't prey.

33

SALLY'S GAMBIT

October 9, 2024, 8:30 p.m.

Water trickled down the rough wall, slick with algae, as Sally pressed her spine to the cold surface. Hurricane Milton pounded against the stadium, a hollow boom rolling through the structure, its echoes thinning into the tunnels. Her muscles burned from holding the position too long, but she stayed still, ears tuned to the voices threading sharp through wet concrete.

The maintenance tunnel stretched ahead like a gray artery, emergency lights flickering to life then dying, leaving pockets of amber-glow and blackness. Each flash caught puddles on the floor, turning them into brief mirrors that broke into ripples. The air carried mildew, damp dust, and a metallic tang—perhaps blood. She steadied her breathing, fighting the urge to gasp at what she heard.

"She has served her purpose." Sarah's Spanish was flawless. "La Reina will appreciate her skillset. Consider her a token of commitment."

El Verdugo's reply was lower, a Portuguese inflection lacing his words. "La Reina does not accept unasked-for gifts. But she may find this one entertaining for a while."

Sally's knuckles whitened on the combat knife, the weapon an extension of her arm. The blade caught a sliver of emergency light, flashing a thin line of fire. Her heart hammered, but her grip stayed steady—years of Special Forces conditioning held the tremor at bay even with adrenaline flooding her veins.

"I assure you, she has qualities La Reina will value." Sarah's tone held the charm Sally had once found irresistible. "She's eliminated three witnesses without hesitation. Her police background and moral flexibility make her an ideal asset."

"Or a liability," El Verdugo countered. "La Reina prefers fidelity never divided."

Sarah's laugh—precise, practiced, never touching her eyes—echoed off the walls. "Everyone's allegiance divides under pressure. Sally responds well to the right incentives. And the others—Nick, Andrea, José Domínguez—Carl has already drawn them to Tropicana Field. Once they fall, every critical witness from the fentanyl pipeline and the Bruth'rs takedown two months ago is erased. Shandra Greene: dead. Hank Kitchens: dead. Quincy Adams … compromised, if not finished. The case collapses with them. After that, La Reina can have Sally as the final proof of my devotion. And my sweet little niece, Jessica, will come to live with me."

The name struck Sally like a blade in the gut. Her breath hitched, a jagged intake of damp air. For a second, she wasn't in the tunnel but back at a memory of intimacy. "I've always wanted a child of my own," Sarah had whispered once, when the weight of their choices pressed too heavy. "A daughter who would look at me without judgment."

Now Jessica wasn't family to Sarah. She was a prize—a possession, another pawn to claim.

"La Reina prefers clean accounts," El Verdugo said at last.

Sally squeezed her eyes shut, fighting the sting of memory. Thomas Lomax—Sarah's husband—smiling as he'd offered Sarah to her, sealing their fentanyl partnership. "My wife will close this deal for us, Officer Hinkins." His casual ownership, the slight stiffening in Sarah before she masked it with perfect composure.

She had watched from across the room. Sarah's fingers tightened on her champagne flute, her smile fixed while her eyes went dead. Later that night, Sarah came to her, vulnerability breaking through the polish like lightning through cloud. "He treats me like property," she'd whispered against Sally's shoulder. "Like something to be bartered."

Now Sarah stood ten yards away, offering Sally to El Verdugo with the identical proprietary confidence, the mirror-cold appraisal of worth. The cycle closing in terrible symmetry.

Grief crystallized into something harder. Betrayal burned through her, shifting from shock to rage to a clarity like ice in her veins. A tremor started in her left hand, but she crushed it against her thigh, grounding herself in the pain. Her lips parted as her breathing slowed, each exhale measured. The sensation was familiar: combat operations, when noise and chaos collapsed into focus, sharp and crystalline.

"We should return to the command center." Sarah's boots clicked against the floor as she and El Verdugo moved off. "Maxwell will want an update once his press conference ends."

"And the Justin problem?" El Verdugo's voice trailed with distance.

"Nick thinks he's found a clue with Hank's body." Sarah sounded satisfied. "By the time he sees it's another dead end, we'll have the weapons shipment secured. And then …."

Their voices faded into murmurs as they rounded the corner, leaving Sally with dripping pipes and her resolution. She pushed off the wall, muscles protesting after the long stillness. The knife slid into its sheath at her hip, the motion automatic.

She was finished with Sarah's games, through with being manipulated, weaponized, and discarded. The realization came not as emotion but as calculation. Following Sarah's orders was now operationally unsound. Sally had survived three tours in South America by knowing when extraction was the only option.

She pulled the burner phone from her pocket. The blue glow lit her face as she opened the map of Tropicana Field's maintenance tunnels. She knew the routes but checked again, finger tracing her escape. No surprises. No one to rely on but herself.

Sally studied the diagram, committing the junctions and exits to memory. Her thumb followed the path to the southeast exit—the route with the fewest checkpoints and closest access to the parking structure. Sixteen minutes at standard pace, factoring in obstacles.

The phone's light caught the scarred tissue on her forearms, burn marks from past missions standing out like pale islands against her skin.

She'd survived worse betrayals and clawed her way back from deeper pits.

Sally pocketed the phone and drew the knife again, feeling it settle in her palm. A vibration shivered through the stadium as Milton surged, dust loosening from the ceiling and drifting onto her shoulders like ash. She knew Sarah's capabilities and had been her instrument too long not to understand the calculation behind every move. But Sarah had made a critical error in her assessment.

She had forgotten that tools could cut both ways.

~

Sally moved through the maintenance corridor, each step placed to avoid the shallow puddles that could betray her. Her breathing matched the storm, measured exhalations under the thunder, quick draws of air in the silences between. Three minutes since she'd left the junction where Sarah's betrayal hardened her resolve. Seventeen minutes until the cartel's sweep of the lower tunnels. Time was passing fast.

Exposed pipes ran along the ceiling like structural veins, condensation dripping at irregular intervals, each drop striking the foundation with a sound impossibly loud. Emergency lights struggled against the dark, their amber glow warped by the storm's charge. Above, Hurricane Milton clawed at Tropicana Field, the groans stretching into creaks that hinted at structural fatigue and foundation strain.

Sally paused at an intersection, pressing her back to the wall as voices filtered from an adjoining tunnel. Two men, cartel enforcers by their speech, mid-level by their assignment. Their radios hissed and popped, the storm's static cutting in.

"Sweep this section again," one said in Spanish with the nasal twang of Colombia's northern coast. "El Verdugo wants confirmation before they move the packages."

The second man grunted, keys jangling as he adjusted his belt. "This is pointless. No one could navigate these tunnels without the maps. And no one has them except us."

WITNESS ELIMINATION

Sally's lips curved in the barest smile, cold and fleeting. Her fingers tightened on the knife, angling the blade for entry under the jawline. The assessment ran itself—two targets, one with a handgun at his right hip, the other with an automatic slung loose over his shoulder. Distance: eleven feet. Ambient noise: enough to cover the strike. Alarm risk: high unless both dropped together.

She inhaled once, filling her lungs, then moved.

The first guard never saw her coming. Sally's left hand clamped over his mouth as her right drove the knife under his jaw, severing his vocal cords before driving deeper toward the brain stem. His body stiffened then collapsed against her, strings cut. She eased him down, lowering him in silence.

The second guard turned at the faint drag of boots on concrete. His hand brushed the grip of his weapon as Sally closed the gap. She shifted angle, slamming him shoulder-first into a vertical pipe. The clang echoed down the corridor as his rifle strap snagged, tangling his rifle against his chest. In the same motion, she dropped to one knee, her left hand trapping his gun hand while her right struck his neck, crushing the larynx. His eyes bulged, breath cut off before sound could rise.

Sally twisted his wrist until the bones gave way with a sharp crack. The noise reverberated off the stone, followed by the thud of his knees hitting stone. She held him as he sagged, his free hand clawing at his neck, nails raking skin in a futile search for breath.

Fifteen seconds from first strike to second target down. Her breathing stayed steady, heart rate elevated but controlled. The copper tang of blood filled her nostrils as she pulled the knife free from the first guard, wiping the blade on his jacket. Crimson pooled beneath him, running along the concrete's slight grade to form swirling patterns in the dim light.

Sally surveyed the aftermath with detachment. Two bodies. Separate pools with distinct flows. IDs on both. Estimated discovery was forty-five minutes, sooner if the next radio check came early.

Thunder rolled overhead, masking the sounds of the skirmish that might have carried through the tunnels. Sally stepped over the second guard, careful to avoid the spreading slick. She paused at a junction box twenty yards ahead, its metal door hanging open to expose a tangle of wires and breakers. Perfect cover.

She pulled out her phone, the blue-white glow lighting her features as she consulted the stolen map. Three exit routes. Northwest through the primary service corridor, high traffic, high risk. East through the electrical tunnels, moderate movement with heavy surveillance. South through the drainage system, minimal presence, but flooding made it the hardest path.

Her thumb hovered over the screen as she reached her decision. Sarah expected obedience, the loyal attack dog no matter the treatment. That predictability was a liability and now a weapon.

Sally opened a new message, José's number recalled from memory. Her thumbs flew over the screen.

The child was cover. Your target the Wrench has not moved from the tunnels.

She attached the map coordinates to Carl's last position, then hesitated.

A pressure groan rolled through the stadium as another band of wind struck. Dust cascaded from the ceiling, veiling her shoulders in a gray film.

She pressed send, watching the indicator shift from sending to delivered.

Sally pocketed the phone and reached for her ankle sheath, drawing a second knife with a recurved blade. Its weight balanced cleanly against the straight blade in her right hand.

The passage ahead dropped into deeper darkness, emergency lights thinning as the tunnel shifted into the drainage system. Sally advanced, each step placed with trained precision. Her senses adjusted to the dark, catching the subtle change in air pressure from a side passage, the varied tones of water running through different pipes, the faint trace of saltwater hinting at the drainage outlets ahead.

A floodlight above the next junction sputtered, throwing harsh white light across the corridor for three heartbeats before flaring brighter, the filament burning with unnatural intensity. Sally froze, her silhouette projected against the far wall like a warning. The bulb gave a soft pop then died, plunging the space into darkness.

Sally moved forward, untroubled by the dark. She'd spent years operating where sight failed and silence decided survival.

34

THE FINAL CONFRONTATION

Water ran down the tunnel walls in sheets, merging into rivulets that snaked across the floor before disappearing into overflowing drains. Nick's flashlight cut through the murk, its beam catching the cascading flow and throwing ghostlike patterns over the concrete. Each thunderous impact from Hurricane Milton above carried through the foundation, a reminder of their precarious position beneath thousands of tons of unstable masonry and steel.

"Junction should be fifty meters ahead." José's phone glow cast his face in ghostly blue as the map flickered, the signal fighting against the storm's electromagnetic interference. "Maintenance hub connects to three primary service corridors."

Andrea moved in silence behind Nick, steady on the slick concrete. The Steyr never wavered in her grip. Her flashlight swept each alcove, her eyes cataloging threats.

"Someone's been through here recently." Nick crouched to examine a section of flooring where the grime had been disturbed. His jeans were soaked through at the knees, cold water seeping into the fabric. "Multiple sets of prints heading the same direction we are."

A metallic groan echoed through the tunnels, followed by the sharp crack of structural failure. Debris rattled through ventilation grates overhead, dust sifting down in their flashlight beams. The Louisville Slugger hung from Nick's right hand like an extension of his arm, its weight both reassurance and promise.

"Milton's downgraded to Cat 3." José glanced at a weather alert on his phone. "Sustained winds of 120 miles per hour. Eyewall's making landfall now, Siesta Key south of us." Their window was narrowing fast.

They pressed forward through ankle-deep water that dropped into sudden calf-high pockets. Their progress slowed as they navigated past fallen pipes and electrical cables that dangled from the ceiling like industrial vines. The emergency lighting system fought a losing battle against the encroaching darkness, amber bulbs flickering at irregular intervals, casting strobing shadows.

Nick's radio shrieked static, freezing all three in place. A garbled voice struggled through the interference. "… evacuation complete … structure compromised … all personnel withdraw immediately …." The transmission dissolved into unintelligible noise before cutting out entirely.

"They're pulling back all first responders," Andrea said. "We're on our own now."

The tunnel widened into a circular intersection where floodwater swirled in deliberate patterns around central grates. Overhead pipes converged at this nexus point, forming a metallic canopy from which water dripped in percussive rhythms. Passages branched outward from this hub, each identical in their brutalist concrete construction, distinguished only by faded numerical markers stenciled above their archways.

Nick knelt at the edge of the junction, his flashlight illuminating a distinctive pattern pressed into the thin layer of silt coating the concrete floor. "Boot tracks." He traced the air over the impression without touching it. His voice hardened. "Verdugo or his mercs, I bet."

The name hung in the damp gloom, weighted with Shandra's disappearance and Hank's tortured corpse. Andrea's posture shifted, her grip on the pistol tightening as her gaze tracked the prints leading down the leftmost corridor.

"Over here," she signaled, moving to the rightmost passage. Her flashlight revealed another series of marks, scuffs along the wall at shoulder height, as if someone had brushed the surface while passing. "The spacing is exact. These are Sarah's." She didn't explain how she knew, but the hard set of her jaw left no room for doubt.

WITNESS ELIMINATION

José's phone vibrated, the screen glowing with an incoming text. "Anonymous text." He turned the display toward them. "Coordinates. Wrench is here."

Nick studied the intel, plotting the location against the maze of tunnels. "That's the central corridor." He nodded at the middle passage. "Storage near the field access tunnels."

His own phone buzzed. One line glared back at him. "The game is not over. It begins now." His jaw clenched, rage and dread knotting together.

He felt Andrea studying his face, as if she knew the words cut deeper than he let on.

José caught the look and nodded curtly, as if to say, "Later."

"One problem at a time," Andrea said, her eyes locked on Nick's.

Nick pocketed the phone, forcing his focus back to the task at hand.

The three stood in silence, the reality settling between them with grim clarity. Their quarry had split, each disappearing down a different path.

"We should stay together," José said.

Andrea shook her head, determination etched in her posture. "We have to separate or we'll lose two of them. There's no time for anything else." Her gaze fixed on the passage marked by Sarah's scuffs. "This ends tonight."

Nick recognized the resolve in her voice, the same tone she'd used when she promised Jessica the people who hurt her would pay. His own resolve matched hers as he stared down the corridor where Verdugo's prints disappeared into shadow. "Twenty minutes," he said. "Rendezvous back here."

José nodded once and moved toward the central passage, his silhouette catching the light before the darkness swallowed him. Andrea's eyes met Nick's one last time. No assurances, no caution. They were past that.

She followed her path, her beam shrinking to a pinpoint and disappearing. Nick turned toward his own tunnel, the Louisville Slugger gripped tight, its wood grain warm in his palm. Above, Hurricane Milton's howl forced its way through damaged vents and shattered windows, reaching even these depths.

The sound trailed Nick as he advanced, swallowing his footsteps, a fitting score for the storm building inside him with every step closer to Verdugo.

~

Nick tracked Verdugo's boot prints through the maze of corridors, each mark fading as rising water blurred the trail. His Glock was in its holster under his arm, while the Louisville Slugger hung from his right hand, its polished grain catching flashes from failing emergency lights. The bat's weight grounded him, a solid counterpoint to the unstable world around him, walls weeping moisture and pipes rattling as Hurricane Milton tore at the stadium above. Every few seconds, the structure shuddered, steel beams groaning beneath the strain as nature tested their limits.

The tunnel curved sharply, descending into darkness where the emergency lighting had failed. Nick paused at the threshold, his flashlight probing the blackness like a surgeon's tool. Water poured down a series of broad steps, a waterfall vanishing into the flooded corridor below.

Nick tucked the flashlight between his teeth and gripped the wall with his free hand, testing each step before shifting his weight. Cold runoff seeped through his boots, numbing his feet as it climbed his calves. An overhead pipe burst, releasing a pressurized spray that blinded him for a moment. He pressed forward, guided more by instinct than sight while his vision adjusted to the alternating dark and light of strobe-like flickers.

Shandra Greene's words echoed in his head. "They killed my Jaquez during a traffic stop. They'll do the same to anyone who threatens them." He remembered the burn in her eyes—the same determination now driving him. And she was gone, her body still missing, her voice silenced by the man whose trail he followed through these flooded catacombs.

The corridor widened into a mechanical room, its walls lined with electrical panels and massive water pumps made useless by the flooding. Runoff pooled ankle-deep across cracked tile, reflecting the erratic flashes of emergency light. Conduits dangled from the ceiling where drywall had collapsed, creating a maze of wires and broken pipes.

And there, with his back pressed against the far wall, waited El Verdugo.

The assassin's posture betrayed no fear, no concern for his cornered position. He remained motionless, water lapping at his military-grade boots, hands resting at his sides with practiced neutrality. His face, half-illuminated by the strobing lights, revealed nothing but cold calculation in his dead, gray eyes. A thin scar ran from jaw to temple, pulsing faintly with each heartbeat—the only proof he was flesh, not stone.

"Lawyer." Verdugo's Portuguese accent thickened the English. "You have come a long way from courtrooms."

Nick stepped into the room, the Louisville Slugger gripped in both fists, its polished surface catching the uneven light. "Where's Shandra's body?"

A flicker, not amusement but something colder, crossed Verdugo's face. "The activist? She served her purpose." His head tilted, assessing Nick with the detachment of a man examining a specimen. "As did your friend Officer Kitchens. Your wife, your sister-in-law, and your child are all loose ends. You're next."

"I asked you a question." Nick stepped closer, the bat rising.

Verdugo's lips curved in something close to a smile, but the expression carried only calculation. "Your sweet Shandra." His voice remained measured. "She never saw me until it was too late. I sent her to her boy."

Jaquez. The name erupted in Nick's chest, a surge of rage and grief that obliterated his restraint. His lawyer's discipline, his passion for control, his careful pursuit of justice—all of it burned away in a single flash of fury.

He lunged, swinging the Louisville Slugger in a vicious arc that split the air with a hollow whistle. Verdugo pivoted, and the bat, missing his head by inches, smashed into the concrete wall, vibrations jolting up Nick's arms. Dust burst from the impact, filling the space with chalky particles that drifted in the flickering light.

Verdugo's counter came fast—a strike aimed at Nick's throat, meant to crush his windpipe. But Nick was already moving, instincts sharpened by months of fighting enemies who dismissed him. He ducked beneath the arm and whipped the bat around in a tight arc that smashed into Verdugo's shoulder.

The blow landed with a sickening crack. Verdugo staggered. Surprise flickered before he settled back into cold calculation. He reached for his belt, but Nick was swinging again, the Louisville Slugger cutting through the water-heavy air.

The next swing crushed Verdugo's forearm, numbing the limb and sending the weapon he'd been reaching for clattering into the floodwater. Another cracked into his ribs, forcing a burst of air from his lungs.

"For Shandra." Nick brought the bat down with savage force.

Verdugo tried to roll, but the confined space and rising water slowed him. The next strike crushed his collarbone, splintering it beneath the skin. Another shattered his jaw, teeth scattering into the murk. Nick kept swinging with brutal rhythm, wood cracking against bone until the bat splintered in his grip.

"For Hank." He slammed the bat into Verdugo's skull. The impact reverberated up his arms, bone and wood protesting together.

Verdugo no longer fought back. His body twitched in the shallow water, blood spreading in crimson tendrils. His dead gray eyes, once empty, stared upward with something akin to shock.

"For Jessica." Nick's voice broke as he delivered the final blow. The Slugger exploded against Verdugo's temple, wood fragments scattering across the flooded floor, leaving Nick with only the jagged handle.

Verdugo's body settled face down, blood pooling from his ruined skull in rings that caught the flickering emergency lights in grotesque patterns. His fingers curled once then went still.

Nick stood over him, chest heaving, knuckles white around the splintered bat handle. Water dripped from his clothes, his hair, and the broken wood in his grip. The reflection staring back from the flood's surface showed a stranger, wild-eyed, blood-spattered, remade by violence into something unrecognizable. Not the lawyer anymore. Not the careful man who built arguments. A man who killed to protect his family.

Time warped, seconds stretching then collapsing before Andrea's voice cut through the fog.

"Nick!" Her call echoed from somewhere in the tunnels, bouncing off concrete walls and water-slicked surfaces until it seemed to come from everywhere at once. "Nick, where are you?"

The cadence of her voice pulled him back from the abyss. He looked at the jagged handle still clenched in his fist, at the blood-streaked water around Verdugo's body, at what he had become. Dread hit him—not fear of Verdugo but of Andrea seeing him like this.

"Here." The word tore from his throat, raw and strange in his own ears. "I'm here."

~

Andrea advanced through the narrow maintenance corridor, each step in balance. Every droplet striking concrete like a distant gunshot. The Steyr was natural in her hand, its weight an extension of her resolve rather than a burden. Her flashlight cut through the murk, revealing scuff marks along the wall, breadcrumbs leading to a sister who had shifted from family to enemy.

Memory tightened her jaw—waking in the hospital after the Gandy Bridge "accident." Sarah's face on the news came into focus: sister, conspirator, and betrayer. The same face that had smiled at Jessica over birthday cakes; had toasted her at the wedding; had whispered childhood secrets long after their parents ordered lights out.

The sister who'd directed Officer Myers to run Andrea's SUV off the Gandy—to acquire Major Slovin's hard drive; to benefit her drug empire. Auntie Sarah, who had arranged the shooting that left Jessica with a bullet scar.

The tunnel sloped upward, leading to a heavy service door at the corridor's end. Water swirled as her flashlight beam found Sarah Brown pressed against the chained exit. Rusted links held the steel door tight in its casing, padlocked on the outside. Sarah's usual armor of composure had fractured. Jeans and boots were soaked through, grime and blood streaked a once-sturdy top clinging to her frame. Her cropped honey-blonde hair hung in wet strands around a face stripped of its mask. For the first time, she wasn't the predator, but a cornered woman.

Recognition flared, followed by fear. "Andrea." Sarah's voice cracked, vulnerability spilling through. Her eyes fixed on the pistol in Andrea's steady hand. "Thank God it's you. I thought—"

"You thought it was one of the people you've betrayed?" Andrea's tone was flat, devoid of emotion. "The list keeps growing, doesn't it?"

Sarah's hand shifted toward her waistband, the outline of a weapon pressed against the soaked fabric. Andrea's response was immediate, the pistol rising to center mass with the smooth precision José had drilled into her.

"Don't."

Sarah froze then slowly raised both hands. "Please," she whispered, "I can explain everything."

"You've been rationalizing things away our whole lives." Andrea stepped closer, her boots finding dry concrete. "A drug dealer. A betrayer. You sold out family for power, for Hinkins. How do you explain that?"

Sarah softened her approach, reaching for the tactic that had always worked. "I'm your sister, Andrea. Your blood. Whatever you think I've done—"

"I don't think." Andrea's finger tightened on the trigger. "I know. Myers ran me off the Gandy Bridge. You kidnapped Jessica for the Slovin hard drive. And you held her at gunpoint, you bitch." She pressed closer, forcing Sarah back against the chains.

"No." Sarah shook her head, wet strands clinging to her face. "I would never hurt Jessica. I love her—"

"The way you loved Thomas?" Andrea's voice sharpened, the name of Sarah's dead husband striking like a knife. "Before you had Sally eliminate him, too?"

A flicker crossed Sarah's expression, truth behind the mask. She drew her gun, but instead of aiming, she turned it, offering the grip forward. It slipped from her fingers into a puddle with a muted splash.

"I'm your sister," Sarah's plea was raw now. "Please."

Memories of shared bedrooms, whispered secrets, and years of tangled loyalty passed between them. Sarah's eyes, so like Andrea's, shone with tears that might have been real.

WITNESS ELIMINATION

"You shot my daughter." Andrea's whisper was jagged with grief and rage.

"That wasn't me. Carl and Verdugo did that." Sarah took a careful step forward, hands still raised. "We're family, Andrea. Blood. That has to count for something."

Andrea's eyes narrowed. "Can't risk you buying your way out of justice." The chain rattled as Sarah shifted, but it held her tighter than family ever had. Sarah's choices had locked her here, with no key left.

"You were family," Andrea said, the past tense deliberate. "You were my sister."

Something hardened in Sarah's gaze, recognition that no words could undo what she'd done. The mask slipped, predator flashing one last time. "If you do this," she said, voice sharpening, "you're no better than me."

Andrea's grip steadied. "I'm nothing like you."

The Steyr kicked in her hands, the report deafening in the confined space. Sarah staggered as the round struck her chest, shock flaring over her face—not at the pain, but at the fact that Andrea pulled the trigger.

She crumpled against the chained door, sliding down until the shallow floodwater pooled beneath her. Crimson spread in fragile tendrils, mixing with the running current over the concrete. Her hand lifted once, reaching for something unseen, before falling into the surface runoff. Her eyes remained open, fixed on Andrea even after she passed.

Footsteps splashed in the corridor—Nick's. He appeared in the doorway, soaked, the splintered bat handle still in his grip. He scanned the body, the spreading blood, the Steyr steady in Andrea's hands.

Both had crossed lines that could never be uncrossed.

Above, pressed into the lattice of pipes, Sally Hinkins watched in silence. She remained still as steel with the recognition that she was outnumbered, and survival meant staying silent, unseen, waiting for her own chance to strike another day.

~

José advanced through the maintenance tunnel, each step calculated to muffle the water sloshing around his ankles. His boxer's stance—

weight balanced, center low—kept him steady on the uneven ground. The phone in his left hand cast blue light on the walls, its screen displaying the anonymous message that had led him to Carl. His other hand clenched a tactical flashlight, phantom pain throbbing where his pinky used to be.

The corridor widened into a service junction marked by a rusted field-access sign. Overhead, the ceiling opened onto an exposed metal framework, Tropicana Field's skeleton laid bare. Through the gaps, violent flashes tore sections of the dome free. Rain poured through the breaches, turning the staircase ahead into a treacherous cascade.

José pocketed his phone and gripped the handrail, testing each step before committing his weight. His tactical flashlight beam cut through the falling water, revealing fresh scrapes on the metal treads, Carl's signature gait, heavier on the right from his limp. José had logged that detail with a thousand others during his investigation of the Bruth'rs, back when he still believed evidence and law could stop men like Carl.

Before they'd taken his finger. Before he learned some monsters required more direct methods of elimination.

The staircase ended at a service door hanging half-off its hinges, wind and spray forcing through the gap. José shouldered it open and stepped onto what had once been the pristine turf. The stadium was apocalyptic now—huge sections of dome ripped away by Milton's Category 3 winds, pouring the hurricane's fury straight down. The field had become a shallow lake, six inches of water rippling with every fresh gust.

Emergency lights on backup power cast stark pulses across the ruin. Home plate floated loose, spinning in lazy circles near a dugout. The outfield scoreboard swung on a single cable, throwing sparks into the floodwater below.

Through the dome's gaps, the storm was lit by near-constant lightning. Rain slashed sideways, stinging his skin like a spray of needles.

Movement flickered near second base. A figure slogged through knee-deep water toward the far exit. Even at this distance, the silhouette was unmistakable: Carl "The Wrench."

José splashed onto the flooded field, abandoning stealth for speed. He rushed forward. Memories rose unbidden as he pursued his quarry:

WITNESS ELIMINATION

Carl's face under a single hanging bulb, detached and clinical as pliers closed on José's pinky. Pressure precise, not severing at once but crushing bone and tendon first. Carl's analytical voice described each nerve and vessel as he worked.

"Better scream now," Carl had advised. "It helps with the shock."

José had screamed eventually. Everyone did.

Carl spotted him halfway across the field. Water churned around his knees as he faced José, his thin face caught in flashes of emergency light and lightning. Recognition flickered in his eyes, followed by something that on another man might have been amusement.

"The insurance investigator," Carl called, his voice carrying through the wind. "Still missing that pinky, I see." He gestured toward José's hand, motion precise. "Still half a man."

José advanced, measuring the distance with a boxer's instinct. Fifteen meters. Close enough to track the calculation in Carl's eyes, the subtle shift as he assessed escape routes and weapons. Too far for a lunge given the water, but closing.

"Nothing to say?" Carl tilted his head, rain streaming down his face in steady rivulets. "I remember you having plenty to say during our session. Before coherent speech became impossible." His tone hardened. "Shandra. Kitchens. Adams. Your lawyer friend and his wife. Even the little girl. Loose ends, all of them. You'll join them soon."

José kept silent, conserving breath. Words would give Carl too much. Better to let silence do the work.

Ten meters now. Through the ruined dome, Hurricane Milton's outer bands loomed, a rotating mass of cloud lit by apocalyptic lightning that turned night into fractured day.

A sound like artillery cracked overhead—another section of the dome surrendering to the hurricane's assault. Metal groaned, concrete crumbled, and a massive chunk of roof collapsed onto the field between them. Carl dove aside, reflexes not quite enough to clear the impact.

Nearly, but not quite.

The debris hit the water with explosive force, sending a waist-high wave across the surface. When it settled, Carl dangled from the edge of a new chasm where the field had collapsed into the maintenance level below. His right arm stretched upward, fingers hanging on by threads to artificial turf torn from its backing.

That same hand—the one that had worked the pliers with clinical precision on José's pinky—was now missing two fingers, severed by falling debris. Blood pulsed from the ragged wounds, spreading crimson spirals through the rain and floodwater.

"Help me!" Carl's voice had lost its mechanical calm, raw fear shredding the persona. His remaining fingers clawed at the turf, his body swinging over a twenty-foot drop onto jagged concrete and rebar. "For God's sake, help me!"

José moved forward until he stood over Carl, looking down at the man who had reduced his left hand to a four-fingered abomination. Water dripped from José's clothes, joining the hurricane's constant deluge as he studied the panic in his tormentor's eyes. He crouched, extending his left hand—the hand missing its pinky—toward Carl's bloodied wrist.

Their eyes locked as José's hand closed on cold, wet skin. For a suspended moment, relief flickered across Carl's face—the animal certainty of rescue overriding the memory of what he'd done to the man holding him.

"Please."

José leaned closer, grip firm but not secure. "Does it help?" he asked, his voice measured despite the hurricane's fury. "The screaming. Does it help with the shock?"

Horror dawned in Carl's eyes—his own words thrown back at him in this moment of extremity. His mouth opened, maybe to plead, maybe to bargain, but whatever he meant to say was lost as José loosened his hold, digit by digit, until nothing connected them at all.

Carl fell without a sound. His body disappeared into the darkness below, the splash of impact masked by the deluge.

José remained crouched at the edge for several heartbeats, watching the spot where Carl had vanished. Rain poured over him, plastering his clothes to his body and washing the last traces of his tormentor's blood from his hand. He straightened, turning his face up toward the hurricane's bands visible through the shattered dome.

For the first time since his torture, the phantom pain in his missing finger had subsided. He flexed his hand. The absence was not loss but completion—as if Carl's plunge had balanced some cosmic equation that had been tilted against him for too long.

Lightning forked across the sky in jagged bursts, illuminating the ruined stadium in stark flashes. José stood at the edge, rain striking his upturned face with cleansing force. The hurricane raged on, tearing at the world with indiscriminate fury, but José held steady, anchored by a weight that had lifted.

The storm would pass, as all storms do. But for now, standing in its heart with the ghost of his missing finger finally at rest, José Dominguez was exactly where he needed to be.

35

THE AFTERMATH

Nick guided his family into Sauvignon Wine Locker, attuned to the contrast between its soft lighting and the devastation outside the windows. Central Avenue was strewn with Milton's aftermath, uprooted palms, scattered debris, and utility crews working with grim determination beneath a sky scrubbed clean by the storm's passage. Inside, candles flickered, and conversation hummed with a fragile sense of normalcy. Nick kept a steadying hand at the small of Andrea's back as she moved toward the second floor.

"Mr. Justin!" Chris stepped from behind the mahogany bar. His smile carried genuine warmth, though new lines etched around his eyes betrayed the two days since Milton had ripped through. "We saved your table. One of the few places in the city that never lost power. Don't ask me how."

"Appreciate it, Chris." Nick nodded, eyes sweeping the other patrons, a habit hardened by months of looking over his shoulder. Each face registered as benign, ordinary citizens seeking refuge from powerless homes and the grind of cleanup. "Good to see you weathered the storm. The wine lockers held?"

Chris crossed himself.

Jessica darted ahead. Her injured arm remained bandaged beneath her favorite blue dress. She clutched the lioness plush to her chest, swinging it as she slipped between tables. Nick noted how she instinctively guarded her arm—a child's adaptation to pain that tightened his heart.

"Uncle José!" Her voice rang above the quiet conversation, bright with the resilience only children found after trauma.

José and Cindi already occupied the corner table, backs to the wall with sight lines on the entrance—an unconscious tactical choice that spoke volumes about what they'd endured. José rose as they approached, hand extended with the familiarity of someone who had seen you at your worst and stayed.

"You guys made it." José's grip was firm. "Roads are still a mess, Southside."

Nick nodded. "Took the long way around. Fourth Street's clear."

Jessica climbed onto the chair beside Cindi, thrusting Zara forward for inspection. "Look! Mom fixed her leg where she got shot." She pointed to a neat line of stitches in the plush's right leg, the thread a slightly different shade of gold than the surrounding fur. "And this is Splash." She pulled a stuffed dolphin from her backpack, holding it with the same protective care she'd once used for her own bandaged arm. "The hospital lady gave him to me because I was brave."

Cindi leaned in, examining both toys. She gave Andrea a knowing glance. "Very nice stitching. And Splash is quite handsome."

Andrea eased into her chair. Nick caught the subtle signs of her discomfort, the way she arranged her legs, the fleeting tightness around her eyes. She met his gaze with a small smile that acknowledged his concern without inviting it.

"I'm fine." She anticipated his unspoken question. Her fingers brushed his before withdrawing to unfold her napkin.

A server appeared with menus and a wine list, her cheerfulness another fragment of normality. "We have a limited menu but plenty of wine. Can I start you with something to drink?"

"Valdicava, please." Andrea's voice was steadier than her hands. "The 2016." She remembered thinking of that bottle the day of the crash—an indulgence she'd never voiced aloud. Ordering it now felt like staking a claim on survival itself.

"Sounds good," Nick added.

Jessica swung her legs beneath the table, heels thumping the chair's base. "May I have a Shirley Temple with extra cherries?" She glanced at Nick for approval.

"Of course." He rested a hand on her uninjured shoulder. The touch steadied him as much as it reassured her.

José studied the menu with theatrical concentration. "Burrata to start, maybe the beet salad. The ribeye's the best here, but the branzino looks good too …."

"You always order enough for three people!" Jessica giggled, the sound startling in its normalcy. "Mom says your eyes are bigger than your stomach."

José clutched his chest in mock offense. "Fighting words from someone who once ordered four desserts."

"That was for sharing!" Jessica protested, her joy bubbling up.

"So is this." José winked at her. "I'm very generous."

Cindi set a hand on his shoulder, her fingers warm. "What he means is that I'll be eating his leftovers for days."

Laughter circled the table like a wound being tested, painful but necessary for healing. Nick watched color return to Jessica's cheeks, and Andrea's smile made her glow. The moment held, fragile yet precious, against the devastation visible through the patio windows.

The server returned with their drinks, setting down a round of French Montrachet. "Compliments of Chris. He said the Valdicava needs time to open." Andrea nodded in thanks but didn't drink. She swirled the wine and let it catch the sunset light streaming through the glass. Her gaze drifted often to the street below, scanning with the quiet vigilance that had become second nature.

Nick tracked her profile against the fading daylight, the familiar lines of her face sharpened by recent ordeals. The woman who once agonized over paint colors now carried a handgun with practiced ease. The mother, who had fretted over Jessica's first fever, now moved with the awareness of someone who knew exactly how much damage a body could take before breaking.

The world outside edged toward rebuilding. City crews in orange vests directed traffic around a fallen oak that had crushed a parked car. A National Guard truck rumbled past, stacked with bottled water and MREs bound for distribution centers. Portable generators hummed from storefronts, their owners selling hot coffee and charging stations at premium prices.

All of it—the destruction, the opportunism, the resilience—formed the backdrop to a fragile peace. This was the aftermath they'd fought for: Jessica's joy, Andrea's vigilance, José and Cindi's steady presence. Imperfect, scarred, but alive.

For now, this careful performance of normalcy was enough, a brief respite in the eye of a different storm.

~

The laughter stopped as Maxwell's voice drifted from the television above the bar. Nick's fork hovered between plate and mouth, stilled by the intrusion. That tone—practiced, polished, precise—cut through their fragile normalcy. Jessica forgot her linguini, and Andrea's hand trembled, then steadied when she set her untouched wine down with deliberate care.

"Thanks to the heroic actions of Sergeant Quincy Adams and his team," Maxwell declared, his tone measured for the cameras, "escaped prisoner Sarah Brown and her violent accomplices will never again endanger the people of Florida. Their remains were recovered in the aftermath at Tropicana Field, closing a dark chapter for our state."

The senator's cadence filled the space, carrying the absolute confidence of a man who believed in his own mythology.

Nick's jaw locked, teeth grinding until a dull ache spread toward his temples. His gaze shifted from his half-eaten filet to the television beyond the doorway. Maxwell stood at a podium emblazoned with the Senate seal, the American flag billowing behind him in a breeze staged for maximum appeal.

"My office has secured an aid package," Maxwell continued, his silver hair catching the camera lights in a halo effect. "One billion to rebuild infrastructure, restore power, and ensure the safety of every family affected by recent hurricanes."

Andrea's knuckles whitened around her unused steak knife, the tendons in her wrist taut as cables. She kept her eyes on her plate, but Nick knew she registered each syllable. The wine in her glass remained untouched, its surface reflecting the last rays of sunset in fractured blood-orange patterns.

Jessica sensed the change, her intuition catching the tension that charged the air around their table. She hugged her lioness plush to her chest, arms cradling it as if shielding it from Maxwell's presence. Her eyes darted between her parents, reading danger in the smallest signals.

"With the storm behind us," Maxwell's voice swelled to fill the restaurant, "we can focus on holding accountable those who would exploit a crisis for personal gain. My committee will prosecute instances of corruption to the fullest extent of the law."

José lowered his fork, the tines tapping china in a sharp, deliberate rhythm that carried more weight than a crash. His eyes met Cindi's, a silent conversation passing between them. She laced her fingers with his, gripping the same hand that had once locked around Carl's wrist before letting go. No words were needed—their understanding ran deeper than speech.

"The resilience of Floridians continues to inspire me," Maxwell declared. "Together, we will rebuild stronger than ever. And I ask for your continued trust in the institutions that have never failed us, even in our darkest hour."

Nick's gaze shifted from Maxwell to the street below, where National Guard vehicles patrolled St. Petersburg's wounded neighborhoods. The irony burned in his chest. The man tied to Shandra's disappearance, to the corruption that had nearly destroyed his family, now postured as savior of the people he had helped victimize. Maxwell talked about accountability, while Myers hid in witness protection. They repackaged Sarah's death at Tropicana Field as justice served.

"This tragedy has revealed the character of our community," Maxwell continued, his voice dropping into the register he reserved for manufactured gravitas. "And I am humbled by the opportunity to lead the federal response to ensure no American faces this recovery alone."

The final light of day gilded the edges of buildings visible from their vantage point, transforming broken windows into blazing rectangles of fire. The sky above St. Petersburg stretched impossibly clear, the storm's passage leaving behind air scrubbed clean of haze—nature's false promise of renewal. Nick knew better. Some stains resisted washing away, even by hurricane-force winds.

Jessica's small hand found Nick's across the table, her fingers squeezing with surprising strength. "He's lying." The whisper was delivered with the unfiltered certainty of childhood.

Nick squeezed back, meeting his daughter's eyes. "Yes, he is."

The simple confirmation seemed to settle her. Jessica nodded once, then returned to her linguini with renewed focus, as if having resolved an important matter. The lioness plush stayed clutched in her left arm, its glass eyes fixed on the doorway where Maxwell's presence still emanated.

Chris appeared at their table, coffeepot in hand, his expression apologetic. "Sorry about that. Some folks wanted to hear the senator's speech. I can have them turn it down if you'd like."

"No need," Andrea replied, her voice balanced between politeness and finality, a tone Nick had always admired. "We should know what we're facing."

Chris nodded and retreated, leaving the five of them on their island of understanding amid a sea of oblivious diners. The broadcast cut off as someone changed the channel, replacing his manufactured sincerity with the blunt cadence of a news anchor:

"Turning now to politics, sources in Tallahassee say Governor Whitman has narrowed his shortlist to fill the late Senator Eleanor Caldwell's seat. With Washington's balance of power at stake, an announcement is expected by the end of the month."

Cindi broke the silence that followed. "What now?" The question carried no fear, only the steady assessment of a woman who had stood firm through hurricanes both literal and human.

Nick's eyes met Andrea's across the table, then José's, then Jessica's. The battle lines had been drawn long before Milton reshaped the coastline. Maxwell remained untouched by the storm that had claimed so many others. But he didn't know what waited in the aftermath, what had been forged in the crucible of their shared suffering.

"Now," Nick's voice was certain, "we finish what we started."

WITNESS ELIMINATION

The evening breeze stirred Andrea's hair as she nodded, her expression hardening into something. The hurricanes had passed, but the war was only beginning.

And this time, they would not fight alone.

EPILOGUE

NEW FACES

The first layer of gauze peeled from her skin with a whisper of pain, adhesive surrendering its grip on flesh still raw from the surgeon's blade. She held herself perfectly still before the mirror, fingers working with measured precision, unwrapping one strip at a time. The apartment's air-conditioning raised goosebumps across her arms, its sterile chill echoing the sterile emptiness of the safe house, a place defined by absence, by what had been cut away.

Sunlight slanted through half-closed blinds, casting prison-bar shadows on the porcelain sink. Sally's hands never wavered as she unwound the bandages, movements precise, unhurried. The final layer clung to her cheekbone, dried lymph fluid gluing fabric to raw incisions. She drew one steady breath through her nose, then peeled it away, ignoring the sting of freshly exposed nerves.

The mirror gave her back a stranger's face, a construct assembled by a Miami surgeon whose clientele included cartel lieutenants and fugitive financiers. A face bought with emergency cash, engineered to evade both facial recognition software and former colleagues. Cheekbones higher, nose narrowed, jaw reshaped into a smoother oval. Even her lips had been altered, the once-distinctive fuller bottom lip, the one Sarah had traced with a lover's finger—now balanced, its intimacy erased.

Only her eyes remained unchanged—pale blue, rimmed by lashes still stained with surgical iodine. The same cold calculation stared back, a predator's focus untouched by the changed flesh around it. Sally leaned closer, tracing the faint suture lines across her fresh face, charting the border between who she had been and who she was now.

Water hissed through old pipes as she filled her cupped palms, the liquid cool against tender skin. She rinsed away the medicinal odor. Drying her face, she spread antibiotic ointment with the same methodical care she once used when field-stripping a service weapon.

Sally stepped into the apartment, bare feet soundless on worn linoleum. The place was in perpetual half-light with the blinds drawn, lamps angled to cast shadows without silhouette. Only the essentials: bed, desk, chair. Everything was arranged for efficiency.

On the desk, a laptop hummed, its screen the brightest object in the room. Beside it lay Sarah's necklace, a delicate gold chain with a small emerald pendant. Sally's fingers hovered then lifted it, the metal cold against her skin.

"La Reina will appreciate her specialized training. Consider her a gift." Sarah's voice echoed in memory, cutting deeper than any scalpel. Even weeks after Hurricane Milton had turned Tropicana Field into a flooded tomb, Sally could feel the cool concrete at her back, pressed into shadows as she listened. Sarah's tone had been casual, dismissive, offering her up like contraband. The charm that once seduced Sally was used to bargain her away.

The emerald caught the lamplight, flaring green to match the burn in Sally's chest. Sarah had given it to her on their six-month anniversary, presented over champagne in her waterfront bedroom. "Green for envy," Sarah had whispered. "Because everyone envies those eyes."

The same fingers that had fastened it at her throat later typed orders for Sally to kill witnesses who threatened her empire.

Sally reclaimed the necklace from their first safe house, not as a keepsake but as evidence, proof that she had survived and would keep surviving. She laid it down with deliberate care, the chain coiled into a circle, the emerald centered like a bullseye.

Her laptop keys clicked softly as she navigated the deep web, threading through layers of security protocols built during recovery. After three redirects and a biometric scan, the contractor contact form appeared. Her new face wouldn't register, but her retina still unlocked the system.

She typed every word fiercely.

Target: "Nicholas Justin."

Location: "St. Petersburg, Florida."

Timeline: "90 days."

Requirement: "Stage as cartel retribution. Family must witness."

She attached the encrypted file, which contained Nick's routines, addresses, and known associates—intelligence gathered during her months shadowing the Justins for Sarah. Payment followed, cryptocurrency funneled through shells no investigator could unravel.

The last field demanded a confirmation code, a verbal commitment:

The lioness still watches.

The reference meant nothing to the contractor, but it locked her resolve. She had seen the child clutching that bloodstained toy the day she left the hospital, had watched Andrea stitch it back together on surveillance feeds. A family that had dismantled everything she and Sarah had built, exposing their network and severing cartel ties....

She sent the message with a decisive click and shut down the laptop. Darkness deepened as the screen's glow vanished, leaving only the desk bulb burning over Sarah's necklace. Sally lifted it, the chain sliding through her fingers like wire before she fastened it at her throat. The emerald settled cold across her collarbone, an anchor and a purpose.

"The war is not over," she whispered, her new lips shaping old words. "We are just getting started."

~

The library smelled of leather and dust, bourbon sharp on the air. A single lamp glowed against rows of law books and framed campaign photos, their glass catching the storm light outside. Gino Myers sat in the senator's chair, body loose, one muddy boot pressed into the Persian rug. A crystal tumbler of Pappy Van Winkle rested in his hand, the bottle uncorked on the desk like an accusation. Its level was already down several fingers—proof he'd been here for hours, drinking at leisure.

The room was otherwise still except for the faint tick of rain against the leaded windows. Silent too was the shape stretched near the door. One of Maxwell's security men lay there, carefully arranged, as if set down rather than dropped. His eyes stared upward, glassy and unblinking. No blood. No struggle.

Myers rolled the bourbon across his tongue, savoring the heat, then placed the glass down on Maxwell's blotter. A dark ring stained the leather desk pad, bleeding onto the senator's stationery.

Beside it was Daniel's badge, its hologram catching the lamplight. The seam in its lamination mocked the ruse. Maxwell had thought to erase him with a counterfeit fed. Instead, Myers sat here now, bourbon warming his chest, proof of his presence cooling on the carpet.

The front doors groaned open. Voices exchanged clipped greetings in the hall, the shuffle of aides withdrawing. Footsteps struck the marble with the measured cadence of a man accustomed to deference. Senator Maxwell had arrived.

The library door swung inward. Maxwell entered, suit immaculate, hair lacquered into place, cufflinks flashing as he adjusted one with habitual precision. His aura of untouchable control preceded him—until his gaze found the body on the rug. His stride faltered.

Myers remained seated, allowing the silence to carry its weight. When Maxwell looked up, Myers raised the glass in a slow salute. His cheek bore raw welts where Daniels's nails had raked him, the marks vivid under the lamplight.

"Your stitching didn't hold, Senator," he rasped. "The badge tore too easily."

Maxwell's jaw tightened. He forced a breath, straightened his shoulders, and a practiced smile slid back into place.

"You've made yourself comfortable," he said, his eyes flicking from the empty tumbler to the open bottle. "I trust the bourbon meets your standards."

Myers leaned forward, poured a second glass, and slid it across the desk until it stopped at the edge nearest Maxwell. The gesture wasn't hospitality—it was command.

He settled back in Maxwell's Himalayan crocodile leather chair, muddy boot grinding deeper into the Persian weave. His brown eyes never left the senator's.

"Shall we talk about La Reina?"

~

La Reina let the silence in her office do its work.

It was the sort of quiet that made men confess, made them offer more than they intended. A hush dense with history: a lacquered rosewood desk inherited from a banker who fled Caracas in '02; a wall of oil portraits—dead presidents, dead patrons, none as permanent as the paint that preserved them; the soft tick of a Breguet carriage clock.

Her phone pulsed once on the blotter. A secure line. No name, only a code she'd memorized before Governor Whitman learned to pronounce hers.

She waited one, two, three ticks, then answered.

"Señor Gobernador." Her voice remained unhurried. "You chose your hour carefully."

On the other end, the governor's warmth tried for casual and landed on careful. "Barely a difference between us, Señora Reina. But a big day. I wanted to share the list before the announcement."

"Hmm." She traced a finger alongside the handset, the gesture half caress, half threat. "Your shortlist to fill Senator Caldwell's seat."

A breath. "Yes."

She didn't ask how he'd gotten her number. He hadn't. Men like Whitman were given her number. That was the nature of power.

He cleared his throat. "My first choice is Franco Martinez. Strong donor base, good on camera, speaks to the I-4 corridor and—"

"No."

He paused. The clock ticked, prissy and precise.

"Franco Martinez is a nonstarter," she maintained her tone. "He has a gambling problem and a brother with a sealed case file in Hillsborough. Every time he smiles, his teeth remind voters of dentures. And he owes people money he unable to repay. He would ask you for favors you cannot grant. He will not be your pick."

She heard the governor swallow the reflex to argue and choose a safer verb. "Understood."

"Raúl Pérez." She named him. "You will appoint him."

Another pause. She could hear him sifting paper he didn't need, buying a second to remember the name. "The software guy."

"Little-known," she agreed. "Young enough to be a generational change. Old enough to look reassuring in a navy suit. His company writes infrastructure code that makes tolls appear and disappear like magic. That matters when bridges collapse and storms reveal rot. He has no enemies yet. Make him yours. Quickly."

A sliver of skepticism crept in—habit, not defiance. "He's never held elected office."

"Then he has never learned to be corrupt in public. He will learn in private. From you."

She imagined the governor's shoulders lower by a fraction. He would picture polling numbers and cross tabs: young Latinos, tech donors, suburban parents who want roads that do not vanish in the rain. He would imagine his next fundraiser with a stage full of laptops and flags.

"Elaborate on the rollout." He maintained professionalism while layering gratitude. "If we do this, I'll need … cover."

She shifted a folder with one manicured finger. She prepared the cover. She always did.

"Leak the shortlist tonight," she said. "Put Franco's name first. Watch the usual voices applaud him. In the morning, new numbers say voters want a problem-solver, not a fundraiser. Pérez becomes inevitable. Business groups will bless him. The League of Something will call him 'a breath of fresh air.' You will say you listened."

"And the donors who expected Franco?"

"Tell them to phone me."

His chuckle was a shade too quick, relief cutting through calculation. "I'm told I should never make you wait."

"Mm." She took a pen and drew a small spiral in the margin of a memo, habit, not art. "There is another matter. Two names in St. Petersburg. Minor fires that need a state breeze."

A crispness entered his voice. This was the part where favors kept their receipts. "Go on."

"A lawyer named Nicholas Justin. An investigator named José Domínguez." She put the accent on the last syllable with deliberate care. "Both have been … enthusiastic. They will not stop. They have found that attention can be a kind of power. You will instruct your people to look into them. Audits. Compliance. Old permits. Friendly reporters asking unkind questions. All within the law, of course. We respect the law."

"You want them charged?"

"I want them occupied." Her fingernail tapped once on the desk. "Find a committee that can send them letters. Let them spend the next six months scanning and redacting while other things happen. They are stubborn men, but even stubborn men must sleep."

"And if they don't tire?"

"Then we revisit."

He hesitated. "They tied Sarah Brown to the fentanyl ring, and now she is dead. The public thinks I solved it. If we poke them too hard—"

"You won your news cycle," she said. "And soon you will win your appointment. The storm has given you a halo. Do not concern yourself with the two men who measure corrosion with their fingers. I will handle the rest."

A beat smaller than a breath. "And the matter of … that name we do not say on open lines?"

She smiled, small and private. "La Reina has many names, Governor. This is one of them."

"I appreciate your counsel," he said. "We'll proceed with Pérez."

"Good," she said. "I will expect his call by noon. He will thank me before he thanks you. That will be useful."

A soft exhale, the sound of a man choosing to be pragmatic rather than proud. "Anything else?"

"Yes," she said, and her voice was almost kind. "Learn to pronounce 'Raúl' properly prior to the press conference. The tongue goes to the palate. Rra-Úl. Not 'Rawl.' We are not electing an appliance."

He laughed, then caught himself, then laughed again because she had allowed it. "Noted."

She ended the call without a farewell. He would not take offense. He would take notes.

For a moment, she sat still, the phone a black oblong on the blotter, the room's filtered late-afternoon light pooling on the parquet like poured cream. From the courtyard beyond the French doors came the low hum of cicadas and the far-off thud of helicopter rotors, a supply run to the private airstrip, on schedule as always. Overhead, the ceiling fan churned the warm air in a slow, stately circle.

She stood and crossed to the terrace doors, carved mahogany panels inlaid with mother-of-pearl depicting a jaguar mid-pounce. The handles were cool against her palms. When she opened them, heat pressed in, tropical and ripe: jasmine, wet stone, the metallic tang of rain starting somewhere on the hills.

The terrace looked out over a courtyard of manicured hedges and a fountain. Beyond it, a private wing flanked by bougainvillea glowed white in the late sun. Two men in linen stood at their posts, eyes forward, hands idle. The hush here was not absence; it was control.

She walked the colonnade, heels clicking, and entered a room kept at a cool hospital chill. Machines murmured. A nurse rose from a chair, head bowed, and slipped out without a word.

On the bed was a shape most of the world believed had vanished into the earth.

Bandages wrapped his forearm like a cast of failed fingers. More bandages circled his ribs, his temple, the place where the field had tried to swallow him whole. The monitors traced his return in patient green lines. The smell was alcohol and cotton and the faintest trace of salt—a man hauled from a wet grave.

She came to the bedside and set her hand on his shoulder. His eyelids fluttered then opened—the flat, analytical gaze of a man who once cataloged pain as if it were data points. Recognition kindled. It bloomed into something like shame, then survival erased it.

"Carlos," she said, using the name few remembered he had. "Qué bueno que despertaste."

His throat worked. The right corner of his mouth tried for a smile and failed. "I fell." His voice was dry as paper.

"Yes." She brushed a stray wisp of hair from his brow, not maternal, not tender—proprietary. "And yet you arrived. My people pulled you from the lower level before the firefighters got brave. We were fast."

His gaze flicked to the window, to the slice of sky, then back. "The hand—"

"Some of it is gone," she said, as if discussing inventory. "You enjoyed removing parts from others. Now you have learned what it feels like."

He blinked. The monitor's green line held steady.

"I will need you again," she continued, her tone turning as cool as the air. "But not yet. You will heal. You will listen. You will not improvise. In the north, a governor will appoint the right man. In the west, two names will discover their time is not always their own." She laid her palm flat. "Here, you will remember who opens the doors and who decides when you leave."

His eyes closed once, opened again—compliance, exhaustion, or both.

She leaned in enough for the warmth of her breath to cross the space between them. "It is good that you have woken up," she said, not quite smiling. "You had me worried."

Outside, the fountain kept whispering. Far away, the phone on the governor's desk lit up with a name he would learn to say correctly the first time. And on a server that did not trace, a file labeled "N. JUSTIN" grew by one more note, as predictable as the tick of a clock that belonged, in truth, to her.

AUTHOR'S NOTE

Although this novel is a work of fiction and the product of my imagination, I want to acknowledge a real piece of Tampa Bay history woven into the story's backdrop. In 2024, our region endured two hurricanes just thirteen days apart.

I used the storms as pressure points throughout the narrative, drawing inspiration from the challenges our community faced during those difficult weeks. While the plot and characters are fictional, the atmosphere of strain, resilience, and disruption reflects what many of us experienced. Tampa Bay came together in remarkable ways, yet the effects of those storms are still visible more than a year later.

During Hurricane Milton, Tropicana Field suffered significant roof damage to the dome. However, the destruction depicted inside the stadium in this novel is entirely a creation of my imagination.

I would also like to offer special thanks to two local businesses that not only survived both storms but remained anchors of comfort and community throughout:

- **Neighborhood Joe's,** home to terrific coffee, great food, and many moments shared in my Facebook posts.
- **Sauvignon Wine Locker & American Trattoria,** another frequent feature in my posts and a longtime favorite local spot. The owner's generosity in supporting area charities is second to none.

Their perseverance—and the spirit of the surrounding community—served as a reminder of the strength that can rise even when the winds are strongest.

DID YOU ENJOY THIS STORY?

Thank you for reading *Witness Elimination: Vigilante Justice.*

If you enjoyed this novel, I'd be grateful if you took a moment to leave a review on Amazon or Goodreads. You can find it easily by searching the title or my name, Scott Johni. Reviews are the lifeblood of authors—your few positive words truly make a tremendous difference.

If you haven't yet read *Personal Injury: A Corrupt Conspiracy,* the first book in the Nick Justin Chronicles, I hope you'll check it out. The third novel, completing the initial trilogy arc, is scheduled for release in fall, 2026.

To receive updates on new releases and bonus content, visit my website or sign up through my free story page:

https://dl.bookfunnel.com/5yrlakk8fg

But the story isn't over yet.

Readers of my series know the name Jaquez Greene. You know his death cast a long shadow over the story. Now, witness the cover-up.

The murder of Jaquez Greene. A missing drive. A meeting in the dark. Officer Mark Mandel is about to learn that crossing the blue line is the quickest way to get buried by it.

Turn the page to enter the shadows.

A LINE DRAWN IN BLOOD

The cool evening pressed against the windshield, the glass fogging at the edges. Mark Mandel drove with both hands locked on the wheel, knuckles pale under the dash glow.

Three nights had passed, but Jaquez Greene still hit the pavement in Mark's mind—body folding, eyes flaring stark, that quick flash of confusion before the bullet took him down. No buildup. No warning. Just the kid's life gone while steam rose off wet asphalt.

Gino called it a routine stop. Mark approved the report and swallowed the bile rising in his throat. The bribe envelopes, the steered traffic stops, the dropped complaints—he let all of it slide. But murder carved a line he never saw until he crossed it.

His phone buzzed on the passenger seat. Gino again. Third call. Mark let it ring.

Internal Affairs wanted him at nine in the morning. Standard follow-up for an officer shooting—paperwork, formal statements, the usual tightening of screws. They knew nothing about the thumb drive in his pocket, the dashcam footage he ripped before Gino could scrub it.

The shot angle came in crooked, the mic crackled with engine noise, but the file showed plenty. It showed too much.

He turned into Bay Vista Park. Late at night, it lay empty. A few lamps along the parking loop cast pale circles across the pavement, and the surf worked the seawall with a slow, steady beat.

The spot offered space—open enough to breathe, quiet enough to talk. He parked near the boat ramp and kept his headlights on, their beams cutting white lines across the sand.

Vasquez arrived a minute later, her silver sedan rolling to a stop twenty yards back. No rush from her. No hesitation. She stepped out and walked toward the light with calm steps, coat drawn close against the chill.

Teresa Vasquez carried a rep for incorruptibility. Internal Affairs pit bull. Strong voice, sharp edges. Mark hoped that reputation meant she could help him dig out of the grave he helped Gino shovel.

She stopped a few feet away, framed in his headlights. "Officer Mandel. You said this couldn't wait."

"It can't."

"Then start."

Pressure climbed through his chest. He drew in a breath that scraped going down. "My partner executed a kid. Jacquez Greene. No threat, no struggle. Just shot him. I backed the story, and I shouldn't have. I helped bury the truth."

Vasquez watched him, logging each syllable. "That's a hard claim to prove."

Mark touched the inside of his jacket. "I know. I brought something."

For the first time, she eased her posture—not soft, not kind, but open enough to signal he should keep talking. She angled her head, scanning the pier. "Tell me everything before you hand over the evidence. I need to know what I'm stepping into."

"Gino lined up the angle, pulled the trigger, and planted the piece. He claimed the kid reached for it."

"And you went along with that."

"I did. That's on me."

Vasquez took a slow step closer, boots sinking in the sand. "Why now? What changed?"

"You know what changed. He killed an unarmed college student. I couldn't keep pretending the uniform stood for anything anymore."

"And Gino? Has he made contact since the shooting?"

"He's been calling."

"Because he knows you're drifting. Men like Gino don't tolerate drift."

Mark studied her face. She wasn't accusing or defending Gino—she was dissecting him, piece by piece. His chest tightened. "I have footage. Dashcam."

She didn't react. Controlled, unreadable. "Show me."

WITNESS ELIMINATION

He reached into his pocket. Her gaze tracked the movement—calculating. He drew the thumb drive out halfway. "It's my only copy," he said, his tone sharp. "This is enough to trigger an investigation."

"That depends. What else did you tell IA?"

"I wanted to come to you first."

"That was smart. Chain of command can crush the truth before it reaches daylight."

"So you believe me."

"I think there's more to it." Her eyes hardened a fraction. "The RADD Squad throws muscle in this city. And that kind of weight draws profit. Gino's part of that stream. You were, too, whether you want to admit it."

"I never signed up for murder."

"No one signs up. They drift. They adapt. They survive. And sometimes people get caught in the gears. You think exposing this changes anything? You think you're the first officer to swing against a current this strong?"

A chill worked through his spine. "This isn't a current. It's a crime."

"You crossed a line when you pulled that footage. Gino called me tonight. Said you slipped, said you might run your mouth. I needed to see for myself."

Realization hit hard. He stepped back without meaning to.

Vasquez closed the distance. "Mark, you should've come to me sooner. We could've managed this."

"Managed what? A kid's murder?"

She didn't answer.

He opened his mouth—to curse her, to plead—and the world slammed sideways with a crack.

A single gunshot. Clean. Instant.

Pain tore through his ribs. His legs folded before his mind caught up. He hit the sand hard, breath ripped from him. The headlights cut across the beach in a white blur, angles spinning.

Vasquez's boots entered his sightline. She stood over him, revolver firm in her hand. Spray streaked her face, and for a moment she stood carved from stone.

"I needed to know what you told and to whom."

Warm blood spread under him. His lungs seized when he tried to speak. She crouched, stripped a glove, and pressed the revolver into his palm. Curled his fingers around the grip.

"Suicide. Officer crushed by the aftermath of a fatal shooting."

His vision warped. The surf pounded somewhere—close, then distant. Vasquez stepped back and fired a second round into the air. The echo rolled along the empty beach.

Mark tried to cling to thought—Jacquez's face, the lie he approved, the truth he carried too late—but the sand pulled at him, heavy and final. The tide erased the space where he had been.

Two weeks later, the department gathered in the community hall, rows of folding chairs facing a small stage draped in flags. Fluorescent lights buzzed overhead. The air carried a mixed scent of polished leather and stale coffee.

A podium stood center stage, flanked by officers in dress uniforms, brass catching the light. Gino Myers stood among them, spine straight, chin set, the grief-stricken hero shaped from stone. His uniform looked pressed by a funeral director—creases sharp enough to cut.

When the chief called his name, Gino stepped forward with measured control, hands resting at his sides like he'd rehearsed the posture in his bathroom mirror. The chief pinned the commendation to his chest and spoke about courage, loss, and the cost of service.

Words rolled out clean, practiced—another ceremony built to keep the machinery running. Officers nodded at the right beat. A few lowered their heads for Mark Mandel, the man the department now claimed drowned under the weight of remorse.

The story held. It held too easily. A fatal shooting. A good cop shattered. Suicide from guilt. The public swallowed it whole. IA closed the file without friction. No one asked why the evidence vanished or timelines shifted. The system digested those parts like it always did.

Gino accepted the plaque with a composed expression, jaw set as if emotion threatened to break through. Colleagues clapped him on the shoulder, murmured condolences. He gave each a controlled nod. Played the survivor. Played it well.

Detective Teresa Vasquez watched from the back wall, arms crossed, badge clipped to her belt. She stood where she could see the room and stay unnoticed. Her gaze kept on Gino while the chief praised his "remarkable resilience" and announced his promotion.

Then she caught it—the slip.

A small smile twitched at the corner of his mouth. Gone in an instant, wiped clean before anyone else registered it.

She caught it because she understood that kind of tell. Satisfaction. Triumph. A predator wearing absolution on his chest.

Applause filled the room. Officers rose in a loose standing ovation. Gino bowed his head with the gravity of a man accepting the burden of duty.

When the room settled, the chief launched into talk of new initiatives and integrity campaigns. Gino stood behind him, framed by flags, the commendation glinting in the harsh glare.

Some predators thrive inside systems built to restrain them. They learn the rituals, recite the lines, and shake the right hands. And the system, hungry for order and clean stories, lets them rise.

Outside, St. Petersburg's streets stretched beneath the morning haze. Patrol cars rolled out from the station, engines rumbled, lights off. Gino would join them soon, carrying his medal, his promotion, his freedom.

The city grew darker beneath men like him—monsters with badges, roaming territory no one challenged, feeding behind the blue line sworn to protect the innocent. And the people who might have stopped them lay in the ground already.

WANT ANOTHER STORY FROM THE SHADOWS?

The short story you just read, "A Line Drawn in Blood," is just a glimpse into the corruption hiding in plain sight.

If you want more, I have another exclusive short story, "José Dominguez," reserved for my subscribers.

Join my readers' list to get:

- The free "José Dominguez" short story.
- Early previews of the next Nick Justin novel.
- Updates on the upcoming multi-book storyline.

Get your free copy here: https://dl.bookfunnel.com/5yrlakk8fg

Ways to Stay in Touch

- Website: www.scottjohni.com
- Instagram: @scottjohniauthor
- Facebook: Scott Johni / Scott Johni Fans
- TikTok: @scottjohni
- Email: https://dl.bookfunnel.com/5yrlakk8fg

ABOUT THE AUTHOR

Scott Johni is a civil trial attorney based in St. Petersburg, Florida, and has been a sole practitioner for over thirty years. He handles complex personal injury cases—including motorcycle and automobile crashes—as well as select class-action matters.

Born in Ohio, he was initially drawn to Florida to attend Eckerd College on the sparkling shoreline of Tampa Bay. After surviving law school in the frigid Northeast, he returned to Florida for good in 1993. Soon after, he met his wife, Lisa, and together they've spent over three decades building his law practice and raising their daughter. The family remains actively involved in community organizations dedicated to improving the lives of children and families.

For Scott, the leap from trial attorney to thriller author isn't as wide as it may seem. Both professions require crafting a compelling narrative, revealing information piece by piece, keeping an audience engaged, and delivering that climactic "aha" moment when every puzzle piece snaps into place. He hopes the Nick Justin Chronicles provide readers with the same satisfying reveal.

When he's not writing or navigating the courthouse, Scott can often be found cycling along scenic trails, golfing beneath blue Florida skies, or pushing himself in the weight room. At home, he's frequently accompanied by two affectionate basset hounds who like to supervise his reading time.

BOOK CLUB QUESTIONS

1. Trust sits at the core of Nick Justin's world—trust in family, institutions, and his own instincts. How does the story explore the fragility of trust, and which betrayal struck you the hardest?

2. Jessica's intuition adds both innocence and tension to the narrative. How does viewing danger through a child's eyes shape your understanding of the family's situation?

3. The author uses Florida's volatile weather to amplify suspense. In what ways do the storms mirror the emotional turmoil within the characters?

4. Andrea's journey blends physical recovery with emotional resilience. How did her evolution shape your sense of strength and vulnerability in the novel?

5. The conspiracy involves law enforcement, politics, cartel influence, and military contractors. Which aspect of this network felt most believable or unsettling to you?

6. The line between justice and vengeance blurs for multiple characters. Where do you believe Nick stands at the end of the story? Does he cross any ethical boundaries?

7. Sarah and Sally are complex antagonists with layered motivations. Did you view them as villains, survivors, or something in between?

SCOTT JOHNI

8. Extreme pressure reveals hidden truths about the characters. Which character's transformation—or breaking point—surprised you the most?